Praetor's Blood

Shattered Peace

Jeffrey MacSporran

GLOBAL
PUBLISHING
SOLUTIONS

PRAETOR'S BLOOD:
Shattered Peace by Jeffrey MacSporran
Published by Global Publishing Solutions, LLC
923 Fieldside Drive
Matteson, Illinois 60443
www.globalpublishingsolutions.com

Library of Congress Control Number:
2022900320
International Standard Book Number:
979-8-9853892-0-3
E-book International Standard Book Number:
979-8-9853892-1-0

Printed in the United States of America

Praetor's Blood

Shattered Peace

Jeffrey MacSporran

Contents

Interlude II: Choices

Arc 6: Hidden Consequences

Prologue: Memories

"This world is old and full of mysteries and secrets."

As a young girl, I would wait eagerly for my father to speak those words. Sat upon his knee, my eyes were filled with expectation as I gazed longingly at his weathered face. I would giggle as I watched his furrowing brow, and smile as he ruffled my hair and looked upwards, almost wistfully at the night sky.

No matter the story, he would start with those same ten words. Night after night, we would walk hand in hand around the same garden paths, sit on the same benches and stare at the never-changing stars, but never were the stories repeated.

Thinking back, his words, full of warmth and wisdom, calmed my restless, youthful heart. I remember the excitement as he regaled me with tales of his youth, where as a young officer, he sailed and fought with our nation's armies across the expanse of the known and unknown world, braving the highest mountains and seas yet uncharted.

He would share with me the memories of those he had met on his many voyages, both friends and foes, as well as the mysteries of the world he had sought to explain. But only when he told me the legends of our people, do I remember his eyes truly glimmering.

Stories of our nation's founding and the uncountable aeons before, when we were nothing more than scattered tribes. A time when Gods, Titans, and mythical heroes trod the same soil as mortal men.

Only now years later, having been betrayed and forced to flee as I am pursued across the continent, do I truly understand the lessons my father was trying to teach me. Lessons I was once too young and naïve to understand.

Arc 1: A World of Myths and Legends

Chapter One

My breathing is haggard due to fear and anticipation as I grip the reins of my horse. The leather straps bound to my hands are wrapped tightly as I ride almost blind through the night, the path ahead illuminated by nothing more than stars and moonlight.

Only when the road straightens do I relax my grip, allowing my horse's strides to shorten as I stare open-eyed at the looming mountain. Mount Tempesta, an aptly chosen name, its peak is cloaked in a thin veil of white mist, the scattered winding paths that follow its contours are barely visible. As the clouds encircling its summit darken, a feeling of dread forms in the pit of my stomach. Swallowing the saliva that begins to form in my mouth, I guide my mount forward.

Despite the fear, or due to it, I begin to remember the various legends that surround its origins. Though there were as many as there were stars in the night sky, my favourite is the one chronicled in the diaries of my father.

⊶——◎◇◎——⊷

It was said that long ago, before the Age of Fire, when Man was young, crude, and barbaric and had yet to receive the blessings of the supreme Gods, they had sinned. In punishment, the Gods abandoned them and plunged the world into an endless winter.

For a decade, the world knew nothing but freezing darkness. As the land grew increasingly barren, the few starving survivors huddled themselves around dying fires whilst praying to their indifferent Gods for salvation.

Those long unheeded prayers were finally answered by a falling star crashing into the horizon. The light that came after a day of tremors was so bright and pure that it pushed back the darkness whilst thawing the oceans of snow and ice. For days the light continued to remain, acting as a beacon for the curious and luring any who were brave or foolish enough to make the journey to find its source.

Individuals, groups, and whole tribes of Man made the journey, a pilgrimage to the source of celestial light. When seven of the great tribes of Man and a hundred lesser reached the source, after braving the treacherous, monster-infested waters that surrounded this island, the light dispersed, as if it had served its purpose.

From the once hidden shadows was revealed a pit, one too dark for mortal torches to light and too deep for a bottom to be seen or heard. But in that darkness, those bravest of Man's warriors heard a sound that chilled them to their very cores.

This joint primal fear forced the gathered elders and chiefs of each tribe to devise a solution, the forging of the Great Seal. Formed from nearby rock, reinforced by ancient magic that had been handed down from generation to generation, what lingered in the darkness was sealed and hidden away.

With winter banished, Man flourished, but prosperity caused them to forget the events which had once united them. Wars were waged and slowly the events of the past were forgotten and lost to legends as those who knew them, took the secrets to their graves.

Three generations would pass before events forced Man to once again remember what was once forgotten, the descent of a God. Haephaestus, Master of the Forge and Smith, came and sought the tribes of Man. His celestial essence overpowered the minds of mortal men, bringing a temporary peace as he asked a single question.

"Where is the hammer that fell eighteen days ago?"

Despite the promises of gifts beyond mortal compare and comprehension, no tribe could answer the God's question. As the God prepared to unleash his wrath, believing those present sought to hide his treasure, an elder on the verge of death awakened. Their name was lost due to the passage of time and remembered only as the "Ancient." They spoke to the God of a youthful memory, of a fallen star and the Great Seal. Easing the man's pain whilst taking their fading memories, the God left after leaving a blessing on his bloodline.

Though no mortal truly knows what occurred, all know that when the God, whose weapons and strength were without peer, attempted to break the Seal, the once fertile plains and forests that surrounded it were burned to ash and replaced by a mountain with the Seal buried in the centre of its valley.

I once disregarded it as nothing more than a child's story, but as my eyes catch the glint of uncut gems and ores on the mountain path, ones normally hidden underground, a tear rolls down my cheek. Smiling, I make a silent promise to continue my father's legacy, to discover the truth hidden within the ancient lore.

Chapter Two

Faster, we need to move faster.

As the mountain trail comes into view, I silently will my steed forward, listening with anticipation as the ground underneath hardens, rock replacing the soft soil of the plains. Now galloping with longer strides, my eyes flicker to the nearby cliff edge, and the sight causes my hands to quiver and the skin to become pale and clammy as I try not to think of the consequences of falling.

Narrow and exposed to the elements, few knew of these treacherous paths. Utilised by smugglers, adventurers, and goat herders, they were unsuited for riders on horseback, let alone those galloping at speed, but our need for secrecy required such recklessness.

Suddenly my horse lurches to the right, and the ground shifting underneath her feet causes a high-pitched scream to escape my lips. Tugging harshly on the reins, I steer her away from the rapidly crumbling edge as the trail ahead collapses, rocks tumbling down the side of the mountain, clacking and echoing before splashing into the waters of the lakes below.

"Sssh girl, sssh."

Thrashing as she rears upwards in fear, I relentlessly try to soothe her, my voice eventually reaching as she relaxes, allowing me to loosen my grip. Breathless, I curse my foolishness, my haste likely alerting the sentries stationed nearby. My eyes scan the shadows ahead, seeking the slightest movement, but finding none.

A faint whistle comes from behind as I let out a sigh of relief, turning, I raise my left hand, extending my fingers as I signal to those behind that I was safe and well. Wrapping my dark blue cloak tighter to my body, the sensation of the soft fabric on my skin calms my shattered nerves. Clicking my tongue, I steer my horse left, continuing as I follow the only path remaining.

Steeper and more treacherous than the original route, the need for concealment forces me to forgo the use of torches and lanterns. Riding slowly, I am guided by the light of the two shining moons and stars. Following the only trail, I soon spot the silhouettes of towers in the distance, their size alone indicating the number of guards stationed within.

Few paths existed into the northern realms, the stretch of mountains and the lakes surrounding it formed a natural border that separates it from the rest of the island. The sentries were whispered to possess the sharpest eyes and ears in all the land, and only the blessed, foolish, or desperate would attempt to enter without the approval of the client kings who rule there.

I hesitate as I question which category we fall under.

Only the caverns which travel beneath the mountains were unguarded, the realm of predators and other indescribable horrors, their presence alone a natural deterrent.

Resolving my conviction, I relax the hold on my reins, allowing my horse to continue at a slow trot. Travelling at her own pace, her once harsh and heavy breathing softens, despite the increasingly thinning air. I knew that she, like those behind her, were exhausted after three days of hard riding with little rest, but the missive I had received days before could not allow for any delay. A parchment containing few words, each however emphasised the importance of urgency.

Go north and seek the commander of the hammer-fall without delay. The Oracle has answered and states your destiny is waiting.

Though risky due to the ongoing war, I had made this desperate journey for this meeting with the Oracle of Artlars. Missing and thought dead after the chaos and bloodshed which had swept through the nation's capital, a meeting no matter how brief could reveal the path to one's destiny. Having long felt lost and uncertain, I needed their guidance if only to ease the fear that continued to dwell within my heart.

As the clouds above darken further, I feel my eyes and limbs grow heavy. Only now as the journey approaches its end do I realise how taxing it had been. The sudden understanding causes me to become sympathetic for my mount's misery. When this journey was finally over, she and those of her kin would enjoy a well-deserved rest.

The wind grows increasingly bitter as we continue our ascent, the dark coloured rock and soil are soon replaced by fresh, crisp white snow and ice. Despite the thickness of my cloak, I could feel the heat slowly leave my body, causing my body to shiver. Breathing into my hands, I can only wrap the cloak tighter to my body as I struggle to stay warm.

Ahead, I spy the daunting palisades which flank the stone tower, the timber thick and impenetrable. As the path widens, I feel a hand on my shoulder as a rider from our group takes the opportunity to ride ahead.

No longer leading, I ride cautiously forward, following their path as my eyes scan the walls for movement. Only the sound of singing and laughter is heard from within. Hopeful that the guards were sitting idle, we inch closer and closer, using the shadows to our advantage as we move towards the open gates.

Suddenly, I hear whistling overhead, my eyes follow the sound and I catch a glimpse of something thin and metallic as it travels through the night sky. Barely visible, it takes me too long to recognise what is approaching.

Reacting on instinct, I pull on the reins, ignoring the boisterous neighing of my horse as I force her to turn sharply back. The movement is barely complete before an arrow impacts and embeds itself into the ground, less than an arm's length from where I was previously riding.

The force of the impact causes particles of snow to rise, coating me in a thin layer of fine powder, before the shaft of the arrow catches fire, burning with a bright light.

Blinding, it becomes a beacon in the darkness, dispersing the cover of the shadows. Soon, angry shouts are heard from the walls and towers, joined by running armoured footsteps on wood and stone. Two of my companions immediately rush forward, drawing their swords and hefting their shields as they linger close to my body, shielding me from any potential harm.

"Your orders?"

"Do we fight or fly?"

Urgent questions quickly escape their lips as they await my commands, but I do not know what to do. The decision is forced however when the bellow of a horn echoes around the mountain, now there was only one path available.

"Stay close and do not move."

"My lady? Surely we must flee whilst we have the chance?"

My eyes linger on the remnants of the burning arrow as I consider his words, the shaft intact despite the flames, it was a blessed arrow used only by elite bowmen. A weapon which was almost unheard of outwith of the hallowed ranks of the Capital's knightly orders, one that brought fear to foreign battlefields. The bowmen who used them would rarely miss, unless by choice, this was a warning, one that should be heeded.

"Stay where you are, do not move."

A booming voice from behind confirms my instincts as a broad-shouldered man rides forward until his shoulders are alongside and touching mine. His tone and presence quell any lingering questions as he glares upwards at those atop the walls. He appears unfazed at the notched arrows aimed at us, making no effort to reach for either his sword or shield.

He only waits as the slow, rhythmic beat of drums grows nearer.

Chapter Three

The symphony of beating drums and marching feet is both alluring and threatening as they announce the arrival of a column of spearmen. Emerging from the gates in their glinting bronze armour, the sound of their footsteps echoes continually from the walls on either side, causing me to feel disorientated.

Without words of command, they begin to spread out, forming line after line that reaches from cliff face to cliff face. Linking their round shields together, they leave no gaps for us to exploit. Coming to a stop, they level their spears, aiming them at us and forming a solid barrier of flesh, metal, and spikes. Only a fool or an immortal would ride forward with horses against a formed phalanx such as this.

"Halt horsemen! You shall go no further."

The shout comes from the shadows of the walls above, the voice of a man that was brimming with authority and power.

"Know this, strangers of these lands, any who enter the northern realms in secret and uninvited face the penalty of death. What manner of fool would attempt such a feat on horseback? Send forth one to represent you and state your business. We will then decide if you be friend or foe."

Murmurs come from the mouths of my companions as they consider the words that have been spoken from the shadows.

"You are trying my patience horsemen. Lochos, ten paces forward march!"

Without hesitation, the phalanx marches forward, their spears level, before coming to a sudden halt. The speed of their actions displays their ability and willingness to dispose of us if their commander so wished it.

Anxiously, I turn to those beside me, before looking back at the track once more. Narrow and covered in snow, we would not all escape in time, it would be best for us to treat with the voice.

Neatening my clothes, I make myself presentable when I feel the heavy grip of strong hands on my shoulders. Turning back, I see the shaking heads of my companions, warning me of the risks whilst the identity and allegiance of the commander were unknown. Nodding in understanding, I assent to their wisdom, causing them to loosen their grip.

Without a spoken word, the broad-shouldered man beside me rides out, performing the duty that was his alone without fear or apprehension. The biting wind blows, causing his cloak to billow, revealing his thick muscular arms. No matter the thickness of the material, no amount of clothing could hide his stature. He was a rarity even amongst his kin, who were renowned for their size and strength.

Over the howling wind, the sound of bowstrings being drawn was heard, the archers on the walls tracking his every movement. Calm and collected, unfazed by the obvious danger, he comes to a stop, showing his outstretched arms.

"Peace, know that we are friends, not foe. I draw no weapon and offer no violence."

"Peace you say? Then is that not a sword hanging from your hip? What business be you in the northern realms?"

Fixing his gaze in the direction of the voice, the man answers.

15

"Only a fool would travel in the wilderness without a sword or other weapon by their side. Surely those of the northern realms, where great beasts and other horrors reside would expect this?"

No voice responds to the question. Taking the silence as an affirmation, he nods and continues.

"Our business is with your lords and king, matters urgent that we need to discuss with them."

"*What manner of business that you must travel the mountain paths?*"

"Sadly that business is for their eyes and ears alone. Shall you not let us pass and be on our way?"

Despite the inquisition, our representative's voice remains soft and gentle, carrying across the distance with little effort as he radiates power. A power that comes from his wealth of experience and age.

"*Beware stranger from the southern realms, we of the north do not take kindly to honeyed words. Two years have passed since we knew true peace, and we do not take words of friendship from strangers who sneak and hide amongst the shadows. Even the*

16

darkness cannot hide the scars and muscles on your arms, you are

a warrior and not a simple traveller.

Lately, many a spy and assassin of the enemy's employ have

attempted to enter these lands. When caught, they expressed words

far better than yours, yet even now their heads rest on spikes on

these very walls.

Until proven otherwise, I declare you a liar and enemy, you shall

not pass these gates unannounced. Prepare for inspection, refusal

will only reveal your guilt."

The words spoken are harsh and challenging, I can only watch

as our representative reacts to his tone. His muscles tense and begin

to shake, not out of fear, but anger. I recognise immediately the

coming danger.

A cold hearty laugh escapes his lips, the sound eerie and

menacing in the darkness, causing the bodies of the approaching

spearmen to tense and quail in terror.

"Indeed, much has changed since the time of my youth, is this

how the north treats their guests? Where is the hospitality of legend?

Forgive this old man for believing that there were still traces of honour within your bloodlines, maybe I should have expected such dire threats and insults from a man who chooses to hide in the shadows and comforts of thick walls.

If you are willing to besmirch my honour and those of my charge with hasty titles of spy and assassin, what be you? I name thee a coward, only one such as they could make such threats and insults without the bravery to speak them face to face. Come out now from the shadows and state once more those words!"

A chill runs down my spine as I feel the grip on my shoulders tighten once more. The challenge made is rash and full of anger. Murmurs and whispers come from the walls and ranks of spearmen.

"*Move.*"

The command is simple, the words forceful, causing the wall of spears and shields to break, separating down the middle and forming a path for a lone figure to walk. As each is passed, the ranks reform, closing the path, ensuring that he cannot turn back. With a torch in one hand and a spear and shield in the other, the man's movements are unhurried and brimming with confidence and purpose. It is clear that this man was no coward.

Stopping, he plants his spear into the ground before standing upright like a statue, glaring at our horseman. His bearing and aura are noble and glorious, reminding me of the ancient heroes of legend. His golden armour gleams in the torch and moonlight whilst his helmet is exquisitely crafted, with a white feathered traverse crest.

The man before us was no mere *lochagos* or company captain, he was an officer of one of the knightly orders.

The cold mountain wind causes his white cloak to flutter, revealing the golden bow placed neatly behind his back. I knew of only one knightly order who used such a weapon, why would a knight of such rank be this far north and guarding a mountain pass?

Lifting his arms, the knight reveals to those around him that he has no weapons before he reaches up to his helmet. Unclipping the straps, he removes it slowly, revealing his face. A scar runs down the left side, from temple to chin, the nature of the wound shocks me due to his youthful features. His long brown hair partially covers the scar as it hangs over his eye, but he makes no attempt to hide the wound.

This is not a mark of shame but rather of honour, one likely earned during the wars of expansion. His features are stern and full of conviction, he would not allow anything but an order from his commander to turn him away from his course and duty.

"So horseman, I have met your challenge, prepare to hear the same words. State now your business or be prepared to be cut down by my sword. Are you friend or foe?"

Our representative sighs, the gesture small but evident. Raising his hands, he shows that he is unarmed before sliding down from his horse. I imagine the ground to shake as he lands, standing upright he towers over the knight. They stare at each other intently, assessing each other as combat veterans before our representative simply nods.

"Even in the moonlight, I can see the scars on your face and body. No coward could earn such wounds, for they have been earnt when facing death head-on. I see the crest on your helmet and bow on your back, know this, I offer apologies for the slight I have given to your honour.

However, I will offer no apologies for my manner towards you for the threats of violence you have made to those behind me. We have stated that we are friends of your lords and masters, this I swear on my forefathers, my patron house as well as to the Gods themselves. Who we are, that is a secret that you cannot know."

A sinister smile appears on the lips of the knight as he looks up at the man who represents us. His laugh is cold, harsh, and hoarse, it sends shivers down my spine.

"Secrets are only secrets if others do not know. You must be a fool to think we do not know your identity, giant! Those behind you we cannot guess, but even this far from the Royal Capital, no one could not recognise the Captain of the Royal Guards."

He stares intently at the other's face, looking for a reaction before he continues.

"Are you trying to deny it? Do you think a knight like I would not recognise the fabled "Silver Lion"?

Do you think I cannot see your armour underneath your cloak? Do you think simple rags could hide your stature? Now let us end this charade Captain, tell me why you have come north with seven others?"

The Captain, his identity revealed, shakes his head, but he remains silent. Even with the penalty of death, he would not reveal our identities willingly. The smile on the knight's face disappears, being replaced by anger as he stares at the expressionless visage of the Captain.

"If you will not answer, then I will guess. Maybe you have grown weary of the comforts of the south? Have you come north to find a true challenge, after all this is where even real men fear to tread?"

The Captain remains silent, he continues to look at the knight who grows increasingly furious.

"Tsk, no? Maybe some noble has sent you here on an errand? I hear the pampered fools of the Capital love the taste of our fine wine."

Seeing no reaction, the knight's lips form a predatory smile.

"Still not willing to answer? Maybe the rumours are true? Maybe the "Lion" has grown soft and fearful, abandoning his duty as he hides away in a cave. After all, what else can we expect of a failure of a knight who could not even protect his king?"

The words have barely escaped his lips before there is the sound of metal striking metal. Despite looking at them both, I had barely glimpsed the movement of the Captain's sword as it was drawn and swung upwards at the knight. The blow, one capable of cutting him cleanly from groin to head was barely blocked by the knight's own. Locked in place by a low guard, it was now a test of strength between the two warriors.

I look in dismay at the two of them, realising the madness that would come if it was not stopped. I look left and right, but no one on either side is willing to intervene. All had heard the insult, no one would intervene in matters of knightly honour. Not wishing for needless blood to be spilt, I push off those who had wrapped themselves around me and ride forward as I shout and wave my hands. My actions gain the attention of both the knight and the Captain.

"Captain Lykon stand down! Cease this madness and sheathe your sword!"

Surprising myself with my actions, my words are unusually authoritative and commanding. Dismounting, soft snow is heard to crunch beneath my armoured boots as I walk towards the two. The Captain's eyes glance in my direction as he continues to face the knight. He nods, taking a step back as he sheathes his sword. The knight's sword remains drawn and I turn and speak to him directly.

"Will you not also sheathe your sword? You know the identity of the great Captain, surely you understand that means we are friends of your king?"

His eyes flicker up and down as he assesses me. His expression softens slightly as he realises my gender. Nodding, he sheathes his sword before taking a step back.

"Now that no weapons are drawn, shall we speak? Sir Knight, surely those words you have uttered are not befitting of a man of rank and station?"

Despite the short distance, my soft and gentle voice barely carries due to the howling wind. It bites deep into my flesh, sending a new shiver down my spine as it chills me to the bone. I pull my cloak tight to my body once again, my every movement watched by the knight who simply nods his head. His dark brown eyes soften as he raises his left hand and opens his fingers. The men behind him relax, returning arrows to their quivers and shouldering their spears.

"You are not a woman of these lands, a noble I can presume due to your manners and how poorly you handle these winds. I will offer an apology to you my lady for the display you have witnessed."

The knight bows slightly, a formality by noblemen to women of noble birth. His eyes, however, remain cold as he turns and stares at the Captain.

"I will, however, offer no apologies for any other actions. The laws of these lands are clear and known to all, the Silver Lion himself should know this. But if he should guard you, this would mean that you are a lady from a Great House. Despite your nobility, without a declaration of purpose and identity, you will be treated like a criminal."

I cannot be angry with the man, despite his harsh words. His actions are to save the people who lie beyond this fort, a duty I fully understand.

"I understand your duty, but know that we have travelled far and further we must go. What we need to do is of great import, can you not let us continue unhindered? I swear by my noble House and the Gods that I mean no harm to your liege or to any who live in these lands."

He shakes his head, his facial features unmoving as he listens to my words. I could expect no other reaction.

"The world has changed my lady, not even swearing by such things is enough. Nobles have turned their backs on much greater oaths, taking arms against those who rightfully have a claim to the throne and Crown. The guises of the enemy are many, we cannot trust those who come from without any longer."

I sense bitterness, regret, and remorse in his tone. His eyes soften further, revealing a warmth that was hidden until now. His words are without malice, the truth is well known to me. I nod, making the decision that needed to be made, I believe I could trust this knight.

"Oaths have been trampled and forgotten, but one stands before me now who has not forgotten his. Our purpose in these lands I cannot reveal, but this will prove our intent."

My right arm, hidden within the sleeves of my cloak rises. My already pale skin grows deathly white as the warmth is stripped away by the cold. My thin, dainty fingers stretch out to reveal a simple ring on my third finger. Made of silver, its design was simple, but the gem in its centre makes it unique.

Spróxte píso to skotádi me tin alítheia tou aímatós mou.

Thymámai ólous ósoi stékontai brostá mou gia tous órkous pou orkístika. [1]

Words of an ancient long-forgotten language echoes through the air, even those who do not understand their meaning can feel their power. This was the language of the Gods. The cold leaves my body, being replaced with warmth as it is basked in a golden light whilst a blinding blue and yellow glow is emitted from the centre of the gem of my ring, an heirloom handed down from generation to generation. Given to my ancestors during the Golden Age of Heroes, it was the symbol for a single family, a family who had the right to rule. No

---

[1] Σπρώξτε πίσω το σκοτάδι με την αλήθεια του αίματός μου. Θυμάμαι όλους όσοι στέκονται μπροστά μου για τους όρκους που ορκίστηκα. - Push back the darkness with the truth of my blood. I remind all who stand before me of the oaths you have sworn.

charlatan could replicate the light, for this was a blessing from a God who would allow no fakes.

The knight shields his eyes from the blinding light, his facial expression changing as he recognises the jewel. He unties his scabbard and places it on the snow in front of my feet as he shouts a single repeated command to those behind him.

"Stand down! Stand down!"

The knight's commands are obeyed instantly, his men following his lead and kneeling, the air is soon filled with the sound of leather and metal scraping against wood, stone, and snow. Tears form on the face of the knight as he begins to speak.

"I have shamed myself in your presence, your Highness. I did not realise your identity and my actions today are unforgivable. Though death awaits me as punishment, spare my men who were only following my orders."

I turn to face the Captain who stands behind me, he watches me carefully, waiting for my command. All it would take would be a simple nod, with that one action he would draw his sword and decapitate this kneeling man and slay anyone I so wished. Instead, I turn away from the man and bend down, picking up the sword contained within its scabbard at my feet. Grasping the sword with both hands, I feel its weight. My hand wraps itself around the grip as I carefully draw it.

The sword leaves the scabbard easily, the blade is beautiful and well made, shining blue in the moonlight. Even my inexperienced eyes can tell this was no ceremonial blade as I scan it carefully. I admire the small notches on its edge, each telling a story, despite the wear, the blade was well maintained and cared for.

Dropping the scabbard, I approach the kneeling knight, the sword grasped in both of my hands as I begin to feel its weight. Hearing my footsteps, he bows his head further, waiting for his apparent death. I feel the growing silence as those of his command wait with bated breath, watching the display and the pending sentence.

I look upon this knight, no, this man, as he prepared for death. Despite knowing his fate, he is unwavering, pleading not for his own life, but those of his command. Traits that were worthy of heroes, traits that have slowly begun to disappear in this new age. Sadly, he has committed the ultimate crime. Adjusting my grip, I angle the

blade towards the man's head and swing.

Chapter Four

With a thud, the blade embeds itself in the snow, mere hairbreadths from the face of the kneeling knight. With one hand still on the pommel, I place the other on the back of his head. My fingers feel the coarseness of his hair as I run through them. A small gasp comes from the man and those around us as he tenses the muscles in his neck, due to the unexpected contact. He does not move his head, maintaining his downward gaze.

"A teacher once told me that you could tell a lot about a man by how he treats his weapon. The same man told me you could tell a lot about a commander by how he treats those under him. Your sword is beautiful and well cared for, and you treat your men the same. You value their lives over your own, even in the face of death. Do you understand the penalty for your actions today?"

"I do your Highness."

"In these dark times, we can ill afford the loss of men of your calibre. You were few and now even fewer, we will need every one of you if we wish to return this land to peace. You have performed your duty, I can ask and expect no more. You wear the mantle of our nation's ancient Orders, I could expect nothing but bravery from one such as you. Rise, I, your Princess demands it."

Rising steadily to his feet, he moves as if a heavyweight has been lifted from his shoulders. His actions are mirrored by those around him as they watch us with open eyes. It was evident to me the love and loyalty that his men had for him. The knight maintains a downward gaze as he speaks, his tone humble.

"I am honoured by your kindness and mercy. As a knight of the ancient Orders, I am relieved that you are safe. Please, your Highness, how can I assist you in your journey?"

"What is your name, sir knight?"

"Helios, first son of Adrian of the House Maleinos"

"Sir Helios, my time is short and I need safe and unhindered passage through these lands. Can you assist in this regard?"

He looks up, his eyes now glinting as hears my words.

"The path you must walk is long and arduous, there are many patrols and another tower ahead. You will be challenged further on your journey, but I cannot show you the hidden paths, for they are dangerous for those not of these lands. An escort however I can provide who will ensure no guards will hinder you."

Turning to face the now idle phalanx, he points at a pale-skinned woman. Her body is toned and defined, her armour and cloak barely hiding her attractive figure. A pair of red and silver braids run down her left side, symbolising her rank of *lochias*, file commander or sergeant.

"First *Lochias* Amynta"

Picking up her spear, she runs forward to stand before her commander. Her movements are swift despite the cumbersome look of her equipment. As she comes to a stop, she kneels and waits for instruction. Standing this close, I see her truly for the first time, her natural beauty is a perfect representation of this feral land. On her back, she carries a quiver and bow, an unusual weapon for a spearman.

"My lord, what do you need of me?"

"A mission of grave import. You will take the Princess and her escorts to wherever they wish. Ensure that none shall hinder or endanger them on their journey. Her identity must remain a secret, take forth my standard and ensure no one will know of your true purpose."

The sergeant bows as she receives her instructions, her actions beyond just mere subservience to her commander.

"I have received your command, my lord. No harm shall come to those I guard and their secrets shall be taken to the Underworld."

Standing, she extends her right arm and salutes before running towards a group of men and women. Her shouts come quickly and they rush off towards the nearby tower. It does not take long before they return with bags strapped to their backs. Watching them, I realise their armour is unusual and different from what I know. Only their breastplates are bronze, the rest of their armour being that of hardened leather. They look like members of a militia who have been dragged from their farms due to the war.

"Will they be sufficient Sir Helios?"

He smiles at my question, his eyes revealing the pride he has in those he commands.

"Your Highness, I have no doubt, they are the best in my command. If I could offer you my whole company I would do so, or even myself, but my duty requires me to remain here to guard this pass. Until you return them to me, I will offer prayers and sacrifices to the Gods for your safe journey."

He smiles as he speaks, a true smile, something that I have not seen in a long time. There is no deceit in his eyes, he believes in the ability of those he commands, what right did I have to doubt them?

"I pray that the Gods are kind to your men as they perform their duties, Sir Helios."

"If the Gods are willing to offer such luxuries, your Highness, I will gladly take them."

I sense a slight bitterness to his words as if I had reminded him of a horrible painful memory. He bows before turning away. Shouting commands, he orders his men back into the tower. I hear the sound of hooves coming from behind me, turning, I am greeted by one of my escorts who is holding onto the reins of my horse.

Placing my feet in the stirrups, I mount her in a single fluid motion. Adjusting my clothes, I ensure I am warm and comfortable before I continue my journey further up the mountain.

As the Captain rides to my side, he tilts his head, his face one of worry.

"Are you feeling unwell Princess?"

I simply nod and look in the direction that we are travelling. The Captain looks at me once more before riding forward to speak with the sergeant who was to act as our guide and escort. Formed in a double file, they hold their shields to their sides, ready to march. Raising his right arm, the Captain soon brings it down, commanding us to move forward as one, the spearman at a slow jog, us at a trot.

But it does not take long for us to become separated from our escorts, their nimble frames allowing them to take routes that we could not. Their torches light our path and we follow behind, keeping their silhouettes in the horizon.

⊷⟨⟩──◎⟍♨⟋◎──⟨⟩⊶

The journey grows increasingly difficult as we get higher, the air growing cold and thin. My hands become numb despite the gloves, as my body aches and grows increasingly tired. As my vision begins to blur, I see our escorts ahead, speaking to another patrol who is in the area. They are setting up a temporary camp and I can see a fire being made. The sergeant is speaking to another person, showing them the standard in her hand. The blue fabric shines in the silver light of the stars and moon and soon the other patrol leaves the area without speaking to us.

The encamped infantrymen come forward carrying bowls of hot soup and cups bearing a hot, sweet, and clear liquid. I take them gladly, the hot drink refreshing as it warms my hands and body. Huddled beside the fire, I watch as the Captain queries the sergeant on how much further the fortress was. I look at the men and women who had formed our escorts, despite the distance we had travelled and the speed of their march, they did not appear to be affected.

Looking at them properly for the first time, I realised my original assessment of them had been wrong. Those before me were not members of a militia but full-time soldiers. Their limbs were toned and defined with muscle. The parts of their arms and legs which were not covered by armour were laced with scars. Their armour though well maintained was dented, scratched and showed signs of frequent repair, the marks of veterans.

As a member of the royal household, I had grown too accustomed to seeing warriors from the capital. Marching along the streets with their armour burnished to a high shine, each piece being custom made and forged by the finest smiths and artificers from the best materials that their families could afford. Only those at the city gates or who guarded the towns beyond the walls were dressed in leather. Their armour was handed down from parent to child, and few were lucky enough to have a bronze cuirass.

Here in the northern realms where the terrain was rocky underfoot, heavy armour was nothing more than a burden. Having only a bronze cuirass, and the rest in leather, a lighter and more flexible material ensured they could move quickly across the terrain whilst still being protected.

"Your eye has indeed improved, they are certainly veterans. In the north where there are greater evils and dangers than men, sometimes you cannot fight alone or at all. Sometimes when facing the beasts of dark magic who live in the untamed forests and caves, it is best to run until there are more of you to handle the danger."

The Captain whispers into my ear as he appears unexpectedly behind me. His breath is ticklish and he speaks in a low voice to ensure the sergeant and those nearby cannot hear.

"Have you become a magician Captain, how else could you know my thoughts?"

"Sadly I have not. I was only watching your eyes, my Princess. It is good to know that you have become curious about those who live within your realm beyond the capital."

"I have never seen warriors like them, who are they?"

"Hunters my Princess. The north does not have standing armies like the southern realms. The soldiers of the north hone their skills by roaming the lands, tracking and hunting the great beasts who threaten small and isolated villages. Every soldier who guards the border has slain at least one, and those who have slain twenty earn the right to the rank of sergeant."

My father used to tell me stories of the great beasts who roam the northern realms. Children of titans or offspring of foul creatures born of magicks, each was capable of destroying small armies. I look at the sergeant who is standing nearby, her skin lined with scars. If what the Captain had said was true, then the quality of those that Sir Helios had assigned to us was appreciated even more.

"I have spent too long hidden in the capital, it is good that I am now learning more about my own people and the lands beyond its walls. Captain, I believe it is time for us to leave once again."

Our escorts quickly dismantle the camp and begin to move once more. I follow them at a steady trot, the sound of hooves clattering on the stone. As we near the crest of an approaching ridge, the sun begins to rise. Covering my eyes, I see white walls in the distance. Finally, after three days, I was within reach of where I needed to be.

Chapter Five

"I never imagined the walls would be so high…"

My words are barely above a whisper as I ride slowly towards the southern wall of the great northern city and fortress of *Sfyri,* a name which meant "hammer fall" in the ancient language. Here according to myths, under the foundations, lay the Great Seal which guarded against the darkness beyond.

A long drawn out horn blast comes from the nearest tower, the sound shrill as it echoes across the entire valley, announcing our arrival before the gates. Soldiers which had previously been hidden or seated stand to their full heights, bows in hand, ready to defend the walls.

"Unfurl the colours!"

Our escort commander gives the command without hesitation as she indicates for us to stop. I watch as the regal blue fabric expands fully, fluttering in the wind to reveal the golden coloured eagle emblazoned at its centre.

"Halt, who goes there?"

Moving forward with only the standard-bearer at her side, she shouts her reply clearly to the sentry at the wall.

"First *Lochias* Amynta, representative of Helios, first son of Adrian of the House Maleinos"

"I recognise thee, prepare to be inspected and state your purpose."

I watch as the Captain subtly leans forwards, his voice barely above a hushed whisper as he gives a single command.

"No sudden movements, keep your armour and weapons hidden until we are within the walls."

"Understood Captain."

I understand his wariness, I could sense the unease and tension which emanated from the walls. He did not truly trust them, despite the welcoming and show of fealty that had already been displayed when my identity was revealed.

"Princess, stay close to me at all times."

I do not have the energy to speak, simply nodding my head in understanding. My already tired body becomes increasingly fatigued and disorientated as I linger near to the walls. Allowing my eyes to wander, I had hoped that this would allow my mind and body to recover. Flickering from side to side, my eyes scan the white stone walls. Even at a distance, I could feel their age and power.

Even before records began, a fortress had existed here to guard the valley. Over the millennia, as the walls crumbled, they would be cast down and rebuilt, until it reached its current form. Easily the height of five men, they had stood proud and unconquered by war and the elements for five hundred years.

Grander and taller than those of the capital, Artlars, using construction techniques long lost to our people, was angled slightly outwards to make it harder to climb. I understood now why the people of the northern kingdoms named themselves the "indomitable". For as long as the fortress walls remained untaken, none could pass into their lands.

Despite its formidable appearance, I could sense something more contained within the stone, something beyond the physical.

Removing the glove from my left hand, I stretch and expose my skin to the air, "feeling" the subtle movement of magic as it flows from the surrounding land and into the stone.

Instinctively drawn to it, I slow my breathing and close my eyes, allowing my inner sight to detect the faint yellow glow emanating from the depths of the stone. Glyphs, long eroded by the elements are visible to me, though familiar, it was written in an ancient language which I can neither read nor understand.

Overwhelmed by the increasingly concentrated magic, my mind wanders and disconnects from my body. Unable to waken, it sways and swoons.

"Help me!"

The thought does not form on my lips, no matter how much I will them to move. Fully disconnected, I can only watch as my arms move on their own accord, instinctively stretching out towards the wall.

"Stop! Wake up!"

As the light from the wall glows brighter, I feel the first tinge of primal fear as I realise the danger of touching the stones.

"Help...."

Suddenly a strong grip on my waist hauls me back, pulling me off my horse despite my body's resistance. I watch as my arms and legs lash out, trying to break free, but my weak body is nothing compared to the immeasurable strength contained within this person's grip

"Princess...wake...up!"

My eyes flutter open and I stare upwards at the hooded face of the Captain. Unsure if I was fully in control of my own body, I reach and allow my fingers to touch his face, the warmth comforting as it affirms I was no longer in a waking nightmare.

"There is great power contained within those walls. Hold onto me until we are past them."

"I am sorry..."

I am drawn into the abyss of his dark blue eyes as I speak those words with a hint of embarrassment. Though stern, they are full of worry and as I feel the heat rising from my cheeks, I turn away, trying desperately to hide the reddening of my face.

The sound of metal striking timber, however, draws the Captain's attention and he turns away, his face hardening as he mutters.

"So it begins…"

Gently releasing the grip on my body, he allows me to return to my horse. I nod as I secure my hood, looking at the gates as they slowly begin to open.

Heavy gates were made from thick oak and covered in sheets of steel screech inwards, revealing the courtyard and the city beyond. As the gap widens, three dozen men and women, dressed in the same style as our escorts march and fan out before levelling their spears. Their movements are punctuated by the sound of bows being drawn at the walls.

A single male figure, his armour burnished, a red braid hanging from his cloak, steps out and walks towards the commander of our escort party. With every step, his eyes move left and right, scanning our escorts, looking for any signs of duress. Finally, when he is mere steps away, his mouth breaks into a smile and he greets his counterpart by the forearm, locking each other in a warrior's embrace.

"Amynta, it has been too long. You are not due to return for another month. Why are you here?"

"Come closer and I will tell you."

Leaning towards each other, they speak in low voices, barely a whisper to ensure no one else can hear. Their conversation is short before they break their embrace, the man looking around, scanning the faces of everyone around him, and stopping only when his eyes linger on the dark blue standard and the towering form of the Captain. Nodding as if satisfied, he turns away.

"Let them through!"

With little fanfare, he waves his left hand in the air. The soldiers at the gate and walls relax and stand straight, shouldering their spears and walking casually back into the courtyard.

"Escort party, forward!"

On cue, the Captain with a single movement of his arm indicates for our party to follow the others through the gate.

The courtyard and the city on the other side are dull and lifeless, the stonework bare and grey, not even weeds or the hardy mountain flowers bloomed here. I had often visited other cities and fortresses, but this was different, the atmosphere felt stagnant. I turn my head in mild fright as I hear the heavy thump of falling timber and creaking of metal as the gates behind are shut. There was no escaping from this city now, I could only trust in the intentions of the sender of the message.

Chapter Six

"Is this a city or a maze?"

Hushed words leave the mouths of my companions, the Captain immediately turning to reprimand the commentator. My lips twitch into an awkward, nervous smile as I understand the sentiment, I had the same thought.

Sfyri was a fortress that became a city and the architect who had designed with an emphasis on defence rather than ease of commerce. The streets were narrow, barely wide enough for two carts to pass, and they were narrower now as the sides were lined with abandoned wagons and carts, forcing us to take detour after detour.

Despite houses lining us on either side, I had yet to see any people in the streets or merchants selling their wares from markets or stands. Everything about this city was eerily quiet, only the sound of coughing and shouting confirmed this city was inhabited.

There were no signs or markers to indicate where we were, and the buildings prevented us from seeing into the distance, only the knowledge of our escorts who we remained close to, ensured that we were not lost. With every turn, my companions grow increasingly wary, their hands remaining close to the swords on their hips, ready to draw if danger presented itself. The lack of sound and life said more about the state of this city than any report my father would have received in the past.

Finally, as we turn another corner, the road widens, and I see the first signs that this is a living city, though the sight is grim. Groups of men and women, dressed in armour huddle around roaring fires, the majority are resting, their cloaks wrapped around their bodies as they eat or lie on the ground, using their shields to rest their heads. Not a single person in front of me was not injured in some way.

At first, I was confused as to why seeing these people increased my anxiety, I soon realised why, and it was due to the silence. These men and women were unlike any soldiers I had met before. Despite being close to each other, none of them took comfort in this companionship. Remaining silent, they simply sleep or eat, choosing not to sing songs, tell stories or even laugh. Despair and exhaustion radiate from them and the taint was suffocating. These soldiers were broken and they would remain so until the end of this war.

A snowflake touches the end of my nose, the flake, soft and gentle, instantly melts as it touches and tickles my skin, covering my nose in a thin film of water. Looking upwards, I watch as more fall from the sky, the shower growing heavier until a fresh layer of snow is added to the ground.

I turn away from the sight of falling snow when I hear the sound of bells and chanting coming from a street to our right. Our escorts upon hearing the sound come to a stop, telling us to wait as a procession of twenty hooded men and women cross in front of us. Their robes are heavy and white, their facial features are hidden and weighty chains made of gold and silver hang from their necks. Walking barefooted, some expose their chests to the elements as they continue to chant, shaking the bells in their hands with every footstep.

Those at the back carry a pair of young lambs, their eyes covered as soothing words are whispered into their ears. Walking past, I watch as they head towards a white-columned temple in the distance. Despite the passing centuries and waning blessings of the Gods, no one would purposely forget to offer sacrifices to them, especially during a period of war. If the mood of this fortress was prevalent, then they would need all the assistance they could get.

Nothing else hinders our path through the remaining streets, not a soul glances in our direction. Our dull grey cloaks hide the finery of our clothing, making us appear drab and inconspicuous. To those living in the city, we were nothing more than soldiers, maybe even merchants who were making our way through.

We follow our escorts to the centre of the city, a grand plaza with high columned buildings on either side. Here and here alone was there true signs of life, merchants selling their wares, bards singing and reciting tales, and couples sitting at the fountain. On the far side was a building grander than any other with guards at the entrance, it was clear this was where we needed to be.

Those who stand guard are no ordinary spearmen, these were hoplites, veterans of war. Chosen to be the personal bodyguard of nobles, they are equipped with artificer-made armour and round *hoplon*-style shields which they hold to their sides. Their appearance of idleness is an illusion, their eyes were constantly watching and the spears in their hands are crossed with those across from them, barring entry to any who approach uninvited.

Even I, a princess who has never experienced an actual battlefield could tell that these men and women were on edge, their hands resting on the pommels of their swords, their fingers twitching in readiness. Looking behind them I could see why, in holders on the steps are the standards of various noble houses, the material fluttering in the wind. With a casual glance, any observer could tell who was in attendance, and there were more than a dozen standards in place.

Spying a nearby stable, we ride towards it, the Captain indicating for our escorts to remain behind. Standing like statues in front of the building, they wait for our return, the only movement coming from the standard as it continued to flutter in the breeze.

A young girl and boy, both no more than ten run out to greet us, their clothes dirty and full of patches. Taking the reins of our horses, they guide us to the entrance. Stepping down from my horse, my boots touch the ground for the first time with a metallic clink. The sound catches the ears of those standing and working nearby who turn their heads. Seeing my shabby and well-worn cloak, they quickly turn away in disinterest.

The Captain stands beside me as he leans down and places a silver coin in each of their hands. Taking the *Drachmas* gratefully, they guide our horses into the deepest and warmest sections, promising to feed them their best stock.

"Are you well?"

The Captain's voice is filled with concern as his towering frame turns towards me, blocking the light behind him. I smile, hiding the growing tremble in my limbs, conserving what remained of my slowly diminishing strength.

I only watch as he shakes his head, a small chuckle coming from his lips as he sees through my façade and extends his arm. Smiling in mild relief, I take his arm gladly, wrapping my body around it as I use his body for support.

"You have my thanks, I will be fine. Let us go and carry out the matter we have travelled for."

"*State your purpose here!*"

Aggressive shouts come from the plaza, causing us to hasten towards the sound, the hands of my companions resting on the pommels of their swords. Soon we are greeted by the sight of our escorts being questioned by three hoplites, their spears levelled as their dark red cloaks are swept behind them.

"I order you to state your business! Speak or face death."

The questioning comes from the man in the centre, his helmet sporting a red traverse crest signifying his rank as a junior officer. Despite the threats, no one from the escort party speaks, their commander only indicating with a wave of her hand the standard that continued to fly.

Growing frustrated, the officer grabs the nearest person, pulling them close and placing the blade of their sword close to their neck.

"As a noble and an officer, I command you to speak."

Breaking away from the group, the Captain steps forward, coughing and clearing his throat. The sound is intentionally loud, drawing the attention of the officer who turns to face him. I watch in amusement as the man's eyes widen as they land upon the Captain's towering frame.

"He is a member of our escort, release him."

Words, though softly spoken contain enough power and hidden malice to cause the man to release his grip. Pointing his still drawn sword at the Captain, he clears his throat before speaking.

"Stop where you are. No one shall approach nor enter the Governor's palace without invitation. He shall not be disturbed for trivial matters."

Pulling back his hood, the Captain reveals his face, a disarming smile formed on his lips.

"Dichas."

A cloaked male responds to the command, stepping forward as he reaches into the hidden depths of his cloak, revealing the gem inlaid sword at his hip. Becoming nervous as they spot the sword, the three hoplites only relax when Dichas pulls a scroll from his pouch.

Purposely keeping his hands away from the sword, he hands the scroll to the officer before stepping back, allowing them to read the contents. The officer, carefully examines the scroll, comparing the seal to the crest borne on his cloak and armour. Reading the contents, the officer sheathes his sword and bows before speaking.

"I confirm the invitation. Please follow me and take shelter in the reception area. I will inform his aide of your arrival."

The previous tension dissipates in the blink of an eye as the hoplite's shoulder their weapons and stand aside, allowing us to pass. I gladly follow the officer into the building as the snow continues to fall, growing heavier and the wind harsher. As I near the inner archway, I notice the lack of movement from our escorts who continue to stand like sentinels outside, waiting for further instruction. Ashamed at my lack of consideration, I discreetly nudge the side of the Captain. Nodding, he indicates his understanding.

"Dichas, relieve our escorts. Inform them that their duty is complete. Ensure they are rewarded for their efforts."

Bowing slightly, Dichas moves towards the standing sentinels, their frames slowly becoming covered in snow. Silent, quick words are spoken with *Lochias* Amynta before salutes are exchanged. Reaching into his belt, I watch as Dichas removes a leather pouch and places a small handful of coins into Amynta's hands before turning away.

With their duty complete, our former escorts turn and begin to march in the direction of the gate, the glint of gold in Amynta's hands are soon hidden away. No small payment had been made to ensure their silence.

Chapter Seven

The reception is warm and dry, giving us a chance to remove our soaked outer cloaks. Huddled beside burning braziers with outstretched hands, we slowly regain the warmth in our bodies that we had lost. The Captain continues to hold onto me, discreetly hiding the growing weakness of my body from the other members. Eight of us stand in the room, but none of us speaks a word as we wait for our host to receive us whilst hiding our features under the hoods of our thick cloaks.

Seeking distraction, I look at the walls and the draped cloth and embroidered tapestry which hangs upon them. The majority depict the legends from the Age of Heroes and famous battles. Our wait is not long before a pair of hoplites and a woman enter the room. Dressed in a low-cut *peplos* that hugs closely to her body, it reveals the various seductive curves of her body, a womanly physique that puts mine to shame. Bowing, she greets us with a smile, the scroll we had provided earlier in her hands.

"Welcome my lords and ladies, I am Eleni, aide to the Governor. He can receive you now in his chambers. However, the room is small and can comfortably support no more than two of your party."

The Captain chooses to answer in our stead, ensuring my identity remains hidden.

"I offer my thanks for your lord's generosity, myself and my companion beside me will be our representatives. Can arrangements be made for our remaining companions to be fed and rested, our journey has been long and our supplies have been depleted."

The woman smiles before indicating the two hoplites beside her.

"Make suitable arrangements, I believe our Lord will wish to accommodate them for the night, ensure they receive something suitable in the east wing."

As the pair salute and disappear into a different corridor, she turns back to the Captain and indicates for us to follow.

"Please stay close."

We walk through the endless dark and quiet corridors, the only sound coming from our footsteps as we follow the flickering torches which hang on the wall. In the darkness, I sense the presence of others, their unseen gazes coming from the gloom. I hold tightly to the Captain's arm, taking reassurance from his presence.

As we approach the end of the corridor, a pair of hoplites standing at the door notice our approach. Recognising the woman in front of us, they immediately react, knocking on the door and allowing us entry.

The room beyond is indeed small, even smaller than expected for the personal chambers of a Governor and it was currently full of men and women huddled around a map-strewn table. Armed and armoured, they speak loudly as they discuss the movements of painted wooden blocks across a map of the region. No one huddled around the table acknowledges or observes our entry, so fixated in their discussion and argument.

The aide indicates for us to wait as she approaches the table, the scroll in her hand as she stands beside the only unarmoured man at the centre of the group. Wrapping her arm around his waist, she whispers seductively into his ear. Taking the scroll from her, he opens and reads the contents before lightly pushing her away. A few at the table glower at the woman, their eyes filled with either anger or disgust.

I blush in embarrassment at her actions as she walks back towards us, giving only a subtle wink at the Captain before stepping out into the corridor. The man, who we realised was the Governor, clears his throat and coughs before turning to those around him.

"An urgent matter has appeared. We will reconvene tomorrow and continue the discussions then."

Puzzled expressions appear on the faces of the huddled men and women, a few of them obviously nobles. Some argue and begin to ask questions, but a single glimpse at the man's face soon makes it clear that he will not entertain any disagreement or discussions. As one, they salute, raising their rights arms before walking out of the room in a single file. A few stare at us, trying to ascertain our identities before leaving the room. Soon only the three of us remain.

The man walks towards us, his facial features immediately changing, becoming warmer as a tender smile appears on his lips and his eyes soften. His hair is grey, his skin sun-kissed and laced with scars, and his clothing, though simple in form is expensive. Both his cloak and chiton are edged with purple thread and his clothes are tight-fitting, revealing his still honed physique.

It was clear that this man had earned his position from service in the military and was not unused to the chaos of war, a suitable appointment for this fortress. My eyes soon move to the gold-plated and jewel-encrusted sword which hung from his hip, something given only to those who held the status of *Syntagmatarkhis* or Colonel.

Coming to a stop in front of us, he effortlessly bends his knee and bows his head.

"Your Highness, thank you for coming. I am Kivos, son of Kastor, I am the governor here."

Checking that no one else is present, I pull back my hood, revealing and loosening my long, golden coloured hair for the first time in three long days. My tired green eyes look upon the kneeling man before I turn towards the Captain who simply nods.

Extending my hand, I allow the man to kiss the ring on my finger before speaking.

"Please rise, Kivos son of Kastor. I have travelled far on request of your missive, tell me more of this matter with the Oracle."

Rising to his feet, the man glances at the Captain who towers over him before returning his gaze onto me.

"Come, take a seat, I am sure you are weary from your journey."

Extending his arm, he indicates the nearby couches on the far side of the room which are placed on either side of a low table. I gladly accept the embrace of the soft furnishings, a welcome relief from the days of horseback.

"Refreshments perhaps?"

The Captain sits beside me, discreetly supporting my body by placing his arm behind my back. Kivos smiles as he watches our movements before clapping his hands repeatedly.

I hastily pull up my hood to hide my features as the doors to the side of the room open and a stream of servants enter, their hands filled with plates of food and amphoras of wine. Their movements are sharp, wasting little effort before they leave as quickly as they had entered.

The Governor smiles the same tender, almost overly familiar smile as he reaches across and begins to fill three goblets with wine.

"Please, sample the food and drink. The wine before us is truly exquisite and will sate the thirst of any weary traveller."

Neither the Captain nor I move beyond pulling back our hoods once more.

"Oh…"

The smile on his face wavers slightly as he picks up a handful of food from each plate and empties the contents of the goblet, making sure I had observed his every movement. Refilling his goblet, he indicates once more to the food.

"I would hate for rumours to spread that I, Kivos, did allow both our Crown Princess and the great Lykon to attend my chambers and receive poor hospitality."

The Captain makes the first move, reaching forward and grabbing the nearest goblet, he takes a sip of the contents before handing it to me. I take it gladly, feeling its weight as I bring it to my lips. The taste of the wine as it flows down my throat is indescribably exquisite and I feel the warmth of the alcohol as it seeps through my body. Feeling refreshed, I place the goblet carefully on my thighs as I pry information from the man.

"I would hate for such rumours to exist, I thank you for your hospitality Warden of Sfyri. However, you and I both know I have not come to sample the wine."

"Ah yes, the matter of the Oracle."

"Now tell me, when is the Oracle due to arrive?"

I only watch as Kivos shakes his head in confusion before answering.

"I must apologise your Highness. There must be some mistake, the Oracle is not expected to arrive."

I look at the man, seeing no deception, only confusion in his words.

"I have your message here, it states that the Oracle has answered and my destiny is waiting. How can the Oracle answer if she is not here?"

"No one has seen the Oracle since she went north to the Temple of Knowledge months ago. Two weeks before today, we received a message from her containing specific instructions and we have followed them to the letter."

"Are you sure you have not changed them in any way? Never has a person received their destiny without being in the presence of the Oracle."

I can see the fear in his eyes as the Captain's hand slowly begins to move, ready to draw his blade at any sign of betrayal.

"I swear, there has been no mistake or deception. Wait, this will explain all."

Standing, he hurriedly moves to a nearby table, removing a side panel and exposing the compartment hidden within. Carefully with great reverence, he removes a pair of scrolls, it is clear that one is still sealed. Returning to the couches, he first hands me the open scroll.

"This contained the instructions."

I unroll the scroll, reading the words carefully. The message is brief, but it was as the Governor had said. I compare the scroll to those I have read in the past, observing the folds in the papyrus, evidence that it had been carried by a bird, one of great size.

Placing the scroll down on the table, my eyes move to the message still contained within his hand. Noticing my gaze, he wordlessly hands it to me. With trepidation, my hands reach out and take it. My eyes scan the still unbroken seal, noting the eye at the centre of a blazing sun, the mark of the Oracle.

"An eagle bearing her symbol arrived two weeks ago. I made all efforts to trace you as soon as I received it. I can only hope it has reached you in time."

I listen to his words before I break the seal, unrolling and reading the contents:

Heed and remember well these words, eldest daughter of those
who are heir to the Sea God's blood.
Long has the prophecy of the end of the scions of Artlars been
chiselled into stone and soul.
Too long have my words been ignored. But soon the great
wheel of destiny must turn.

During the blackest day when the sun is swallowed, death will

stalk the land,

With the coming of death, there shall fall a seven-tailed star.

Fear not its coming or power, for within its light is hope not

doom,

Within its embrace is the heir of Europa, unblessed by Gods,

but whose blood promises victory

A King and general from an endless time and place, his heart

and soul shall decide your salvation or death.

My eyes scan the words again, reading them repeatedly, but each time causes my confusion to only grow. Turning the scroll over, I seek further words beyond those I have already read, but I find none. Contained within the message, my apparent "destiny" was only the final verse of a prophecy that had been chiselled into stone at the birth of our nation.

Prophecy, I had grown to despise to the word, the same prophecy had started this war. Anger, sadness, and disappointment begin to grow within me and despite my efforts to rein in my emotions and maintain my dignity, tears form in my eyes, the liquid running down my cheeks. Looking down, I hand the scroll to the Captain, to let him read the contents.

During the silence, I glance upwards at the face of Kivos, it is full of expectation as he waits to hear the contents. I cannot hate the man, I had similar expectations before my arrival. I decided to ask the only question that mattered.

"Did anything accompany this message?"

The simple shake of his head shatters what remained of my hope. He sees my tears and the wretched look on my face and his facial features begin to change.

"Is something wrong?"

Slowly, I am swallowed by the growing despair that had begun to settle within my heart. With a gasp, I realised that I no longer cared for the prophecies of the Gods.

"Nothing…"

The words that leave my lips are barely above a whisper.

"Is there no message? I do not understand."

"Captain, if you are finished, show him the message."

He takes the scroll eagerly and begins to read the contents.

"As you can, the "destiny" which I have been given is nothing more than verses from the Prophecy of Two Kings. Only a repeat of those same words that began this war."

I watch as Kivos shakes his head in denial, his words are mumbled as he tries to argue against my words. Despite his various attempts, there is no hope lingering within my heart.

"Surely the Oracle would not send this without reason. Surely this means a saviour is coming?"

My fatigued limbs recover their strength and I stand, ignoring his pleading. It is clear that he is one of the many who still believe fully in the power of prophecy and the blessings of the Gods.

"Listen well, you know like I do that Europa is nothing more than a myth, a tale told to children."

"But…"

"For more than a thousand years that prophecy has been chiselled into stone, do you honestly believe that it applies to us now? I tell you now, the time of our reliance on Gods and prophecies is over, and they will not aid us now nor in the future. A fool started this war because he listened to these childish stories, only his death will end it."

"Your Highness, please restrain…"

The Captain tries to speak, but I cut him off, ignoring his pleas.

"I will not base the results on this war on the empty prophecy that a saviour will come in the form of a king from a land of myth. I believe only in what I can see and feel. My body is weak, I cannot hold a sword, but even I know this war will be won by blood and sweat alone.

The Gods might as well be dead…"

A pair of gigantic hands reach across and grab hold of my shoulder, pulling me back as he spins me around. A hand covers my mouth, preventing me from speaking any further. I look at the face of the Captain as he looks down at me pleadingly.

"Princess! Take back your words, you condemn yourself and your bloodline with your blasphemy. Let us make haste to a shrine and offer a sacrifice, they will forgive you if you repent quickly."

My eyes soften as I look into the eyes of the man I consider family, the raging torrent of anger and despair which had dwelled within me begins to dissipate. Despite his words, I cannot agree with them, I have chosen my path.

"No it is far too late, I have chosen to walk this path and forge my own destiny. My bloodline is already cursed my dear Captain, is it not the same blood that has brought misery and destruction to my people?

What matters now is doing what is right for my people, our actions, not the Gods, will remove the Usurper from the throne and restore peace to this Isle."

The Captain sighs as he looks at me, he was used to my stubbornness, a trait that I had inherited from my father. My iron will compensate for my weak body. Behind me, I hear the silent whimpers of a man who is on the verge of grief.

"What shall I tell the men, everyone here has seen the arrival of the eagle? They expect a miracle..."

Taking hold of the Captain's hand as he stands beside me, I wrap my fingers around his own as I look down at the man sitting before me, a mere shadow of who he was only a few moments ago. Even a veteran of his standing could be overwhelmed by despair after two long years of relentless war.

"Know that I am not my brothers, I am neither a politician, a warrior nor a priest. You alone know what is contained within their hearts. Tell them what they need to hear, even if you do not believe it."

"I understand. I only wish the Oracle had given us something more. The people of this land need hope."

I understand the words of the crestfallen man as he tries to rally his own heart. Despite this sympathy, I have no remorse for my words and actions. This journey had been a waste of time, a commodity I had little remaining.

"Winter is about to end and the season of war is about to begin. My brothers have tasked me to rally as many soldiers to our cause as possible. I intend to ride south in the morning and can afford no delay. Can you offer rooms for me and my companions to rest for the night?"

Standing to his full height, he bows before clapping his hands once more. The door behind us opens, and the woman from earlier returns. Standing between us, she bows before greeting us once more.

"Our guests will be leaving in the morning. They will require rooms for the night, ensure their needs are met."

"My lord, I have already made preparations. Suitable rooms have been allocated within the east wing."

Turning towards us, the Governor picks up his goblet and drinks the last of the wine.

"I will pray for good fortune in your journey. Please excuse me, but I have much to do before the morning. I will leave you in the care of Eleni."

I thank him for his hospitality before following the woman out of his chambers. Despite my wish to offer him words of comfort, I can find none within me. Taking hold of the Captain's arm, I use him to remain upright, my body growing increasingly weaker with every passing moment.

Every day I curse the weakness of my body and wish for the strength necessary to continue, but every day my prayers were never answered. The priests during my youth had examined me, explaining to my parents that it was the price for the other gifts I had received. My physical weakness ensured I could never leave the palace as a young woman and I had never experienced the outside world until recently.

My destiny was to be a figurehead, and when this war was over and one of my brothers ascended to the throne, a bargaining tool for marriages of convenience. I had known this fate since I was old enough to understand my position and role in life. Ironically this fate had been delayed due to the onset of war.

Chapter Eight

Eleni leads us to the east wing, the corridors here brighter than those we had entered earlier. As we approach a pair of double doors, she opens them carefully and guides us within. I find Helena, my lady in waiting, already inside. She bows as a pair of servants finish placing plates of food and amphoras of wine on a table near the window before leaving.

The Captain waits for everyone to leave before he excuses himself, leaving me with Helena as he closes the door and follows Eleni to his room. Helena locks the door behind him, ensuring no one else can enter without our knowledge or approval.

Making my way to the bed, my limbs begin to tremble and I grab hold of the table, steadying myself as I catch my breath. Helena rushes over and takes hold of my body, steadying my own with hers.

"Your Highness, are you feeling unwell?"

I click my tongue in annoyance as I hear her words, despite the years we had spent together, she continued to be formal even in private, despite my express wishes.

"I have told you before Helena. When we are alone use my name."

She whimpers in apology as she hears my scorn.

"I am sorry Selesia, but are you feeling unwell?"

Shaking my head, I indicate the bed.

"No it will pass, I just need to rest."

"Would you want help to remove your clothing?"

Stubbornly I prepare to refuse her service, but, I sense the growing tremble of my arms and reluctantly nod my head. As we reach the bed, she carefully sits me down and begins the removal of my outer layers. Each piece of clothing is carefully folded or placed near the fireplace to dry until I am dressed only in a light chiton.

Guiding me under the blankets, I watch as she goes to her own bed and begins to disrobe. Whilst her back is turned, she tilts her head and asks what she had been desperately waiting for the answer to.

"Was this journey worth it?"

I hear the eagerness in her voice, the wish that my grand destiny had been revealed and that a saviour was coming to end this war. But I cannot lie, I shake my head and give her an answer.

"No, I did not find the answer I sought."

"Oh"

A single sound was enough to reveal her disappointment. I knew she was not alone, I had sensed the same disappointment from the Captain despite his attempts to hide it from me. Everyone who had come had hoped that the message would be the revealing of some divine intervention that would end this stalemate and swing the momentum of this war in our favour.

I listen to her breathing as she slips further under the blankets, pulling up the thick, pure, white, and fluffy fleece and turns her back to me. I can tell by the subtle movements of her shoulders that she is on the verge of tears. Turning away from her, I look towards the open window, staring into the clear night sky. In the silence, I remember the words of the message, a single word returning to my thoughts.

Europa

"Selesia, have I ever told you the Epos of Europa?"

"No father, is that today's story?"

I watch as my father nods his head in satisfaction before looking up once more.

"Always remember, this world is old and full of memories and secrets, our nation was once powerful, possessing a power unrivalled by any other. Our leaders blessed with divine blood, led our armies beyond the oceans.

Though we were few, we were equal to a thousand others, our strength coming from the weapons and armour of Haephaestus himself. But our ancestors though blessed were still Men, bound by pride and we challenged those who should not be challenged.

Using the Pillars of Haerakarles we crossed the divide which had been made by the three supreme Gods and we sought to rule those on the other side. We who were blessed broke the Covenant.

But those who lived in the land of Europa united against us, pushing us back until our very own Isle was on the brink of invasion.

80

But when our fall was certain, the Gods took pity and intervened in our affairs for the final time. But this came at a price.

The skies above us became filled with ash and lightning as earthquakes shook our lands. The rising waters sunk and scattered the invading armadas, but also shattered the Pillars we had once used, forever closing the gates to the domains beyond and our access to the Gods."

Europa.

It was a word that had become a metaphor for the unobtainable, but today was not the first time I had heard it mentioned. Many believed the lands had once existed, but I had visited the Pillars of Haerakarles and they were nothing more than a dozen columns of shattered stones with nothing beyond them bar an empty ocean.

I certainly did not see a mystical land filled with mythological warriors who could fight as equals to our ancestors. Even if the myths were true, it was clear we had not learnt our lessons, for my ancestors led our people into a millennium of war.

Even before the year of my birth and before the ascendency of my father to the throne, we had lost domains and colonies as our armies were broken, scattered, and pushed back until our very Isle was faced with the threat of invasion. Only the fear of the final gifts of our patron God which had been sealed away within the Vault of Haephaestus had prevented our enslavement and conquest by the barbarian hordes who lived across the oceans.

My father had often spoken of the folly and mistakes of his predecessors and had sought to end the cycle of war. Seeking peace, attempting to build ties with those who were willing, trading resources for research and technology, ever seeking to restore our nation's place in the world. Those in my father's Court however did not see the wisdom of his actions. Being too short-sighted and narrow-minded and believing in the ethos of our supremacy, they condemned him as a traitor and a fool.

Knowing that his enemies would soon make moves to depose him, my father had acted with great foresight and wisdom. Using the last of his might and knowledge in the ancient art of high magic, he sealed the vault and prepared for us, his children, to escape from the capital.

But on that same night, more than two years ago, he was murdered by his brother, my uncle who usurped the throne. I remember that night well, saying goodbye to my mother as she remained behind with the smell of burning and the cries and screams of the victims of the massacre which followed. But my father's sacrifice had not been in vain, even now those legendary weapons were still sealed away, and could not be used against us in this war.

I feel the flow of tears running down my cheeks and I wipe them away before they can soak into my sheets. Staring out into the night sky, I bask in the light of the twin silver moons and begin to appreciate the softness of the covers and bedding underneath my body. It had been months, maybe even a year since I had last slept in a bed of such comfort.

As I remember the faces of my parents, I choose not to fight the warmth which was beginning to seep into my body. Surrendering myself, I slowly enter sleeps embrace, closing my eyes, allowing my mind to wander into memories of happier times. I remember the voices of my mother and father, of them, reading me stories, of a

time when I still believed that heroes would come to save me.

Chapter Nine

I feel the sensation of soft small hands shake my shoulders repeatedly. Opening my eyes slowly, I see the shadow of a woman on top of me, their voice full of fear. My still sleeping mind takes time to understand the words they are speaking, but soon I hear them clearly.

"Princess, Princess Selesia, please wake up!"

"Helena?"

Rubbing my eyes and blinking repeatedly, I stare up in confusion at Helena as she continues to shake my body. The fear and urgency in her voice and the horror that was etched onto her face revealed that something was wrong.

"What is wrong Helena? Why are you terrified?"

"The drums!"

"What drums? You are not making sense."

"The drums in the distance, can you not hear them?"

I turn my head, listening for the sound, but the silence only adds to my confusion. Just as I am about to question her further, I suddenly hear them.

THUMP! THUMP! THUMP!

Understanding instantly the reason for the terror on her face, it was a sound I had grown to know well over the last two years. A sound that has continued to haunt my every waking moment as it pursued me across the land.

"Get me my clothes."

The simple yet normal request breaks through the fear that has come to grip her. Hesitating at first, she reacts to my words, nodding her head in understanding as she moves to the table beside my bed. Sliding across to the edge, I slowly clamber to my feet, holding onto the table as my limbs tremble. Despite sleeping, I was still exhausted and needed the assistance of Helena to slip on my clothes.

Opening a tied satchel, she exposes and unpacks a set of silver armour. Turning her head towards me, she looks on with a face full of expectation.

"Only the cuirass and grieves, my body can handle no more today."

Removing only the pieces I had asked for, she packs the rest away before strapping and tying the pieces to my body. Standing to my full height in front of a mirror, I admire the armour as it glistens in the sunlight.

My father had commissioned the armour to mark my sixteenth birthday, crafted in the belief that my body would not develop any further. Three years had passed and their prediction had been correct, my physical body had remained unchanged since the day I had received it, my mind, however, had not. Gleaming like silver, it was forged from the lightest and rarest metals, lighter than anything issued to a knight. But even this was still heavy for my frail and easily fatigued body.

Leaning on the table, I rest my limbs as Helena affixes my cloak with trembling hands. Dyed in a rich purple, it would reveal to even a casual observer my lineage. I watch as her hands continue to shake, the intensity increasing with every beat of the approaching drums.

Before the final pin is secured, the brooch slips from her fingers and falls to the ground. With a soft chink, it rolls away. Helena panics, falling to the floor, tripping over her clothes as she manically reaches out, trying to stop it from slipping beneath the bed. With the brooch grasped in her fingers, she looks up with tears in her eyes. My face softens as I reach down, taking hold of her hands with both of mine and help her to her feet.

"That is enough Helena, I can do the rest myself. Go and get dressed."

I continue to speak words of reassurance, steadying her nerves as she fights back the tears. Blushing in embarrassment, she breaks from my embrace, walks to her bed, and begins to disrobe. Carefully attaching the final brooch, I watch as she begins to get dressed, her youthful and energetic body a contrast to mine. Her pale yet unblemished skin possessed a healthy glow, a contrast to her long, silky, flowing brown hair that touches the small of her back. Though not yet sixteen, I admire her curvaceous body, knowing that if given the opportunity she would someday blossom into a woman who would be the envy of all.

Watching her dainty movements, however, fills me with guilt and sadness as I realise how hard the last few years had been on her. The first daughter of a country noble, she had been born and raised in the relatively peaceful southern realms. Her childhood like mine had been sheltered from the harsh reality of poverty and conflict. Mere months after being presented as my lady in waiting, she had been forced to bear witness to constant bloodshed, her eyes as a result had lost their original lustre and youthful innocence.

My cloak finally fastened, I walk across, assisting her as she struggles to fasten her own. She looks downwards, her pale skin becomes tinged with red as she blushes in embarrassment, and her words as she speaks are barely above a whisper.

"Thank you Selesia."

A frown forms on my lips as I reach out, lifting her chin with one hand as I stroke her hair with the other.

"It is okay to be afraid Helena. But know that the Captain and those under him will never allow anything to befall you.

Nodding her head, she looks into my eyes as a thin, faint smile forms on her lips.

"Do you know where the Captain and my sister are?"

Nodding her head, she clears her throat and stands with her back straight.

"The Captain awaits outside, those of his command are escorting your sister as we speak."

I smile as she regains her composure, her words and news were as expected. The Captain had acted quickly and had begun to make all the necessary arrangements for our departure. During moments of crisis, I could think of no one more reliable than him. Helena secures a short sword to my waist before a pair of daggers to her own. Bowing slightly, she turns and walks to the door, but her attempts at elegance are ruined when she trips over a rug, a high-pitched squeal leaving her lips as she falls.

The heavy wooden doors immediately open and a pair of arms, coated in silver, reach out and take hold of her, stopping her descent. With a smile, her saviour stands to his full height, his heavy armour shining in the sunlight. Cradling her in his arms, he holds her carefully as he kneels before me, allowing Helena to place her feet on the ground and leave his embrace.

Mortified, her face flush, Helena steps away, standing by my side as the silver giant draws his equally large sword, placing the tip on the floor as he awaits my command and acknowledgement. I smile, it has been months since I had seen the Captain in his full armoured might, for too long we had to hide in the shadows.

His armour was, in form, the equal of my own, crafted by the same master artificers with the same rare ores, but it was superior in practice. Behind the etched murals of ancient legends were hidden glyphs of protection, invisible to all who did not possess the aptitude of the sight.

My eyes follow the etchings, admiring the design on the breastplate which depicts the battle of the demi-God Haerakarles against the Lycurgus Lion. The artificer's work was intricate, depicting the flowing hair of the lion's main as it makes its final leap. No one could look upon his armour and not realise the identity of its wearer, nor those he guards.

"Stand my Captain."

"By your command."

Returning to his feet, he sheathes his sword as his eyes scan my body.

"Have you rested my Princess?"

"I have rested, though my body is still fatigued. Captain, are those the drums of the Usurper?"

He nods his head in response to my question, confirming what Helena had said to me. My left arm begins to tremble in response to his words. Grabbing hold of it with my right, I steady my voice before speaking.

"How…many have come?"

"Twenty thousand."

I feel his eyes boring into me as he answers my question. My legs begin to tremble and Helena reaches out, holding onto me as I feel my legs buckle.

"That is impossible…"

The number is incomprehensible, even I who was ignorant of military strategy knew the importance of numbers. But never has such a host marched on our blessed Isle, especially not in the middle of winter.

"The scouts appear to be reliable, I do not doubt what they have seen."

"How did such a host approach unnoticed? Even we who were few could not approach this closely."

"They have used the recent storm to hide their movements, marching despite the risks. It is also believed that they have magicians within their ranks."

"Sit me down, Helena."

She assists me to the nearby bed, allowing me to sit as my body continues to tremble from the shock of what I have heard. I hear the rapid beating of my heart and feel the clamminess of my hands as I begin to sweat uncontrollably, fear had gripped me.

"Can…this fortress be defended?"

My words are barely above a whisper, but I know the Captain has heard them. I can hear the movements of his armour as he moves his head, I do not need to look up to know his answer.

"The Governor and those under him are experienced, the walls are thick and high, but their numbers are too few. Three thousand will not be enough to push back the enemy."

"What do you advise my Captain?"

"I have already made plans for our escape if the opportunity should arise."

I blink in astonishment at the Captain's unexpected words. In the years that I have known him, he has never spoken openly of the possibility of defeat, though I knew he always made plans for it. Such words ran counter to his warrior's pride, I knew this was due to the presence of me and my sister.

"If we should escape, where would you take us?"

"Those of the northern kingdoms appear to be loyal to you and your brothers, I do not believe they will surrender us to the enemy."

"We however cannot remain here, my brothers need me in the south."

"No my Princess, your brothers need you and your sister to remain alive. We will go south when the opportunity allows. There are other paths beyond those of the mountain."

I shudder as I hear those words, knowing the paths he speaks of.

"However, due to the peril, we will need others to join us, for even we would struggle to defend against the hidden horrors whilst defending three others."

I am filled with shame as I look into the Captain's face, knowing that I was a burden to the Captain and those he commands. He sees my expression and walks across, taking hold of my shoulder as he shakes his head.

"Even your brothers who are skilled with bow and sword need to be protected. You have never been a burden to me, believe in your own greater destiny. You have a role to play in this war and what happens after."

I blink, fighting back the tears as I look into the Captain's eyes, appreciating his kind words. My lips begin to move when I hear the sound of clinking metal and running feet. I look past the Captain and watch as a young girl dressed in chainmail enters the room. Running towards me, she leaps with outstretched arms.

"Sister!"

I catch her before her body impacts against my breastplate, her momentum knocking me onto my back as I land on the bed.

Wrapping my arms tightly around her small and delicate body, I allow her to burrow her head into my chest. Through the armour, I feel the tears that are streaming steadily down her childlike features as her body quivers in fear.

"They have come for us!"

"Sssh, I am here now."

Younger than Helena, her youth had been stolen away by the horrors she had been forced to endure and witness. Despite my own fears, I bury them deep inside me as I act as an older sister, gently stroking her soft golden hair as I wait for her sobbing to end.

"Do not be afraid. Lykon would never allow anything to happen to us."

She looks up immediately, a look of expectation on her face as she turns towards the Captain who simply nods. Guilt and various other emotions flow within me once more as I look at her damp puffy red eyes.

"Your sister speaks the truth. Never would I allow another to harm you."

The Captain's bold but truthful words cause my sister's grip to slacken as her body relaxes. Pushing her off gently, I slowly sit up and turn towards the still-open door. I see the backs of the other members of the Royal Guard, their actions allowing us a degree of privacy.

"Little sister, you must always remember, you are a princess. We cannot allow others to see us cry."

"Uh-huh"

Nodding her head in understanding, I continue to stroke her hair as Helena removes a silk cloth from the inner lining of her cloak. Moving slowly, she dries away the tears and makes my sister presentable once more. Turning towards the Captain, I indicate that we are ready.

"Princesses, follow me."

Taking the hands of my sister and I, he helps us off the bed as he guides us to the door.

"Artemesia, at the front with me. Dichas, lead the rear guard. We make for the Governor's quarters."

"By your command."

Chapter Ten

Using the route shown to us the night before, we hasten through the myriad of corridors without a single challenge. The few hoplites remaining sheathe their weapons and kneel upon gazing at the silver armour and flowing purple cloaks.

Ever vigilant, the Captain rests his hand close to his sword as his eyes flicker, searching for assassins in the darkness. Exhausted by the speed of their march, I cling to my sister, relying on her to keep me upright as she squeezes my hand.

Though they linger in the shadows, murmurs follow our movements.

"The Silver Lion! The Silver Lion has come…"

"It is the Crown Princess. Surely the rumours are true, we are saved…"

Despite the efforts of the Governor and his aide, whispers of our attendance had been circulating during the night. With our sudden appearance in regal garb, those rumours would soon quickly spread beyond the walls of this mansion.

"I am telling you it is pointless. The fortress is lost!"

"Coward!"

"Never in our history has this fortress been abandoned. We cannot do so now!"

Angry retorts are heard from the other side of the thick wooden doors ahead of us. Noticing our approach, a pair of hoplites guarding the door draw their swords as they motion for us to stop, but upon hearing the Captain's wolf-like growl of displeasure, they hurriedly step aside.

Placing his gauntleted hands on the twin doors, he pushes them open with minimal effort, the sudden creaking of the door causes a single person from those huddled around the table to look up.

"How dare you…"

The words are caught in the man's throat as he blinks before opening his eyes wide in surprise. His unusual actions cause those around him to look up, and soon whispers are heard from those at the table.

"The Lion! Why is he here?"

"Is that the Princess? Is that why the enemy has come?"

Approaching the table without breaking his stride, the Captain's eyes are drawn immediately to the map and coloured blocks on the table.

"Tell me, how bad is the situation beyond the walls?"

The Governor clears his throat, he alone remaining unshaken by the Captain's sudden appearance. Glancing left and right, he looks into the eyes of those around him.

"By the Gods, I cannot lie. The fortress will not withstand a siege."

The honest response causes a growl to escape the Captain's lips.

"How long?"

"The enemy is mostly infantry and cavalry, with little or no siege equipment. We believe they will try to besiege us, sadly our supplies have not been replenished due to a poor harvest. We have food to last two, at most three weeks."

Picking up a coloured block that represented a segment of the enemy's approaching army, the Captain turns it repeatedly before placing it back on the map.

"Your kingdom has always been few in number, can you afford the loss of three thousand? Have you thought of abandoning the fortress?"

The Captain's words cause comments of displeasure to leave the mouths of half of those around the table. The Governor raises his hands, indicating for everyone to remain silent.

"Sir Lykon, honour alone would prevent us from taking such action, but we have another reason to remain. It is no longer the season of war and our winters are fiercer than those known by the south. Only the three thousand stationed within our walls remain, the other home armies have been disbanded to wait the coming of spring..."

"And you need time to muster."

The Captain speaks the final words, a cold chill sends shivers down my spine as I watch the expressions of those at the table, faces of resignation as they prepare for the ultimate sacrifice.

"And how long will it take for the north to muster and march?"

The Governor directs our gazes to a woman who stands beside him, dressed in burnished bronze armour, her red cloak decorated with the rank of a *lochagos*. It is my turn to be surprised as I recognise the face of the woman wearing it, Eleni, the aide of the Governor. Her armour hides her womanly curves and her long red hair which had previously hung loose was now pleated and hanging down her back, a sword sheathed at her waist. She bows her head towards me and the Captain before speaking.

"I have sent doves and riders to the nearest settlements, but we do not expect an army to arrive for four weeks."

"Too long…"

I barely hear the mutterings of the Captain despite being beside him. He steps forward and places his extended finger down on a section of the map, far from any blocks of wood.

"This path, is it still passable?"

All eyes follow his gaze and nod as if understanding the Captain's intent. It is the Governor however who answers the question, his words hesitant.

"Our scouts state the forest path is still open and unopposed. However…"

"However?"

"I wish to make a request before you and the princesses leave."

"Request?"

A deep-throated snarl leaves the Captain's lips as his brows furrow, his glare being directed not at the Governor but those behind him who shuffle nervously.

"I wish for the princesses to delay their escape for three more days."

The words have barely left his lips before the hands of every member of the Royal Guard are drawn to their swords, ready to unsheathe their blades as they shield my sister and me between them. I sense the growing tension in the air and push past those in front of me, placing my hand on the Captain's forearm, a gentle press to indicate my wish to hear their reason.

"Sir Kivos, you have made an extremely bold request, especially in our current circumstance. Now with an army at your gates and with all that has happened, surely you understand why my guards are prepared to strike you and everyone in this room down? I would speak plainly and quickly."

Upon hearing my words, he steps away from the table and his advisors and kneels. Looking up, he ensures his eyes are looking directly into mine.

"Your Highness, forgive my presumptions, but have you ever lived amongst the common people?"

I look intently into his eyes before shaking my head in response.

"Soldiers on the brink of battle, when faced with death become superstitious, they seek omens either bad or good. Despite our attempts at secrecy, rumours of your arrival have already spread, and now there is an army beyond our gates. Many have begun to remember the coming of the eagle bearing the message with the Oracle's mark."

He chooses to pause, allowing the implications behind his words to be understood. Guilt swirls within me, but despite my inner turmoil, I refuse to allow my emotions to appear on my face.

"I have listened to your words, tell me, what is your request?"

"I ask, no beg of Your Highness to remain for three more days. On the morning of the fourth, we can proclaim that you are riding north to lead our relief."

Never during his passionate appeal did his eyes waiver, nor did he break contact with mine, but I had seen and heard better liars during my time at Court, men and women whose tongues were more potent than any poison. I however could sense nothing but conviction and sincerity in his voice.

Closing my eyes, I know the choice I wish to make, but my decision would decide the fate of others as well. Calming my beating heart, I isolate my mind as I stare into the very essence of the man kneeling before me.

"Sir Kivos, is it true you were once a knight of the ancient orders?"

"I was, a long time ago."

"Why are you not one now?"

His essence flickers upon hearing my question, the colour changing, becoming dimmer as if he is remembering a painful memory.

"As a young man, I was chosen to wear the blue of the Trident. I wore it with pride but I was young and foolhardy, forever rushing into danger without a second thought, always seeking glory for personal gain.

The Gods' however judged that a fool such as I should be punished, and on the field of battle, my actions led to the death of seven of my sword brethren. I was cast out, discarded, and dishonoured, I have sought to atone for my shame ever since."

A harsh memory, but despite his pain, despite the revelation of his dishonour to those beside him, he has told not a lie.

"Do you still honour your vows?"

"I do your Highness."

"As a loyal knight, give me counsel."

"Ignore the request I have made, flee, and never look back. Your life and your sister are worth more than ours."

Satisfied, I finally understood the character of the man before me. Opening my eyes, my decision is made.

"My father often spoke highly of those from the northern kingdoms. I understand why your loyalty and honesty are much

106

desired. Know that your request is made to I, Selesia of the Royal House of Theaolus. I am not my brothers nor am I, my father. I have no skill with words nor bows and sword, but the divine blood still flows through my veins. I have a duty to my people so I grant your request but on one condition. My sister and I shall remain only as long as my Captain deems it so."

A sigh of relief comes not from the lips of the Governor but those behind him. It was clear from his words that the request was not his own. I turn and look at the Captain, noticing the small movements of his fingers in his right hand.

"Princess Selesia has made her choice, but know this, we leave when I command. Ensure our horses are made ready with our requested supplies."

Though his words are directed to everyone in the room, his eyes remain fixed on the still kneeling Governor.

"By my honour, I will ensure it so."

With our agreement struck, the Governor stands to his full height and sweeps back his cloak. Revealing his burnished armour and honed physique, before extending a hand in my direction.

107

"Your Highness, would you accompany me as I address the garrison?"

I hesitate at first, unsure of what to do, but I catch the subtle nod of the Captain in the corner of my eye. Accepting his hand, I feel the dry, roughness of his skin as his fingers gently wrap around my own. Standing beside me, he guides me through the open door and into the corridors. Only the Captain follows me, the others remaining with my sister and Helena.

⚜ ⚜ ⚜

Shielding my eyes from the blinding sun as I step out onto the central plaza, I allow them to adjust before gazing upon the sight of rank after rank of bronze armours soldiers, their weapons grasped in their hands as banners fly in the breeze.

Taking my hand, the Governor guides me into the shade, before leaning forward and whispering into my ear.

"Please wait here, Your Highness."

Taking slow and steady steps, he climbs the raised podium that has been prepared in advance. I soon hear the roar of the crowd, the respect and admiration they had for their Governor and commander.

I stare in admiration as he simply raises his hand, the motion enough to silence the crowd.

"Warriors of the north, my brothers and sisters, listen to my words.

The oath breakers have come to our lands once again. They come to pillage, murder, and destroy, but today as always, we stand against them. For ten years I have led you, not once have I lied to you and I will not start now.

The enemy has come in great numbers, you will see this truth with your own eyes, but that means nothing before our walls. Not once have our walls been taken, not whilst we draw breath, not because we are braver, not because we are stronger, it is because we fight for something more than gold and riches.

We fight for those we love, our families in the lands beyond these walls. Today, like every day, we will declare to the very Gods our remembrance of the oaths of loyalty we have sworn, the same oaths that they have spat on and forgotten."

Turning his head towards me, a smile on his suddenly youthful face, he extends his hand, asking me once again to take it. Slowly, I walk up the steps until I am standing beside him, looking down on the faces of those below.

"Silver armour…"

"She is wearing purple…"

"Is she not the Crown Princess…?"

The crowd grows eerily quiet as if enchanted by my presence. Only the whispers of those close enough to the podium are heard.

"Crown Princess Selesia stands before you now, unlike the Usurper who has chosen to remain hidden in the southern realms. She has not come alone, beside her stands the Silver Lion, the greatest living warrior our lands have ever known."

Upon hearing the Captain's epithet, the crowd shatters its earlier silence with cheers as they shout repeatedly the Captain's name. I smile in amazement at their reaction. I knew the Captain was famous, but only now did I understand the extent and effect of his fame.

"Show him and the ever-watching Gods how you fight, show them deeds to earn your place in Elysium and when this war is over,

let bards sing of them so even when your bones are dust, you are not

forgotten. Go now, to victory!"

The words have barely left his lips before the crash of shields, beat of spears, and cries to victory escape the mouths of those in the plaza. Nodding in satisfaction, the Governor turns and guides me down the stairs and hands me back to the Captain.

A pair of hoplites emerge from the mansion, a second spear, shield, and helmet held in their hands. I watch as the Governor's face changes, the smile remains but the intensity and emotions behind it are different, becoming almost regal and reassuring. Taking the helmet, he places it carefully on his head, securing it in place with the chin straps. My eyes open wide as I admire the unusual colours and design of his helmet, the crest possessing alternating stripes of red and white plumes.

With a deep bow, he turns and addresses me once more.

"Your Highness, I have prepared a tower in the northern sector of the city, it should meet your needs. I have also made arrangements for your horses to be moved to a nearby stable and for your supplies to be restocked."

111

I part my lips, a reply on the tip of my tongue when the Governor's gaze moves to the Captain.

"A dozen of my own guards are now yours, treat them like your own for they will serve you well."

I watch as they stare at each other as if having a silent conversation before coming to an understanding. I smile and bow, returning the favour that had been shown to me.

"I thank you for your consideration. I will pray to the Gods that your battle goes well, Sir Kivos."

No further words are spoken as he turns and takes the shield and spear that have been presented to him. With a single wave of his spear, he marches in the direction of the great southern gates, his bodyguard following a few paces behind him. I watch the shrinking outline of his back as his blood-red cloak billows behind him, the sight majestic yet filling my heart with sadness. Too many brave and noble warriors would soon have their threads cut in the coming days.

"The people are lucky."

I hear the Captain's words and turn towards him, my face etched in confusion. A twinkle appears in the Captain's eyes as he smiles and chuckles.

"You are blessed with a kind heart, Princess."

I repeat the words silently as the Captain continues to chuckle, his features growing warmer with every passing moment.

"We, who wields a bow, spear or shield know our possible fate, give us not tears of sorrow, but remember our deeds, that is what we ask."

"I understand, but still…"

"Do not worry about that man. He has changed much since his youth, but his skill and prowess have not."

"I suspected you knew of him, but I did not realise you had a shared history?"

"We did…"

The Captain looks at me, hesitating before he continues.

"He once served your birth mother, pledged to stand by her side until the day of her betrothal to your father. Believe me, his thread will not be cut easily."

My eyes widen as I hear the revelation. Quickly I look south, my eyes darting left and right as I desperately look for the Governor's distinctive crest, but he is gone. A frown forms on my face as I turn questioningly towards the man beside me.

"Why did you not tell me sooner?"

I stifle the mixed emotions that are swirling within me, the anger and disappointment in the lost opportunity to know more about my past, to know more about the woman I never knew.

"I feared your decisions would have become influenced if you knew."

Those simple words bite deeply and I cross my arms in umbrage, insulted, as I speak coldly in response.

"I am not a child…"

Despite my retort, I see my reflection in his eyes and realise immediately how immature and child-like I appeared. Cheeks reddening in embarrassment, I quickly turn away and look down at my feet, seeking to preserve my dignity as much as possible.

"Still, I would wish to speak to him again someday and learn…"

Mumbled and barely above a whisper, I knew no one would hear those words, a child-like wish that continued to linger in the deepest recesses of my heart. I feel the Captain's gauntleted fingers on my shoulders as he slowly turns me away from the sights and sounds of the southern gates.

"I apologise my Princess. When the time comes, let me tell you of what I know. There is much still that he and I need to discuss before either of us enter the fields of Elysium."

"Lykon!"

His foreboding words are spoken almost absentmindedly and they shake me to the core. My words, my face, and my voice reveal the emotions I have tried to hide. Seeing the Captain's face as he hears my retort, I attempt to recover.

"You cannot let others hear such things, think of our nation's morale. You who has no equal in strength or skill...."

A hoarse and hearty laugh escapes the lips of the Captain as he hears my hurried recovery, causing me to puff my cheeks and scowl at him. The laughter continues until he finally stops on his own accord, tears in his eyes.

"Still you treat me like a child!"

"I apologise my Princess. However, when I saw your face, it reminded me of the words you spoke as a child."

Despite his words, I see no changes in his face or even the hint of remorse.

"No one has ever bested me in battle, but not even I can escape death. It is only the young who would believe it so. Death will claim me someday, whether I have a sword in my hand or when I am old and within my bed."

Looking down, he smiles a true and genuine smile at me, one filled with warmth and hope. The sight alone causes my heart to race and disperses the earlier mood.

"Once I thought only of dying on the battlefield, but now, I would not mind being within my bed and surrounded by those I love."

Turning away, he looks north at the tower in the distance.

"Come, let us go and watch the battle in comfort and safety. Your sister will hopefully be waiting already."

Nodding, I lean against him, wrapping my arms around his own as I allow him to guide me through the streets. A feeling of warmth is spreading through my body as I think of his words.

Chapter Eleven

The cruel wind that sweeps across the rooftop knocks back my hood, exposing my already pale skin and hair to the chilling elements. I feel the cold instantly as it bites deep, the warmth leaving my body before I can even shiver as my skin whitens further. Quickly, I pull up my hood and nestle deeper into the cloak of the Captain who stands beside me.

Standing on the roof of a tower in the north of the city, far from the southern walls whilst wrapped up in the arms of the Captain, I feel like a nesting bird that is perched up high. My eyes scan the streets below, listening to the shouts that travel across the city as officers quickly herd their companies into position.

I suddenly feel the Captain's grip tighten as another strong gust threatens to knock me down, protecting my frail and light body once more with his own. The warmth of his body spreads due to how close we are standing, and despite the pending chaos, I feel at ease.

Subtly, I tilt my head upwards to have a better view of the Captain's face underneath his hood, I gaze at his strong, square jawline and his short cut, brown but greying hair. The sight of his features up-close causes my heart to race. I feel my palms become clammy as I realise we are alone, the others sleeping below in the warmth of the tower's chambers. I close my eyes, imagining how we would appear to others, did we look like a noblewoman and her bodyguard, parent, and child, or did we appear as lovers? The final thought causes my heart to flutter and my cheeks to redden.

The moment soon passes however as the Captain speaks, his voice and demeanour becoming that of a teacher as he narrates what is happening below. His personality was ever-changing, dependent on the circumstances, easily becoming my teacher, my guardian, friend, and confidante.

Pointing to the nearest movement of soldiers, he explains the importance of placement, how due to the width of the walls, only a quarter of the garrison could man them, requiring the remainder to wait in reserve. Despite his explanations, I doubted I could ever become a successful military leader. As my eyes scan the ranks of burnished bronze, I notice something unusual.

"I had thought Sir Helios' garrison was unique, but I see everyone here is armed with bow and spear. I have never seen the like before."

A long *hmm* escapes the lips of my teacher as a bemused smile appears on his lips. His tone causes me to glower.

"Our people are famous for their use of spear and shield within a phalanx, a wall of flesh and metal that crushes anything in its path. But this is not the only way to fight, our way is slow and ponderous, a legacy of our ancestors which has remained unchanged after a thousand years.

The belief that our traditions are superior had caused many to consider the bow as a weapon for cowards on the battlefield, the skill only for sport and luxury, but for the northern kingdoms, it is different.

What do you see beyond the walls, my Princess?"

I look beyond the walls onto the still clear horizon and see mountains and oceans of forests. A sound passes my lips as I understand a little better.

"As you see, they do not share our vast open fields, but instead within these mountains and forests lie the great beasts. Skill with shield and spear is not enough, so here the bow is also prized. Their need for flexibility has led to their own style of warfare."

The heavy beat of drums in the distance however brings the lesson to an abrupt end, the sound resonating and echoing through the valley, causing a feeling of dread to settle into the hearts of all who hear it. I imagine the ground trembling due to the heavy tread of marching feet as the enemy finally appears on the horizon.

A single horn blast causes the enemy to suddenly stop, standing in long and deep ranks, their dark coloured banners flapping in the wind. My heart beats for a different reason when I see them, the feeling shared with those in the city below as the less experienced soldiers let slip their cries of fear. Their panicked cries are cut short as officers and veterans lash out with barbed tongues, fists, and canes held in their hands, the snap of breaking wood a warning as it strikes soft flesh.

How could any man or woman retain their courage when they see such a monstrous spectacle, how could they not be awed? Question after question begins to cloud my judgement and my body trembles until I feel a reassuring hand pat my shoulder. Turning, I look up at the Captain, staring at him in interest and confusion as he holds a strange cylindrical device in his right hand. Smiling, he waits for me to take it, but its purpose and design are alien to me.

"What is that?"

My fingers tremble as I slowly wrap them around the object, feeling the cold touch of metal as I look in confusion. I feel the softening gaze of the Captain as he chuckles.

"Hold the thin end close to your right eye and look through it. Do not forget to close your left eye."

I notice the transparent glass on either side and follow his instructions with trepidation. The object is heavier than I expected and my arms tremble as I look through the narrow end. My vision changes instantly, the city landscape is replaced by the up-close glimpse of dark coloured armour. A shriek escapes my lips as I try to step backwards, barging straight into the Captain as I nearly drop the cylinder in my hand.

I feel the grip of the Captain's hand wrapped around my own, maintaining my grip on the object as he stops me from moving. I push against him, trying to get away, not understanding why he remained as still as a statue despite the closeness of the enemy.

"Let me go! The enemy is close."

The sound of a deep, hearty laugh however causes me to stop struggling, I look up in worry, wondering whether the Captain had grown mad due to the enemy's number. Only the glint of a mischievous twinkle in his eye made me look in the direction he was pointing.

Turning my head, I find the enemy once again far in the distance, far enough away that they were nothing more than a large black blob. With a quizzical look, I ask the question.

"Magic?"

"Not quite."

Shaking his head, he answers my question cryptically.

"Decades ago when I was a younger man, I once travelled to the southern continent, I found this at a simple market. It is a tool to allow the user to see things in the distance as if they are near."

"I never knew you possessed such a thing. What did you mean by your answer, how is this not magic?"

The same mischievous twinkle once again appears in his eyes as he gives me a knowing smile. The smile is both charming and irritating.

"There are many mysteries in the world, every land has its own knowledge and magic. The shopkeeper I bought this from described her lands magic as *al-aloum* or science."

I repeat the words, forming them in my mouth as I attempt to duplicate the pronunciation. Despite my attempts, it is not perfect and I still do not understand their meaning.

I turn the object in my hand slowly, examining it in detail, my curiosity piqued.

"What do they call such a device?"

"*Al-tilskub* is how I believe they pronounced it. I choose to call it a telescope."

Telescope, I repeat the word silently, nodding my head in satisfaction as a wry smile appears on my lips. The Captain always chooses simplicity.

"I returned with a pair of these devices, the second of which I gave to your father. He saw instantly the potential in the wisdom of others."

"And that is why he was so desperate to seek peace..."

Having heard the origins of the object in my hand, I now look at it lovingly, admiring its simple design and craftsmanship. I smile as I return the cylinder to my eye and peer through it once again, happy that I had learnt something new about my father.

"They are surely blessed by Artheana and Haephaestus to readily have such items."

"Blessed they may be, but not by our Gods, they worship Gods of their own."

I hesitate upon hearing his words, I had never known the world to know other Gods beyond our own. Sweeping aside my ignorance, I concentrate on what I was seeing. My vision centres on the black pinions being flown from the top of the spears, the design of twin

125

white snakes wrapping themselves around a blood dripped sword, the personal heraldry of the Usurper.

"My father's dream must live on, when this war is finally over and my brothers replace me and ascend the throne, we must convince them to seek this knowledge."

⊰────◦◦────⊱

A deathly silence fills the valley as the enemy comes to a stop beyond our walls, beyond the range of even our artillery pieces. The rectangular shields they were holding were a stark contrast to the round shields that were held in the hands of those at the wall.

I watch as a ripple appears in the centre of the orderly ranks as a trio of armoured knights ride out. Their armour and even their horses are black, the only contrast coming from the blood-red cloaks and the white fabric flying from their lances. The archers on the wall nock and pull back their bows, following the movements of the riders. Their release is only prevented due to the recognised symbol of an envoy negotiating under the symbol of truce. All knew the foul fate of any who broke this hallowed law.

I focus on the lead rider, peering at him through the telescope in my hand. His facial features were hidden underneath his helmet, but his long flowing golden hair is familiar to me. I move to the heraldry on his shield and see a single golden coloured winged claw, the sight causes my heart to stop. A symbol of one of the great noble houses whose sons and daughters often married into the royal bloodline. I could no longer doubt the words of Sir Helios when one of the royal family's staunchest allies was in league with the enemy.

The hammering of wood announces the slow opening of the fortress city's gates, from the shadows of the walls emerge three armoured figures dressed in bronze with red flowing cloaks. They close the distance between them and the riders, their movements unhurried. I recognise immediately the leader of the group, spear in hand as the feathers of his distinctive red and white plumed helmet fluttered in the cold breeze.

Sir Kivos, flanked by his retainers, plants his spear into the ground as he greets his counterpart. The wind and distance make it impossible to hear what is said, but their body language is telling. Standing like statues, Sir Kivos and his retainers listen to the words

127

being spoken, but it is clear they are wary due to the small movements of their hands.

The noble however makes no attempts to feign interest, riding his horse backwards and forwards, seeking to intimidate as he points back at his standing army. The negotiations come to a swift end when the noble points at his retainer who hefts up and throws down a sack that had been hanging on his saddle. The sack lands at Sir Kivos' feet and I see a dark fluid seep out into the snow. The enemy's envoys do not wait for the contents of the sack to be revealed before riding back to their battle lines.

A sword sweeps down, cutting through the knot tying up the sack, I watch as the contents spill out and I immediately begin to wretch, emptying my stomach of its contents. I had seen them, the severed heads of scouts and sentries who were stationed beyond the walls. An angry shout and command are given and the archers on the walls loose their arrows at the fleeing riders.

I feel the Captain's hand gently rub the centre of my back, the comforting motion easing my nausea and I regain my composure. He takes the telescope from my hand as he replaces it with a waterskin. I gladly take the water, pouring it into my mouth as I cleanse it of the foul-tasting bile.

"This is the ugly truth of war, it is far from the stories that you have been told. Behind the veneer of chivalry and nobility are barbarism and savagery which are barely held in check. The enemy has only chosen to abandon any pretences."

"That desecration…"

The image appearing in my head causes the nausea to return, but I hold it in.

"Surely the Gods will curse them!"

Shaking his head, the Captain's action causes my heart to darken. Though, only the night before I had said that the days of the Gods were over, I still lived in the belief of their existence and wrath.

"Will Kharon still allow them to make the journey?"

"No, the laws of the dead are clear. Only those who are whole and receive the proper rights may cross. Someday we may give them the service they deserve."

The Captain's words are emotionless as he replies, I feel however the anger hidden within them. I direct the whirlwind of emotions, the sadness, despair, and anger in a glare towards the retreating riders. Only two had managed to reach their lines, the other screaming in pain in the middle of the battlefield having been thrown from the saddle. His screams cause my anger to subside, and a cheerless smile begins to form.

I stare at the noble and feel only disappointment. How could men and women of such privileged birth allow themselves to partake in such disgrace? I think back to the lead rider and my anger swells, knowing that such a man could have been my suitor if the war had never started fills me with disgust.

The steady beat of drums is joined by the sound of wood and metal clashing as the great armoured gates are closed once again. All pretences of a peaceful resolution are over, the battle was now about to start.

Chapter Twelve

The crack of whips is followed by the screams of pain and fear as the enemy makes its first move. Thousands of men and women, dressed in nothing but rags that hide little of their modesty, move to the front. Behind them stalk figures dressed in elegant robes, bloodied whips in their hands. Neither of their clothes is suited for the winter climate, let alone the battlefield.

The sound of cracking whips is joined by the shout of words in an unknown language. Harsh and filled with bloodlust, it causes shivers to pass down my spine. They were words of a language not heard within these lands for a millennium, the barbaric mother tongue of the slave masters of the western kingdoms.

In response to the whips, the men and women surge forward without discipline and coordination. Without shield or armour, their hands filled with only crude daggers, ropes, and ladders, they are vulnerable to the archers stationed on the walls.

Loose

A shower of white-tailed arrows rains down upon them, cutting great swathes as hundreds fall. Despite their early losses, they continue rushing forward, showing reckless indifference and abandonment to the danger. The only sound to leave their lips are the squeals of pain and fear, but the fear is not of the enemy to their front, but of their masters who stalk behind them. I feel only sympathy as I watch them fall, their wrists and ankles still bound by chains.

The jingle of bells and the singing of hymns soon drown out the sounds of death as priests make themselves known to the defenders. Hymns to the Gods, they seek blessings for those who are about to face death. Their soft and gentle tones are soon joined by raw, untrained, and harsh voices as the veterans lead by example and sing. Their pure, yet heartfelt words are uplifting and they are soon joined by others in their entirety.

Unmoving, unafraid, they strike their spears on shield and stone as they prepared to stand before the barbaric horde.

Draw, Loose

The command is repeated until the voices of the officers grow hoarse. Arrow after arrow is being released with great discipline and effectiveness. I did not need to use the object in my hand to see the great chunks that were appearing in the enemy line, despite this, the number of dead did little to slow the enemy advance.

I catch the glint of something flying, it is soon followed by the faint clunk of metal as the first grappling hook lands on the battlements. A veteran moves quickly, drawing his dagger and cutting the rope, sending the bold climber to the ground below. Soon, however, it is joined by another until a hundred hooks and ladders are in position.

With daggers and axes drawn from their belts, those at the battlements move quickly, cutting the ropes and shattering the ladders as quickly as possible, but the enemy is already scaling the walls. The first to clamber over is impaled by a spear held in the hands of a figure dressed in a red cloak, his helmet crest filled with a mixture of red and white feathers.

Spears and shields

Sir Kivos' voice cries out, and his command is obeyed instantly as those at the wall set aside their bows, placing them on their backs as they grasp the massive round shields and spears placed neatly at their feet. The flexibility of their style of warfare is evident, allowing them to switch quickly, not needing to step aside to allow others to take their place.

Turning his back to the enemy, he points to the massed ranks standing within the city, their bows drawn and aimed skywards. Without a glance at the enemy, he shows his disdain as he sweeps his arm downwards. A thousand white-tipped feathers soon fill the sky, travelling downwards in a great arc.

The enemy advance, which had become emboldened as the vanguard had reached the wall, falters and slows for the first time as they see the looming shadow. Robed figures mercilessly reach out, grabbing hold of their wares as they use them as living shields, but the mass of arrows pass over them, landing in the ranks of spearmen and archers who had followed slowly behind.

The battlefield, already slick with blood and the dead, is thrown into confusion as the second wave falters, stops, and splinters as they

134

clamber over their own dead. The shrill shouts of the enemy officers are heard as they try to restore the earlier discipline and formation.

Catapults and ballistae, third marker!

Artillery commanders who had remained unusually silent make themselves known, as if in anticipation of this moment. Normally the first to bombard the enemy, their weapons exceeded the range of hand-drawn bows, but a poor harvest and recent snowfall had ensured the bolts and heavy stones for their pieces were scarce.

With a hunter's patience that was born from experience and discipline, they had delayed until now, waiting for the enemy to be in a disarray for maximum effect.

Unleash!

What semblance of a formation was instantly shattered as bolts and rocks hammer into the enemy lines. Their light armour and wicker shields do little to dampen the damage or potential of death as men are impaled or crushed.

The first wave, alone and now isolated continue their climb, clambering over the battlements due to the fear of their master's whips. I watch as the defenders lock their shields together, becoming a golden coloured wall of metal and flesh that effortlessly blocks the stones, javelins, and arrows coming their way.

Facing death to the front and no way back, the rag-wearing enemy charge forward with desperate, heartfelt cries on their lips, their crude daggers doing nothing but scratch the shields as they are held in check. Spears lash out, piercing and skewering their near-naked bodies before they are thrown back over the wall. Like a swarm of insects, they are relentless in their assault, uncaring of the danger, swarming until the last of them is wiped out before the ragged remains of the second and third waves arrive to support them.

The cycle of death and bloodshed continues until the sun is high in the sky, I watch the carnage and chaos through the far-seeing eye of the telescope. Just as my heart was on the verge of breaking and I could watch no more, a crude horn blows from the rear of the enemy's line, signalling their first retreat.

Relief washes over my body as I watch the ragged and bloodied soldiers of the enemy withdraw from the walls, running across the blood-churned snow and mud, their withdrawal unchallenged as the defenders collapse from exhaustion, choosing to rally, rest and resupply.

Hope, the smallest hint of it flutters in my heart, but the feeling is shattered as I glimpse the sight of the enemy archers. Lined up with their bows drawn, their aim is not at our walls, but at their comrades who had fought bravely until moments ago. A scream forms on my lips, but no sound escapes as a shrill horn signals the release of hundreds of black-feathered arrows. My knees collapse as a feeling of nausea washes over my body, I could not understand the callous action which had just occurred.

Why? The question does not leave my lips, only tears that stream down my face. Tears for my enemy.

"Your kindness is both a blessing and a curse."

I feel the rough hands of the Captain as he takes hold of my head, wiping away the tears with a cloth. Through the tears I see his face, there is none of his usual charm and smiles, only a steely determination.

"A warning that has cost them nothing."

Those words, cold and emotionless, cause a look of shock horror to become etched on my face. The Captain turns towards me and our eyes meet; they are as cold as a frozen tundra, and it causes a chill to travel down my spine.

"Slaves and prisoners to wear us down, their deaths are a warning to the rest of the price of failure. They can spare the death of thousands we cannot."

Those words, though harsh and emotionless, are the truth and I cannot find the will to challenge them.

A howl travels across the battlefield, ominous and filled with bloodlust, the sound causes our eyes to separate. My body begins to shake at an instinctive level. Biting my lower lip, I raise the telescope to my eye with trembling hands.

On the other side is the next wave arrayed in ranks with their skin sun-kissed, crisscrossed with scars, and coated in red and white paint. Their clothes and armour are heavy, covered in thick pelts, within their hands they hold black stone-based weapons and wooden shields. It is not their appearance, but their very presence that causes my heart to sink.

"Barbarians…"

The name was given to the nomadic, seafaring raiders who continually raid and ravage our nation's shores. United under no single leader, they seek only the weak and undefended to enslave and plunder. For centuries they had been a plague, taking advantage of our nation's strife. They were a people that my uncle, the same Usurper, had argued tirelessly for extermination. Now they were here, in our heartlands, fighting in my uncle's war, his hypocrisy knew no bounds.

But it is the armoured figures who stand behind them, fewer in number, which causes my heart to beat rapidly and my palms to sweat. Dark heavy armour that is caked in dried blood, within their hands and strapped to their backs are oversized swords. Their helmets formed into the features of a snarling wolf, they are the source of the ominous howl. Despite the distance, despite their faces being hidden, I could sense the barely repressed rage and anger.

"Lykanthropos."

The Captain gives voice and name to my fear, these almost legendary wolf-headed warriors who were infamous for their skill

139

and savagery. Their appearance here meant only one thing, there would be no mercy for any who lived within the fortress walls.

What follows is chaos of a different intensity from what I had seen before. I already knew the ability of the soldiers who defended the wall with discipline and resolve to push back the initial waves with minimal losses, but the competence and experience of the barbarians made me realise that nothing was certain in battle, especially victory.

Their equipment was crude but suited for the battlefield, their discipline belied their nature as barbarians, allowing them to emerge relatively unscathed from the barrage of arrows and missiles. Despite their shields and armour being cushioned in white-feathered arrows, they soon reach the walls and begin to climb.

Clambering onto the battlements as if the walls did not exist, they soon clash with the golden line of shields and spears which were raised to face them. Shields, swords, and axes in their hands, they fought with a zeal I had never seen before, not even from members of the knightly orders.

I watch with pride as the line of golden armoured warriors hold, their spears punching out, skewering, and piercing any who came near, and their shields were unbroken despite the relentless barrage. But I soon saw the effects of continuous battle, their discipline wavering as those at the front became exhausted, the fanaticism and relentless assault of the enemy not allowing them to rest.

With fanatical zeal the barbarians continue to swing their weapons, howling in ecstatic delight whilst singing hymns to their unknown Gods. Even when injured and on the verge of death, they continue to fight barehanded, crawling forward, grabbing hold of feet, and pouncing on shields.

The air is soon filled with the almost constant shout of "Doru, doru!" as spears snap and shatter, their replacements swiftly brought forward whilst the veterans switch to their short swords. The walls are soon slick with blood and offal, and even here from the tower I can smell the growing stench of death as it begins to spread. Slowly the once impenetrable line of shields begins to buckle as the number of defenders dwindles. No amount of skill, discipline, or bravery can last indefinitely against such relenting numbers.

"Like ants, their numbers are without end."

My own words sound distant as my eyes grow weary. The darkness grows as the sun begins to set and with it is the coming of the cold blistering winds. It batters my body, piercing through my cloak and sapping away my strength and warmth. My teeth soon chatter and I wrap my cloak tighter to my body.

My limbs are growing weary, but I continued watching, knowing that I could not turn away from the chaotic scenes until the battle ended for the day, no matter how much I wanted to. Despite my resolve, my vision begins to blur and my thoughts become muddled and cloudy. Like a puppet whose strings have been cut, I feel my body crumple.

Strong, large, and coarse hands grab hold of my body, wrapping me up in their arms as I am effortlessly lifted up and sheltered by their shadow. Though I cannot see, I smell the scent of the person and know it instantly as the Captain. My hands reach out, moving up his armoured chest. I wanted him to know I did not want to go indoors yet, that I had to see this battle to the very end.

"It is enough my Princess."

His warm words cut through the fog in my mind, despite the kindness they were clear and stern, in the tone of a father disciplining their child.

During moments of clarity, I feel and hear various things. Heat, I feel it wrapping around my body, warming my cold and tired limbs. I can feel something soft underneath my body as I am gently lowered. I feel soft hands reaching out, touching my skin, moving up and down as they slowly begin to undo the clasps on my armour and cloak.

"Stop."

"...My Lord?"

"Leave her be in her armour."

"My Lord Lykon, she is sick and will not rest properly with it on."

"Her body must grow accustomed to wearing it."

"Surely it is..."

"The enemy continues to assault the southern walls, she will wear it until I say otherwise."

"I understand, my Lord."

I hear the argument between Helena, my lady in waiting, and the Captain. I cannot speak nor move, my fever is too strong and my body is hot and flush as I sweat underneath my armour.

Coarse hands touch my face and gently pull back my hair, stroking it slowly. Their soothing voice is comforting to me, it reminds me of my father. Listening to the voice with closed eyes, I feel a single tear form and roll down my cheek.

"Rest Selesia, you will need your strength in the days to come."

Chapter Thirteen

For three days I had remained trapped in this tower like a maiden of lore, entrapped not due to chains or magic spells, but due to the weakness of my own body. During moments of delirium, where I lingered in a state neither asleep nor awake, I would hear the sound of battle that carried across the winds, causing me to envision vivid dreams and nightmares.

Even now, my body remains weak, the cold air enough to send shivers down my spine. I silently curse my body, knowing it was the cause for my sister's and Helena's looks of concern. Taking a bowl of medicine and soup from their open hands, I swallow the contents gladly.

The bitterness of the medicine is washed away by the richness and warmth of the soup, though the ingredients are simple, I savour every spoonful, admiring the texture and taste. War had taught me many things, but none more so than the appreciation of a warm meal, even if the quality is less than what I was used to.

The door creaks open as I finish the bowl, the Captain entering with a scroll held tightly in his hand. Noticing my wakefulness, he approaches the bed and kneels, allowing me to look at him without straining my neck.

He speaks to me simply, I was not military-minded and did not need the full details, but I knew enough to know the siege was going in our favour. The high walls and the bravery of those who defended them were holding the enemy at bay, but the casualties were growing, especially amongst the veterans who bore the brunt of the fighting. It was their skill and experience which ensured the enemy's numbers counted for little.

Feeling the warmth of the sun through the open window, I stretch out my arms, basking them in the golden rays. Drawing strength from the natural magic which lingers in the aether, my skin begins to glow. As magic seeps into my body, the tiredness is washed away as it is steadily reinforced and rejuvenated.

"O ilios kai o asteroeidis fotismós, mou dínoun dýnami"[2]

Drilled into me since childhood, the chant effortlessly leaves my lips. A simple ritual, it was enough to compensate for my weak constitution, allowing me to live an almost normal life, though the price was great on my mind.

Slowly, with shaky movements, I shuffle towards the edge of the bed.

"Sister! Stop, wait."

"Princess, please remain still."

Hysterical shrieks leave the lips of my sister and lady in waiting as they rush towards me, placing their hands on my shoulders as they try to force me back onto the bed. My body, now invigorated, easily brushes them aside. Planting my feet on the ground, I slowly begin to rise.

"My cloak."

My voice, unusually authoritarian echoes within the now silent room as I chastise them. Helena, with her head drooped, drapes the

---

[2] Ο ήλιος και ο αστεροειδής φωτισμός, μου δίνουν δύναμη - Sun and starlight, grant to me strength.

147

cloak over my shoulders and fastens it in place. On trembling legs, I take a determined step towards the door that leads to the roof.

As sweat drips from my brow, the Captain stretches out his arm, a tender, almost fatherly smile on his lips as he turns his gaze to the others in the room. Consenting under an unspoken command, everyone steps back as I gratefully take the outstretched arm. Pulling close, I coil around him like a snake as I lean on him for support.

"Are you not planning to stop me?"

Hesitantly, I whisper the question as a knowing smile forms on his lips.

"After seeing that face, I did not think it wise to stop you. You have your reasons, do you not?"

Those simple, but heartfelt words cause the dam of emotions within my chest to nearly burst. Digging my nails into the palm of my hand, I fight back the tears that were beginning to form.

With his large hands, the Captain opens the door and allows me to feel the bitter elements once more.

For two whole days, the Usurper's army had chosen to sit idle, choosing to wait rather than press their attack. The ballistae and catapults had long fallen silent, the scant ammunition spent, and what few archers remaining on the walls were nursing half-empty quivers. But despite this respite, the enemy's lack of resolve made everyone ill at ease.

"Why are they…?"

"Singing."

Upon hearing the Captain's half-spoken mutterings, I stop asking the question mid-sentence. I had heard the rumours circulating the city that the Usurper was preparing to starve us out, that the armies before us were only the vanguard of the battalions prepared to subjugate the northern kingdoms. But I did not want to hear the theories and rumours of strangers, I wanted to know the Captain's thoughts.

"Do you believe them to be true, the rumours?"

There is a pause before he answers, choosing instead to stare into the distance, as doubt forms on his normally unmoving and unrelenting features. That face unsettles me.

149

"No, I suspect something more sinister."

"Sinister?"

"The singing."

His cryptic, incomplete sentences are like a series of riddles, ones I know not the answer. Instead, I strain my ears, listening for any sound in the air. Soon I hear it and the expression that Helena had shown days earlier formed on my face.

...ypárche... skotádi.... elpída...

Faint, surrounded by an unnatural buzzing, the words are broken and barely understandable. Despite this, a sense of anxiety, no not anxiety, something much worse, dread washes over my body. Unable to understand the reason for this feeling, I hum and sing, copying the sounds I was hearing.

With each repetition, the song grows increasingly familiar.

"Ópou ypárchei fos, ypárchei skotádi.

Ópou ypárchei elpída ypárchei apelpisía.

Ópou ypárchei zoí, prépei na ypárchei thánatos.

Móno me thysía boreí na gennitheí i néa avgí.

Eláte to skotádi"[3]

My eyes widen as I gag mid-verse, spluttering as I gasp for air, I realise the meaning of the words, the true purpose of the song.

Death.

"Captain, stop their singing!"

Hopelessly, I implore the Captain, screaming at him as I grab his hands, but I already knew it was too late. We were powerless to stop what had already begun.

An icy chill runs down my spine as the air grows still. Afraid of what I would see, I slowly turn. A mist of darkness descends on the valley, billowing from the centre of the enemy camp. My limbs tremble as I sense its unnatural and unholy nature.

A feeling of revulsion forms in the depths of my stomach as I sense the very life, contained within the air and land, carry itself away on unnatural currents towards the epicentre of the darkness.

Something was coming.

---

[3] Όπου υπάρχει φως, υπάρχει σκοτάδι. Όπου υπάρχει ελπίδα υπάρχει απελπισία. Όπου υπάρχει ζωή, πρέπει να υπάρχει θάνατος. Μόνο με θυσία μπορεί να γεννηθεί η νέα αυγή. Ελάτε το σκοτάδι - Where there is light, there is darkness. Where there is hope there is despair. Where there is life, there must be death. Only with sacrifice can the new dawn be born. Come the darkness

I was not alone in reading the omens, across the city, bells begin to ring, the heavenly chimes carrying over the howling winds, briefly dispelling the taint of the unholy hymn. Priests, carrying the symbols of their patron Gods rush to the walls. Their uncloaked bodies wet and exposed to the biting cold, faintly glow as they begin to pray.

THUMP!

The single beat carries across the valley, echoing on the mountain walls. The *thump* is joined by blasts of horns and marching feet as metallic figures emerge from the darkness. Arrayed in deep ranks which stretched across the width of the valley floor, they spread the miasma with every forward step.

Death! Death! Death!

Blood-curdling war cries escape their lips as panpipes are played in response. Though unsettled, the sentries rouse and rally those beside them, waking them from their opportune slumber.

Hastily donning their armour as they clear their eyes of sleep, the northern soldiers once more stand in ranks of gleaming gold, ready to face the latest onslaught. Though they had repeated this cycle a hundred times, I could tell at a glance that something was now different.

"Soldiers are superstitious and they look for omens whether bad or good."

The words of Sir Kivos ring heavily in my ears as I watch the defender's wavering resolve, despite their brave appearance, they stank of fear.

Pinpricks of silver light flicker in the looming darkness as priests wade through the press of bodies to stand at the forefront of the defenders. Though barely clothed and unarmoured, the spearman rally beside them, taking heart from their selfless bravery. Mouthing prayers, they offer their bodies and eternal souls to the Gods as they seek their wrath and salvation from the blasphemy they were witnessing.

As tendrils of black fog reach the walls, shrieks come from the ancient stone as the long-dormant glyphs awaken, crackling as they defend *Sfyri's* inhabitants from the malign influence.

My instincts scream, warning me, telling me to flee as the words that linger in the air become clear. The buzzing, akin to a hive of

153

bees, grows louder as it rings in my ears, causing me to feel suddenly isolated.

I scream for the Captain as the magic within my body is forcibly torn away. A sharp pain pierces my chest as I fall to my knees, coughing and wrenching.

"Princess!"

Wrapped in his arms, I begin to chant, seeking strength as I grow increasingly weaker.

"O ilios kai"

The first syllables have barely passed my lips before I cough and wretch once more. Covering my unsightly mouth, I feel something wet and sticky coat my fingers. Tasting bile interlaced with an unfamiliar metallic tang, I look down and see bright red patches.

"Blood…"

Motionless, I lie as limp as a ragdoll as the Captain carries me away. Struggling to stay awake, I feel the air around me thicken, becoming sicklier to the touch.

"…stop, the, chanting…"

The words are forced as I raise a trembling finger, pointing into the distance. The Captain follows my gaze, not in the direction of the battlefield, but upwards towards the sky.

The twin moons were beginning to move.

Chapter Fourteen

"Blood! Why is there blood?"

My sister's shrill, panicking voice echoes within my ears as the Captain carries me downwards into the warmth of the tower's inner chambers. Ignoring her cries, he places me carefully on the bed whilst commanding the fires to be stoked and fuelled.

The voices around me are faint as I feel the touch of small, dainty hands, wiping away the cold sweat and returning my limbs to life. Unable to focus, I watch as the shadow of the Captain grows darker. Weakly, I reach out, grabbing hold of his wrist with a pitiful grip.

"We must leave…"

Pausing upon hearing my plea, the Captain gently plies away my fingers before stepping out of the room, I can only listen as others join him.

Flashing lights and the deafening roar of thunder causes my eyes to flutter open. With my head still spinning, my eyes are drawn to my right hand as I feel something warm wrapped around it. Beside me, sitting on a chair is the slender form of my sister with a blanket wrapped around her. Asleep, her hands are tightly wrapped around my own.

"Not long. If you are wondering, you have not been asleep long."

Hidden by shadows, a man's voice comes from the corner of the room, followed by the creak of wood. Recognising the voice, I remain silent and smile wryly.

"The eclipse is nearly complete."

With my eyes downcast, I stare out of the rattling window, watching as the last remnants of the sun's rays begin to disappear and the nightlike sky is lit by lightning. The windows and doors continue to rattle as they are struck by the howling winds and lashing rain.

The fire behind me crackles as the Captain adds another log, poking and stoking it further. Basking in the warmth, I feel only guilt, knowing the suffering of those who remained outdoors.

Despite my concern, I can hear singing. Faint and shaky, it grows in strength with every passing moment. I recognise the tune, it is one of victory and courage.

"Rest while you can, we will be leaving soon."

The Captain speaks without looking at me, his words intercepting my internal thoughts. Not wishing to disturb him, I lie back, ashamed by my ineptness and gently squeeze the hands of my sister. Noticing my gentle embrace, she begins to stir and slowly her eyes begin to open.

"Sister?"

Mumbling her words, she coughs and clears her throat whilst wiping away the drool around her mouth. Smiling, I stroke her hair, wordlessly easing her fears. Standing up, she reaches out and wraps her thin arms around my body, nuzzling her face into my bosom.

Suddenly the door opens and slams into the wall, the fire flickers as the cold northern wind follows the two members of the Royal Guard who enter the room. Breathless, their cloaks and bodies drenched, I knew instantly that they were harbingers of urgent and terrible news.

"An avalanche has made the northern trail impassable."

Remaining calm whilst furrowing his brows, he directs them to the fire, allowing them to dry their clothes.

"Great evil is coming Captain, we cannot remain within these walls."

My ominous words are punctuated by the crack of thunder as lightning begins to strike the ground. The silence that follows is thick in melancholy. My words only emphasise what their warrior instincts were telling them.

A strong gust of wind forces open the windows and doors, extinguishing the fire and torches, plunging the room into darkness. Moving quickly, the Captain and his men force the windows and doors shut. Outside, the entire city was in darkness, the only light emanating from the bodies of the priests as they continued to pray.

INTRU...!

A cutthroat scream is interrupted, and soon the sound of battle is heard nearby. Lighting a torch, the Captain orders one of the Royal Guard to investigate. It does not take long before running armoured footsteps are heard and the same guardsman returns in a state of mild panic.

"Battles on the walls my Lord."

"You, escort Lady Helena.

You, carry the third princess. We head to the stables now."

Giving his instructions quickly, he scoops me up within his arms and carries me to the door. Joined by the remaining Royal Guardsmen, Helena, and our assigned hoplites, we begin to descend the stairs to the streets below.

"What is happening?"

Helena questions those beside her as she hears the sound of screams within the city walls. My eyes scan the darkness, noticing the rapid disappearance of the scattered pockets of lights.

"No time for questions. Hurry to the stables. Stay close."

Obeying the Captain's commands, we stick together, moving through the narrow streets to the nearby stables. Around us, the sound of battle was getting louder and nearer, but in the unlit streets, we could not see who was fighting.

The sound of footsteps echoes behind us, no, as I listen closely I hear them encircling us in the shadows. Their movements are synchronised and with a purpose, causing me to grip the Captain tighter. Sensing the malevolent stares, a hoplite throws his torch ahead, the light piercing through the gloom to reveal the glint of red glowing eyes.

"Protect the princesses."

As if born from nightmares, their appearance is almost incorporeal and akin to daemons as they blink in and out of the shadows. Their sinister laughter coming from all directions only serves to prove their existence as they continue to taunt us.

Frantically waving their torches, the hoplites beside us whimper as they speculate on who or what they were facing. But the flickering light only serves to deepen their despair as they catch only a glimpse of lifeless figures.

"As min krývoume kakó apó ména, na apallagoúme apó to skotádi"[4]

---

[4] Ας μην κρύβουμε κακό από μένα, να απαλλαγούμε από το σκοτάδι - Let no evil hide from me, banish back the darkness.

Growing weary of their taunting, I invoke the magic contained within my ring. Stretching out my right hand, the light emanating from the gem banishes the nearby darkness, revealing the figure of three armour knights.

"Oh my, what a pretty ring you have there."

"Oh yes, is that not what our patron desires?"

"Shall we take it, brother? After all, it is far too pretty to belong to her."

Words dripping with malicious desire cause my body to flinch in revulsion. Sensing the disgust emanating from my body, the Captain carefully places my feet on the ground and hands me to another Guardsman as he steps forward. Drawing his sword, he aims the tip at the three figures as he spits on the ground.

"Such filth shall not be spoken in my presence. Go back to your foul lord, traitors like you are not welcome."

"Not welcome are we?

"Oh, but we are, we are always welcome."

"The Lord of Death demands that souls be claimed."

"You shall find none here that belong to you or your Lord."

"An aged lion is still a worthy prize. Shall we claim it?"

As distorted laughter emanated from their blackened blood-stained armour, no one had any doubts about their identities. Wielding twin darkened blades, the deeds of this Order were infamous. Gatekeepers, knights dedicated to assassination and subterfuge, were the secret shame of our nation which placed pride in honourable combat.

Piercing screams and clashes of metal on metal continue to come from the walls, the clamour of battle revealing the harrowing truth. More than three of their Order had come, utilising the cover of the unnatural darkness they had infiltrated the fortress city, and soon it would fall.

We are trapped

Helena's silent quivering speaks volumes as she tightens the grip on my shoulder and pulls me close to her, deeper into the centre of the circle which had formed around me.

Stepping forward with vile and hollow laughs, the three assassins taunt us, playing with our emotions, twirling their blades as they move purposely slow. In fear, my hands move to the daggers on my belt, my fingers wrapping around their grip as I earnestly wish to never use them.

"PRINCESS!"

A breathless, hurried shout comes from the darkness behind the advancing figures. Emerging from the gloom is a haphazard gathering of men and women, bronze armour dented, red billowing cloaks torn, and bodies slick with blood and sweat, it was clear they had come from the battles on the walls. Despite their ragged appearance, their arrival is welcome and causes my heart to rejoice.

Running, they slow as they notice the presence of the assassin knights wielding blades dripping in blood. Their commander, wearing a red and white plumed crest, does not hesitate, raising and aiming his sword at the three, he orders a charge with a war cry on his lips.

"For the Crown!"

Locking their shields, they become a behemoth of bronze and flesh, capable of trampling and crushing all in their path. The appearance of the phalanx causes the confident swagger of the three assassins to disappear. Standing back to back, they spin their weapons nimbly, preparing to receive the charge. Sensing the shifting tide, the Royal Guard and hoplites beside them launch an attack of their own.

With a skill and ferocity that was a match for even the swordsmanship of the Royal Guardsmen, the assassins intercept the thrusting spears and swords. Like cornered vipers, they evade and parry, their twin blades passing through the smallest gaps to cut through flesh and sinew.

Swords, shields, and spears are dropped from lifeless fingers, but this was not the assassins' chosen battlefield or style of warfare. Though knights, they were dedicated to the darker arts, outnumbered, they knew their looming fate, and after a short, deadly, and brutal melee, the last of them falls, their bodies and armour sundered, pierced, and torn. As a testament to their skill, their corpses lie alongside sixteen others.

Breaking formation, the survivors plant their shields and spears into the ground, resting their exhausted, shaking limbs. Sir Kivos steps forward, removing his helmet as his men form an ad hoc semicircle around us. Movements hampered by a shallow cut to his thigh, Sir Kivos kneels before me, with his head bowed.

"I saw your light, are you unharmed your Highness?"

"I am, I extend to you my gratitude."

His expression hardens at the sound of nearby battle, both of us knew our conversation would have to be cut short.

"Tell me, what is happening?"

"Foul magic and blasphemy your Highness. The traitors are slowly taking our walls and soon the gates will be open. I fear the fortress is lost."

"It is as I feared…"

"Your Highness, flee this place, we will hold them for as long as we can."

Standing, he looks up at the nothingness of the darkened sky. Not even the eternal stars were visible.

"Join us…"

My voice quivers as I hesitantly speak my selfish wish, despite knowing it would be rejected.

"Your Highness's offer is kind, but we must remain, for the realms need more time."

Gently shaking his head side to side, he grasps my hands with both of his own and places something small within them. Looking down, I notice the appearance of two scrolls, each bearing his personal seal.

"There are things I still wish to do, but I have no regrets about my fate. Go north to the lands of my father, you shall find sanctuary there."

With a wry smile, he looks upwards to the heavens.

"Your Highness, if he should ask, tell them I fought bravely to the end."

Upon hearing his earnest wish, I wanted nothing more than to return the pair of scrolls and command him to survive, to deliver them himself, but I knew I could not speak those words. He had embraced his destiny.

"Eleni"

The words are spoken tenderly and Eleni appears from the darkness to stand beside him. Dressed in armour, her normally

167

picturesque features are hidden by the shadows of her helmet. Leaning close, Sir Kivos surprises us all by openly embracing her, causing her body to stiffen.

He whispers into her ears and discretely places something within her open hands. Though the words spoken are too soft for me to hear, I notice the hand-carved wooden lion that was now being placed in a satchel on her belt as she strokes her stomach.

"Your Highness, I give to you my aide. She will guide you north. None will challenge you needlessly."

Ending the embrace, he stands straight and proud, causing me to remember the statues of the heroes of lore. Straightening my own back in response, I return the kindness he had shown me.

"Fight and die well Sir Kivos, son of Kastor, Warden of Sfyri. All that you have entrusted to me will be delivered."

Enemies coming from the shadows, Lykanthropos!

Cutting our farewell short, he turns away, hiding his moistening eyes by placing back on his helmet. Securing the straps, he swiftly shouts a series of commands, those around him hefting once more their shields and spears.

Stopping for only a moment, he turns back towards me, a radiant smile on his face.

"Princess Selesia, you have your mother's eyes as well as her heart. Though you may deny it, this world still has a need for Gods. You were sent here for a reason, it is your destiny to live on."

His words root me in place, forcing the Captain to sweep me off my feet and forcibly carry me to the stables. With tears streaming down my cheeks, I peer over the Captain's shoulder, watching as Sir Kivos draws his sword and his fifty remaining hoplites lock their shields in response to the overwhelming number of glowing red eyes.

"Show them the courage of the north! Let us earn our rest in Elysium."

His final command is roared as those beside him clash their weapons against their shields. Unable to watch, I turn away as the enemy emerges from the shadows and pounces upon them, listening with regret as the air is filled with the clash of metal.

Having hauled me unceremoniously onto my horse, the Captain mounts his own before sweeping down his arm, commanding us all to ride north. Kicking open the stable doors, we gallop through the myriad of narrow streets, our path illuminated by the flames of the nearby burning buildings. Hectic and panicked shouts come from all directions as the chaos of battle continues to rage. There was no longer any discipline or cohesion, only confusion as the defenders offered their final resistance.

Citizens of the fortress city shuffle aimlessly, crying and wailing for sanctuary, the last vestiges of hope had left this place, replaced by despair. Heartbreakingly, I ignore their plight, burying my face deeper into the depths of my hood.

The notching and drawing of bows draw my attention to the hoplites riding beside me.

"No time, keep riding."

The Captain's tone is commanding as he urges us forward. Reluctantly they obey and I follow their gazes, noticing the dark silhouettes moving on the rooftops, effortlessly keeping pace despite us being on horseback.

Overhead

A calm shout warns us of the coming threat and my escorts raise their shields, forming a protective shell that shelters me from the rainstorm of stones being launched from slings in our direction. Frantically we continue to ride, ignoring the pitter-patter of their bombardment as we manoeuver around the various obstacles which hinder our path. Finally, we escape the labyrinth of the streets and approach the still open northern gates.

A thin line of bronze forms our welcome party, a single company of spears and archers, the ground around them is littered with dozens of enemy dead. They were now the final guardians of the gateway to the northern kingdom.

Realising our identities, they separate their shields, forming a causeway for us to safely pass. Now safely behind a human wall, the Captain comes to a stop with little ceremony.

"I am Lykon, Captain of the Royal Guard. The great fortress has fallen and we are riding north. Will any of you join us?"

None of the assembled men and women answers, turning instead to their own *lochagos*. A veteran, his scarred skin and greying hair

171

were testament to his long service. Sensing the trust and expectations being thrust upon him, the man's brow's furrow as he bows to the Captain and Lady Eleni.

"Look not to me, but your own conscience. Fight here, or fight out there, I do not care which."

Free to make their own choice, ten step forward, presenting themselves to the Captain's service. Without delay, they gather their scant belongings, and mount the few remaining horses, riding double where necessary.

"Ride now, and when these gates close, forget all who have chosen to remain and look not back."

The *lochagos'* ominous words are not a statement of resignation, but instead a conviction for revenge, one shared by all those beside him.

Arrows whistle past me as the archers spot the oncoming enemy.

"Go now! Close the gates!"

Without hesitation we ride towards the closing great gate, the last of us have barely passed through when they are sealed with a heavy thump of falling timber and metal. Dejected, I follow Eleni and her hoplites, never looking back as they guide us through the biting bitter winds, following paths known only to them.

I am glad of the wind, for they drown out the screams that come from the city. Even when they are faint and barely audible we continue to ride, riding until our horses could move no more.

Now hidden within a mountain hollow, I finally look back at the once-great fortress. Even at a distance, the still-raging fires were clear, acting as a flickering beacon in the darkness. Filled with guilt, I close my eyes, offering my first prayers to the Gods in months, wishing that others had escaped beyond the two dozen who had joined me.

The air here is clean, the sickly taint which had once tinged my taste buds, was replaced by the sweet freshness of the nearby pines.

A sound not dissimilar to thunder causes me to look skywards. The dark clouds are pierced by something silver, shaped, unlike anything I had seen before. The once hidden sun shines through the gap, the rays growing stronger now that the twin moons were beginning to separate, signalling the end of the unnatural eclipse.

173

Basked in golden rays, the unknown object continues to fall whilst radiating its mesmerising white light. Bewitched by the sight, I move closer to the edge of the path, uncaring of the danger as my eyes track its descent.

Knowing the destruction a falling star would cause, I should have felt despair and sorrow, but within my heart, I only felt peace. How could something so enchanting bring death?

As if responding to my thoughts, it changes direction, its unnatural movements reminding me of a bird gliding on the currents. Childishly, I imagine it to be a chariot, like those my father once spoke of, one commanded by the great Sun God.

I already knew that the star would fall far to the north, beyond the nearby forest and horizon. As I look away, I gasp as the single white trail splits, not once or twice, but seven times, each leaving behind a different colour of the rainbow.

"Princess are you all right?"

Shocked, I barely register the tears rolling down my cheeks until the Captain touches them. Joined by the others, we stand shoulder to shoulder, following my gaze as the star falls beyond the horizon and into the distant mountains.

A blinding flash and a sound akin to the wrath of the Gods cause my heart to flutter. I continue to cry, not in sadness, like those I had shed for the last year, but in joy. The written prophecy echoes within me once more.

With the coming of death, there shall fall a seven-tailed star.

Fear not its coming or power, for within its light is hope not

doom,

Within its embrace is the heir of Europa, unblessed by Gods,

but whose blood promises victory

Fate and destiny, was this the real reason why I was summoned here? Despite everything I had experienced, despite everything I had thought, I wanted to believe that the Gods had finally answered. Closing my eyes, I begin to pray. If the Gods were listening, let this be the salvation we were seeking.

Arc 2: Legacies of the Old World

Chapter Fifteen

Classified

Classified

0415 hours, 09-08-2177 C.E.

Whilst emitting auras of behemothic strength, three humanoid figures emerge from the darkness. Announcing their presence only with the crunch of crushed stones, their movements could hardly be described as graceful. Encased in layers of steel and ceramic, their limbs were heavy, their stomping footsteps causing spider-like fractures to appear in what remains of the asphalt road.

Speaking not a word, their coordination is sublime as they move as one, maintaining an unbroken line across uneven ground. Emitting only barely audible hisses and clicks, they march, ignoring the dying embers of scattered flares that served to illuminate the weathered signs.

MINES

Emblazoned in multiple languages, the word is underscored by the worn image of a skull and crossbones, even a glimpse would be enough to deter all but the determined and foolhardy. Whether due to confidence or arrogance or some other unknown reason, the figures continue without hesitation. Step by step they march until they reach the outer limits of a ruined and desolate city.

Clunk

As a testament to their recklessness, the sound of metal impacting against metal is followed by a series of loud pops.

⸎————◦◦◦————◦⸎

Hidden under a blanket of freshly lain snow, I watch the chain of explosions in the distance. With a burst of blinding light, the three figures are engulfed by a cloud of rock and ash.

Remaining still, the only movement comes from my eyes as they flicker from side to side, reading the stream of data that appears on my Heads-up Display. IBAS, my Integrated Battlefield Assistance System had already begun the calculations on their chances of survival, but I did not need to wait. Decades of experience had already told me the answer.

Trudging forward like an unstoppable juggernaut, the first of the three emerge from the cloud before it disperses. Their armour barely scorched let alone damaged, they continue, their movements unhindered.

Aiming the crosshairs of my rifle, I remove the safety with a flick of my thumb. My heart rate slows as my breathing becomes shallow, each thump was the countdown of a ticking clock that was nearing zero. As the first of the prepared markers is crossed, I pull the trigger.

◆◦───◎◦◦◎───◦◆

The still air is broken by a whip-like crack, as a single bullet crosses the distance and lands with a heavy clunk. Impacting on their chest, the central figure staggers, swaying side to side before regaining their footing.

Lit by flickering street lights, I watch as the now compressed bullet slides down the still intact chest plate, the panel barely misshapen by the impact. Coming to a halt, the three quickly spread out, adopting an open formation as they turn systematically in different directions, hunting for the source, me.

I watch as their cumbersome, almost unwieldy weapons are raised purposely as they scan every rooftop and open window, before centring on the belfry of the derelict church. Exposed, with my position bereft of any true cover, I remain motionless. Aiming for the head of the central figure, I watch its unchanging eyes as it peers in my direction, the intensity of its stare growing with every passing moment.

With legs braced and its right arm raised, it exposes the multi-barrelled weapon system secreted within. Compromised, I act, my finger moving rapidly as a stream of bullets is unleashed. Sparks fly in the distance as each land with a *ping* that resonates in the air, the sound alone telling me everything I needed to know about the thickness and composition of their armour.

Arm, leg, body, I cycle through the target areas as I search for a weakness. Each causing dimples to appear on the armoured skin as I delay the inevitable counter-attack.

Click

The ominous sound is followed by the rearward movement of the bolt as it locks open, empty. Before me, the enemy lies sprawled on its back, motionless, the other two accompanying it lost to sight.

With well-rehearsed, fluid movements, I eject the spent magazine, pulling another from my vest and locking it in place in a blink of an eye. As the receiver slides forward, my rifle is shouldered once more.

The ground churns as the enemy hauls itself to its feet, the asphalt and stone buckling under its slow and purposeful movements. Stomping the ground, it digs itself in as it braces its legs. Arms raised, its protruding weapon is aimed in my direction once again. Matted black barrels begin to whir and spin, picking up speed with every rotation.

Danger!

I did not need to wait for the words to appear on my display. Standing, I turn and run, my rifle cradled in my arms. A high-pitched wail follows my every movement, as a stream of high-velocity slugs bombards the tower. Though inaccurate, the volume is deadly as they chip away at the nearby pillars, causing them to crumble, bringing the roof to the verge of collapse.

Chalked in dust, I avoid the falling masonry as I push my body further, aiming for the building across the street. Adrenaline surges through my screaming body as my armour responds, assisting as I make the five-meter leap.

Curled into a ball, whilst embracing my rifle, I aim for the open window as I prepare for a heavy landing. A delayed *blurt* punctuates a series of painful blows on my right shoulder, jolting my centre of gravity and changing my trajectory.

Bracing, I prepare for the inevitable collision as my encased flesh crashes through wood and masonry, the contact causing me to spin out of control and land awkwardly on the ground, the rifle escaping my grasp.

The respite is fleeting as a stream of lead follows me, ripping through the thin, flimsy walls and pouring light into the dust-filled room. Remaining low, I avoid the incoming fire, crawling and slithering towards the nearest cover, gathering my rifle as I seek shelter behind a heavy stone pillar.

Slowing my breathing, I watch and listen to the enemy's sweep as it moves from side to side, the fluorescent red tracer revealing the enemy's still entrenched position. Confirming the pattern, I wait for an opening before twisting my body and opening fire.

My armour absorbs the heavy recoil as the rifle barks fiercely, sending round after round into the darkness. The response is instantaneous as sparks are soon joined by a distinctive crack and tinkle. Waiting with bated breath, I watch as a small fracture appears, then grows as an armour panel sloughs off and lands with a heavy thump on the ground.

Faltering as their whirling gears and delicate tubes and wires underneath are exposed to the open air, the incoming enemy fire grows increasingly inaccurate as they begin to withdraw. Sensing victory with every backward step, I become relentless in my pursuit. My rifle was a surgeon's knife compared to their unwieldy mallet as I slice and thrust, gouging and opening the wound further before they move behind cover and are lost to sight.

Another magazine spent, I eject and reload before ducking down, scanning the nearby doorway leading to the corridor on my left. Sensing no one nearby, I use the lull in combat to activate the map on my HUD. Memorising the nearest landmarks, I deactivate the image with a flick of my eyes.

Moving swiftly and silently, I leave the room, following the degraded blueprints contained within the archives of my armour. Formerly a hospital, the once clean walls were now damp, caked in mould due to the constant drip of water from the floors above, the previously bright lights were now barely functioning, buzzing as they cast eerie shadows.

Navigating the narrow confines, I check and clear room after room, noting the changes in the blueprints due to the passage of time. Finally, as I turn a corner I find a dusty, disused stairway, the only route to the floors beneath.

Gently placing my rifle on the grime encrusted floor, I kneel and remove a grenade and lengths of wire and tape from the pouches on my harness. Embedding the grenade in the wooden frame, a length of wire is looped around the pin as it is stretched across the walkway, creating a simple yet effective trap.

A tremor travels from the floors below, causing ripples to appear in the nearby pools of water. Slow and rhythmic, I calculate the distance as I slowly stand, picking up my rifle and blending into the shadows.

Rifle-shouldered, I peer down the unlit stairway, searching for movement in the darkness, finding none. Time, was a commodity in short supply and I choose not to linger. Cautiously I move backwards, each step silent as I continue to stare into the gloom. Waiting until the last moment to turn, I move further into the building's depths.

⚬◦━━━◦ ❧ ◦━━━◦⚬

The door is chained and bolted shut, the metallic parts long lost their lustre. Slathered in rust, the chain offered little resistance as I thrust downwards with the butt of my rifle, snapping instantly with a metallic tinkle.

Wedged in place, the door offers little resistance as I shoulder my rifle and kick it open. Looking left and right, I find the roof empty and deserted. Turning, I heft the steel door, bending it back into shape as I force it back into the frame.

With my back secure, I stalk the rooftops, my movements cat-like as I search for my escaped prey. I soon hear the sound of heavy footsteps from the streets below. Peering over the edge, I catch sight of a single figure, my armour instantly highlighting the damaged sections of the now limp right arm.

Slicing through the air, a flurry of shots impact the mass of ceramic cables and plastic wires, slicing and shattering them as a geyser of black, viscous fluid erupts from the damaged panels, spluttering and falling like rain as it drenches the entirety of the suit.

With its lenses coated, it reacts by firing blindly, sending a stream of bullets harmlessly into the brickwork on the lower floors. Second by second, the aim is slowly forced downwards until it is aimed directly towards the ground. Round after round hammers into the suit's own leg with its unusual almost inhuman design making it vulnerable as piece after piece of its armour is chewed and stripped apart.

Wires, cables, and finally the support pillars are exposed and disintegrated until the leg is incapable of supporting its own weight, collapsing and falling on its back. The barrels continue to spin, glowing red hot, long after the last of the ammunition had been depleted.

With my finger resting on the trigger, I wait, my rifle aimed at the body of the suit, waiting for a hatch to open. Seconds pass, but there is no movement and I tilt my head, shifting my sight to the damaged leg.

Shredded and barely recognisable after being removed below the knee, dark coloured fluid leaks and pools underneath the body. Too dark to be blood, it matches the colour and texture of the fluid which had emerged from the internal workings of the arm.

Straining, I listen for cries of pain or screams of anguish, but there is only silence. Staring ahead, my helmet clicks as the lenses clean and magnify what I am seeing. There is no bone, no flesh, nothing organic, pieces begin to fall into place as I see only metal and plastic.

Erupting with an earth-shattering explosion, the overworked motors of the still spinning barrels overheat, showering the air with white-hot metal and flames. The shrapnel lands in the pools of dark fluid, sizzling before setting it alight. The flames take hold quickly, engulfing the suit, cloaking it in intense blue flames.

Igniting with high pitch squeals, the suit sparks as it liquidates, losing all semblance of its previous form. Anything alive was likely dead now.

An almost inconsequential *pop* causes a minor tremor to shake the roof, distracting me from the spectacle that was the death throes of the fallen suit. Immediately recognising the source as the grenade I had placed earlier, I begin to run.

Almost as an afterthought, the fingers of my left hand wrap themselves around a small metallic cylinder located on my belt. Pulling the pin, I watch as it flies through the air before I drop the grenade behind me. Rolling back, it hisses as it scatters a thick black fog that envelops the entirety of the roof.

Filtered air enters my lungs as the seals of my helmet close, preventing the inhalation of noxious fumes as I leap from the ledge, falling to the building below. Softening my landing with a roll, I duck behind a low wall as the roof door is torn from its hinges. The intruders are making their entrance with heavy footsteps.

Escaping under the cover of the still billowing smoke, I move into the building's interior, the maze-like corridors masking my movements. Rifle held close due to the proximity of the enemy, I move cautiously for the location of the third was still unknown.

Strewn with debris, the corridors are a mess, possessing little semblance to the designs contained within the archives. Sunken and subsided floors with chasms too wide to cross and collapsed sections of walls cause detours, only my compass ensured I was continuing south, guiding me to the fall-back position that had been decided in advance.

Slow, trudging footsteps approach from the corridors ahead, too close for me to backtrack. Caught in the open, I sidestep into the shadows of a nearby room, a shallow hollow breaking the contours of my body. Pressed flat, I flick the selector of my rifle as a large shadow emerges.

Standing still, my breathing and heart rate slows, becoming almost non-existent as the giant inches closer with every step. Its cold, emotionless red eyes turn, scanning left and right as it peers into the rooms, its form too large to enter. Exuding an aura of violence, the only sound to leave its body is the whirl of motors and the hiss of pistons.

I feel its gaze as its eyes bore into the room, scanning before turning away and continuing down the corridor. Exhaling and breathing slowly, I allow my heart rate to slowly increase as I slink back into the corridor, my rifle in hand.

Shouldered and using the offset iron sights, I follow the enemy, watching its broad armoured back as my finger hovers over the trigger. Observing its movements, I notice something that could not be seen until now. The thick armoured panels which appeared to have no visible seam possessed a small gap. Too small for a bullet to enter, but large enough for a knife to slip through.

Red lines appear on my display as my armour scans the enemy, assessing its weapons and abilities. Designed for close-quarter battles, it was different from what I had previously encountered. Wielding a four-bladed mace in its right hand that was designed to crush and maim, in the other was a three-pronged pneumatic talon, made to grab and eviscerate. In the confines of this cramped city, they were fearsome and deadly.

But it was not their strengths that drew my attention, but their fatal flaw, my presence was not being noticed. Possessing no sixth sense or instincts of a human pilot, it was being deceived by my slow movements. Recent hardware developments were not easily misled, suggesting what was contained within was obsolete and dated.

Moving my hand slowly to my shoulder, I reach for the blade fastened there when a high-pitched squeal sounds nearby, joined by the steady, rhythmic thump of approaching footsteps. My eyes dart towards the target, the gap enticing and tempting as it steadily grows smaller with each footstep.

Patience was the virtue of a seasoned hunter. Soon to be outnumbered in the narrow confines of the corridor, I stop and decide to withdraw, allowing the enemy and my target to turn the corner and be lost to sight.

Patience, we would soon meet again on a battlefield of my choosing.

Chapter Sixteen

Silence.

My eyes scan the streets which were once vibrant and teeming with life but were now empty except for the husks of burnt-out vehicles which are strewn across them. Relics of a bygone age, they had long ago been stripped of anything useful.

Remaining in the shadows, I move from cover to cover, my eyes ever watchful as I search for anything out of place. Ahead, behind a wall of detritus is my destination, a building of simple design. Constructed in the middle years of the Twentieth Century, it was built for a simple purpose, to house and re-educate the undesirables of society.

Though long abandoned, its walls were thick and far from decrepit, its windows and doors boarded behind inch thick wood and sheets of stainless steel. This was to be the battlefield of my choosing.

My fingers gently run across the doors and windows, testing their durability as I search for a means of entry. Though aged and coated in a film of rust, their construction remained sound and would take too long and cause too much noise to remove.

Instead, I look up, noticing the window on the fifth floor, which due to some quirk of fate had been forced open, the bolts used in its fastening snapped. Scraping away the thin film of moss, I reveal the small hidden gaps, large enough for a finger to slip into.

Probing the gaps, I test the strength of their hold before I begin to climb. My muscles burn as my fingertips hold not just my own weight, but also that of my armour. Following an unseen path, I continue unmolested until the border of the third and fourth floor. Here the nature of the stone and brickwork changes, becoming brittle and crumbling to the slightest touch.

Falling would not be fatal, but the chances of injury were high. Seeing no other option, I abandon any pretence of stealth and secrecy as my fingers form a spearhead. Like a lance it plunges into the brick and stone, forming a hollow for my fingers to enter.

Blow after blow, the sound carrying across the air, I continue my climb until I reach the open window. Grasping the narrow ledge, I pull myself up and slither into the building before lying flat and motionless on the floor. Straining my ears, I listen and search for the distinctive heavy tread of the enemy.

Hearing nothing, I shuffle to the window and peer out. Scanning the horizon, I confirm with both my senses that I have not been followed. Standing to my full height, I unhook my rifle, holding it close as I begin to explore the prison's interior.

Floor by floor, room by room, every inch of the building is checked and secured. Every inch is etched into my own memory as it is recorded in the archives of my armour. In battle, where every second matters, none could be wasted by reading a map.

Pressing my thumb against the soft timber frames, I mark each doorway until only the entrance to the basement remains. The sound of trickling water is heard as I force open the door and take my first steps into its depths. Step by step, I continue my descent until I am sloshing in a pool of dark, putrid water. Submerged to my waist, it is clear that what flood defences had once existed were now compromised and no longer operational.

Beams of light shine out from the sides of my helmet, casting awkward shadows as scraps of wood glide over the surface of the water.

Clang

Turning left, I follow the echo of metal striking metal and soon find a half-submerged shelf. Canisters of propane gas, once used for heating and cooking, bob up and down, tethered in place by lengths of rope.

Moving closer, I check the contents of each canister, confirming the existence of their precious cargo as I tap each dial. Worth more than gold during the wars that followed the nuclear winter, it was likely their submersion which had ensured they had not been plundered.

Hauling the canisters from the shelves, I drag them behind me as I stride to the stairway. Resting them on my shoulders, I confirm nothing else of value remained. Pressing my thumb against the wooden frame, I mark the area as checked.

Like a second skin, I carefully peel away the harnesses and holsters strapped to my body, the materials drenched with water. Carefully, I remove the contents of each, placing them on what was once a kitchen table, the room long lost its original purpose. Twisting and squeezing, droplets of waterfall-like rain as I place the still damp fabric on the shell of an antiquated generator, the residual heat drying them slowly.

Formed in a series of lines, what few possessions I had remaining were arrayed before me. My food supplies were nearly depleted, and the land had little to forage. There were six grenades, a mixture of fragmentation, smoke, and incendiary, five magazines, two for my rifle and three for my pistol, and whatever remained within the weapons themselves. It was too little for a major firefight.

Seated on the floor, I allow my body to rest as my eyes flicker constantly at the wall of data appearing in front of them. Blueprints of the prison from the year of its construction, much of the interior had changed in the decades since, with many of the rooms unsuitable for my needs. Only those on the upper floors, accessible from a single winding stairway on the third floor, would allow me to corral the enemy to where I wanted them to go.

But it is the IBAS analysis results that garner the most attention. Having scoured through thousands of records, comparing hundreds of designs, it had sought the closest match to the armour worn by the enemy.

Nothing matched exactly, but this was to be expected, decades of strife had ensured that records were incomplete as knowledge was lost. This did not include those purposely omitted, being developed and researched in secret.

Three however were close matches, legacies of an ill-fated experiment into automated soldiers which began and ended six decades ago. The similarities were too uncanny to be a coincidence.

⋅⊰──── ᏋᏂᏬ────Ᏸ⋅

Strapped, pinned, and secured at chest height, incendiary grenades are carefully placed on the two stairways leading to the second floor. Silver cylinders no larger than the palm of my hand, the intense flames created by their exothermic chemical reactions were likely the most effective means of breaching the armour worn by the enemy. With an almost invisible wire wrapped around each pin, the grenades had been angled to ensure maximum exposure if the rudimentary traps were ever activated.

Hauling the canisters to the upper floor, I forcibly pry open the seals, allowing the contents to saturate the rooms with flammable gases before sealing the door, ensuring nothing would be allowed to escape. The scene set, my eyes settle on a plain wooden cabinet nestled in the corner, made of cheap veneer, it was nothing more than an example of mass-produced furniture from the previous era.

Twitching my right cheek, I send a short-ranged signal, beginning the countdown as I effortlessly lift the cabinet and move it towards the nearest window. Too wide to pass through freely, I force it through, the glass shattering and wood breaking under the impact as the cabinet falls to the street, five storeys below. The sound of splintering wood is distinct and loud enough that it could not be considered accidental.

With the trap set and baited, I wait in the unlit corner of the nearby room. Kneeling, my body relaxes as I meld into the shadows, my heartbeat and breathing slowing as I shut my eyes. Soon I become almost inanimate as I wait for my chosen prey to arrive.

Chapter Seventeen

The distinctive clash of metal against wood echoes through the air, the shockwaves of each blow reverberating through the walls and floors until they reach my fingers. Slowly, I open my eyes, reading the time displayed on my screen, barely fifteen minutes had passed.

The crash of wood and the crumpling of metal soon announce the destruction of the barriers on the ground floor. Heavy, rhythmic footsteps vibrate through the building, revealing the enemy's location as it begins to search the building systematically, their timings indicating they were alone.

A pair of gentle pops is followed by a series of explosions as the grenades placed on the northeast stairway are detonated. The sound is soon joined by the shrill shriek of cracking, melting metal, and the stench of burning wood as a trail of thick smoke seeps upwards from the lower floors.

Silently counting, I wait, listening patiently for the tell-tale heavy, trudging footsteps to ascend and reach the top floor. Soon I hear it, the shriek of metal, the hiss of pneumatics, and the click of turning gears.

Toxic – Low Oxygen

Dismissing the symbol that appears in the corner of my eye with a flick, I watch as the room and corridor are quickly saturated with a blanket of thick black smoke.

00:00:00

As the display reaches zero, a hollow ringing comes from the nearby rooms, cutting through the silence like a hot knife through butter. Lured by the sound, the enemy immediately reacts, ploughing its way through the door and wall like a battering ram.

An earth-shattering explosion follows, shaking the entire building as the once trapped gases are ignited. The walls dividing the various rooms are torn, and from the chaos, a dark towering figure emerges, their appearance daemonic due to their cloak of bright blue flames and glowing red eyes.

Concentrating only on the movements of the enemy, my heart rate and breathing slow further as the enemy advances into the room, its left three-pronged claw opening and closing like a nervous twitch as its head turns systematically left and right. Its radiating eyes stare into the darkness, looking in my direction before turning away.

Remaining in the shadows cast by the flickering flames and the mass of furniture, I begin to move. Adrenaline enters my bloodstream as my heart rate and breathing slowly increase, readying my body for combat. My right hand moves across my body, slowly reaching and drawing the combat knife sheathed on my shoulder. Twenty inches of steel and titanium composite, its blackened blade ensured no careless glint of light would alert the enemy to my presence. Its size made it more comparable to a short sword than a knife or a dagger.

Step by step, each movement camouflaged by the enemies' own, I creep closer until I am within striking distance. My muscles tense, ready to move in an instant as I watch and wait for my moment.

The moment comes quickly as the enemy's head tilts downwards as it examines an object on the ground, the act widening the gap between its helmet and torso. Pushing off, my arms are outstretched as I plunge the blade upwards and deeply into the helmet. Gripping onto the enemy's shoulder with my left hand, I anchor myself in place as I punch the knife deeper, cutting through what little resistance remained.

The enemy's reactions are swift as it jerks erratically from side to side, trying to throw me off and dislodge the embedded blade. Gripping tightly, I begin to move the blade left and right, cutting through cables and wires before pulling the blade free. Changing the grip, I plunge it downwards into its body, where a human spine would have resided.

Forced down to the hilt, sparks begin to fly as something vital is hit and an electrical current travels up the length of the blade before being absorbed by the insulation contained within my gauntlets. Its movements slow as I continue to stab, each thrust performed with deadly precision and purpose. Components contained within the torso begin to rattle as the light being emitted from its helmet fade, revealing the loss of power to its eyes and ears.

Blind and deaf, its movement becomes sporadic as it fights like a cornered, injured animal, jumping up and down as it flails its arms. The mace held within its right arm punches out, cutting great gouges into the nearby walls and sending debris in various directions. As its movements become harder to predict, I tighten my grip on its shoulder, the act leaving an imprint as the metal buckles under the pressure.

My ears alert me to the sound of cracking as the floor beneath us begins to break due to the heavy impacts of its jumping. Planting my feet on its back, I push off, freeing my knife as I acrobatically flip and land across the room, away from the growing fissure.

When the floor finally collapses, it takes the armoured suit and half the room with it. A sound akin to a clanging bell resonates from below due to the impact of metal on stone and wood.

Peering down into the newly formed chasm, I look upon the sprawled-out frame of the armoured suit. Spreadeagled on the ground floor, its descent had barely slowed from the impact with the floors above. Panels torn apart, its delicate innards exposed, and black fluid leaking onto the cracked stone floor, there was no doubting its nature as an artificial construct.

Suddenly a high-pitched scream is emitted as the suit thrashes, the frequency and pitch growing in intensity, causing me to double over in pain as my enhanced senses are shocked and overwhelmed. Disorientated, I reach for my helmet and manually shut off the receivers built into them.

Comparable to the cries of a baby animal on the approach of a predator, I knew it was a call for aid, one that could only come from a single source. With my ears still ringing, I shake my head, clearing my vision as I drop from the ledge, falling three floors and land softly with bent legs.

Advancing on my deaf and blind prey as it unsteadily rises to its feet, my knife is held close, ready to strike as my eyes look over its broken armour. With inhuman speed and ferocity, I pounce, my blade slicing at the back of both of its knees, cutting through the thinly armoured carapace that guarded its cables and wires.

Lashing out its arms in response to my strikes, I barely evade as the four-bladed mace slams into the ground, sending shards of concrete into the nearby walls, peppering them with holes. Lingering back, I allow a steady stream of black viscous fluid to flow down the back of its leg, coating the panels as it collects into a pool underneath its feet.

Soon its legs grind to a halt, the limbs straight, rigid, and immobile as the last of the fluid dribbles out. Rotating its body, its arms swing manically in wide arcs to act as a deterrent as I begin to encircle. Though inorganic, it realises its fate and emits another high-pitched scream. Too close, despite my receivers being deactivated, I could still feel the vibrations, and the ringing returns to my ears.

Compartments, hidden within the armoured torso, slide open, releasing canisters that roll in various directions, emitting clouds of smoke that blanket the entirety of the room in thick green smog. Stepping back, I allow my helmet seals to close, isolating me from the outside air.

Not entirely toxic, the smog's low oxygen content would eventually affect even my body if exposed too long. I look upon the shadow of the paraplegic enemy as it continues to swing its arms, cutting great gouges into the floor. Despite sending shrapnel in various directions, it was no longer a threat.

Lingering back, I wait for the smoke to dissipate before advancing. Sensing my movement, the immobile figure emits one final scream before its limbs lock down by its side and it becomes as still as a statue.

Stopping mid-stride, I watch as dust and small pebbles fall from the damaged floors above, sensing the subtle movements of the floor as the foundations of the building continue to weaken. This place was no longer suitable as a stronghold or a battlefield.

Staring at the freshly made statue, I decided to leave, its deactivation was equivalent to its destruction. My eyes flicker left as I activate the map and set a waypoint to the east, choosing another destination I had chosen in advance.

Turning to leave, my eyes are drawn to my fingers and limbs, noticing the dark viscous fluid coating the panels. Bringing my fingers to my eyes, I rub them slowly, feeling the sticky resistance with no hint of drying. I knew this fluid was far from benign, having seen the destruction it had caused to an armour system much heavier than my own.

With the back of my blade, I begin to scrape, running it across the panels as I remove the tar-like fluid, the excess pooling near my feet. After several minutes, I flex my fingers, testing their strength and grip, before returning the blade to my shoulder. With my hands now idle, I twist the manual switch on my helmet, re-activating the receiver and ending my isolation.

As sound returns to my ears, I feel a sudden tingle in my fingertips as I sense an ominous presence directly behind. Not doubting my instincts, I react using movements born from countless battlefields against innumerable foes, turning and drawing my rifle.

Chapter Eighteen

Shockwaves travel down the length of my arms as I use my rifle as a quarterstaff against the downward swing. The weight and momentum of the heavy strike cause the rifle's plastic and metal components to buckle as I lock it in place.

My eyes look upon the source of the blow for the first time, an oversized dark-bladed sword held within the grasp of a towering giant. Bearing down with its red glowing eyes, I feel the pressure increase as the servos enclosed within its arms begin to whirr, the ground cracking as I am forced downwards to my knees.

Barely struggling to brace my arms and legs, I am drawn to the menacing whine of spinning blades. Turning towards the sound, my vision is soon filled with a series of circular serrated blades being swung in my direction.

With little time to think, I push against my rifle, sacrificing it as I slide across the ground, barely evading the spinning discs. No longer opposed, the dark sword hammers into the stone floor, crushing my rifle as the shockwaves of the strike cause dust and debris to billow in my direction.

Clearing my helmet of dirt and dust, I slowly rise, my hands reaching to my holstered pistol and sheathed blade as I prepare for the advancing enemy.

⊷⊶——◯◟◞◯——◉⊷

Retracting its arms, my armoured foe stands to its full height, towering even an unnatural giant such as I. With its sword-shouldered, it slowly moves forward, each footstep causing the already unstable building to shake, loosening masonry and wood which falls from above.

My eyes are soon soaked in amber as IBAS scans the armoured plates, highlighting individual sections as it attempts to find and exploit a weakness. The enemy however refuses to give me such time as it surges forward, charging as it swings its arms, each capable of a force beyond mortal men.

With little grace, my hands move, parrying the incoming blows with my blade, but soon scratches and shallow gouges appear on my armour as I slowly surrender ground. With each swing, its movements grow increasingly faster, becoming less robotic but natural and fluid.

Sparks fly from my blade as it grinds against the spinning discs whilst my pistol barks repeatedly as I fire at point-blank range with little effect. With my limbs growing weary, I desperately seek an opening and sweep under the machine's guard to aim my pistol at the eyes of its helmet.

Feathering the trigger, shot after shot rings out, hammering into the glass until it cracks and penetrates the inner workings. Damaged, the suit rears up, causing its incoming swings to go off target, crashing into the wall and opening a route into the room next door.

The glint of silver in the darkness draws my eyes to a cylindrical object lying on top of a pile of rubble. Recognising its distinctive shape immediately, I move towards it after ducking under the guard of the half-blind machine.

Sprinting, I lean down and in a single motion sweep up the cylinder and pull the pin, allowing it and the hinge to fly through the air. Without turning back, the grenade rolls gently from my fingers, billowing smoke as I continue to run towards the door.

"Locate, Incendiary."

My voice rings out, causing waypoints to appear on my display, directing me to the last known locations of the grenades I had placed. With my rifle shattered, only they could even the odds in this unfair conflict.

The details I had etched into my memory were useless now, the earlier struggle had caused sections of the building to collapse, once clear corridors were now blocked by fallen pillars and chunks of masonry caused by caved-in roofs. Changing my route, I navigate the newly formed maze, but each mistake and detour cost me precious seconds that I could not spare.

The crash of something battering through metal, wood, and masonry directly behind, confirmed this as fact. My enemy did not care about subtlety, only the fulfilment of its mission, it would use its body to plough through, uncaring of the risks.

Finally, after turning endless corners, I find what I am seeking. The grenade attached to the wooden frame on the stairway is undamaged. The *whirr* emitted from the spinning blades is close, too close for comfort, preventing a delicate extraction.

Forming a fist, I punch through the masonry, ripping away a section of the wooden frame with the grenade still embedded within. Slicing away the thread attached to the pin, I extract the cylinder and place it carefully into my harness. Peering down the stairway, which once led to the lower floors, I see only rising, flowing water.

A black blade punches through the wall behind me, causing me to duck and roll to narrowly avoid being skewered as it becomes embedded in the wall in front of me. The enemy, its underhanded strike avoided, crashes through the wall, corralling me into a dead-end corridor.

Too close to use my ace, I was as likely to burn through my armour as the enemy's, instead I reach for and draw my pistol. Aiming and firing quickly, round after round ricochets from its thick armour as it shields its helmet with both of its arms.

Stepping back with every pull of the trigger, my heel soon touches the wall behind. As the pistol clicks empty, I duck, pushing myself away from the wall as I avoid the incoming sweep of the black blade, nimbly dodging the strike as I slide between its splayed legs.

Rising to my feet, I run, my eyes centred on the exposed wooden struts on the sides of the corridor, splintered and barely able to support the weight of the roof above. Swinging my arms wide, I strike out, shattering the wooden frames, causing the roof to tremble and shake as it begins to give way.

Heavy footsteps follow me, the vibrations caused by the giant's tread shift the already unsettled roof further. Reloading my empty pistol, I sweep my right arm behind me, firing blindly as I continue to run. The *ting* of ricocheting bullets confirms the impact of each despite my lack of aim.

The giant's movements slow as it shields its head, increasing the distance between as my left hand strikes another strut. The rumble grows as amber warnings lights appear, cautioning me as I weaken the structure further. Ignoring the warnings, I concentrate on the strut ahead, buckling as it struggles to act as a cornerstone.

Pistol raised, I switch it to fully automatic as I unleash what remained into the timber, watching as it splinters with each impact. The rumble turns into a roar as the roof collapses, with wood, masonry, and steel falling, first as small pieces which bounce off my armour but quickly growing in size.

05.00m

The displayed distance shrinks with every step as I run to the end of the corridor, but time was against me. The tempo of the tread behind me quickens as the giants attempt to catch me within its embrace. Straining my already weary muscles further, I leap to the end of the corridor. Rolling over my shoulder, I turn to face the oncoming dust cloud with my pistol raised.

As the rumble comes to an end, the cloud dissipates, revealing the once open corridor buried under a mass of stone, wood, and metal. The sound of scraping metal beneath the rubble warns me of the hidden threat. With the enemy delayed, I eject the nearly spent magazine and slide another into place as my eyes scan the surroundings.

Now trapped in the building with no obvious means of escape, I turn in the direction of the route I had previously taken. Without time for preparation, I would rather fight instead in a room I already knew. In my mindset, I run towards the shimmering lights, knowing it was likely to be my last stand.

Chapter Nineteen

Water cascades from the now porous roof, the evening light reflected from each falling droplet before it strikes the floor. My heartbeat and breathing are slow and steady as I linger by a pool of dark, thick fluid. Standing before a dormant armoured colossus, its hanging limbs hint at its original potential. The fingers of my left hand glide up and down the ridges of a grenade held within its grasp.

My eyes and ears focus only on the sound in the distance, the shifting of heavy rock as something heavy hammers it repeatedly. I knew it would not be long now.

The sound of approaching, trudging footsteps causes adrenaline and other stimulants to course through my bloodstream, pumped into my system from both natural and unnatural organs. The sudden surge of biochemicals heightens and focuses my senses as I prepare for the coming fight.

My eyes scan the room, noting every minute detail, every crack, every hole caused by the earlier struggle, everything is processed and memorised. The fingers of my right hand twitch as I loosen the muscles, releasing the tension as I prevent the onset of cramp.

My eyes flicker downwards, lingering on the pistol as I consider its limitations. Chambered in 9x19mm, the munition had remained the standard for a century and a half of war. Graded as armour piercing, the term had little meaning against my current enemy.

I glare at the door as I sense the approach of an inhuman presence, their silhouette outlined by the residual light from the corridor beyond. Ten minutes, thirty-eight seconds, that was all they had been delayed.

I react as the armoured colossus crashes and tears through the wooden frame and surrounding wall. Pulling the pin from the grenade, I allow it to fall as I grip tightly to the hinge, waiting for the opportunity to strike.

A distorted *whirr* cuts through the silence as the cracked and shattered circular blades slowly begin to spin. Building momentum,

217

it leans forward and charges like a rampaging bull, its arms swinging as it seeks to gouge and eviscerate.

Relying on skill and instinct, I dance outwith of its reach whilst luring it closer and closer to the pool of fluid. Pistol raised, the fingers of my hand move endlessly as it sends round after round into the enemy's armour.

Aiming high, I force it to shield its eyes, blinding it as I drag it into the black tar. With one leg trapped, it changes stance and lunges forwards whilst swinging its sword, the momentum causing the other to become soaked in the dark viscous fluid. Sensing my opportunity now that my prey was trapped, I throw the grenade, watching as the hinge flies through the air as it crosses the narrow distance.

Turning quickly, I run, barely glimpsing the blinding explosion as I seek cover behind the dormant weapon system. The light from the detonation illuminates the room as the volatile chemicals react to the air and to whatever they land.

Burning, glowing flames land on the enemy, bathing its armour panels, wires and tubes, causing them to hiss and squeal. Cracks soon appear on the melting, oxidising panels as they vainly resist the heat being released. As more particles fall, they land in the black tar, setting it aflame with a deafening bang. Shielding my eyes from the bright blue flames, I watch as the molten panels flow downwards, pouring into cracks and joints as it emits high-pitched squeals.

Taking a step back from the intense and uncomfortable heat of the blue flame, I continue to fire bullet after bullet into the now unarmoured shell, splitting and shattering its innards. As more fuel is added to the flames, the system slowly frees itself from its sticky prison and begins to walk, dragging its legs as it continues to swing its sword.

Wreathed in a cloak of flames, it charges forward, abandoning all pretences of protecting its weakened shell as it aims its sword, seeking to skewer me with its blade. Smiling, I watch its clumsy movements whilst flipping backwards, elegantly evading the strike as its sword becomes embedded into the torso of its statue-like counterpart.

Awakening, the statue responds immediately and blindly strikes out with talon and mace, cutting great furrows in the armour panels of its perceived enemy. Locked in a deadly embrace, the two titans violently unleash blow after blow, each mortal for an organic foe. Neither has a clear advantage as the talon of one and the spinning blade of the other squeeze and cut, but soon an oversized arm falls with a heavy clang.

As dark fluid spurts out from the wound, the spinning blades which had caused it, shatter, sending shards of metal flying through the air. Sensing victory, the still mobile titan continues its offensive, plunging the remnants of its spinning discs deep into the torso of the other. The clawed giant's resistance wanes as its innards are ripped apart and gradually it grinds to a halt.

A cry of triumph blares from the hidden speakers of the victor as it pulls free its arm and finishes its opponent with a flourish, ripping it apart and scattering the pieces across the room, before turning its single red eye towards me once more.

⚜ ━━━ ◎◦◎ ━━━ ⚜

I had watched the barbaric display with little satisfaction, the damage caused to my opponent was below expectations. Outclassed, I raise my pistol and continue to fire, the last of the bullets effortlessly cutting through the now fragile armour plates. Clicking empty, I return the pistol to its holster as I change stance, switching the knife to my right. Despite being ambidextrous, there remained a degree of dominance and preference.

Its single red eye glares with an almost baleful look as it charges forward, its limbs hissing with each step. Gaining momentum, it charges into me with the force of a freight train, the spinning discs clashing with the blade of my combat knife, sending shockwaves down the length of my arm.

Stepping backwards as sparks fly from the constant grind of metal, my eyes are drawn to the remnants of the sword arm, hanging limp and useless. Using the advantage of an extra limb, I slam the palm of my left into the torso of the enemy.

Switching effortlessly between offence and defence, my knife acts as both sword and shield as I parry and cut. Each movement born of repetition and instinct, ingrained into the fibres of my body from years of war. Cracks appear in what remained of the armour as the hammer-like blows of my hand continue to rain.

Time however is not on my side, as my stance deepens, the incoming swings become faster and increasingly fluid as my muscles grow weary, highlighting the gulf between mechanical and even enhanced organic limbs. Biochemicals surge through my bloodstream, compensating for the tiredness of the muscles, but it is not enough. My avenues of escape shrink as I am pushed back with every blow until I am trapped.

Unable to take another step back, the enemy's increasingly erratic movements become harder for me to predict and soon shallow gouges appear on my armour as my parries slow. Turning its body whilst raising the stump of its sword arm, it covers my helmet in black fluid, blinding me despite my efforts to quickly clear it. Now blinded, I do not see the incoming kick, the single strike enough to send me crashing back into the wall.

Pain surges through my shoulder, as flesh encased in armour impacts against the reinforced stone. Tumbling through the wall, I land on the other side in a crumpled heap, my right arm numb. Red warning lights illuminate the interior of my helmet as I feel the pressure of something sharp resting on my shoulder blade. Power surges cause my display to flicker as I feel my armoured limbs grow increasingly weaker, I knew instantly that my power supply had been penetrated.

Moving slowly forward, I push off the floor, hearing the shriek of metal as I pull away from the metal spike that had impaled me. The narrow stream of light emanating from the hole in the wall illuminates my armour, allowing me to see the cracks in my cuirass, the damage extensive and unlikely to handle another impact.

Dust continues to fall as heavy impacts come from the other side of the wall, the enemy ruthless in their pursuit. As the light entering the room grows with every new crack appearing in the wall, I knew I did not have much time.

My right arm hangs limp and useless at my side, dislocated. With few options, I decided to force the limb back into position. Reaching across, I pull down on the dangling limb, sweat dripping down my face as I clench my jaw. Slowly, the joint re-articulates and re-enters the socket. The excruciating pain lessens, as small pinpricks occur on my skin, announcing the flow of pain suppressors as my armour injects them directly into my muscles and bloodstream. Moving my arm, I find its movements dull and possessing little of its usual strength, it would take time to fully heal.

As a section of the wall collapses, an armoured giant steps through, its tread sending swirls of dust into the room. Outlined by the light behind it, it enters the remnants of the storage room, the shelves and wooden crates empty. Pillars line the centre, likely the only things maintaining the integrity of the building despite the widespread damage.

Drawing my combat knife for the final time, I hold it in my left hand, changing my stance as I shield my right arm due to the throbbing pain. The route to survival lay before me, the only obstacle is the enemy in front. Pouring the remnants of my armour's power into my arms and legs, I rush forward, countering the charge of the enemy as it moves towards me.

Moving through the gaps, the knife in my hand cuts into whatever it could reach. Every burst of movement causes orange lights to appear on my display, the charge remaining shrinking as the armour is pushed to its limit, the limbs growing heavier as the power-assisted systems begin to seize.

As the legs grow heavy, I redirect what little remaining power into them as I leap, plunging my knife into the enemy's left arm, wedging it into the motors, and bringing the discs to a screeching halt. Abandoning my weapon, I spin, kicking out as my right heel hammers into the torso, causing the cracks to widen.

Landing with my feet apart, I push all my strength into the next strike with my left hand. Aiming for the already crumpled and white panel, it shatters under the impact, my momentum carrying me deeper into the innards of its body. Pushing past the entangled wires and flimsy plastic, my fingers seek something vital. Finding something hard and cylindrical, my fingers wrap around it and pull back, ripping it free as I drag it out into the open air. Without even a glance, I crush it before throwing it away.

Damaged, the giant changes tactics, lunging forward instead of swinging with their left arm. As the arm draws close, I watch as the now still blades retract and fold away, revealing a hidden reaching hand. Weighed down by my unpowered armour, my body reacts too late, failing to leap back in time and become caught in its grasp.

With its fingers wrapped around my torso, it begins to squeeze, the sound of metal and ceramic plating cracking and crumpling carrying over the whine of servos. As the pressure grows, the bitter tang of metal appears in my mouth as biochemicals concentrate in my blood. Punching downwards, I try to break its vice-like grip as it effortlessly picks me up and pulls me closer.

With my armour nearing its limit, I reach and punch out, striking the looming helmet. With a heavy *clang*, the already broken metal bends. Striking again and again, my arm moves like a piston, mechanically striking the helmet until it breaks and becomes misshapen. No longer smooth, I form almost animalistic claws to reach out and wretch the helmet free, exposing the frame underneath.

Now vulnerable, the single red artificial eye widens, almost in shock as it concentrates on my approaching fist. Realising its looming fate, it emits a high-pitched wail. Too close, I absorb the full brunt of the sound as it carries through my helmet, overwhelming my senses, causing my vision to blur and upsetting my balance.

My strike misses, hitting the shoulder as the giant seizes the opportunity. Charging forward with the full weight of its body, it smashes me into each pillar, using me as a club as it throws me around like a rag doll. Each impact causes blood to splutter from my lips as the ground and roof begin to tremble, each strike causing masonry to fall as the entire building is brought closer to collapse.

Using what little strength remained within my arms, I punch and force open the grip. Pushing off, I land heavily on the ground, barely avoiding being trampled as the armoured suit shatters the sole remaining pillar like a battering ram.

An earth-shattering crack announces the collapse of the building. As chunks of stone, metal, and wood fall, the already weakened ground splits open, revealing a chasm that grows with every passing moment.

Standing on unsteady legs, I begin to run towards the opening in the wall. Willing my body onwards, I force air into my lungs as the ground beneath my every footstep collapses. The distance is far and

227

I know I will barely make it. Leaping, I outstretch my arms, reaching for the nearest ledge. My fingertips brush against the loose stone, sending me sliding down until I grasp a firmer hold.

Hanging in place, I can only watch as the room and building around me collapses. Large sections of timber fall from the roof as the building begins to lurch to the left. Seeing the falling rubble, I attempt to pull myself up, but the stone crumbles in my hands.

Unable to climb higher, I look up as the creak of metal draws my attention to the roof and the swinging metal girder directly above me. With little time, I leap to the ledge to my right, trying to avoid its descent, but it's too late. The girder falls, striking my body and sends me into the darkness.

Knowing that my fate was already decided, I cross my arms and legs, embracing the dark as I fall into the unknown.

Chapter Twenty

The crash of waves and the squawking of birds cause me to open my eyes. Blinded by the radiant sun, I squint and turn, allowing time for my helmet to adjust as I concentrate on the circling shapes. Gulls, their wings and bodies a mixture of white and grey, fly openly in the clear blue, cloudless sky.

The ground underneath me is different from the stone and asphalt I was expecting, feeling soft and soothing. Digging my fingers into the ground, I scoop up a handful of sand, white with no impurities, it is unheard of in this age. Rubbing the grains together, I find them smooth, despite their coarse appearance.

Bewildered, my eyes catch the glimpse of subtle green light bathing my helmet's interior. The display, which should be covered in red warnings is clear, is indicating my armour and body are in top condition. Pushing myself upright, I turn and look, finding myself at the edge of a white sanded beach, with green fields behind.

Where am I?

How did I get here?

Opening and closing my hands, I feel strength unfelt in decades. Standing, I feel the same strength coursing through my limbs and body. Spying a pool of still water, I move towards it, using its shining surface as a mirror. Staring back at me is something that should not exist, of something lost and never to return.

Figure-hugging black armour, the panels sleek, curved, and moulded to fit the body, it was a design so complicated and expensive that it was never created in mass numbers. Resilient and near impenetrable, anything less than weapons designed to counter heavily armoured vehicles would be deflected.

The War had ensured no undamaged sets remained, leaving only half-completed prototypes which were sealed away in time-locked vaults. Never to be opened until humanity's technological achievements returned to pre-War levels.

I reminisce as I spot the white symbols painted on my shoulders, symbols of an age of peace, an age which would never return. Turning slowly, I find that I am unarmed, with neither blade nor

230

firearm on my body. Despite this, I sense no danger, instead only the feeling of déjà vu.

A sudden chill in the air announces a change to my surroundings as a mist approaches from the sea. Too fast to be wholly natural, the thin, tendril-like fingers are filled with the scent of burning coals and salt. Slowly enveloping my body, it becomes thicker until anything more than a metre ahead is hidden.

I regain my bearings as a soft breeze blows from behind, lifting the fog to reveal a tower in the distance. Alone, it stands on the edge of a cliff, like a needle, its exterior glints with the sheen of steel and pure white stone. I recognise it immediately, a place where humanity's greatest minds once met, to share knowledge as they performed miracles, a place I once called home.

I understand.

Nodding, the existence of the tower had confirmed my suspicions, everything around me was an illusion, a dream. This beach, the water, and the sand beneath my boots were nothing more than memories from the distant past, my past. These memories could never be forgotten. They were my earliest for everything before this day when I set eyes on this building and were blank as if they were purposely wiped from my memories.

A sudden gust of wind causes the sand to swirl, growing faster and stronger with every second until it becomes a storm that obscures my sight. Shielding my helmet, I wait for the storm to die down and when it does, the once pristine and gleaming walls of the tower in the distance are now black, the stone charred as a burning inferno rages within. Dark smoke rises from the broken windows, the glass shattering due to the heat. The air is filled with ash as everything around me burns, even the sand beneath my feet becomes glass. This was how I remembered this tower, a place of lost beauty.

The high-pitched wail of a bullhorn carries through the air, the siren a warning of impending doom. Knowing what to expect, I look upwards, catching the glint of something metal plummeting from the heavens, bright and beautiful like a falling star. Breaking apart, the star sends trails of destruction in different directions.

An orbital research station, it was once the hope for all Mankind, now it would announce its destruction. I kneel, bracing my body as I wait for the inevitable impact. The station crashes into the

Mediterranean Sea a moment before its sabotaged reactors detonate. Closing my eyes, the dazzling flash of light pierces even the protective lenses of my helmet and eyelids as I feel the shockwaves and heat wash over me.

The crackle of shattering glass and the scent of charred meat is the cue to open my eyes. Flaring my nostrils, I breathe deeply as I look around me, everything is black. The cry of twisting metal draws my attention to the tower in the distance, I watch its death throes as its foundations crumble and it falls into the sea with a splash.

The finger-like tendrils of fog return, cloaking me fully as it hides the destruction in the distance. The fog does not linger long before a gentle breeze carries it away, gone were the tower and evidence of chaos, all that remained was a clear white beach.

Having better understood my situation, I relax. This place was many things, but it was not real, for everything within it was a figment of my imagination and memories. I had chosen to not enter this realm for decades, for it contained sealed away aspects of

233

myself, aspects which could achieve the extraordinary, the impossible, and the terrible.

Concentrating on the series of flashing memories, I collect and stitch them together. Though pieces were missing, enough of a picture remained to remind me of my last waking moments.

Pain

Gritting my teeth, the feeling soon dissipates as my mind recovers from the shock. The agonies of the body had no meaning here.

A hundred different questions appear within my head, yet none of them mattered. On the verge of my death, my body had done what it was designed to do, forcing itself into a comatose-like state, to allow it time to heal. To answer any of the questions, I would have to force my body awake, but this would cause more harm than good.

But as I look around, I sense a falseness, a lingering uncertainty that this place was chosen for a reason, as if some external force had chosen to bring me to these specific pages of my life.

Unlocking the seals, I allow the various sections of my helmet to expand outwards and sideways before exposing my flesh to the elements for the first time. With my senses no longer filtered, I breathe in the fresh air, tasting the scent of the sea and nearby meadows.

Glancing down at a pool of still water, I look upon my face, noticing that despite the passage of time, my features had remained relatively unchanged.

As I turn the now empty helmet, I allow my fingers to feel every curve and crevasse of its long-forgotten shape. It was a design that was both elegant and subtle, in my eyes it was beautiful, but to others, it would be ugly for it represented death, destruction, and terror.

Placing it carefully on the sand, I use my attachment to the armour to anchor myself to this time and space, before beginning my walk.

As I head towards the distant cliffs, I listen to the soft *squelch* that comes from my armoured boots as it tramples the sand. Extending my senses, I find nothing unusual, nothing existed here which was not already a figment of my memories.

Having walked in this realm in the past, I would come upon persons I had once known. Often fated within untimely deaths, they would act as my guide, leading me to discover the secrets that they had been unable to share. The appearance of the living was rare, for only one had ever met the conditions necessary, and they were tied to me by a bond stronger than blood.

Suddenly my fingers tingle, my instincts warned me of a new presence. Turning sharply, I am greeted by an armoured figure, one who had not been present moments before. Wearing raven black armour like my own, it was however designed to fit the frame of a fairer form.

Recognising the armour, I leisurely walk towards them, acknowledging their existence with a wave of my hand. Due to the presence of the anchor, the figure could be only one, but I begin to wonder why they had entered this realm. Long ago they had suffered a horrific trauma and had vowed to never again return to this place.

Slowing my movements to a crawl, I sense that the aura emanating from the figure was unlike anything I had experienced before, and did not match that of the woman I knew. Turning, the figure acknowledges my hesitation with a tilt of their head, before reaching for the seals of their helmet. Pulling upwards, I watch as long black hair cascades from the interior, the volume was an amount that was impossible to fit within. Flowing down their shoulders, it soon reaches the small of their back. Their facial features were feminine, and despite being partially hidden by the bangs of hair, she could only be described as beautiful.

I search through my memories, but I cannot recall ever meeting them. Was she someone who was contained within my still unreachable memories, or was she something else?

"Who, or what are you?"

Wary of their identity and intentions, my voice booms across the distance separating us. Despite my challenging tone, she does not react, instead, she carefully collects and ties back her hair into a ponytail. Her face no longer covered, reveals a gentle, innocent smile that could disarm lesser men.

My wary eyes scan her appearance, noting the subtle traces of purple within her apparent black hair, the streaks barely visible in the sunlight. I sense no malice from her calm demeanour, but my wariness causes her to watch me with an expression of sadness and disappointment.

Slowly she turns away, whilst extending her right hand, inviting me to take hold. I did not understand why, but her movements were eerily familiar. After taking a few steps, she waits, her lips moving as tears form within her eyes. The words spoken were unheard as she continues towards the water.

Her movements are graceful, too graceful to be human, her every footstep light and soft, barely leaving a mark in the sand. As the sun's rays wrap around her body, bathing her in golden light, her outline becomes hazy and slowly begins to change.

Piece by piece, the black armour disappears, changing, being replaced by pale white flesh and soft green cloth. As her clothes begin to change, so does her stature, becoming more feminine and petite.

Now no taller than an unenhanced human, she dances along the sand, the blowing wind revealing her clothes' silk-like qualities. Her dress is unlike anything I had seen before, appearing weightless and semi-transparent, it was close in design to those worn by the ancient Greeks.

With one foot in the sand and the other in the water, she turns towards me with a radiating smile on her youthful features. The simple act is alluring, but I can clearly see the exhaustion and tiredness contained within her eyes. Despite her spotless skin and child-like movements, she was older than her apparent twenty years. I stare into their depths, sensing the wisdom and knowledge contained within. Eyes such as those were earned from living a long life and experiencing countless tragedies.

Sensing my continued reluctance, she twirls and dances on the waterline, her feet kicking out as her hair spins around and around until her movements become a blur. When she finally stops, her appearance has become more regal, her hair now tied in a French-style pleat that reaches the small of her back and topped with a silver crown.

Despite her unknown identity, her attire, her personality, and demeanour remind me of another. Decades ago, I had been assigned to the sole heir of the last Queen of Britannia. Young and full of life, the young princess's promising future was cut short by a needless quarrel.

Shaking away the memory, I notice the lurching movements of my feet as I unconsciously step towards her beckoning hands. I fight against the compulsion, forcing my body to come to a stop. She watches my resistance, tilting her head, silently questioning me as her eyes soften in sadness.

Her lips open and close, forming words that are drowned out by the blowing wind, one that smells of meadows and forests, unlike anything I had smelt before. But soon I hear it, also carried within the wind is a soft and distant feminine voice.

O ippótis mou, se vríka teliká.[5]

Despite sounding familiar, the words, their meaning and origins are unknown to me. Gradually, my mind, which has been moulded to the heights and beyond of human ability deciphers the meaning of the words.

Greek?

---

[5] Ο ιππότης μου, σε βρήκα τελικά. - My knight, I have finally found you.

No, though the harsh tones appeared to have Hellenic origins, they had diverged and distorted along an unknown path.

"Knight?"

The appearance of the familiar word, though laced with confusion, spoken in the High Language stops my chain of thought. As the woman's lips move once more, a new wind swirls around me and with it the return of the same voice.

"Do you understand me now?"

Though heavily accented, the words are understandable. In response, I cautiously nod.

"Please, do not be afraid, I mean you no harm. Will you not enter the water with me?"

Her soft, feminine voice resonates deeply within my very being, her pitch and tone for unknown reasons, were familiar to me.

There were too many questions surrounding this woman, and I would find none of the answers if I continued to resist. As if sensing my change in resolve, she raises her hand once more, inviting me into the tide.

My movements are heavy as I step forward, each stride causing me to sink into the soft sand with a *squelch*. As I close the distance, the sun's rays strike my body, coating the black armour in a layer of white light. My limbs grow light as the barely noticeable weight of my armour disappears, each piece being replaced until I am clothed in a dark blue tunic.

Glancing down on my sleeves, I notice the woven and embroidered symbols, the insignia of my first unit. Glancing back up, I am confronted by a mirror that stands to my full height. I stare at the reflection, resisting the urge to touch the epaulettes on my shoulders and symbols on my chest. Each represented a more civilised, peaceful era.

Thin, dainty fingers appear slowly from the side of the mirror as the woman peeks out. A giggle escapes her lips as her eyes lock upon mine. Smiling, she slinks away, disappearing behind the mirror as I rush forward. Despite following her movements, there is no one there.

I soon feel the gentle touch of fingers on my arms as the woman appears once again. Sensing no malice, I offer no resistance as she wraps her limbs around me. Her fingers follow the shapes of the embroidered symbols on my right arm, a Corinthian helmet and the symbol of lambda.

None alive bar me and one other should know the meanings of these symbols, the others having taken the secrets to their graves. But the warm smile and loving look contained within this woman's eyes hinted that she knew.

As another girlish giggle escapes her lips, she breaks the embrace, stepping out and takes hold of my right hand with both of her own. Her hands are small, barely able to cover half of the area as she pulls me into the water.

The strength contained within her body is unexpected, a near match for my own. Dragging me forward, I am soon submerged by the rising tide. Closing my eyes, I allow the water to wash over me, each passing moment causing the weight on my body to lighten.

As the tide retreats, I feel the warmth of the water and the softness of the sand between my toes. Opening my eyes, I confirm what I already knew, the water had washed away all traces of my clothing, leaving me naked.

Silently approaching me from behind, she embraces me once more, her dry, clothed body wrapped around my right arm. Holding me close, she embraces me like a lover as her eyes stare at the now setting sun.

With her actions dictating my own, I watch the scenic view and feel something stir within me, something I had never felt before, contentment. I feel her gaze and look down, meeting her bright green eyes. But before I can speak, she stretches out her hand and places her index finger on my lips.

Her gaze is stern, and not wishing to disturb the world's serenity, I simply nod, doing nothing as she leans close and buries her head into my chest. As a soft sigh escapes her lips, I feel her warm breath drift over my bare skin as she places her ear on my chest, listening to my heartbeat.

"Unfair."

The words are barely a whisper as I feel a sudden wetness on my skin. But before I can look upon her face, she breaks the embrace, wiping away the tears that had formed within her eyes as she places both of her hands on my chest.

Her bright green eyes change colour, becoming golden as the skies above darken. In the far horizon, a shadow appears, its form faint and incomprehensible.

"The darkness is coming, there is little time until it is here."

Within her golden eyes are emotions I have seen but never experienced, regret, sorrow, sadness, and fear. As the golden radiance spreads to the rest of her body, I feel the warmth of the light as it basks my skin. With a gentle push, she sends me flying backwards and I land at the edge of the sand and fields.

Winded, I try to catch my breath as I look upon the woman in confusion. Shaking her head, as if apologising, she steps backwards, hovering over the water as her hair scatters like tendrils in a non-existent wind.

A warm wind blows, engulfing me as her lips once again move.

"For countless centuries I have searched, and only now have I found you. But as you are now, you cannot help me, for you are bound by the weight of chains that you alone have wrought. Only when you are free of guilt will you be ready for the war that is coming."

With those words, finely wrought silver chains appear on my chest and limbs, anchoring me in place as their weight drags me to my knees. With grinding teeth, I strain and fight against them, struggling to my feet as I try to break free.

"Who…are…you…to…me?"

I cough out the question as the intensity of the wind increases and sand enters my open mouth. As the storm bites and gouges my exposed flesh, the woman turns away, unable to look upon my blood slick flesh as tears form within her eyes.

"I am no one and someone, an observer of your past, present, and future. Long have I searched for one who has known grief beyond those of mortal men, yet remain uncorrupted by it. Long have I waited for a knight such as you, who can decide the fate of our two worlds."

Unsatisfied by her cryptic answer, I form another question, but she indicates with the wag of her finger, that she will answer no further.

"I can hold back the darkness no more, go, you must leave this place. You and I will meet thrice more in our lifetimes. Do not search

for me, for no matter how far or how long you look, you will not find me.

Only when the last of this world's knowledge is gained and the once broken bridge is restored, shall I be found. Go! Sleep no more, for your duty is yet unfinished."

Blinded, I am slowly buried by the sand as it enters my mouth and nostrils. My chest grows heavy as I struggle to breathe. Falling, I feel the weight of the sand on top of me as my world is once again replaced by darkness.

Chapter Twenty One

Spluttering, I force air into my burning lungs as my eyes snap open. Awakening to darkness, I lick my dry lips, tasting the tang of metal as I notice the weight on my chest. The interior of my helmet is tinted red as layers of warning symbols appear on the display. On top is a timer, the bright red numbers counting down with every breath I take.

Running low on air, I turn my head left and right in an attempt to find my bearings but I am greeted only by blackness. The entirety of my body aches and I attempt to lift my arms, but only the left responds, the other buried and trapped under layers of rubble.

Looking down, the chin of my helmet strikes the object sitting on my chest, the surface hard and metallic. Gripping it with my left hand, I begin to push, the muscles of my arm straining under the pressure. Inch by inch the object rises, until with a roar I cast it aside.

A stream of dirt falls from the layers above, coating my helmet in a layer of dirt and grime that I claw away.

A series of low-pitched clicks sound from the interior of my helmet as it slowly peels away the darkness. Absorbing what little light was available, it reveals the broken pieces of metal, wood, and stone that had formed my makeshift tomb.

Carefully, I reach across my body and begin to dig, the fingers of my left hand forming a makeshift shovel as I slowly claw away at the rubble. Visually, I knew the right arm was still physically connected, but the level of trauma that the nerves had suffered had disassociated it mentally. As I continue to dig, the grip on my arm loosens until finally, I pull it away.

With my right hand in front of my face, I watch as the fingers respond to my commands, but I cannot feel their movements. Sighing, I rest it on the ground as my eyes flutter in various directions, cycling through the multitude of warnings. One by one, each is cleared as I confirm the extent of the damage. Though my armour was torn, ripped, and pierced, the flesh underneath was merely bruised and with time would recover.

With my eyes closed, I spread my consciousness across every fibre, muscle, and neural pathway. Whilst concentrating on the areas of pain, bio-chemicals surge through my bloodstream as artificial and natural organs begin their work, easing the pain as torn muscles and sinew are reknit and reformed. Though the process was faster than those of unenhanced men, it was still too slow.

A high-pitched ringing causes my eyes to flutter open as a new orange symbol appears on my display.

Air Low

Scraping away the dust which had collected on the grills of my helmet, I find it to be dark and sticky, the air here was too noxious and thick in debris to be breathable. I did not know how long I had been asleep, but it was long enough for my air supplies to reach this level.

Injured and without the strength to change my predicament, I can only ration what little air I had remaining. Slowing my heart rate and breathing, I enter a state akin to hibernation, straddling the realms of consciousness and dreams.

A gentle backwards and forwards rubbing sensation on my wrists, causes me to awaken. The timer on my helmet displays zero, confirming that thirty minutes had passed. The pain in my body was now gone and my limbs were filled with newfound strength. Bringing my hands close to my face, I open and close them, my right, which had once been a stranger, was connected to me once more.

With barely five minutes of air remaining, I shuffle and place my back against the slanted roof of my ad-hoc tomb. Legs braced, I push, the muscles in my thighs and back groaning as they strain under the weight. Teeth gritted, I fight against the resistance until finally the stone panel crumbles and gives way with the creak of metal and snapping of wood.

A ray of light pierces the gloom, showing the path to the surface, but it soon flickers as a stream of stone and gravel cascades downwards. Blinded by the dirt and grime, I instinctively reach out, grabbing whatever I can find and begin to climb.

Fighting against the seemingly unending stream of rock and dirt that slams into my body, my hands become shovels and picks. With little grace, my arms and legs flail as I continue upwards, unable to stop for even a moment due to fear of being carried away.

My movements slow when my hands touch nothing but air, but only when my chest slams onto the surface do I completely stop.

Sensing the change in the environment immediately, the grills on my helmet and armour unlock, sliding open to draw fresh air into their interior. In a matter of seconds, the once stale air has a hint of freshness and the bright red warnings disappear.

But my moment of respite is short-lived as the creak of splintering wood warns me of looming danger. Ahead, a crude wooden dam shatters, sending a tidal wave of water crashing into me, threatening to send me back into the abyss I had just escaped.

As the current clear away the silt that had clogged my joints, I grab at a coil of wire that sways side to side. Wrapping it around my forearms, I drag myself towards higher ground.

Flopping onto an embankment of dry, solid rock, I allow my shattered body to rest, arms and legs shaking as the adrenaline surges out of them. Rolling onto my back, I clear the grime from the lenses of my helmet and stare upwards at the dark sky.

The entirety of the building had collapsed. The once formidable walls were barely upright and without a roof, and I was exposed fully to the elements.

A dim light appears in the corner of my interior, drawing my eyes to the descending numbers as the scant power within my armour is depleted. Unsealing my helmet, I cast it aside as the armour grows heavy, its final task being the administering of pain suppressants by a series of pinpricks that are felt on my skin.

Willing my exhausted body to move, I struggle to stand, my spent limbs now weighed down by the deadweight of my armour. Gritting my teeth, I stand straight and to my full height as I gain my bearings from the tower on the horizon.

Trudging forward with heavy, dragging footsteps, I barely cover ten metres before my legs collapse beneath me. With clawed hands, I crawl and drag myself towards a low wall and pull myself up.

Though my eyelids were growing heavy, and my body longed for a true rest, my instincts were warning me that I could not remain here. Taking slow and deep breaths, I regain my composure before making another attempt.

A tremor causes the ground beneath my feet to shift and tilt left, the suddenness causing me to lose my footing. Landing heavily on the ground, my dulled and dazed senses immediately sharpen as adrenaline courses through my veins. Turning towards the epicentre of the tremors, I knew instantly that this was not the result of the building's instability, but something else.

The tell-tale scrape of digging is soon joined by those of hammered stone and tearing metal as a dark mass erupts from the ground. A mere shadow of its original form, heavily damaged with its panels torn, its identity however was unmistakable. As dark fluid seeps from its open wounds, it turns its head left and right, searching. Finally, it's one remaining eye turns in my direction and focuses.

Gone were the lithe and fluid-like movements, replaced with slow, jerking lurches as it shuffles forward, dragging and scraping its left leg across the ground. With each forward step, it swings its remaining arm left and right in a criss-cross pattern. The once intimidating ranks of spinning blades were now cracked, shattered, and still, but I could hear the spluttering of the motor as it attempts to restart its movements.

Though battered and on the verge of destruction, this foe was beyond the ability of the current me. My body had been pushed to its physical limits and beyond, I could not fight here even if I wanted to. I only had one option, to withdraw.

Turning, I make to move, but my tired, barely healed limbs, encumbered by the dead-weight of my armour, make little progress. After twenty excruciating steps, my legs finally give way. Unable to support the weight of my frame any longer, I fall into the mud. Punching my fists into the ground, I prop myself up as I will my limbs to move, but they remain lifeless.

As the sound of scraping metal grows nearer, so does the intensity of the shaking ground. Turning my head, I look upon the looming shadow of my nemesis. Closing my eyes, I accept the fate that had been thrust upon me, but the wait is long and arduous.

A sudden damp breeze brushes past me, wrapping itself around my body as it cleanses and strips away the exhaustion and cold. My nose twitches as it catches the faint whiff of forests and meadows, scents which were unnatural to this place. The smell reminded me of the bewitching woman within my vision.

"Why do you surrender so easily?"

Her voice appears within my head, sounding both distant and close.

"It is not your destiny to die here or now. If it were, how will you find me?"

Gently she questions me, her tone neither judgemental nor disapproving. With my eyes still closed, I expand my senses, trying to follow the voice back to its source, but there is none, as if it is disembodied from anything nearby.

Impossible

I shake my head at the thought, the voice was nothing more than a delusion created by my damaged body.

"Why do you hide your true self? Release the chains, stop hiding what you truly are."

An onslaught of cold air causes me to open my eyes, the warmth surrounding me was gone, and I was now alone, as I always was. Shaking my head as I rationalise and dismiss the voice and vision as nothing more than delusions of my injured body, I focus on what was before me.

An awkward smile appears on my lips as I begin to laugh, despite the passage of time, the giant had barely made any progress. Belittling myself, I slow my breathing and begin to concentrate, feeling time itself begin to slow. As my eyes track the slow descent of droplets of water, I concentrate my remaining will into a single point.

I feel the weight of the metaphysical chains bound to my body, despite the passage of decades, they were still as sturdy as the day they had been forged. Wrought by my own hands as penance, they were constructed for a single purpose, to curb my strength and ability to bring death and destruction.

Words, long forgotten from the tongues and memories of Man, escape my lips, passing through them as naturally as breathing. Within the depths of my mind, I feel the first of a dozen chains begin to crumble, but there is not enough time to truly unbind myself. Concentrating on the smallest and weakest, the chain shatters with a sound akin to breaking glass. Though minuscule, it is more than enough as a sliver of the decades' old guilt is lifted from my body.

No longer encumbered, my limbs are filled with a newfound energy that washes away the exhaustion. Standing on sturdy legs, I feel the narrowing of blood vessels on the areas of exposed skin as the temperature of the air around me plummets. Opening my eyes, I watch as the droplets of water in the air freeze mid-descent, turning into ice that shatters on the ground. Frost forms on the walls and floor as the breeze passing me becomes colder than those found in the Antarctic.

A familiar, tingling sensation condenses on the fingertips of my right hand. Seeing and sensing everything with greater clarity, I watch as my would-be executioner's movements become almost non-existent. With its arm raised, it intends to deliver an earth-shattering strike, but I already know where it is going to land and casually move away.

Raising my right hand, I stretch out my fingers and expose my palm as the final words of an ancient song passes my lips. As the final syllable is sung, the energy collected within my fingers is unleashed. Arcs of electricity strike the suit, piercing through the armour and melting the metal frame underneath as it slowly pushes the figure back.

The dark fluid which was seeping out catches fire, bathing the figure in a cloak of flames. Despite being on the verge of destruction, it continues to step forward, swinging its arm downwards to deliver a final strike.

Chapter Twenty Two

WARNING, THRESHOLDS BREACHED, WARNING!

SAFETY PROTOCOLS REINSTATED.

An artificial woman's voice blares from hidden speakers, carrying over the klaxon that wails in the background. The warning is reinforced by flashing red lights that illuminate the walls and roof.

The downward strike comes to a stop, mere inches from my face as I flick my wrist, dissipating the energy that was contained within my fingers. Standing upright, my would-be executioner retracts its arm before taking a step back. It remains still as its frame continues to melt, the molten metal flowing downwards and coiling around its legs.

With my reserves spent, I collapse to the ground, my consciousness lingering long enough to hear the sound of doors being forced open and the pitter-patter of running heeled shoes. My vision grows dim as I feel the touch of hands reaching underneath my body, lifting and dragging me before carefully placing me on the ground.

I barely register the cold and wet ground as wires are placed on various points of my skin and armour. The faint outline of a woman stands above me, her voice faint and incomprehensible. Sensing that she was someone I could trust, I nod in response and allow my eyes to close, ending my resistance to sleep's embrace.

Wake up!

A semi-recognisable voice calls out to me, causing me to open my eyes. Lying on my back, I stare up at the woman hovering over me. Her fingers move effortlessly over a tablet held in her hand as she retracts the lengths of wires attached to my armour. Sensing that I was awake, she looks down, her face emotionless as she casually places the tablet in an inside pocket of her tunic.

"Alive and awake."

A statement rather than a question, her words contain little to no warmth.

"Can you speak?"

My mouth and lips are dry and I struggle to form the words, what emerges is hoarse and barely above a whisper. Kneeling, she cracks open a ration pack and places it between my lips. I suckle on the tepid but welcome fluids, quenching my thirst as I restore moisture to my dehydrated body.

Draining the contents, I study the face of the woman who kneels resplendent in her uniform. It is a face I know well, despite her lack of expressions and words, I could feel the anger and concern that was being contained within.

A flicker of a smile appears on my lips as I continue to stare at her face. Her eyes catch the subtle movement and immediately her facial features harden in response. I understood the reason for the fury that was being hidden beneath her cold visage, I could expect no other reaction from my adjutant, Colonel Amelia Brendt.

Gracefully extending her hand, she waits for me to accept before wrapping her fingers around my own. With a single fluid motion, she pulls, hauling me to my feet as I am caught within her embrace.

Waiting no more than necessary for me to find my footing, she steps back, straightening her posture and tidying her clothes as she prepared to reprimand me.

"With all due respect sir, what do you think you are doing?"

Though sounding like a question, her tone makes it clear that it is rhetorical, she does not expect, nor wish to hear an answer. Despite being aware of this, I whimsically give one.

"Is it not obvious? A light training session?"

The remark is met with a light impact on my right shoulder, the action alone saying more than any words. Despite her calm expression, I could see the smallest, barely noticeable quiver in her upper lip. Despite my apparent lack of remorse, I understood the meaning of her words. Sensing my true thoughts, the muscles in her face relax.

"You never change."

Barely a mutter, the comment is spoken underneath her breath as she shakes her head.

"Surely after all this time, you should know me better?"

"There is a thin line between heroic and reckless actions, I believe it unwise for a senior official to endanger themselves needlessly."

Her rebuke ends with a barely audible *tsk*.

Slowly stretching, I find the muscles in various parts of my body to still be tender. Though most of the soft tissue damage had already been repaired, I knew how close I had come to a mortal wound. I feel the gaze of Amelia, her eyes tracking my movements, searching for irregularities.

"I checked your inputs, disabling all mandatory safety measures, do you place little value in your life?"

Sensing the heavy, dour mood, I place my hand on her shoulder. The concepts of guilt and remorse are alien to me, but I understood their concepts.

"The Confederation can ill-afford to replace you."

A hoarse laugh escapes my lips as I listen to her final remark. Shoulder to shoulder, she and I had fought on countless battlefields across the decades. I knew how her near-emotionless, analytical mind worked, and the true reason behind her concern. Since my "transfer" from the frontlines, I had developed an insatiable "hunger", one that only grew with every day of inactivity.

"This place was designed to test the limits of a soldier's abilities. Anything less would have been pointless."

"This facility however was not designed for our needs. What would have happened if I had not re-activated the fail-safes?"

"You know better than I that there are no second chances, no safeguards in battle. Your eventual report would have stated the realism of the scenario."

"And the choice of subpar equipment?"

Her comment highlighted the true issue, the equipment was unsuited for this type of opponent.

"Not everyone has access to Praetor grade, what I used was the best the Confederation had to offer. This shows the need for heavier calibre weapons."

"Does proving this justify the risk?"

She tilts her head slightly, three degrees to the left. A trait since childhood, it was an indication that she disbelieved my political answer. She knew that though my response contained nothing but the truth, it was not the entire answer.

Since the end of the last "true war", the world's technological levels had regressed to an almost pre-Industrial Revolution state. Gone were the large standing armies, and those armies which remained no longer wore armour that could resist our standard-issue weapons. Without a true enemy, one which could challenge our martial strength, weapons, and armour development had stalled as there was no need to adapt and innovate.

But this, the experimentation on artificial soldiers, capable of wielding heavy weapons and armour, concerned me. Today was proof that preparations needed to be made for the day they would be used against us.

"Now Colonel, your other reason for coming here?"

My previously playful undertone disappears as I change the topic of conversation. Sensing the change, Amelia's body straightens as she stands to attention.

"I come in regards to three matters."

"Relax and brief me in order."

Her stance relaxes slightly as she begins her brief.

"The Lord Marshal requests an audience with yourself, to discuss the projects you are overseeing."

"He received this already, three days ago."

"He wishes to discuss, *all* of them."

Her emphasis on the word "all", allows me to understand the political undertones behind the request.

"Then Colonel, prepare my refusal if you have not already done so."

The request out of context is not unusual, for the Lord Marshall was the de facto leader of the Britannic Confederation, but I did not trust the motives behind the request. Not when the success or failures of humanity's future could be determined by them.

"And the second?"

"The regional Council wishes to confirm the rules of engagement."

"Their reason?"

"Disruption to buildings supplying Facility 04 have increased since your departure, they have exceeded earlier expectations."

Having anticipated the question, she reaches into her tunic and removes a tablet. Handing it over, she reveals the current and projected casualties. I scan through the various logs and graphs before making a decision.

"It is within acceptable levels. My orders remain as they were until my return."

Returning the tablet, I watch as her hand makes a single movement, confirming that she had anticipated my response.

Callous

The word was how the non-Praetorians under my command would often describe me. Always questioning how I could disregard the lives of so many, so easily. But this was a war and casualties were to be expected. A few hundred dead now could spare hundreds of thousands in the future, I only had to ensure that the lives sacrificed were not wasted.

"Emphasise that we are at a tipping point. I will not allow any Insurrectionists to become martyrs."

Confirming my command with a biometric signature, I watch as Amelia returns the tablet to her tunic pocket. Her movements allow me to glimpse the red envelope secreted within. Understanding the final matter, I extend my hand, requesting that she hand it over.

After placing the envelope in my outstretched hand, she immediately takes three steps back. Raising my free left hand, I beckon her forward.

"Amelia, you are my aide and successor. The contents of this letter will be made known to you either way. Disregard protocols, would it not be better for you to read it directly, removing any possibilities of misunderstandings?"

I had purposely chosen to use her name, an act rarely performed outwith of the privacy of my office. There were few I trusted as indefinitely as her, for aeons she had remained by my side, fighting back to back across countless battlefields. That reason alone was enough for the trust, as well as a thousand others.

Checking her surroundings by glancing left and right, she steps forward, standing behind me as I begin the process of checking the numerous seals on the envelope. As my fingers and eyes move, I muse on the symbolic meanings of the letter.

In this age of regression, it was a representation of our technological might. The ability to communicate instantaneously, despite the vast distances. It was an advantage that allowed us, despite our limited numbers, to sweep aside all resistance during the Wars of Reclamation.

But this letter also symbolised the shadows, the secrets that were at the heart of the empire we had built. Every form of communication was encrypted, from the lowest within civilian households to the highest used in governance.

At the apex were these simple red letters, existing within an independent network that was linked to only eight structures. Any messages sent from within those eight guarded rooms were decoded, printed, and sealed within the envelopes by machines, with no living eyes except those of the intended recipient entitled to see the contents.

In an age where sophisticated cyber warfare was non-existent, the system was effectively impervious. Those entitled to handle and deliver the letters were few, their status earned after numerous, rigorous checks. Any person, regardless of rank, who attempted to hinder the delivery or tamper with the contents were dealt with by summary execution.

Satisfied that the letter had not been tampered with, I break the seal and remove a single sheet of folded red paper, the contents written in large black ink.

OMEGA PROTOCOL AUTHORISED

Underneath is the seal of the Lord Marshall, ensuring the meaning of those three words were clear, an escalation in anti-insurgency tactics.

Returning the envelope and its contents to Amelia, I stand straight, reaching my full height as I remove all traces of emotion and familiarity.

"Colonel dispose of this letter.

Make arrangements for an audience with the Lord Marshall and a transport for the Capital leaving at 2100 hours."

Like an emotionless doll, Amelia acknowledges the command with a crisp salute, before turning and marching towards the exit, her parade standard movements as natural to her as breathing. Only when she reaches the door does she stop and turn her head towards me.

"Are you feeling lighter?"

I hesitate before answering her cryptic words.

"Colonel, in regards to the second instruction."

"Commander?"

"Until I say otherwise, they remain unchanged."

"Understood."

Though her back is turned to me, I sense the lightening of her steps as she opens the door.

Now alone with my thoughts, I consider every tactic, option, and consequence of this command. Every outcome was the same, an increase in disorder and violence. A single emotion wells within me, anger, one of the few not removed by the decades of implants and psychological indoctrination.

Why now, when it would jeopardise all that had been sacrificed already?

Arc 3 – New Truths and Old Secrets

Chapter Twenty Three

Training Facility Alpha "Thorian Academy", District 6

63.16, 14.63

1700 hours, 09-08-2177 C.E.

The blaring klaxons and red flashing lights disappear as the sliding doors, leading to the corridors beyond, close behind Amelia. In their place are bright white lights that banish the darkness of the battlefield, revealing its full size and splendour.

Six miles wide and eight long, at its centre were the ruins of a twentieth-century city. One of eight simulation rooms within the Academy's compound. Here and at sister facilities located elsewhere within the Confederation were the future guardians of the empire trained.

No expense had been spared in their creation, collecting the best instructors and tactical minds to ensure that the recruits were trained in the latest tactics and equipment.

I turn my gaze back to my final adversary, an automated soldier so fundamentally new that even I was not aware of its existence. I held no doubt, that in time they would replace soldiers of flesh and blood, but this was still years away.

Even at the height of humanity's technological advances, there was a single unresolved problem that prevented their widespread use on the battlefield, power. If I had chosen to wait another hour, I would likely have won the simulation by default.

Standing at attention, the once towering giant is a shadow of its former glory. The flames which had once cloaked it had been extinguished by the overhead downpour, revealing the full extent of the damage.

A series of thin metallic wires descend from the shadows, each held in the grasp of a partially hidden multi-armed machine. Attaching themselves to what remained of the frame with hooks and magnets, they gently hoist the now slumbering giant skywards.

Climbing a set of nearby stairs to follow the sound of rumbling in the distance, I watch as large, hanger-sized doors open. A mixture of men and women wearing orange and white coveralls emerge carrying tools and handheld devices. Splitting into groups, they search the ruins of the city, recovering the wreckage of broken suits and placing them on the back of tracked vehicles.

Though their movements were quick and their searches thorough, I sensed a feeling of confusion and unfamiliarity from their actions. I could only deduce that the armoured suits, under normal conditions, would have returned to storage under their own power and with minimal assistance.

Below me, a team of twenty finish excavating the final suit, its scattered parts buried under the rubble of the collapsed building. As each limb and part is recovered, it is immediately hoisted or towed to the distant room, a warehouse that contained rank after rank of armoured suits of various designs, enough to fight the initial phases of a war.

Having recovered all they could, the various groups converge and begin their return to the open hangar doors, but a single figure lingers behind. Sensing my inquisitive gaze, he turns back and looks upwards. His eyes gawp open at my battered silhouette with a combination of respect and fear. I read the unspoken words formed on his lips, knowing that today's events would be exaggerated by half-true rumours.

As he turns and hastily leaves, the white lights which had illuminated the room are extinguished, returning the battlefield to darkness. Alone, I have little to distract me from my various thoughts, but even my martial pride could not ignore the damage to my armour and body. Even a casual glimpse was enough to know I was combat ineffective.

A single beep sounds from my left forearm, making me aware of the trickle of power that had been regenerated from my pierced power supply. With no reason to remain within the room, I walk off the edge of the roof, falling three stories before landing with a thump on the now cracked tarmacadam.

Recovering my discarded helmet, half-filled with water, I tip it out before rotating it slowly in my hands. Scanning the various shallow and deep cuts, each evidence of my brushes with death, I force open the respirator and place it on my head.

Looking at the room one final time, as my armour reboots, I walk towards the exit and the corridor beyond.

⊶⊰——⊙⋑⊘——⊱⊷

Clean and sterile, the corridor is the opposite of the post-apocalyptic environment I had just left. Noting the time and date on the digital displays scattered on the various walls, I realise the full extent of the time I was away.

Backtracking on the route I had taken two days prior, I pass offices and storage spaces, their interiors filled with men and women in white uniforms. The few that pass me give me a wide berth, their only acknowledgement being their fear-filled gazes.

This borrowed armour displayed none of my usual insignias, only my stature hinted at my Praetorian heritage. The brief period of respite and anonymity is short-lived as I arrive at the armoury doors.

Like all armouries in the Confederation, it was secured against unauthorised intrusion, for the weapons within were capable of outfitting a medium-sized army. Waving my right hand over the access panels, the transponders beneath my skin cause the display to change colour as it confirms my identity.

Stepping through the open doors, I am met by the stern, emotionless face of a man who reluctantly greets me from behind a desk. His lifeless voice is still as monotonous as the day I had signed out the armour and weapons. But the eyes of the quartermaster are not idle as his gaze follows my every movement. Though his facial features and body mannerisms have not changed, I could sense the displeasure emanating from him as he visually inspects the damage.

"One armour returned, rest destroyed."

Muttering inaudibly as he hears my report, the quartermaster hands over a tablet, requiring me to confirm the losses before directing me towards the adjacent room. Like the main chamber, the armour station was empty, all those involved in training had long left.

Stepping onto the nearest station, I wait as the platform rises and mechanical arms descend to take hold of my wrists and lock down my feet. Pulling my arms skywards, I stand like the Vitruvian Man as emerging drills meticulously unwind the locks and bolts which connect the individual panels of my armour.

Piece by piece, each is removed and transferred to a nearby rack, until I stand only in my black under armour and helmet. With my arms now released, I unlock the seals of my helmet, allowing it to expand before stepping off the platform and placing the helmet carefully on the stand.

Able to see the full extent of the damage for the first time, I run my fingertips down the length of the panels, examining each cut, gouge, and bullet hole. Only its resilience and the protection of the under armour had spared me from further injury or death. Gently tapping the cuirass, I listen, finding that despite its appearance, it was still usable.

I knew the capabilities of the Mark V armour well, designated the Light European Battlefield Armour (LEBAR), it was the latest in a series that I had assisted in the development of. Issued to all those who served on the front lines, it was a cheaper, simplified variant of the "light" armour worn by Praetorians.

Though it was referred to as light armour, to any unenhanced human, it was almost too heavy to be wearable. With panels composed of a mixture of Kevlar, steel and ceramic, it gave unmatched protection from firearms, blades, and blunt force weapons. What was issued to the Confederation armies was lighter and modular, able to be adapted for specific roles.

Satisfied with my inspection, I wave my hand on a nearby panel and watch as the rack slides back and disappears behind a series of closing doors. Turning away, I follow the illuminated arrows to the showers and changing facilities.

The sound of tearing fabric echoes across the room as the figure-hugging under armour is peeled from my skin. Slick and sticky due to the layers of clinging sweat, the pieces are not easily removed.

Placing the three sections into a self-sealing bag, I send it away to be washed, sterilised, and inspected for damage. Though I had praised the LEBAR system, it was the under armour that made it near indomitable.

Expensive and timely to manufacture, it was not yet available in large enough numbers to be a standard issue, with only specialised units being granted the privilege. Its relatively thin nature belied the protection that it granted from the elements, vacuum and ordinary threats. Possessing a double-layered weave of Kevlar and titanium, with a silicon-based composite between them, it was able to absorb and resist the penetrative forces of anything but the heaviest calibres. When worn with hardened panels, it provided protection to the areas where they could not be placed.

The showers were empty, not even a warm mist lingered to suggest that persons had been there recently. Like all military compounds, they were unisex, the battlefield allowing no opportunities for luxuries such as gender-specific rooms.

Stepping into a cubicle, I run my hands across the multiple panels until I feel the touch of warm water on my skin. Recognising my name and rank, it had applied the pre-designated settings for temperate and pressure.

Closing my eyes, I steady my breathing as I allow the warmth of the water to soak into my skin. Slowly the tightened muscles begin to loosen as my body returns to normality, purging the lingering remnants of biochemicals from my bloodstream.

My fingers forcibly press and squeeze, stretching and massaging every limb and muscle as I assist the flow of fresh blood into them. I feel every scar across my body, mementoes of the countless wars I had fought in, the majority long forgotten by others. Ignoring the discomfort as my fingers press on areas of bruised, welted, and reddened skin, I find no fresh injuries which would cause me to remember today's events.

As my hands reach my chest, painful memories flow through me as I feel the various crisscrossed scars, the wounds of the last true war. Turning off the water, I stand silent as I allow the memories of that bloody time to fade away. Stepping out, I grab hold of a towel from a nearby shelf and walk towards the lockers. It, like the showers, is empty.

Chapter Twenty Four

A faint mechanical *click* is heard from the locker door as the light from the panel changes from red to green. Reaching in slowly, my fingers meticulously disarm the stun grenade which I had placed within the interior.

Placing the now disarmed grenade onto a nearby shelf, I allow the towel that was wrapped around my body to fall onto the floor and remove the items contained within. My fingers rub against the material of the carefully folded bodysuit, the fabric soft and gentle to the touch.

In style and function, it was similar to the LEBAR's under armour, but its construction was different. Lighter, more comfortable, and breathable, it was designed to be worn daily. One of a dozen prototypes designed by myself, its unique, experimental weave made it too costly to manufacture in large numbers.

Checking the seals of the three individual pieces with meticulous care, I reach into the locker and remove the hanging black dress uniform. Tailored from a unisex, standardised design, it consisted of a shirt, tunic, trousers, and peaked cap. It was a functional uniform made from an artificial weave, reminiscent of Egyptian cotton, granting ballistic protection against small calibre ammunition.

Tying the laces of the gleaming black shoes, I stand before a mirror with my back straight, inspecting the clothes for defects. Aesthetically, all ranks wore the same uniform, but officers were entitled to embellishments that matched their status. My own tunic's interior was lined with red silk with discrete internal pockets for storing additional pistol magazines.

Though my epaulettes bore five silver threaded stars encircling a red ruby, denoting my rank of Field Marshall, it was the emblem on my arm that often brought fear and admiration. A subdued green triangular patch located at the top of my right sleeve featured a side-facing Corinthian-style Greek helmet impaled by a spear. Borne by less than a hundred across the entirety of the remaining world, a glance of it was enough to reveal my heritage.

Having finished the scrutiny of my uniform, I check and load my pistol, inserting it carefully into the holster attached to my right hip. Exiting the room, cap in hand, I am once again greeted by the unchanging face of the quartermaster as he stands straight behind his desk. Greeting me in the same monotonous voice, I acknowledge him before striding out of the armoury and into the corridor beyond.

Still too early to attend my scheduled meeting, I leisurely walk the empty corridors whilst monitoring the time. Arms outstretched, I allow my fingertips to brush the whitewashed wall, feeling the texture of the paint as I admire the simple aesthetics of the building. Possessing tall archways, the architectural style was unlike anything else within the Confederation, but one that would likely define the architecture of the modern era.

Ten thousand men and women were stationed here, but due to the size of the compound, I had yet to encounter another soul after leaving the armoury. My footsteps alone echoed along the corridors, disturbing the eerie silence.

Situated in what was historically known as Scandinavia, it was once the northern frontier of the United European Federation. But three decades of conflict and the aftermath of the First Thermonuclear War had whittled away the population until they were nothing more than a footnote.

Isolated due to its harsh Arctic climate, it was still a territory of vast mineral wealth. But only recently did the Confederation make use of the land. Not only for training their future and current recruits but also as a firing range to test their conventional and experimental weapons.

The walls suddenly change as I turn the next corner, no longer empty but lined with paintings of famous historical battles. Replicas of originals long destroyed by conflict or lurking within hidden vaults of now dead collectors, the majority depicted battlefields of the nineteenth century, an age where cavalry was still dominant.

My ears perk as I hear the distinctive sound of a young woman's laugh, a sound rarely heard. I follow the sound and watch as a trio of young women dressed in matching black uniforms carrying tablets enter a room. Rankless, their epaulettes instead had sky blue slides, denoting their status as students.

Not wishing to disturb those within, I loiter in the shadows as I peer into the room. Inside are three dozen young men and women, no older than sixteen, standing and sitting behind desks arranged in the style of a lecture theatre.

As a chime sounds, a woman enters from a door on the opposing side, her presence causing those within to stand straight until they are given the command to sit. I observe the newcomer's movements as she purposely adjusts her glasses and places a tablet on a nearby table.

Clearly, their instructor, three chevrons, and a pair of crossed rifles decorate the shoulders of her sharply pressed uniform, matching her black shoes, bulled to a high shine.

With the appearance of a woman no more than her late twenties, her expression is stern and she wears little to no make-up. Her tanned complexion hinted at her southern European heritage and her long hair, though tied into a bun, has a pair of thin wisps hanging on either side of her face. With a glance, it was clear from her physique that she was a woman in the prime of her life, likely a transferee from the units stationed at the frontiers.

Adjusting my stance, I listen carefully to the lesson, with the sergeant's pronunciation revealing her Germanic descent. A series of images appear on the display behind her, each depicting a moment of recent history, events that I have lived. Each was chosen carefully to boost patriotic ideals.

Twenty minutes have barely passed before the screen turns black, the sergeant sliding her finger across her tablet before coughing and clearing her throat.

"We will now continue your modern studies, concentrating on the events of the twenty-second century and those following the First Thermonuclear War."

Intentionally punctuating her sentences, she scans the class, taking note of those she believes are distracted.

"Before attending, you were instructed to review the pre-read. Any who have failed to do so, I advise you to complete this before the end of the day. Failure of this module will lead to your immediate expulsion

Now, why is this topic the easiest but also the most difficult to study?"

Afraid of the silence and the increasingly frustrated facial features of the sergeant in front of her. A young woman hesitantly glances at those beside her before raising her hand. Wearing thick-framed glasses which hide the majority of her features, her voice is barely above a whisper as she stutters an answer.

"Is it due to the war destroying any records and that the survivors did not make efforts to record their memories for future generations?"

"Cadet Silva. Are you asking a question or providing an answer?"

Visibly shrinking into her seat under the intensity of the sergeant's glare, she trembles before replying timidly.

"An answer, Sergeant."

"Your answer is acceptable. But always remember, clarity and discipline."

Mildly satisfied, her gaze turns from Cadet Silva to the remainder of the class.

"Now, who shall expand on her answer?"

Ignoring the series of questions and answers, I consider the enigma of Cadet's Silva's presence within the facility. Physically and emotionally timid and frail, she was unsuited for the frontlines and would be unlikely to survive the mandatory two-year period before she was transferred to an administrative role. Why had she chosen to study here?

A series of chimes announce the passing of the hour and the sergeant begins to summarise her lesson. Having listened in dismay, I shake my head at what had been taught. Due to no fault of her own, she was teaching a syllabus designed by others for their own agendas and she was too young to know the truth behind the lies.

Roughly a decade older than her charges, she had not experienced the events she was teaching, likely remembering only the conclusion of the Wars of Reclamation. But it was clear she was far from inexperienced, her eyes were dull, symptoms of a veteran who had borne witness to loss and suffering, but enough life lingered within them compared to those who had experienced the age of true horror.

The undiluted truth, when spoken by those who truly knew them, were treated as nothing more than stories to scare unruly children. No one willingly accepts the depths that mankind had fallen. Could future generations imagine a world without governance, where artificial concepts such as "state", "country" and "community" were replaced by primal, animalistic urges?

History is written by the victors and the survivors wished for nothing more than for that truth to be replaced and hidden by something more palatable.

⊷⊱————◌◦⊰◦◌————⊱⊶

Are there any questions?

The mentally fatigued students have asked few questions, hinting at their desire to return to their rooms. Those asked are simple and answered vaguely. In a sea of unmoving black bodies, the restless fidgeting of a single student draws my gaze.

Male, young, his uniform ill-fitting compared to the others due to his thin limbs and gaunt face, symptoms of recent malnutrition.

All indicated his status as a former inhabitant of lands newly reclaimed. His raised hand draws the immediate ire of the sergeant who stares in his direction. Pausing, she turns away, ignoring his question.

"How much of this is true?"

His heavily accented words are spoken loud and clear, causing a collective gasp to sound, followed by a silent lull as the sergeant's eyes bore into the youth. Undaunted, he expands upon his question with a stream of others.

"Surely, I am not alone in noticing the gaps in history? What is the purpose of the Praetors? What do they have to gain by creating this?"

"Cadet Janko! Your questions are inappropriate, take a seat!"

The sergeant barks her retort as the youth looks at his peers. Shaking his head, he ignores their spirited pleas as he continues.

"Why do we not question whether they are even human?"

"Sit down now!"

The shrill shriek of the sergeant's voice sends chills down the spine of everyone in the room as she edges forward, her hand on her belt.

"Everything they teach us is a lie, we are nothing more than sl..."

The youth's speech is interrupted by a tablet hurled in the direction of his head as the sergeant rushes forward, her fingers tightly wrapped around the baton on her belt. Extending it, she prepares to deliver a strike when I purposely knock loudly on the door.

The distinctive sound of flesh striking wood echoes across the room, breaking the tension as dozens of eyes turn towards the source of the sound.

"COURSE!"

Spotting the epaulettes and braiding, a sharp-eyed cadet announces my presence. Like a well-honed machine, the class stands to attention. Unable to move, their eyes follow my movements with trepidation as I walk into the room.

All had heard the treasonous outburst and knew the punishment. A few forget to breathe, growing pale and only remembering when they are on the verge of collapse, whilst other sweat profusely as they stare fearfully at my towering frame.

Stopping before the now still sergeant, my eyes glance downward at the baton still in her hand. Paralysed by fear, her quivering lips whisper a single word repeatedly.

"Why?"

Unable to escape from the endless cycle, I assist her with a stamp of my right foot. Upon hearing the sound reverberate across the room, she instinctively clicks her heels together and salutes. Acknowledging her eventual response with a single nod, I watch as her gaze is drawn to the ribbons on my chest and green patch on my arm.

"Praetor"

Finally remembering the baton still in her hand as she stutters the word, she carefully returns it to her belt before timidly greeting me.

"Good Afternoon….Sir...how can I help you?"

"I hope I am not interrupting your class?"

"No Sir, the class was about to end. Can I assist you?"

Her frequent glances at the pistol at my hip cause her heart rate to spike, betraying her inner thoughts.

Did he hear those words? Are we to be executed?

"No, on the contrary, I am here to answer that cadet's question".

Cutting to the heart of the matter, I point in the direction of Cadet Janko. My words and actions cause the sergeant's already fast-beating heart to skyrocket as she sways side to side.

"Sergeant, you appear unwell, take a seat in the corner."

Directing her to the only chair in the corner of the room whilst claiming her space on the podium, I gesture for every student except Janko to take a seat. Appraising the cadet causes a smile to form on my face as I find his heart rate, though fast, was calmer than those around him. Not yet indoctrinated, his still sharp mind was unbound from dogma. He would be of use to me if he survived till graduation.

"Choose your questions wisely, Cadet."

Swallowing the saliva that had flooded his mouth, he speaks, his mental fortitude allowing him to accomplish the task without a stutter, something his peers had not yet achieved.

"This history, how much of it is true?"

"All of it, none of it. Only time will tell."

The unexpected answer causes a series of silent gasps to escape the lips of the assembled students.

"Winston Churchill, a political figure you should be familiar of, once stated, 'History is written by the victors.'"

Purposely pausing to glance at the faces of those around the room before continuing, I find the entirety of the class enraptured.

"But in the last war, there were no victors, only those left behind. Everything being taught now is the truth that has been recovered. With time, what was once known as "fact", may become falsehood. That is the uncertainty of history."

Though the majority accept my words, the clenching and unclenching of Cadet Janko's hands beneath the table, reveals his dissatisfaction.

"Are you even human?"

A dry laugh escapes my lips as I consider the question. With a perfect smile, I point at a pair of female cadets sitting at the rear of the room.

"I will answer that question if any of you can answer one of mine.

Do you know who I am?"

Shaking their heads, the pair answer with a whimper before I repeat the question to others in the room.

"Disappointing, but you will come to know me well. I am Field Marshall Archean, Commander of all forces within the Britannic Confederation and Governor of the Fourth District. I answer to no one but the Lord Marshall."

My revelation sends ripples of fear through the seated students and they begin to fidget, cracking their thin veneer of discipline.

"As you can see, I am nothing more than a soldier, not a god nor an angel. Do you truly believe I stride into battle whilst unleashing lightning from my fingers?"

My apparent jest causes a few to twitch nervously in their seats.

"Cadet Janko, you question our intention, but do you know the purpose of a soldier?"

"Fighting those who threaten the nation."

An almost predatory smile returns to my lips as I hear his immediate response.

"But is it truly that simple? What if a soldier has nothing to protect?"

As expected, the engrossed cadets lean closer, eager to hear the answer. Having captured their attention, I steer them towards the path of least resistance, their only route to survival.

"Know that my answer is not hypothetical, history has already shown us the answer."

A momentary pause allows my sombre words to resonate within their minds.

"In society, Governments guide the people, making decisions and choices both necessary and unpopular. The soldier's role is to protect those their Government represents.

But what is a soldier without a country, a home, or a purpose?

Sadly, everything you have heard of the world of the past is true, many did choose to become something barbaric. For us Praetors, even without a "master", we believed in our duty. We made a choice, not because we desired prestige or power, but because there was no other choice.

That choice, though imperfect has given us a decade of peace and stability. But more importantly, a chance for you, the next generation to dream of a better future. When you are ready to bear our mantle of responsibility, we like all that was old will fade away."

As I continue, the students are overtaken by patriotic ideals that cause them to weep, cheer and meet the end of my oration with a round of applause. Even the eyes of Cadet Janko soften, as the earlier hostility towards me and my kind disappears. But I knew that this was nothing more than a brief respite, his inquisitive mind would soon question the various half-truths. Until the day he graduates, he would be observed and monitored. Despite the dangers, I could only see his limitless potential.

A heavy knock shifts the student's gaze as they turn towards the figure standing at the door. Dressed in black, with the image of an eagle fighting a two-headed serpent emblazoned on both arms, rifle in hand.

"Excuse me, Field Marshall. The station commander has asked me to find you."

With his arrogant tone gruff with hints of violence, a warrant officer of the station's security detail was used to having his instructions followed without delay. Ignoring his presence, I turn and speak to the sergeant who has remained rigid within her chair.

"I believe my visit has answered the question, would you not agree?"

Irritated, the warrant officer stomps into the room and directs his ire towards the sergeant.

"Sergeant Adamson, the station commander has been made to wait. Dismiss your class and allow the Field Marshall to be on his way."

Turning my disapproving gaze towards the man, the smirk on his lips disappears as he senses my displeasure. Glancing at the sergeant and seeing her hesitation and fear, I knew instantly the personality of the man before me and how the hierarchy was maintained.

"And he shall wait, warrant officer. The students are the priority here, surely they would benefit from my experience."

"Err...yes...please take your time, Sir."

"Sergeant?"

With the spell surrounding her finally lifted, she stands and faces the class.

"Any further questions?"

Acknowledging their silence, she turns and salutes.

"Sergeant, I believe today's "matter" has been resolved. Dismiss your class after I have left."

Ignoring the sergeant's sigh of relief, I face the warrant officer and gesture towards the door. Acting as my guide as he walks beside me, I contemplate the true answer to the question as my heavy footsteps echo down the corridor.

With recent events, were any aspects of our original plan still true?

Chapter Twenty Five

Command Centre, Starlight City, District 4

52.03, 11.56

1730 hours, 24-08-2177 C.E.

Counting down to the tenth "Day of Foundation", we at BCBQ News will now end our coverage with a special report.

A series of images appear on the terminal as the propaganda machine that was the Office of Executives reinforced the notion that the Britannic Confederation was the height of civilisation.

Though the world had changed for the better in the last decade, having lived in the world that was, I knew this was far from true.

The wars of that age are forgotten and meaningless to the youth of today. For many in government, they were events that should not be remembered. The Second Great War, the Third World War, the First Thermonuclear War, it had many names, but each described the same thing, the fall of civilisation and devastation of the world.

Though more than a fortnight had passed, the questions posed by Cadet Janko continue to plague my thoughts. His progress reports confirmed what I already knew, it would not take long before he stumbled upon the truth. The Confederation was nothing more than a by-product of our original aim.

The "Day of Emergence", celebrating the appearance of Praetors and United European Federation soldiers from time-locked bunkers, was the result of a flaw. An unforeseen fault in their construction forced their opening decades ahead of schedule.

Our military campaign was never a crusade to spread enlightenment, but rather a means to gather resources scarce on the Britannic islands. But as our forces ventured further, we found the world more devastated than expected.

Areas of habitation were few, and resource-rich lands were too contaminated to be safely utilised. Unable to venture further, we sacrificed what little resources we had remaining, to cleanse the land, making them habitable so that the materials could be mined and refined.

As our makeshift settlements grew, so did the number of survivors who flocked to them. In exchange for our protection, food, medicine, and water, they gave us their bodies, to work, to farm, and mine.

Months and years would pass, and more land was decontaminated and reclaimed. Our cities grew, increasing our workforce, but it was still not enough and our original purpose was delayed as we realised that decades would be needed.

Needing permanent structures, we tore down the old cities, building new, better, dedicated cities in their place, until all traces of the "Old World" were removed from the foundations up. No one argued for the preservation of the old cities as no one remembered them, for the past was nothing more than a time of legend.

And with all legends, the truth would remain buried and hopefully forgotten.

⊷⊶────◌⟍♨⟋◌────⊷⊶

Swivelling in my chair, I turn and gaze at the sky as the sun prepared to set on my capital, Starlight City. Two million citizens lived within its wall, though a far cry of the populations of the "Old

World", it was a significant number considering the world's remaining population.

Dedicated to scientific research and manufacturing, its skyline was dominated by two towering buildings, both of equal importance. The first, standing at its centre was the "Crown of the Confederation", Facility 04, known locally as the "Sky Elevator".

Once a project of the United European Federation to transport material and personnel to orbit without spaceports and rockets, it was found damaged and incomplete, halfway through the "Reclamation". One of five designed, the others around the world never went further than the laying of their extensive foundations.

Though its generators were destroyed by the electromagnetic pulses caused by the fall of nuclear warheads, its structure remained intact. Though we dedicated all our resources and remaining scientific minds to its completion, it took another two decades to become operational. Now with easy access to zero gravitational environments, technology long thought lost, as well as new, were created and re-discovered.

Owing to its importance, a permanent garrison of men and women of the National Defence Force (NDF) were stationed within, supported by squads of Military Police and Commandos seconded from units on the front line.

Smaller in scale, though no less daunting was the District Headquarters, located to the south of the City. Within its black stone and glass walls, hundreds of citizens worked, performing roles necessary for the running of the empire.

Housing the Governor's office and the highest courts, it would normally stand at the centre of the Capital, to remind all of the power of the Confederation and the rule of law, but here, that "honour" was surrendered to another.

Learning from the faults of the "Old World", the laws and legal systems of the Confederation were simple. If libelled charges were proven, the punishment, depending on the severity of the crime, would either be death or forced labour.

Even after a decade of peace, the Confederation could not waste resources by allowing a person to languish in prison. Every citizen, even prisoners had a role to perform. For minor crimes, they would be transported far beyond the safety of the borders of the empire, to mine until they gathered what they owed to society. Once the debt was paid, they would be returned to their district, reintegrated into society, and their crimes forgotten.

For more severe crimes, the punishment was death. Chained and dragged to the lowest levels of the tower, they would be confined and executed the following morning. Their remains would be used in scientific research or broken down and used as fertiliser. The bodies of the condemned were not a resource to be wasted.

There were no appeals to sentences and the longest that a person had remained confined was twelve days before trial, an abnormality caused by the complexity of the investigation, the average being seventy-two hours.

Currently, a hundred Insurrectionists linger at the lowest levels, awaiting their imminent trial. Despite the escalation of attacks, none had been foolish enough to attempt a rescue.

❖———◉\ঌ/◎———❖

A fortnight had passed since my attempts to have a private meeting with the Lord Marshall were rejected. The confirmation of

307

my fears were the various reports, graphs, and testimonials that were strewn over my desk.

In the streets below, the citizens of my district were continuing their daily lives, the infrequent attacks were nothing more than an inconvenience. But in the west where the Insurrectionists were deeply rooted, the attacks had become daily occurrences and the effects had been devastating.

Reinforcements from outlying cities and those stationed at the southern and eastern borders had managed to restore order, but beneath the surface, there remained a deadly undercurrent.

Weary, I stretch my limbs, the proof of my efforts as I crossed the width and breadth of the empire to see what had been "forgotten" from the daily reports. The bravery of the men and women of the Army and Defence Force had given us time, but my instincts warned me of the long-term dangers as resources were syphoned away. The bureaucrats within the Executive did not understand that the resources of the Confederation, though vast, were still finite and would eventually run empty.

Only my district had managed to retain its strength, my rank allowing me to refuse the endless requests. But the whispers of political unrest from the central capital had reached me, soon the Lord Marshall himself would intervene to force my hand.

The rhythmic clicking of military dress shoes draws my gaze to the sliding door as a familiar face enters. Coming to a stop five paces from my office desk, she stands to attention as she awaits my acknowledgement.

As always her uniform is finely pressed and pristine. With her long hair tied neatly into a bun and her deep green eyes hidden behind thin-framed spectacles, a person's attention would instead be drawn to the ruby epaulettes that glint warmly in the light of the setting sun.

"Colonel Brendt."

Having acknowledged her presence, she relaxes slightly and places another pile of documents and tablets on my desk. Observing her still rigid form, a small sigh escapes my lips as I indicate once more for her to relax. In the privacy of my office, I did not desire the normally rigid adherence to regulations surrounding superiors and their subordinates.

Catching the glint of blue as Amelia moves her arms, my eyes flicker to the date on the wall. A true smile forms as I notice the subtle change in her uniform and aura. For others, the difference would be too minute and unnoticeable, but for me, the difference was as apparent as night and day. Silver cufflinks, partially hidden by the sleeves of her tunic, the simple design belied the expense of the inlaid Royal Blue Sapphires.

Walking past her, I head towards a cabinet on the right side of the room. Undoing the locks of the main compartment, I reveal row after row of glasses and bottles of various shades and shapes. Every bottle contained a different alcoholic beverage, some having been distilled during the age of the Old World and were irreplaceable.

Hovering over the tops of the various bottles, I search for something specific. Having found what I was looking for, my fingers wrap around the neck of the bottle as I remove a pair of crystal tumblers.

Having understood my intent, Amelia gives me the slightest nod as she carries the latest pile of papers and tablets and places them on a table located on the opposite side of the room.

Choosing a chair close to the window, she sits upright, her legs placed together as she rests her hands on her thighs. Her movements are silent as she waits for me to join her at the table.

Basked in the golden rays of the setting sun, her skin is youthful and ethereal in appearance. An avatar of unrefined beauty, her appearance is perfect, with no obvious blemishes despite the many life-threatening experiences she has faced.

Carrying the bottle and glasses to the table, my eyes never leave her face as I swiftly remove the cork, allowing the scent of aged oak to enter the air, an aroma only smelt once a year, on this very day.

With steady hands, the contents are poured into each glass, the first being given to Amelia as she places the glass gently on her lap, ensuring not a drop of the amber liquid is spilt or sipped until I had taken my seat. A flicker of a smile forms on her lips as she gazes almost lovingly at the object nestled between her hands. Every movement is performed with nostalgia, for each had been repeated year after year, decade after decade until only a single bottle remained of our mentors' gift. After a century, few remained who knew the origins of the Praetorians.

More than a century ago, when humanity truly expanded beyond the frontiers of their terrestrial home, they discovered the hidden secrets of the universe. Gripped by the fear of extinction, the greatest scientific minds of humanity were made to realise a dream, the creation of humanity's next stage of evolution. Despite knowing their achievements would be used in war, the scientists funded by the United European Federation initiated the "Praetorian Project".

At first, the dream appeared to be beyond their grasp, despite their countless attempts, the results were too unstable to be deemed a success. No natural human source could meet their strict demands as they sought to create their perfect being, an individual who would be the match of a hundred others. Whether by chance, or fate, when the Project was on the brink of termination, an accident occurred.

No one knows what started the fire, but when the destroyed laboratories were searched for survivors, they found only two in the deepest recesses. One boy, and one girl, unharmed where others had perished, possessing no memories, only the rags on their bodies hinted at who or what they were. Children of unknown lineage, they were the Project's only successes. The progenitors of all those who followed were given the names of Primus and Altera.

The remaining scientists were ecstatic as test after test revealed the unlimited potential of the children. After a decade of countless failures, they had two living successes, but how they had achieved this were lost to the fires. Desperate to replicate the results, they treated the children as something less than human as sample after sample was taken.

Despite having two living templates, the years would pass without success, as if the children's creation were a fluke that could not be repeated. Three hundred candidates, their genetics marking them as the best of humanity, were lost during the decade-long trials. But from the tragedy came a single success, a young woman known as Tria. Lithe, agile, and possessing physical strength comparable to those before her, there were however limits to her mental abilities.

Three successes after two decades, it was only their proven achievements that prevented the dissolution of the Project once again. Faster, stronger, and with minds sharper than the greatest strategists, they achieved the impossible, turning the tide in battles that were deemed lost.

The military seeing the potential, no longer cared for the scientific community's original aim in developing the next stage of evolution, humans possessing both body and mind beyond the current status quo, they wanted soldiers.

Using Tria as a template, they redesigned, simplified, and adjusted the procedures. Caring nothing for mental attributes, they enhanced only the physical. This, the Project's third attempt was a success, creating an army of Praetorians, but they were only a shadow of the first and second generations.

But this army of "super-soldiers" was found to be unleadable, for unaugmented humans could not understand the scope of their abilities, which were beyond the rational and reasonable. Only those like them could lead them and the "firstborn", Primus, Altera and Tria would become the first commanders. Though ten companies were planned for the regiment, the outbreak of war would divert the needed funding and resources, the first company would become the first and only.

⋘───◈───⋙

The memories fade as I continue to admire Amelia's cufflinks, their simple design emphasising her unadorned beauty. Smiling as our glasses are raised, I remember the moment she had received them. Always the perfect soldier, she had surprised our mentors when she was asked to choose between them and a gold pendant with diamond inlays. When asked to explain her choice, she had simply responded that she could wear them with her uniform.

"For the living."

Speaking the words together as our glasses come into contact with a crystal chime, we complete the ritual which had remained unchanged and unbroken despite the decades.

"And to the next year."

"The thought of another year by your side is rather depressing. Is this something I should be celebrating?"

Amelia's comment is said with a hint of a smile as I consider the meaning of time. Time as a concept had become almost meaningless to our near ageless bodies, but with its passage, even our once frozen minds were slowly changing.

For many of her subordinates, Amelia was cold and expressionless, but as I watch her softening features, I believe that with each passing year, aspects of her humanity were being slowly drawn to the surface. I hoped that in time she would become the person she would have been if not for the intervention of the Project.

Leaning back in my chair, I relax as Amelia and I discuss our shared history, remembering those who no longer live, as well as the events and missions that only we can remember.

Chapter Twenty Six

A soft melody carries across the room as an antique clock announces the end of another day. Empty glasses and bottles sit on the table, their irreplaceable contents gone and never to be tasted again. With the anniversary now passed, I wordlessly beckon for Amelia to explain the reason for her original attendance.

Noting the change in atmosphere, she stands and straightens her uniform with a downward tug, before picking up the handful of documents from the table. Though both of us had consumed multiple bottles, neither of us were suffering from ill effects, the alcohol having long been metabolised from our blood.

Methodically, she informs me of the various requests that she had already disposed of, before drawing my attention to those remaining. Barely a dozen, the scant number a testament to her efficiency, one at a time, she places the documents in front of me.

"Commander, there is also one further matter."

Shifting my gaze from the documents to her moving fingers, I watch as she types rapidly into the display of her tablet before lifting it to her eye. The movement was enough to reveal the seriousness of the subject. Multi-layered encryptions were only used by Praetorian commanders to share information that was of national importance.

Accepting the unsealed document, I begin to flick through the contents, my eyes scanning over the passage of text and images. In a matter of minutes, dozens of pages are processed, but as I prepare to swipe to the next page, an image causes me to stop.

Nothing more than a photograph of an ill-lit damp room, one likely beyond the confines of the empire, but it was not the room, but what it contained which drew my attention. Using my fingers, I expand a small section of the image to reveal something which should not exist.

A highly detailed cross-sectional drawing of a triangular object, a component of something much larger and complicated. It was not something that anyone should know of, let alone have blueprints.

Turning the page, I scan the recovered blueprints, examining every line, number, and word. They were far from perfect as if the blueprints had been hastily drawn from memory.

"Colonel, take a seat."

Standing, I move towards my desk and place my hand on the biometric scanner. Blue light illuminates the room before a single *beep* is followed by the locking of my office doors and the descent of metal panels as the windows and doors are fortified and secured.

With the threat of unwanted "guests" removed, I input a code and the walls behind me retract and reveal a heavily armoured door. Rolling up my sleeves and placing my now exposed arms on the access panels, I wait for the sensation of needles entering my skin and the drawing of blood. With a *click*, the door swings open, causing a rush of cold air to escape the room.

Shelf after shelf of folders lines the side of the temperature-controlled room, ensuring the preservation of the Confederation's and its predecessor's greatest secrets. Beside them are weapons and armour systems of a bygone age, items from my personal collection.

319

Entering the room, my eyes scan the various shelves, seeking the location of a specific file. Soon they are drawn to the thickest, the word "ORION" emblazoned in bright red script. Grasping it carefully with both hands, I carry it out and place it on the table beside Amelia.

One by one, the blueprints contained within are scattered across the surface, lined in order of creation. Initial drafts, amendments, and finally the current version, each is compared to those that had been recovered.

Only one copy of each iteration should exist, located here in this file, for the others were destroyed with each amendment, to ensure that no one could replicate the process without my knowledge.

Amelia stands over my shoulder, casting her experienced, analytical eyes over the documents as she assists my appraisement. Despite our efforts, none of the originals matches what has been recovered. The inaccuracies only confirmed my suspicion that they had been drawn from memory over a long period of time. The closest being those from a period, two years prior.

Scanning the access logs for the three closest iterations, only four names appeared repeatedly, Amelia's, the Lord Marshall, his adjutant, and mine.

"Where were these recovered?"

"Kursk."

A place of personal significance, it was now nothing more than a desolate ruin, having once been a great city on the western frontier of the Novoyan Russian Federation. Its armaments production facilities and military barracks made it a priority location for precision strikes during the opening phases of the War.

Taking a seat in my chair, I cross my legs as I wait for Amelia to elaborate on her answer.

"Seven days ago, the First Expeditionary Wing performed a sweep fifty kilometres east of District Five. During this, they observed significant vehicle movement near the ruins of Kursk and its abandoned military compounds.

Commander Hecate and three full squads performed a preemptive strike, discovering a previously unknown facility buried beneath the ruins. A sweep of the interior was performed once all hostile forces were eliminated. Within were stockpiles of weapons belonging to the Novoyan Federation, confirming its identity as a former weapons research station.

It was Commander Hecate and her personal squad who recovered the blueprints."

"The size of the enemy force?"

"The number of enemy dead were logged at five thousand and thirty-two."

The disclosures cause my troubled brows to arch upwards. Since the end of the War, no person had managed to rally the various factions under a single banner in significant numbers. The various "reavers" and "warlords" care only for their own personal gain than standing united. If this was the start of a new trend, our border armies would be placed under increased pressure, endangering the expansion efforts in the future.

But this was insignificant compared to knowing that highly confidential information had managed to fall into the hands of external forces, far beyond our borders. Our complacency in treating those from outwith as "savages", had allowed them to infiltrate our ranks.

"How many are aware?"

"At this time, eight. Commander Hecate has already debriefed her squad."

Illya Hecate was someone I knew well and trusted, second only to Amelia. She knew the importance of minimising the spread of this information.

"Send my appreciation to Illya. We shall not inform the Offices of this incident, not yet."

With information control secured on the eastern border, it was left to me to manage it here. Removing an unused and sealed tablet from a drawer from my desk, I remove the protective casing and activate the device.

Placing the tablet beside Amelia's, I connect both with wires. Perceived as redundant and crude, there was no more efficient method in terms of speed and security to ensure the transfer of data.

One by one, the files appear on my tablet, just as they are deleted from Amelia's. With the process complete, I remove the connections and confirm that no fragments remained on hers that could be pieced together. Satisfied, I return Amelia's as I place the other securely in my desk.

Standing tall, I prepare the words that needed to be said, words that if said to another could be regarded as high treason.

Blueprints pertaining to Project Orion have been discovered beyond our borders. At this time, there are only two possible sources…"

"You suspect the Lord Marshall is directly or indirectly involved."

Having arrived at the same conclusion, she speaks the statement plainly.

"That is the current theory based on available information. But it is unknown why he would endanger the project and the Confederation."

Though the source could be the Lord Marshall's adjutant, both of us know that little happened in his own Office without his knowledge. The shrewdest and most politically gifted of the Praetors, he knew how to use the system to his advantage.

The blueprints contained errors, errors matching the suggestions of the Lord Marshall, rejected due to the increased risks with little benefit. Even the enhanced mind of Praetors could not remove personal bias from memory recollection. But this evidence was circumstantial, it was not enough to remove him from his position.

"How will you proceed?"

The smallest spasm in Amelia's cheek is enough to reveal her inner thoughts that this situation, theoretically, should never have occurred.

"I require proof before I can confront him with charges."

Making my way to the storage room, I remove a black, steel container from the deepest shelf. Sealed by simple welds, I place it on my shelf before forcing it open.

Within is a carefully folded navy blue uniform, a memento of an age long past. Lifting it ceremoniously from the box, I tenderly place it on the desk. Amelia's eyes sparkle as she gazes almost reminiscently at the clothing. Beneath, at the bottom is a small titanium box, no bigger than the palm of my hand. Pressing my right thumb down on the lock, I wait to hear the triple *click*.

325

With the locks disengaged, I open the container and remove a golden amulet. Gazing nostalgically, I allow my fingers to follow the various contours, tracing the engraved symbol with a glowing gem embedded at its centre. For many, this was nothing more than a piece of extravagant jewellery, but for Praetors, it had a special meaning. The Greek symbol of lambda engraved on its surface, if shown to the right people, could grant near immeasurable political power.

"Colonel."

A single word whilst holding the amulet is enough to change the atmosphere of the room. Amelia stands to attention, adopting the position as if it was as natural to her as breathing. What was about to be said had to be ordered, not asked.

"Alpha priority mission.

Objective, ensure that information contained within facilities, past and present relating to Genesis and Orion are secure.

Rules of engagement, black."

"Orders received."

There is no hesitation in her voice as she monotonously acknowledges the order.

"Deployable resources?"

"Squad Gorgo will be yours to command."

Whilst giving her the final piece of information, I reach across and take hold of her right hand, wrapping it in mine. Placing the amulet within her palm, I wait for her fingers to take a firm grasp before I take a step back.

"Commander, Squad Gorgo is…"

"Your mission is of the highest priority. You cannot fail."

Aware of what she was planning on saying, I interrupt her before she can finish. Her mission would determine the future of the Confederation and no person, not even a Praetor could be allowed to bar her path. With the amulet, her authority would be absolute, but it was a tool of last resort. She could not do this mission alone and I could ask and entrust no other than my own bodyguards to join her.

"I will not require their protection whilst you are away."

Hearing my words, Amelia's lips twitch. Though small, it is not easy to miss.

"I will contact Illya and ensure her fourth squad is available if required."

Accepting the small consolation with a nod, she responds to my command.

"Mission accepted, First Commander."

Clicking her heels together, she turns and uplifts her tablet, placing it carefully into her inner tunic pockets before making her way to the door. Disabling the panels, I wait for her to leave when she stops and turns. Though her lips move, the words spoken are unheard. Understanding her simple sentiment, I give her the only possible reply.

"I will await your return, Amelia."

⊷⧉——◉\♨/◉——♨⊶

Now alone, I lean back in my chair as I re-read the contents of the tablet in greater detail. With each page, my concerns only grow, as I consider the implications.

How far had the rot spread?

Were the decisions, my decisions, of the past to blame?

For the first time in a decade, I truly felt alone.

Interlude I: Pursuit

Chapter 27

"Keep riding, no matter what, don't stop, don't look back!"

The Captain roars his warning as we spur our horses through the rough terrain, evading the low hanging branches of the forest path. Arrows are launched behind as we seek to deter those hounding us, but the darkness created by the canopy makes it hard to aim.

Four whole days would pass before we had noticed the dark shadows trailing us in the distance. Foolishly, I had hoped that the chaos would buy us more time to travel north and that our trail would become unfollowable. The appearance of the Usurper's hounds however had brought me back to the harsh reality.

All of us were survivors of the fortress, we knew the identities of these black armoured knights, we knew first-hand what they were capable of and none of us wished to fight them unless we had to. Though only three had appeared so far, we knew that more would follow. In the confines of the forest, our numbers meant little, we had to flee.

Weighed down by armour, our horses were growing breathless after two days of harsh, continuous riding. It would not take long for them to falter and collapse, we would have to make the decision soon on where we would stand and fight.

"Clearing ahead!"

The shouts from the scouts reveal an opening in the canopy as they turn and loose another series of arrows from their bows. Riding past them, we enter the clearing, one filled with purple flowers blooming in the tall grass. If not for the approaching enemy, this place would have been calm and serene.

"Halt!"

Quickly determining the conditioning of those around him, the Captain makes the decision and bellows a series of commands.

"Draw your weapons and form a circle. Protect the Princesses. This is where we fight."

The scrape of metal is heard as swords are drawn from their scabbards. Red cloaked hoplites position themselves in between members of the Royal Guard, their bows already drawn. Huddled behind them in the centre, are Helena, my sister, and I.

The wait feels like an eternity before the passing wind brings the stench of dried blood and death. Emerging from the treeline are three riders, their armour the colour of midnight black. As they silently trot forward, I hear the whispers from the hoplites as they prepared for death.

Drawing their twin short swords, they hold them in each hand as they steer their horses with only their knees. The black blades were so steeped in darkness that not even the sunlight could escape their grasp. Turning their heads to look upon us, not even their helmets could hide the deathly piercing gazes as they settled upon my sister and me.

No side offered words of parley before the battle, we knew they were here to kill, nothing more, and upon our deaths, they would desecrate our bodies and use them however they so wished.

The enemy's location now known, the Captain reforms the circle into a straight line and waits.

"You two, stay behind."

With a simple command, two members of the Royal Guard break away, their duty to protect us for as long as possible. If the nine in front of them should fall, they alone would decide whether we should flee or stand and fight, whichever option gave us the greatest chance of survival.

Sorrowfully, I look upon the men and women who were willing to risk their lives for us. As my eyes seep with tears, my heart burns with rage at my uselessness. Scrunching my eyes, I hold myself back from reaching out with magic. The land here was cursed and there were no blowing winds from the aether, what remained within my body was barely enough to keep me upright.

Why? Why do I not have the strength to protect those dear to me? Why did the Gods bless me with such gifts if my body was unable to wield them?

As I have such depreciating thoughts, my father's reassuring smile surfaces, I knew the words he would speak if he heard what was within my heart. Knowing what is expected, I open my eyes and stare at the advancing enemy, my hand resting on the pommel of my dagger.

"Encircle them."

With a simple flourish, the Captain orders the advance of the hoplites, who unleash arrow after arrow as they ride to the flanks. Dark blades sweep through the air, spinning so inhumanely fast that they could barely be seen. One by one the arrows are cut down, the split shafts clattering to the ground.

With wide-open eyes I watch the display of swordsmanship, feeling both fear and wonderment at the breathtakingly beautiful, but deadly sweeps.

"For the true King of Artlars!"

Locking down his helmet, the Captain unleashes a battle cry as he gallops forward. The cry is repeated from those beside him as they level their swords and lances and join the charge.

Responding only with a sinister laugh, the Gatekeepers counter the charge with their own. Steering with their knees, their blades sweep left and right as they aim for the centre of the silver armoured knights. Soon the battlefield is filled with the clash and clang of metal as sword meets shield and armour.

As the fighting grows more desperate, the long heavy blades of the Royal Guard become a hindrance as the Gatekeepers enter their guard. Narrowly deflecting the incoming strikes with their small crescent shields, the Royal Guardsmen awkwardly pull on the reins and try to turn.

Though known for their skill with sword, shield, and spear, each Guardsman was also a proficient horseman, but against these knights, they appeared amateurish. Like a flowing river, the Gatekeepers turn and ride through the gaps, whilst unleashing the fury of their twin blades.

Encircling the melee, the northerners continue to unleash their bows, each successful draw a result of instincts honed by decades of warfare and generations of passed down knowledge.

So used to fighting the great beasts within the confines of the forests, they know when and where to strike, making most of every opportunity and exposed vulnerability. Though every arrow flies accurately, the skill and agility of their foe are too great. When striking thick armour or cut down with a sweep of their blade, none find their intended mark on human flesh.

Amateurs

The humiliating remarks cause cries of fury to escape the lips of the northern men and women. Each a veteran of countless wars and hunts, they could not stand for their skills to be deemed inadequate.

Limbs trembling with rage, they shoulder their bows and draw forth their spears. With a savage cry, they level and use them as short lances as they ride forward. With thunderous hooves, they worry not about death, only wishing to impale their foes at the end of their spears.

Distracted by the presence of the Royal Guard, not all of the strikes are evaded and a single Gatekeeper is impaled on a pair of spears. No cry or moan escapes his lips as he lashes out, his swords slashing the throats of the two hoplites before succumbing to his wounds.

Having watched their comrade fall, the ferocity and bloodlust of the remaining two black armoured knights intensify. Their dancing blades spin faster, becoming invisible as they strike out, causing two more hoplites to fall from their saddles as they grasp at their torn throats. Bathed in warm blood, the knights laugh haughtily as they continue to swing.

Unused to fighting other humans from outwith of a tight formation, the hoplites' skills as warriors were lacking and their light, leather armour made them too vulnerable. Realising that their foes were beyond their skill now that their spears were shattered, they turn and ride away.

No, no my little pets. It is still too early to end our little game.

Manic laughter escapes the confines of the helmet of the nearest knight, their sultry feminine tone distorted by the underlying cruelty.

"No, your fight is with us.

With a swing of their swords, a pair of Royal Guardsman bar the pursuing Gatekeeper's path. Breathing heavily, both sides realise the end of the battle is near and pour the entirety of their being into their swings.

Near them, a single dark knight toys with his opponents. Disarming one with a flourish, he turns and cuts through the triceps of another. Effortlessly stealing the sword from their opponent's now lifeless fingers, he stabs them in the chest and turns away with a passing remark.

Pitiful

Bleeding and humiliated, the dying man draws a small dagger, something normally gifted to a child. Lunging forward, they plunge the blade into the neck of their killer, who turns in surprise and wraps his gauntlets around the man's neck and squeeze. With an audible crack, both then fall to the ground, dead.

Now alone and surrounded, the remaining knight backs away, their sword sweeping out in careful circles. Glancing left and right, they look for a path of escape, but their encirclement is complete and they are trapped. Slumping their shoulders, they allow their swords to fall to the ground before raising their hands in the air.

"I wish to treat."

Hearing the unexpected words, the four nearest riders stop, their weapons aimed warily at the knight. Turning, they look to the Captain who simply nods. Satisfied by the response, the knight lowers her hands and removes her helmet, revealing her pale skin and long hair of argent shade.

Beautiful, perhaps due to her near white skin, her features were more in keeping with those of the Royal Court than a knight, let alone an assassin. But any illusion of gentility is shattered by her cold, leering sapphire eyes and sadistic smile.

"Oh Lykon, Captain of the Guard and feared Silver Lion, will you allow one such as I to speak my terms freely and without fear, or will I be cut down whilst unarmed?"

Despite her sarcastic and challenging tone, the Captain maintains his distance and sheathes his sword, showing caution for any signs of deception.

"Tell me, traitor, why would I wish to besmirch my honour by treating with one such as you?"

A sinister laugh escapes the woman's lips as she stares unafraid at those around her.

"Oh, do you truly believe this battle is over?"

"Do you believe you can win?"

Sniggering, the woman stares straight at the Captain, her plastered smile both seductively alluring and frightening in equal measure.

"Are you ready to pay the price? I swear by my God, that I shall reap two more souls before I fall. I am prepared to die, but can you, the mighty lion spare such losses?"

Glancing at the dead who litter the battlefield and those beside him, bloodied and tired, he knows that he cannot spare anymore and simply nods his head.

"You speak truthfully, I have lost many, but I will not allow you to continue to hound those I guard. What do you offer, if you wish for me to spare your life?"

"How about my word as a noble and a knight that I will not pursue?"

Peering down at the woman with a look of disgust, the Captain spits at her feet.

"That is what I think of your word. I will accept none from oath-breakers. Your word is nothing more than lies."

Growling in displeasure, the Captain reaches for the grip of his sword. His anger is growing as the woman laughs in response.

"Here I thought you were a fool. You have indeed learnt the value of honour in this age."

"My patience grows thin, Gatekeeper. Speak your terms, or we end this."

"Have I angered you?"

"It is growing thinner, speak quickly."

With his sword drawn, the Captain aims the tip at the woman's throat.

"Though my master is greedy and his thirst for souls is endless, I have much to do before I greet him at his throne. I bargain my weapons and my horse for safe passage away from this battlefield."

"And tell me, what shall you do once we leave your company? What would stop you from revealing our location to those who follow behind you?"

"These terms do not stop you being my prey, but it is twelve days on foot to Sfyri. Think of what you can achieve in that time?"

Confident that we would accept, her smile grows wider as she tilts her head almost coquettishly to the side. I sense the turmoil within the Captain's soul, but the benefits outweigh the negatives.

"For your weapons and your horse, I accept your terms."

"Age does indeed bring wisdom. May you grow old and die comfy in your bed."

Mockingly, she begins to disarm, removing the small daggers hidden, discretely around her body. One by one, she throws them to the ground, tip first. Her skill with throwing weapons was evident, it was no lie that she would have killed two more before her death.

Allowing her hands to be bound by rope, she giggles as a Guardswoman confirms no other weapons were secreted on her person. Disarmed and horseless, she is allowed to leave, but as she stalks silently towards the treeline, she turns and looks lovingly back at her horse.

"Her name is Skia, use her well in your travels for she is both obedient and swift. If you do not trust her due to her former master, set her free at the next town."

Her eyes show the first and only hints of warmth before she directs a cold glare towards me. Boring into my soul, the stare causes my body to shiver.

"It is refreshing to see your face, Princess Selesia. Long has it been since I saw you last at your father's Court. You have grown into a beauty, but know this, though you and your sister have escaped tonight, others are coming. Your cage is growing smaller and you will soon become the bride to our new king. That fate has been ordained, my Queen."

Turning, she melts into the shadows and disappears from view. The Captain and those around him wait, watching the treeline before nodding in satisfaction.

"We have no choice but to trust the words of a traitor. Be wary until we are far from here, she may choose to follow us and her kind is skilled in a thousand ways of inflicting death."

"My Captain, what shall we do about the dead?"

Turning to his second in command, he answers with a hardened face.

"We do not have the time to bury nor burn them. Strip them of their weapons and armour, drape them in cloaks, and place coins in their mouths and eyes, we can offer them nothing more."

⊶⧫——◎◟♃◞◎——◈⊷

Covered by their red cloaks, the dead are lined side by side. Scurrying between them, my sister and I place a small bouquet of

343

gathered flowers at their feet. Compared to the silver coins to pay for the Ferryman, they were nothing more than a beggar's gift, but we could offer nothing more to show our appreciation.

Only the corpses of the two Gatekeepers are left untouched, though their weapons and armour were of fine quality and valuable, no one wished to touch the grimed bodies which reeked of death.

With the grim task complete, we mount our horses and prepare to leave the clearing, guided by our sole remaining hoplite. Wiping away the tears, I make a silent vow, I would become stronger, strong enough that no others would be sacrificed so I could live.

Looking up at the clear night sky, my heart flutters as I think back to the silver star I had seen days before. Only the Oracle could truly tell me what I saw that day, but the emptiness and hopelessness within me had been replaced with a passion and warmth I had not felt in years.

Riding into the darkness, I pray to the gods for an end to this pointless war.

Arc 4: A Shattered Peace

Chapter Twenty Eight

North Sea

55.75, -00.92

0940 hours, 15-09-2177 C.E.

The subtle movement of the aircraft banking right causes the ordered papers on my desk to slide towards the edge. Reaching out, I carefully collect them and place them beside me on the vacant seat. Rolling my shoulders, I stretch as I gaze onto the dark blue waters of the North Sea and watch as they are replaced by the dark sands of the Isle of Britannia.

The pop of bottles and laughter draws me away from the window and onto those seated across from me. Having rarely ventured beyond the borders of the fourth district, today's invitation was likely a once-in-a-lifetime experience for them.

For nine consecutive years, I had avoided the journey, the pomp and ceremony to celebrate the nation's founding a needless diversion, but this year was different. Not even I could ignore the personal summons of the Lord Marshall without consequence.

Unwilling to bear the inconvenience of the event alone, I had chosen two representatives from the District Council to accompany me, the highest-ranking officials after Amelia and myself.

The first, dressed in a black tunic lined with silver thread was Colonel Stefan Maczek, commander of the District's security forces. Few knew his real age, for his youthful appearance could deceive any who did not look into his eyes.

Born before the end of the Thermonuclear War, he had grown into adulthood amongst the ruins of the Old World. A volunteer for the Praetor's newly created army, he was a veteran of the Reclamation and every medal on his chest was earned from personal sacrifice.

Beside him, though less imposing in his simple, tailored grey suit was Magistrate Albert Black. Nominated leader of the Council he was a man of great influence and nothing happened within the district without his knowledge.

Nearing his eightieth year, he had the privilege and the curse of being an adult when the warheads fell. Ravaged by malnutrition and tumours due to the radiation, he was found on the brink of death in the ruins of London.

A former lecturer, his value was immediately recognised, but not even the advanced medical facilities available to the Praetors could restore his body to its former youthful self. Though physically frail, his sharp mind and insight were beyond those of his nearest peers.

I choose not to listen to the conversation of the two men, the topics being of no interest to me. Instead, I glance down at my wrist, watching the swishing of the three black hands as they turn on a pearl white face. Once regarded as an everyday consumable, mechanical watches such as these were now a rarity.

Few engineers and even fewer watchmakers survived the devastation of the major cities and their areas of industry. Barely a dozen artisans now remained who possessed the skill necessary to repair, let alone create watches such as these.

Symbols of status and prestige, each was prized by those with disposable incomes. My own was a relic from before the War, a gift from a long-dead acquaintance who performed a futile final duty.

For the everyday citizen, watches such as these were unnecessary, the technology to manufacture digital watches was plentiful and every city had displays at major junctions, allowing a person to know the time with a glance.

Soothed by the gentle ticking, I turn my gaze back to the tablet in my hand. Despite the various requests, very little required my full attention. Signing the last document, I turn off the tablet and place it beside me on the vacant seat.

My right hand moves instinctively to my forehead, rubbing my temple as I lean back and close my eyes. Nearly a month had passed since I sent Amelia away, and there had been no contact from her or squad Gorgo. Though their mission required the greatest secrecy, the lack of contact disturbed me.

I knew for certain that the mission was not compromised, for there was nothing that she, let alone an entire squad could not best.

The silence only indicated the extent of the infiltration that had occurred in the empire.

The view out of the window changes as the sea and sand is replaced with rich green meadows, land which four decades ago was desolate and devoid of life. Confirming the time of arrival, I unlock my briefcase and place the tablet and sheets of paper carefully within before sealing it shut. Placing it in an overhead alcove, I sit back and allow my body to relax as I dream of a time long forgotten, and promises I still had to keep.

Chapter Twenty Nine

Air Force Facility 01, Alpha City, District 1

55.95, -3.20

1050 hours, 15-09-2177 C.E.

Awakened by the gentle backwards and forwards rubbing sensation on my wrist, I stretch my limbs, loosening the muscles which had grown tight whilst asleep in the chair. Allowing my eyes to adjust to the oncoming stream of sunlight, I watch as the green fields are replaced with concrete walls, tarmac, and anti-air batteries.

A small ripple in the air announces the departure of our two escort aircraft as our own prepares to land on the airfield. With our descent nearly complete, the engines rotate until they are almost vertical and with a gentle bounce, the wheels touch the ground.

As the engines wind down and the flight crew prepares to disembark, I grab the briefcase from the alcove above, checking the seals before placing it on the seat next to me. Outside, groups of figures scurry about, locking the wheels in place as a black armoured convoy parks in a nearby yellow chevroned area. Grey armoured figures emerge from the vehicles, their features hidden by their helmets as they grasp rifles tightly to their bodies.

Grabbing my tunic and cap, I make myself presentable as the doors are unlocked. Greeting the flight crew who stand to attention, I step out into the open air. The sensation of rain splashing my face is both soothing and refreshing after hours of sitting in the dry air of the aircraft's cabin. Placing the cap on my head, I purposely make my way down the steps.

The *clack* of metal announces the presence of my honour guard as their well-drilled movements cause them to stand in two files, each facing the other. Their commander, his three downward facing chevrons prominent on his chest, salutes me as he welcomes me to the airfield.

Dressed in the urban variant of the LEBAR series, his armour was suited to the relatively peaceful environment of the city. The under armour had been replaced with normal battledress, maximising comfort over survivability as the vitals were only protected by the standard plates.

His helmet, which would normally resemble a respirator, was instead a hard shell with a hinged polycarbonate visor, granting a less restrictive view and allowing easier communication. Exchanging pleasantries, I examine the ribbons moulded onto his front plate; long service, valour, distinction, and campaign medals. He was a veteran that I could relate to.

"Governor, please allow my men and I to escort you."

Having spoken in a tone befitting a veteran non-commissioned officer, I respond, indicating with a wave for him to lead the way, noticing the hesitation in his movements as he catches sight of my holstered pistol.

"Is there a problem, Sergeant?"

"Governor, I must apologise, but I have received instructions that all guests must attend unarmed."

Mentally sifting through the various messages which I had received in the last seventy-two hours, I find none which had mentioned this diktat.

"I have not received this instruction."

"The instructions were issued by the Executive in the last hour for all guests to surrender their arms and armour. I must request that you and the Colonel surrender your side-arms, we are also required to inspect your briefcase."

Turning my towering gaze downwards, I watch as the Sergeant and those behind him flinch. A central pillar of the Confederation since its foundation was for all senior officers, the majority being Praetors, to be armed at all times. Practically this was to reduce the chances of successful assassinations, but also to administer justice.

Being unfair to be overly critical of the sergeant as he follows his issued order, I turn to the Colonel and indicate for him to disarm. Nodding as he understands the political agenda, he removes his pistol and holster, handing it to the nearest escort.

"And your sidearm and suitcase, Governor."

Extending his hand expectantly, he waits for me to comply, but I have already made my decision.

"I refuse."

My response causes the sergeant to hesitate in shock as his mouth flaps up and down.

"If you refuse, we can take them by force."

A predatory smile forms on my lips as I stand to my full height, causing those in front of me to quiver in fear. Few had witnessed a Praetor in combat, even fewer survived being the target of one, and we had a reputation earned from countless battlefields. Even unarmoured, the sergeant was doubting whether he had sufficient resources to force my compliance.

"Do you recognise me, sergeant?"

"Yes, I served with you on the Eastern Fronts before the creation of the wall."

"Then you know that I outrank everyone in the Executive Office, they and their diktats have no authority over me."

Hearing the cold, monotonous words, devoid of emotion causes the sergeant to swallow involuntarily as he glances at my medals and gold braid. Leaning forward, I wait for his eyes to settle on the pair of gold "I"s on my lapels.

The creation of the Office of Executive was meant to be the first step in many in distancing Praetors from matters of daily governance. Holding influence comparable to those of individual Governors, only in matters of security, both internal and external did they hold no sway, the matter reserved solely for Praetors.

But instead of a controlled transition over years and decades, the emboldened Executive had started to make moves to unsettle the "balance", manoeuvring in the shadows to usurp and weaken the Governors' influence.

"The "I"s on my lapels confirmed my appointment as First Commander of the Britannic Confederation, the highest-ranking officer whose influence was second only to the Lord Marshall. I had ignored their movements until now, but today's actions had earned my ire.

The sergeant squirms unconsciously as he bears the brunt of my gaze, it is clear that his superiors had failed to brief him thoroughly. Weary of the delay, I press the issue, forcing the man to make an instinctive decision.

"Only the Lord Marshall can request that I disarm and allow you to inspect the contents of my suitcase. I am sure your commander will "happily" disturb the Lord Marshall for such a trivial thing."

Furrowing his brow, the sergeant glances at the men and woman intently listening behind him. Pride prevented him from appearing weak and indecisive.

"Yes, it is a trivial matter. Field Marshall, please allow me to escort you and your retinue, I apologise for the unnecessary delay."

Pivoting to face his squad, he gives a series of short commands before directing me to the trio of parked vehicles, the Colonel and Magistrate following behind. Despite standing six foot two, the sergeant is still dwarfed by my unarmoured frame, forcing me to take shorter strides.

Speaking no more than necessary, he stops in front of a vehicle with pennants flying on its bonnet and a corporal standing by the open door. Ugly, its red leather interior did little to hide its origins as a military vehicle.

Returning the series of salutes, I move to the furthest point from the open door, allowing the Magistrate and Colonel to sit across from me. As the door is closed, I am left alone with my thoughts.

Having waited till the mid-point of the journey, I glance upwards at the driver, ensuring he and the front passenger's attention was elsewhere before I opened the suitcase. Sitting on top is a pistol which I secrete into the holster sewn into my tunic. Spying the glint of brass, I consider taking the four magazines tucked into the sides, but I knew the limits of the tailored suit, anything more would create a suspicious bulge.

I catch the eyes of the Colonel as I redo the locks, a worried smile on his face as he watches my movements. Though no words are spoken, his eyes tell me he too is confused as to why the Executive had disarmed the guests.

Unable to answer the question, I instead allow my mind to wander as the city I had not seen in a decade comes into view. My instincts warned me that this series of unusual events was a precursor for something beyond my ability to predict or control.

As my right hand comes to rest on the pistol holstered on my hip, I settle on a single fact. No matter what happens, I would trust in its cold metal and react accordingly.

Chapter Thirty

Assembly of the Britannic Confederation, Alpha City, District 1

55.95, -3.20

1200 hours, 15-09-2177 C.E.

As the convoy enters the central boroughs, a melody that can only be described as regal carries over the air. Curious, I glance at the men, women, and children lining the streets.

"Seeing them like this makes all the sacrifices worthwhile, does it not?"

More a statement than a question, the Magistrate emotionally reaches across and touches the window with outstretched hands. The mirrored glass prevents those on the other side from seeing his actions.

"If the world was as it should have been, it would never have been necessary, Albert."

Seeing the tears forming in his eyes, I sympathise with his situation, everyone had lost something when the Old World collapsed. Both of us had lived through the disaster, but his losses were deeper than mine.

The density of the crowd increases as we draw nearer to our destination, the masses huddled around stalls and vendors, hawking food, memorabilia, and other wares. The crowd parts as our convoy approaches, their faces filled with smiles as they continue to wave the flags in their hands voraciously.

"A few more minutes Governor"

The driver's voice blares from nearby speakers as she prompts our attention to the bronze armoured gates, gates I had once designed.

A squad of five step out from the guardroom, standing in the middle of the road as our convoy comes to a stop. On the walls, armoured figures hold their rifles and machine guns close, the weapons aimed at the bonnets and windscreens of each vehicle. I had no doubts that they would fire without a moment's hesitation.

Despite the apparent threat, there is little tension in the air, the actions of everyone here a formality as the sergeant in the lead vehicle hands over a tablet to his counterpart.

"*Hmph.* Utterly pointless, their weapons would not even scratch the paintwork."

The Colonel's eyes glint as he scans the movements of everyone at the gate. I understood his sentiment, for the capabilities of the soldiers garrisoned in the eastern cities had been called into question lately.

"They rely too greatly on the walls. I wager a thousand credits that if the enemy was even half credible, they would be slaughtered."

Worryingly, I could only nod in reply to the Colonel's comments. A high level of security was necessary here, for the Assembly of the Britannic Confederation lay beyond the gates. Offices that housed the highest tier of government officials and managed the day-to-day running of the empire.

Designed as a fortress within a fortress city, the walls stood five meters high and were patrolled by select regiments of the Defence Force. Every inch of the compound was covered by an intricate

361

network of cameras ensuring no blind spots for unauthorised persons to enter. Only three routes existed into the inner sanctums, by air or by the two armoured gates at the front and rear.

Despite the recent intensity of the Insurrectionist movement, none had yet dared an attempt on this place. Not because they feared the three companies of men and women stationed within or the nearby city garrisons and airfields that housed wings of gunships, but the Praetors who formed the personal guard of the Lord Marshall. Only a fool or a martyr would plan an attack on such a place.

The *creak* of metal announces the end of the checks as the convoy once again begins to move. As the gate swings open, the modern urban landscape is replaced by something akin to an aristocratic estate. Finely cut grass stretches as far as the eye can see and the branches of the trees which line the road sway side to side in the autumn breeze.

My face hardens as I spy the fountains which sit at the junctions which criss-cross the compound. Each is magnificently sculpted with images of heroes from myths and classical history. The unnecessary ostentation were departures from the militaristic simplicity which I had grown accustomed to.

⸺◦◦⸺

The convoy takes fifteen more minutes before it arrives at the main building, a reception party already formed on the stairway to greet us. Dressed in their ceremonial uniform, the argent sheen of their swords and shields contrasted sharply with the black.

A prim, smiling corporal opens the door, her voice chirpy as she greets me. Returning her greeting, I step out and breathe the fresh air.

"Welcome to the Assembly. I hope your journey has been uneventful."

A young officer steps towards me, a clipboard in his hand. A lieutenant, his rank new, the twin pips unblemished, and his clothes wafting the scent of inexperience. The muscles in my face form an awkward smile as I provide the most suitable response. The lieutenant does not sense my discontentment and continues to make small talk as he slowly leads me up the stairs.

"You are the last to arrive, please follow me to the reception area."

Intentionally taking smaller strides, I turn slightly back to watch as the Magistrate's frail frame is assisted, by the same corporal who opened the door, up the stairs. His jovial voice carries the short distance as he speaks happily with the woman who would have been the same age as his granddaughter.

Now if you follow me this way...

I barely acknowledge the lieutenant as he guides us through the maze-like corridors, his voice growing increasingly excited as he draws closer to the reception. My eyes scan the surroundings, assessing the changes to the blueprints I had drafted a decade before. But it is the guards which line the route which causes my gaze to linger. Dressed like those lining the stairs, their weapons and lack of armour made them unsuitable for their role.

Perhaps in centuries past, there would have been a purpose to this grandiose display, but who was there now to impress with ivory-painted walls, purple velvets, or catalogues of historical paintings?

Each was originals recovered and salvaged from derelict museums, warehouses, and private storage, the names of once famous artists and battles etched on brass placards beneath each; Thermopylae, Cannae, Gaugamela, Waterloo, and a dozen more.

But it is a painting, hidden in the shadows, that catches my eye, causing me to stop. New, the paint barely dry, and depicting a battle from the modern age, it is still too far in the past to be remembered by anyone here. Gritty, the atmosphere is heightened by the simplistic and minimalistic palette, something no photograph could recreate. The Second Battle of Kursk, an engagement of tanks that had not been seen since the Second World War and the last major victory of the United European Federation.

"Beautiful is it not?"

A cheerful, naïve voice comes from behind as the lieutenant appears at my side, his eyes full of wonder as he stares longingly at the painting. It is a look that only those who have not experienced war can show.

"I would never call anything of such nature, beautiful."

"I mean rank after rank of men and women giving their lives willingly for their people, surely such heroic sacrifice is blinding?"

My features remain passive as I gaze at the lieutenant who thinks of nothing but romantic notions. It was not my role to educate him on the truth of war, he would learn soon enough when he entered the battlefield.

"I have seen all aspects of it, it is nothing more than a necessity of last resort."

I walk past the lieutenant as he stands silent, considering my words.

"Would you like to meet the artist, Sir?"

The words from behind caused me to slow my pace. Turning, I face the lieutenant as he repeats the question.

"Do you know them, lieutenant?"

"Yes, she is a former colleague who is currently studying here in the Capital. Do you wish me to make arrangements for an introduction?"

I consider his request, was it to curry favour for future promotion, or something more pure and simple? Staring at his naïve face, I believe it to be the latter.

"I am currently busy for an extended period. Make contact with my adjutant and something will be arranged for the future."

Pleased, he returns to my side and continues to guide me to my destination. As I respond to his new attempts at small talk, I think back to the painting and remember the battle that changed the world.

Chapter Thirty One

Statues line the walls that lead to the oak door, but not all of them are inanimate, standing on either side are giants, their armour as black as midnight as they rest shotguns in their gauntlets. No one would question if their armour was ceremonial, it and those beneath were battle proven.

I feel their glare as they sense our approach and as one they step forward, their seven-foot forms towering over everyone but me in the corridor.

"Halt"

All obey the command, not daring to cross the line marked on the laminated floor.

"Purpose?"

The lieutenant's voice wavers despite his knowledge of their presence and style of questioning.

"I present the final representatives, attendance by invitation."

The nearest giant acknowledges the information and directs us to the green glowing panel on the wall.

"Identification."

Making no sudden movements, the lieutenant places his hand on the scanner, the panel instantly lighting and confirming his identity. Satisfied, he is directed to the waiting area as one by one the process is repeated by the other members of the party.

Waiting till last, I approach the wall, noticing the subtle shift in the warriors' movements as they watch my steps, the grips on their weapons becoming slightly relaxed. As my identity is confirmed, the two giants' stamp their feet together and shout in unison.

"Vronti"

A smile appears on my lips as I remember the old watchword. Standing tall, I face the two Praetors with my right hand formed into a fist over my chest and the other in the small of my back.

"Astrapi"

With the tradition complete, they move to the side of the door and in sync, input the access code. With a *clunk*, the doors behind open and reveal the sights and sounds of those on the other side.

As I walk past the Praetors towards the sound of music and laughter, I hear the almost silent words coming from beneath their helmets. A genuine smile appears on my lips as I simply nod, the sentiment is enough to be understood.

Finely dressed employees, their clothing inspired by those worn by high-class establishments from the Old World, offer us glasses of wine as we pass. Taking a glass, the flute appearing ridiculously small in my hand, I sample the bubbling, golden liquid.

Despite the size of the oval chamber, there is little room to move freely, hinting at the number of guests present. Many of the faces are unknown to me, or only known from photographs I had seen from a computer screen. Few make an attempt to reach out and greet me, those that do, do so with a mixture of fear and admiration on their faces.

Moving to the side of the room, I isolate myself from the rest of the guests as I sigh in exasperation. Nothing had changed in a decade. Suddenly my senses warn me of a presence approaching me

370

from behind, their movements silent and their intent unlike any other in the room.

"Still not good enough, maybe next time."

With a smile, I turn and greet the well-dressed giant.

"Tsk, were you even remotely surprised?"

A light-hearted chuckle escapes my lips as I greet my counterpart from the first district.

"Even if I was stuck behind a desk for a hundred years and lost both of my ears, your skills would still be lacking."

With a hearty laugh, the man steps closer and drags me into a friendly embrace. His action draws the attention of others, so unused to seeing a friendly spectacle between Praetors. Some choose to turn away, whilst others continue to stare and murmur in amazement.

"It has been too long First Commander, your voice has been gravely missed here in the Capital."

"So I have been told, but I do not miss it. You are correct, it has been too long Commander Nelson."

For the majority, Praetors were nothing more than giants, and they did not wish to see our differences. Though his uniform was an almost carbon copy of my own, the number of medals on his chest were significantly reduced, hinting at the extra decades I had spent on the battlefields. But it was his face, which regrettably was his defining feature. Though he wore a smile, half of his features were permanently immobile due to a scar that ran down the entirety of his left side, through his eye, and down to his chin.

Though half a century has passed since the battle and the advancement of technology, the eye would forever remain white and cloudy. But he did not see the wound as shameful, instead treating it as a memento of a battle lost to history. But his pride and vanity existed in other forms as I smell the subtle scent of ammonia coming from his short, blonde hair. Age was finally catching up within him, despite his apparent youth.

"It is rare for you to appear at events such as these, perhaps even rarer for you to be without Amelia."

His question is one of genuine surprise, rather than as an interrogation, so I reply in kind.

"Regrettably, she stated that I should experience the company of others and would remain at home"

A smirk appears on his face as he hears my words, the grin doing little to hide his imaginative thoughts.

"So continues your marital bliss."

Laughing, he slaps me repeatedly on the back, the force sufficient to cause the sound to travel across the room.

"Here I was, expecting you to remain hidden in your laboratory, tinkering away on your next project. Do you not miss the frontlines?"

"If I did return, you would never catch up."

I watch his widening grin, the movement natural despite his deformity. Many Praetors since the end of the War had embraced their human heritage, regaining their emotions, for others, it was harder.

"Well, I did hear about your little "exercise" at District Six, breaking all those expensive machines. Have you grown bored of your office yet?"

I choose to remain silent, knowing I could never truthfully answer.

"Ah, you never change, still a man of few words. I truly have missed your company, James. James Archean, that is what you call yourself these days?"

"I do not recall you being as boisterous Victor, were you always so?"

Picking up a pair of glasses from the tray of a passing waiter, he takes a sip from both before he continues to speak.

"I have only embraced the freedom you gave us, you did state you wanted us to become more human."

I can only wryly smile in response to his statement.

"Victor, I need a moment of your time."

Hearing my tone causes his jovial personality to disappear in an instant as his smile turns into a frown. Glancing left and right, he creates a false pretence of happiness before leaning in and speaking softly into my ear.

"Your questions usually mean trouble, this is not the best place."

"I think we will have no other opportunity."

Sighing, he grips my shoulder and guides me to a quiet corner, his perfect, effortless false visage enough to hide our intentions as he greets officials along the route.

"Make it quick."

"Were you involved in the planning for today?"

Understanding immediately what I was asking, he shakes his head as his eyes settle on the pistol holstered on my hip.

"As you suspect, everything was planned by the Executive."

"Still you obeyed?"

Pretending to sip on his glass, he leans in close and whispers his answer.

"The original bore the high seal, none of us could challenge it."

It takes a moment for the meaning of the words to take effect, if the original command bore the Lord Marshall's seal, this was more than just an attempt to usurp power. This was something bigger, something which could change the core of the Confederation.

"None of us could challenge it without consequence, but at least you managed to retain your pistol."

"Why would…"

The barest hint of a question forms on my lips when the sound of clapping and applause from the other side of the room interrupts our conversation. Armoured footsteps marching in unison echo on the wooden floor as a formation of black armoured giants cause the crowd to part.

Separating only when they reach the balcony, they allow the man in the centre to step out. Wearing a uniform similar in style to my own, the fabric was instead white with greater flourishes of red and gold. Standing below the skylight, he clears his throat, causing the room to quieten as the crowd eagerly awaits his words.

Though no introductions are needed, he makes them anyway, his every sentence planned and laced with politics. The end of every sentence is met with the sound of applause as those in the room vied with each other for his favour.

Seeing this, Victor separates from me, stating that he would continue the conversation later. Even at this distance and with the noise of the crowd, it was still possible that those with enhanced ears could listen in.

I settle my gaze on the man, his smiling face a contrast to the man I once knew. Here before me was the most powerful man of the Britannic Confederation, who with a word could unleash the might of the world's last empire. A man whose whim controlled the destiny of a third of the world's surviving population.

Lord Marshall Alexander Corsica.

Chapter Thirty Two

Hours after the departure of the Lord Marshall, the announcement is made that the next venue is ready. Meeting the news with great fanfare, the guests down their drinks, and surge towards the exit, eager to be the first to reach the destination.

Following their guides, they are led in groups through the corridors of the Assembly, the route lined with men and women of the Defence Force, standing as still as statues with weapons slung on their backs.

Choosing to linger at the rear of the room, I wait for the initial rush to settle before moving towards the door. On route, I spy Colonel Maczek holding up the Magistrate, his lethargic frame the likely result of excessive alcohol consumption.

A series of squeaks is heard from the door as a petite woman pushes her way through the crowd in the opposite direction, her movements scurried as she protects a tablet held close to her bosom.

Having broken through, she barely catches her breath before running in my direction.

"Com…man…der…Arch…ean?"

Forcing the words out of her mouth as her chest rises and falls, she appears to be on the verge of collapse as I place a hand on her shoulder, indicating that she should catch her breath before continuing.

"Are you Commander Archean?"

"How may I help you, corporal?"

"Commander, I was requested to find you urgently, there have been last-minute changes to the seating, you are now at the front of the stage."

Having unexpectedly been brought to the fore, I bite down my irritation and follow the corporal as she directs me to a different exit.

"Where have you been stationed previously, corporal?"

Having shortened my strides due to her still ragged breath, I sate my curiosity as I notice the lack of ribbons on her tunic and her apparent youth, traits which together were unusual for her rank.

"Oh, I have always been stationed here, with the Assembly garrison, Sir"

"Are you planning a transfer to another garrison?"

"Oh no, Sir. I will probably remain here. Most do,"

"Then I hope your time in service is rewarding."

Forming a wry smile, I bury my concerns under a veneer of serenity. The questions would come later, with persons of accountable rank.

Banners and flags of various sizes flutter on the rooftops and from the top of poles. The majority bear the emblem of the Britannic Confederation, its domains in Northern Europe outlined in white, surrounded by eight five-pointed stars on a royal blue background.

Designed more than a decade ago, its purpose was to show the borders of the Confederation, frontiers which have since expanded, as well as the representation of the Lord Marshall and his seven Governors who governed the seven districts. In time, the design would change again, but this could wait until the end of the next war of expansion.

Ahead lies a newly built, multi-layered stage, the white paint still fresh to the smell and touch. Made to accommodate a hundred with room to spare, it was quickly being filled by ranks of representatives.

Behind the stage stand three poles, the middle flying the colours of the Confederation, but standing proudly on either side are the emerald green pennons of the Praetors. Rarely seen in public except on our uniforms, at the centre is a Corinthian Greek helmet of antiquity, impaled on a spear. Forever looking left to the future, each helmet is surrounded by downward striking lightning bolts.

Few remained who knew the meaning let alone the origins of the design. If they did, they would only be disappointed in the dream that never came to be. All it represented now was the might of the few remaining Praetors.

The corporal's movement grow increasingly timid as we near the stage, glancing ahead, I soon see why. Standing next to the speaker's podium are five Praetors, but not just any, each was my Governor counterpart.

"You are excused from your duties corporal, I can find my seat from here."

"But Sir…"

Her protests are quickly cut short as she notices my subtle wink.

"I will be nearby if you require me again, Sir"

With a look of relief, she hastily leaves my side and disappears into the crowd of black. I could not fault her manner for the physical and political might of Praetors were often viewed with no small hint of fear.

Due to making no effort to hide my footsteps, my peers quickly turn and greet me with open arms as I enter the stage. I welcome their embrace, for it had been too long since I had felt the touch of those present, those I could call my friends.

Not once in the last decade had this number of high ranking Praetors been present in one place, due to the risk of assassination. I could only wonder at the Lord Marshall's vanity in requesting our attendance.

Ladies and Gentlemen, could you take your seats.

The announcement cuts our reunion short as we are forced to our seats at the front of the stage. Basked in sunlight, I wait, waiting for the next sequence in this pointless charade.

What decadence

I hide my growing disgust as my eyes sweep the horizon. White stone paths snake across the lush green lawn, connecting the scattered gardens and orchards in a complex weave. Standing at its centre is a fountain, larger than any other in this new world. Twenty feet high and crafted from white marble, at its base stand gold plated effigies of Greek deities, their arms raised skywards to a single figure sitting upon a throne, thunderbolts in hand. A sight which would have been home in the estates of old royalty.

The whir of motors and the crackle of static causes my gaze to shift towards the nearby teams of technicians and engineers working non-stop as they check the screens, cameras and speakers.

The Lord Marshall's intentions were only too clear, the desire to drag the once mysterious, hidden leaders of the Confederation from the shadows and into the public eye. No longer would we have the freedom of anonymity, forever would we be chained to this world.

Forward!

The shout followed by the rhythmic beat of drums draws the attention of the crowd to the garden's left as three companies of men and women march towards us in a column. Dressed in black with white gloves and courlene belts, their polished shields held tightly as they sweep their right arms up to shoulder height. Every movement is sharp, showing their dedication as not even a single step is out of time.

Halt!

Rounds of applause come from those seated behind as they enjoy the pomp and ceremony, something near unseen in decades. With the clunk of metal, the companies once again move, breaking into platoons and squads until they form an open square that has the fountain at its centre.

Those behind me can only cheer as my instincts warn me of danger. My experienced eyes knew instantly that this formation was not one for ceremony, but for something more practical. The subtle nods of those beside me only confirm my fears, this was to funnel and cordon large groups.

⋇⋇————⊙⅋⊙————⋇⋇

The screech of rusted metal and the grind of turning gears announces the opening of the distant gate. Barriers made to be immobile except in times of emergencies were slowly being opened as the silhouettes of men and women appear in the growing gap.

Gasps and murmurs of confusion come from the stand as they question what is happening. The lack of activity from the soldiers at the wall only confirm my suspicions and my hand moves instinctively to the pistol on my hip.

With screams of excitement, ten thousand men, women, and children surge into the Assembly's garden. Waving flags and banners, their voices are joyful as they sing songs glorifying the Confederation.

Question after question comes from those behind as they find no answers to what was happening. No one attempts to control the crowd as they approach the stage, no attempts are made to perform checks or sweep for weapons. My senses grow increasingly restless as I realise the complacency which had entered the minds of the organisers.

All that stood between us and the crowd was an over-reliance on goodwill and eight hundred members of the Defence Force. Standing in ceremonial uniform, they did not have their usual complement of weapons and armour, instead, a small round shield, baton, and an unloaded rifle slung on their back. A loadout is unsuited for spontaneous incidents. Without walls for protection, they would be quickly overwhelmed by the crowd's numbers.

Having already naively overestimated the ability and judgement of the organisers, I turn towards the high-rise towers in the distance. Used for business and habitation, the clear blue skies only served to emphasise the lack of patrolling aircraft and guards on the rooftops. With the right weapon, a skilled marksman could overcome the three-mile distance. Discreetly I lean down, brushing my fingers against the lock of the suitcase at the side of my seat until I heard the subtle *click*.

The crowd reaches its crescendo as it makes contact with the cordon. In their excitement, a few begin to push against the wall of flesh as they vainly try to get closer to the stage. Only settling when they are pushed back by the thrust of shields and hear the playing of percussion and wind instruments.

Words of a long-dead language languish in the air as the national anthem, Ode to Joy, is sung to Beethoven's 9th Symphony. Once known as the "Anthem of Europe", little had changed from its days when it was played across the entirety of the United European Federation and its predecessors. An unwanted legacy of the "Old World" retained in the "New World" we were creating.

As the band reaches the final verse, a uniformed figure appears on the podium. Purposely clearing his throat, he makes his presence known by speaking softly in the direction of the crowd. Appearing as a man in his thirties, his peaked cap hides his short, brown, greying hair. Few would know his identity, but those in power would recognise the meaning of the golden "X"s on his lapels. This was none other than Major Anthony Oates, adjutant, to the Lord Marshall.

With his image broadcasted on the various screens around the garden, he whips the crowd into a frenzy, his passionate, energetic words an opening act before the main event. Soon the expectant words are spoken.

"I present to you the Lord Marshall of the Britannic Confederation."

On cue, the band plays a slow melody as the cameras turn from the adjutant to the six figures approaching the stage. As if hypnotised by the group's movements, the crowd's earlier frenzy is forgotten as they stare in silence.

Reaching the steps, the group splits into two, two taking their place at the foot of the stage, whilst the others follow the Lord Marshall to the podium. As the wood creaks under their combined weight, the Lord Marshall casually picks up a glass of water and sips it before speaking. His every movement is calculated as he looks directly at the camera.

Every inch of his apparent eminence is broadcasted across the entirety of the Confederation as the camera centres on his unblemished face, deep blue eyes, and short brown hair.

"Today we are here for a single purpose, to celebrate the founding of our fair nation. For ten long years, we have worked and strived to make a success of these once barren lands. I ask you all, do you not feel pride in the accomplishments earned by your blood and sweat?"

Like a composer, he plays on their hearts and minds. One by one, they are awoken from their apparent slumber and begin to cheer.

"I have watched you all my children, as you worked and prospered, celebrating your achievements as if they were my own. Every sacrifice, every life lost in the wars of yesteryear has been for the realisation of a dream, a dream that has saved innumerable lives.

Now we have enjoyed ten years of peace, a peace which has allowed us to declare as one people this land as our own. We have become a beacon of light for the darkness that exists beyond our borders, of a land where the vestiges of true war have been forgotten."

Like a skilled demagogue he plays on the crowd's emotions, his words though simple evoke powerful images within those listening. By purposely adopting an accentless manner, he ensures no one ignores his words due to bias. Despite all this, I sense the insincere, artificial emotions that lace his every word, ones based on patterns exhibited by dictators during the early twentieth century.

"Now my children, let me tell you of a new dream."

Chapter Thirty Three

"Now my children, let me tell you of a new dream. One that will allow us to conquer the very stars."

The utterance of those precarious words, causes me to turn away from the podium and look in the direction that he is pointing. Understanding his treachery, I return my gaze to the Lord Marshall, watching his eyes burn with triumph as a sinister smile forms on his lips.

Alexander…what have you done!

No more than a glint in the afternoon sky, few in the garden had anything in hand to realise the true form of the heavenly body that drifted above us. Few were trusted to know of its existence, even fewer its significance to the survival and progress of humanity.

Suddenly aware of its presence, the crowd begins to murmur, querying how they could have missed an object hidden in plain sight. Few however question its origins, believing it to be a legacy of their forebearer's wasted potential.

"Long has mankind gazed at the stars in wonder and awe, the darkness being both a source of fear, trepidation, but also hope and salvation. What I wish to offer once more is hope, hope that will offer your children's children a better life."

Few understood the true meaning of those words and the crowd remains silent, waiting for the Lord Marshall to continue.

"Long ago, our people reached the very stars and sought to make the moon and planets our own, and we will strive to do so once more."

The almost childlike ambition causes the crowd to murmur in disappointment, they had expected something more tangible, more within their reason and probability.

"Oh, I hear you even from here, you ask me, 'How is this possible?'.

Well, let me show you the chariot that will make this possible."

Stretching out his arms, he directs the crowd to the monitors behind him, the image of the Lord Marshall replaced by utter darkness. At first, the crowd stare at the screens in confusion, questioning if there was a fault, but soon their confusion is replaced by gasps as the images begin to change.

My hands clench into fists as my fear becomes a reality. Before the eyes of every citizen of the Confederation and those beyond is a silver triangular-shaped object, one that few had seen outwith of blueprints.

"Orion." As its name passes through my lips, I glare back at the Lord Marshall's arrogant features. I had seen this look before, on dictators and tyrants who believed in achieving victory by any means. In his pride, he had chosen to claim the greatest prize as his own, exposing our greatest secret, uncaring of the consequences.

As the image behind the Lord Marshall changes, so does the mood of the crowd as they are greeted by the appearance of exposed wires, cables, and engineers floating in zero gravity. Finally understanding what they are seeing, the crowd cheers as they raise their hands to the sky.

Satisfied by their response, the Lord Marshall turns to the cameras, his expression once more of a gentle father than a smiling conqueror.

"This is our gateway to our empire in the stars. But we have much to do before we can claim them as our own. This land that we hold dear is not enough and we must go beyond our borders and into the wasteland. Our armies must once more march forth into the darkness and bring those lands and those within it to our fold."

As his desire for conquest leaks into his words, the militant fervour of those below is roused.

"All must dedicate themselves to the cause, not just those who fight on the front lines. With the fires of industry, the miracles of science, and our iron fist, we will make this world our own. Are you ready my children, to unite mankind under one banner?"

Metallic *thumps* echoes across the gardens as the soldiers strike their shields with their batons. Caught up in the fervour, the crowd clap, cheer and sing songs of victory and martial pride.

After the declaration of war, I notice unnatural movements in the centre and sides of the crowd, too large to be a mere coincidence.

No longer making efforts to blend into the crowd, the groups cluster into a formation the size of a small company.

Instinctively, I stand and move to draw my pistol, the Praetors on stage also beginning their movements. A warning forms on my lips as I prepare to aim, but it is interrupted by the sound of whips cracking in the air.

Chapter Thirty Four

Driven by instincts born from decades of war, my body moves in response to the sound. As I roll forward towards the nearest cover, a round impacts on the chair I was sitting on, causing it to shatter as the heavy calibre projectile passes through the bodies of three others before embedding itself in the stage.

Not even my enhanced senses can follow the path of the incoming fire, my ears are only able to tell me the number as five more impact on the stage. Screams of hysteria and fear follow as the Praetors shoulder their weapons and return fire, their rifles aimed at the distant tower. The sound is deafening as anti-material ammunition is unleashed into the distance.

The dead and dying litter the stage which is now awash and stained in red. Screaming in agony, they desperately try to slow their bleeding as the wood around them is splintered by heavy impacts.

"Medic! Medic!"

Old, young, male and female voices desperately cry out for help, but no one is coming. But it is not these dead and dying which draws my eyes, but the three still figures closest to me, their uniforms distinct even in the sea of black. Forms belonging to the Lord Marshall and two governors.

Moving quickly, the armoured Praetors stand in front of the Lord Marshall, though they had already failed in their duties with the first impact, they would not fail him further, shielding him with their very bodies.

Who dare...! Infidels...Unbelievers...

Coughing up blood, the Lord Marshall suddenly opens his eyes and splutters incoherent words as he reaches for his left shoulder, the remainder of his arm lying three feet away. As his enhanced body fights against the shock and makes attempts to stem the bleeding, his words grow increasingly disillusioned with religious dogma.

Whilst the Lord Marshall clings to life, those near him are a different story. Where his was a mere glancing blow, theirs had struck directly, collapsing and rupturing their chests.

With wounds too horrific for even their enhanced bodies to stem, they twitch and spasm as their breaths grow increasingly arduous. Their Praetor peers struggle to pin them down, knowing that every twitch would break the ad hoc seals formed on their bodies, applying strips of clothing and anything clean to dress the wounds.

Despite everything they had suffered, no screams of pain escape their lips. Having been raised and reborn into Praetors, they had expected a life of pain, they would now meet their end with dignity and without fear.

⊸⊱─────◎◟♨◞◎─────⊰⊸

The echo of footsteps from behind, announces the arrival of the first wave of reinforcements, dressed in full armour and carrying shields that are presented to the approaching enemy. Lingering in their shadow are the lightly armoured medical teams, their bodies weighed down by life-saving equipment.

"Alpha grade casualties. Go, go, go!"

Linking their shields together, the squads rush forward and stand in front of the three hulking Praetors. Now relieved of their primary duty, the Praetors shoulder their rifles and begin to move freely, engaging the approaching enemy with round after round of light ordnance. Behind them, sheltered from the incoming storm of bullets and shrapnel, the medical teams perform their vital work.

I listen to the cries of the dying grow in intensity as they notice the presence of the medics, who purposely ignore them, concentrating instead on the three Praetors, knowing each was worth more than the others combined.

⋯⊰⊱⋯

Soon the bodies of the medics are lathered in blood and sweat, the wounds of their patients being treated as best they could. With the Lord Marshall finally stable, they reinforce the seal around his shoulder and place his amputated limb into a container.

But the efforts of those working on the governors is interrupted by the crack of whips, as the distant tower which had remained silent since the opening salvo unleashes a fresh payload that cuts gouges into the shield wall. I watch as the heavy projectiles cut through the armour of the soldiers holding them before embedding themselves into the ground beneath the increasingly unstable stage.

I see the widening eyes of those behind the shields, something that not even the helmets could hide, the fear of death. Knowing their protection was becoming scant, the medics still working apply liberal amounts of biomedical foam into the wounds. Described as a battlefield miracle due to its ability to quickly seal wounds and prevent infection, even this could not stem the blood from wounds this grave.

In desperation, the medics use high powered lasers to cauterise the still gaping wounds, filling the air with the waft of burning meat. Few had a working knowledge of Praetor physiology, their bodies too far removed due to the presence of implanted organs, instead, they buy time until specialists could arrive.

But I know time is running out as I listen to the increasingly shallow heartbeats and breathing of my friends. My heart is filled with sadness at the latest milestone, it had been five decades since the last death from amongst our ranks.

⊶⊰──◖◍◗──⊱⊷

"Alpha one stable, two and three needing urgent evac."

"Understood, team on route, E.T.A. fifteen minutes."

"Negative, too long. We need evac sooner."

The hectic radio chatter blares into my ear as I listen to the communication between those on the ground and the control room. The medical teams could only wait, the muscled bodies of the Praetors were too heavy to be carried, not without assistance, especially in their current condition.

I watch as a dark spectre approaches the medics, causing the team leader to look upwards into the skull-like visage of the leader of the bodyguards, Captain Michael "Reaper" Andros. Glancing down at the prone bodies of the Lord Marshall and the governors, he makes a swift decision as he places his rifle behind his back.

"We withdraw, now"

Despite the fear etched on the man's face, he gives a firm response.

"We cannot move them like this."

As a stream of bullets *pings* off his shoulder pads, he shakes his head.

"We are out of time."

401

As new gouges are cut into the shield line, the Praetors returning fire indicate they are running low on ammunition. Sweeping out his arm, Captain Andros points in the direction of the Assembly building.

"Move them now."

The deathly gaze radiating from behind the Captain's helmet cuts short any words of protest.

"Our kind is beyond your skills now."

Grabbing hold of a limb each, the medical teams try to move the prone giants, barely moving two metres before setting them down. Having watched their struggle, the three still standing Governors emerge from cover, throwing away their scavenged weapons and assist in lifting their wounded colleagues.

"VIP secured, fall back!"

I watch as the majority take this opportunity to leave the warzone, knowing it would be some time until the next wave of reinforcements could arrive. Those not willing to brave the gauntlet instead dig deeper into their scant cover.

I have no hesitation as I begin making my way to the rear of the stage. Having heard the continuous *cracks,* I knew the identity of the weapons being used, weapons once heard on the battlefields of the Europa-Novoyan War. Weapons that should not be heard in the heartlands of this new empire.

But my movements are halted by a flash of blinding light.

Chapter Thirty Five

Blinded, I fall and land heavily on the blood-soaked grass as an earth-shattering explosion causes the weakened stage to collapse. With my ears still ringing, I rub my eyes, waiting for them to re-adjust. Around me, looking like they had been thrown around like rag-dolls belonging to an unruly child are the bodies of men and women, crumpled in unnatural positions.

An acrid smell of metal and burnt flesh carries in the air as the once beautiful gardens are desolated. Gone were the hedgerows and finely cut grass, replaced with blackened, circular marks. Anything within their charred circumference was incinerated with little trace.

Those caught on the periphery slowly stagger to their feet, their movements dazed as they recover from the shock. Across the gardens, booming voices and the shrill shriek of whistles are heard as officers attempt to form a defence.

Using themselves and their brightly coloured epaulettes as rally points, they haul men and women to their feet, shoving shields into still confused hands as they attempt to reform the cordon, but the now shattered line is not ready for the emerging threat.

Having taken advantage of the chaos to approach the stage, the menacing group cast aside their hooded cloaks. No longer bound by the need for secrecy, they reveal their secreted weapons and armour. If not for the red hammer encircled by flames emblazoned on their arms and chest, they would, in form and function be the equal of those worn by the Defence Force. The symbol of a once declared extinct Insurrectionist order, the chatter of machine guns and rifles however makes a lie of their apparent demise.

The latest bout of violence breaks the already fragile crowd's mentality. Screaming, they scatter or prostrate themselves, begging for mercy as they curl themselves into balls, shielding them and those they cherish from harm.

A heroic or foolish few instead rush forward, trying to buy time as they wrestle and attempt to pry away the weapons from the

Insurrectionists' hands. Behind them, soldiers form a desperate rearguard, raising their shields and rifles, but they too fall quickly, the resistance quelled by the butt of rifles and glint of metal.

Marksmen from the enemy's ranks aim at the few remaining officers, easy targets due to their bright epaulettes. With each death, the chain of command breaks further, until it is beyond repair.

Effectively leaderless, men and women form individual squads, some withdrawing whilst others act as forlorn hopes. With every passing second, it was becoming clear that the battle was becoming no more than a drawn-out massacre.

My body reacts as the stench of blood saturates the air, chemicals once more flowing through my bloodstream as it prepares for combat. But without armour, even my skills and enhancements were meaningless.

My eyes flick left and right, searching until they find the object of my desire, an ebony suitcase which had fallen off the stage. Half buried in the grass and outwith of my reach, I tear apart a section of black cable, forming a makeshift grappling hook and throw. As the hooked end catches the handle with a metallic *clink*, I carefully drag it towards me, ignoring the chaos until my fingertips brush against the locks.

Tearing away the hidden partitions within the interior, I reveal the dark coloured ceramic panels concealed within. Curved and rectangular, individually they were too small for their role to be obvious, but each was a segment of armour, moulded to fit my chest, back, shins, and forearms.

Heavy

The single thought enters my mind as I clamp and slot each segment into place. Offering barely half of the protection of the armour I usually wore, but compared to the garden defenders, I was a walking tank.

VIPs secured

The update blares into my ear as I slip on a pair of gloves and begin assembling the helmet. My eyes are first met with darkness as I slip it on my head, but as the interior is filled with light, I note the status of the already dwindling battery.

Extending the side panels of the holsters to protect my thighs, I attach the spare magazines onto the pouches on my chest before removing the remaining contents of the suitcase. Broken into three sections was a basic carbine, light and easy to assemble, it was not suited for prolonged combat, but ideal as a weapon for defence.

Standing from cover, with my rifle shouldered, I make my presence known.

"Ares on all channels, requiring immediate assistance at Alpha Two. Insurrection forces within the perimeter, danger close, rear guard insufficient."

Moving forward as I request assistance, I begin to rally the remaining survivors, their numbers barely above a company and a half.

"Rally on me."

The scattered wide-eyed defenders rush to my position, drawn by my towering frame and presence as I bellow the command.

"Hold this position, dig in."

No time for anything more complicated, I give the simple command. Stacking whatever they could find on top of the concrete walls, the defenders obey my command as they hunker down and return fire, every shot carefully aimed due to the lack of ammunition.

Seeing the instantaneous change in the level of resistance, the enemy directs their ire towards me. As round after round impact relentlessly on my chest and limbs, I answer with the bark of my rifle and pistols, each volley cutting down the enemy like a scythe. As my weapons click empty, I duck down and assess the damage.

"Maintain that rate of fire, we are holding their advance."

Amber light illuminates my helmet interior as I unload and reload my rifle with little flourish, bullets continuing to fly overhead as the enemy inch closer and closer. The *zing* of a bullet flies past my ear as a bullet embeds itself into the wooden panel beside me. Curious, my fingers probe the indent and extract the barely damaged bullet. Turning it repeatedly, the scant examination confirmed my fears and suspicions.

I had suspected the weapons in their hands to be from the eastern borders, but how had they managed to acquire so many and bring them into the Confederation heartlands unnoticed? No more than another piece of the puzzle, too many were still missing to complete the picture which connected the defunct Novoyan Russian Empire, Insurrectionists, and the blueprints recovered from Kursk.

"Running low!"

The bitter words are heard from the lips of those at the forefront of the line, their scolding rifles proof of their efforts. A pair of shrill whistles are heard as those at the front begin rotating with those at the rear. A distance of only five metres, it was the only respite that could be offered. Despite outnumbering the remaining defenders initially, the price had been steep for the Insurrectionists, every metre gained bought by pools of blood. Despite appearances, the decades' old armour provided little protection to modern rifles.

"Relief One, ETA ten minutes."

As the welcome words are heard in my ear, the latest enemy assault delivers an unwelcome message.

"Dry"

First spoken by one or two, they are soon repeated from the lips of the remaining defenders as their rifles click empty. Laughter escapes the lips of the advancing Insurrectionists as they empty magazine after magazine, their actions almost gloating as they fire indiscriminately in our direction.

"For the Confederation!"

The battle cry escapes the lips of the squads nearest to the enemy, thinking fast, they rack their extendable batons, heft their shields, and charge. A sight reminiscent of ancient battlefields, it is an act that is both reckless and glorious. Too few reach the enemy lines, but those that do engage in hand-to-hand combat, buying us a smidgen of time.

"Collect what ammo you can, withdraw to the next line."

Loading the last of my magazines, I prepare for the final stand.

Chapter Thirty Six

"Vronti"

The war cry is blared from the helmets of tall, dark shadows approaching at speed. Moving impossibly fast, two armoured giants leap and land in the middle of the enemy ranks, scattering them as their weapons bark. Lethal at even extreme ranges, this close, they are devastating and the enemy is torn asunder.

Nothing can stop this new irresistible force, those that try are the first to fall. Silent and merciless, more akin to machine than man, they make no sound as they scythe down those around them. Their once polished armour becomes drenched in the splatter of blood as the enemy's courage falters.

Though the enemy does not know it, the battle had been lost before a single shot had been fired. All on the battlefield recognise what they are, Praetors, decades of myths and legends, both true and embellished etched their prowess into the common psyche. But not even a lifetime of stories could prepare them for what they were seeing.

With movements too fast, too fluid, and inhuman to be real, those witnessing the slaughter can only watch, their mind's shocked into inactivity.

Praetorian Petrification

Informally, this was the name of the phenomenon which has appeared since the conception of the Praetors, explaining the disruption of the delicate nuances of the human mind upon seeing the perceived impossible.

Few however alive today had seen the days of the Wars of Reclamation, when hundreds of Praetors fought like this, cementing the phenomenon's existence. Today's events would once again confirm the horrific truth of the myths.

"Astrapi"

With a tilt of my head, I open a private channel to the titans performing their methodical slaughter.

"Andros Three and Five, what are you doing here?"

"Answering the call."

A genuine smile appears on my lips as I hear their words. Swiping my left hand across my helmet visor, I convey my gratitude, knowing that if not for a personal appeal to their squad leader, their presence here would have been impossible.

"Buy us time to evacuate."

Responding with only a pair of blinking lights, they wordlessly advance towards the retreating enemy. I watch as the Insurrectionists grow increasingly desperate, emptying magazine after magazine with no obvious effect before drawing their knives or striking out with the butt of their rifles.

Treating the attacks as nothing more than a nuisance, they continue to stride forward like mythical titans, their bodies impervious to everything thrown their way. Soon, the ground behind them is littered with crushed, eviscerated dead and empty casings.

As exhaustion and fear begin to drain their resolve, many choose the coward's path, falling to their knees and begging for mercy or using nearby women and children as hostages. Neither is successful as the emotionless Praetors cut them down with only looks of disdain.

"Get moving…"

Overwhelmed by the slaughter, too many of the garden defenders fail to hear the commands being given, unconsciously standing and staring. Squad leaders quickly apply physical stimulus, grabbing hold and pushing them back as they evacuate the injured and civilians.

Only I can willingly watch the dance of death performed by my brethren. Techniques designed for Praetors, honed over a century of warfare, each was a master of their craft which had remained relatively unseen for a decade. With blades glinting in the sunlight, they seamlessly switch from sword to pistols and rifle. Who would not be entranced by their elegance?

But as the evacuation nears completion, a series of cracking whips is heard from the direction of the distant tower. Heavy calibre slugs impact the armour plates of the Praetors, the once devastating projectiles were now insufficient, barely scratching the panels before falling, crumpled and broken, to the ground.

415

Made to counter weapons from an advanced age, they were not easily pierced, but even they cannot ignore the laws of physics as the continuous impacts cause the Praetors to stumble.

Having brought the titans to their knees, the Insurrectionists rush forwards, firing their weapons manically as they take advantage of their enemy's perceived vulnerability. But their reckless endeavour is ended by wide sweeps of a pair of swords. Those watching their display are either filled with hope or dread, but as the Praetors begin to rise above the press of bodies, a streak of green light causes one to fall.

Chapter Thirty Seven

My hypersensitive eyes watch in slow motion as the Praetor's left arm is torn away at the elbow, sending a stream of blood spluttering into the air as a second slug hammers into his stomach, doubling him over as he tumbles through the grass. The projectile, having travelled faster than the sound behind it, is followed by an explosion a few seconds later.

"Impossible…"

Dismay escapes the lips of those who still linger behind, never had they imagined that they would witness the fall of a "Battlefield God."

"Keep moving, get out of here!"

Requiring no unnecessary witnesses, I lash out with my tongue, commanding them to leave as I shoulder my rifle. With barely half a magazine remaining, I fire indiscriminately into the swarm of howling beasts as they pounce on their stricken prey.

Injured but far from dead, the Praetor sluggishly shakes them off with sweeps of his remaining arm and legs, but they pin down his limbs through sheer weight of numbers, before firing point-blank or stabbing hysterically into the joints and seals of his armour. Unable to support his stricken comrade, the still-standing Praetor moves from cover to cover, evading the incoming fire from the tower as he turns his ire towards them.

As craters begin to pocket the grass, memories of forgotten battlefields return to me. Grabbing a fallen shield, I charge forward, my legs burning as the final trickle of power is drained from my armour. Step by step, I move towards the stricken titan, his resistance slowly fading as his vice-like hand crushes the skull of an insurrectionist and tosses them away.

Swinging my now empty rifle like a club, I clear the area of threats before hammering the shield downwards into the ground. Barely protected by its shadow, I examine the wounds as I tap the helmet of the fallen warrior.

"Report."

With his mouth filled with blood, his words are garbled and distorted, but a series of flashes appearing on my display answers my questions as his armour status is sent to mine.

Pain surges through my right thigh as a stray bullet misses the scant armour, embedding itself in my clothing as the bodysuit underneath stops it from penetrating.

"Andros Three, cover fire."

Even with my knowledge of Praetor physiology, the battlefield was too chaotic to attempt to stem the bleeding, let alone remove the still embedded slug. Taking hold of the Praetor's armpits, I drag him in the direction of the barricades.

Staying close, Andros Three uses his body and armour to shield my own, his rifle and pistol barking continuously as he cuts down those foolish enough to follow. Barely conscious, Andros Five does his best to assist, kicking and pushing out with his remaining good leg as the other dangles useless, the injury a legacy of the swarm.

Buoyed by their victory, the insurrectionist's hound our every step, firing from cover as they relentlessly pursue the greatest imaginable scalp.

Tumbling behind the makeshift barricades, I throw my pistol to Andros Three and check on the casualty.

"Hold them."

Nothing further is needed as the Praetor swipes his left thumb across his visor, his interpretation of a smile, before standing and delivering volley after volley.

My hands become slick with dark red blood as I check on the wounds of Andros Five, with every passing second his breathing grows increasingly harsh. Though the opening in his armour is no more than an inch in diameter, there are no signs that blood flowing from his abdomen is slowing, the coagulating agents in his blood inactive due to the still embedded foreign object.

Unable to do anything without removing his chest piece, I pry open the compartments built into his thigh, extracting the rudimentary first aid kit. Beginning the operation, I crack open the silver tube, and with a hiss, a bright blue flame forms as I press the opening to the armour plate. Cutting through the near impervious metal compound like a hot knife through butter, it only takes a matter of minutes before a square section is cut and pulled away, exposing the torn flesh underneath.

Grabbing the forceps, I dig them into the wound, pulling away the flesh as I search. Though camouflaged by blood, it does not take long before I am greeted by the glint of cold coloured metal. Awakened by the pain, a groggy murmur escapes the lips of Andros Five as his hand unconsciously closes and opens, revealing the pain that he was trying to suppress without words or sound.

As the tips of the forceps grip the smooth edges of the metal, I pull, prying it free and dropping it onto my lap. Placing the nozzle of a green canister into the depths of the wound, empty the contents, watching as the blue foam expands and flows into the crevasses before changing colour. Reacting to the oxygen in the blood and air, it quickly hardens, turning black and forming a seal. No more than a stop-gap, it is enough to stem the bleeding and stabilise his breathing. I had done all I could, only a true medical facility could do more.

"Status."

Bellowing the command over the roar of explosions, Andros Three answers me promptly.

"Running low, enemy utilising grenades."

Short and to the point, I knew we would be overrun in two minutes when the last of the pistol ammunition was expended.

"You should withdraw Commander."

I consider the words as my eyes are drawn to the extracted piece of gold-tinted metal, too different in shape compared to bullets used in standard warfare., Though distorted by the impact, I recognise its origins immediately, another legacy of a dead empire.

"Praetor-killers."

The hated words escape my lips as I reveal the threat which the enemy posed. Circular discs of a tungsten-based alloy, they had been used in the closing days of the Europe-Novoyan War as the Novoyan Russians used everything, even experimental weapons from its arsenal.

Magnetic acceleration rifles, colloquially known as railguns, designed for the sole purpose of killing us, were the only force beyond heavy field artillery capable of slowing our advance.

422

I had thought the technology had been destroyed in the final months of the war when we raided their research facility. Destroying all blueprints and examples except those we captured and sealed away in time-locked vaults for future research. Where had this example been recovered?

The reminiscence is cut short by the audible click of two empty pistols as Andros Three ducks behinds the barricades, his action announcing the commencement of the end game.

"Oh monsters, will you not let yourself die?"

The taunting goad is shouted across the distance of the two opposing lines, as the enemy believes they have the upper hand. A single man stands out with cover, his smile evident as he encourages the forty men and women behind him to advance.

"Abominations like you should not exist, this world belongs to humanity, it shall be ruled by..."

His rhetoric is cut short by a knife slamming into his chest, thrown by my hand as I stand to my full height.

"No you are wrong, it is your death that has come."

Chapter Thirty Eight

From the southwest comes the roar of rotors, causing the smiles of the Insurrectionists to disappear as they realise what is coming. The order that once existed is extinguished as they panic and begin to flee, heading towards the rapidly closing gates in the distance.

Seeing their avenue of escape disappear, some stop and drag out the frightened civilians hiding nearby. With knives and pistols placed against their trembling flesh, they make threats and demands as they negotiate for their lives.

"Reaper One to Squad Andros, seek cover, initiating strafing run."

Coming from beyond the walls, they are still too far to see the hostages mixed into their ranks, but the lives of the civilians are a secondary concern to me. Though callous, what I wanted was the information contained within the heads of their remaining commanders, information that could complete the still incomplete picture.

Ares Commander to Reaper One, abort, abort. Standby and provide overwatch."

"Requiring authentication code"

Though the cannons are still locked onto the crowds, the incoming gunships slow their approach enough to allow me to respond.

"For the strength of the pack is the wolf, and the strength of the wolf is the pack."

"Authentication confirmed. Reaper One to Reaper Wing, abort, abort."

⸺◦◦◦⸺

Heavily armoured and armed gunships hover over us, encircling the Insurrectionists. The sight of turning rotary cannons cause all but three of the riflemen to surrender their arms and fall to their knees. Those still standing defiantly shout at their colleagues, encouraging them to stand fight, but even their grips loosen as they realise they are trapped and have nowhere to go.

Looking at their faces, I realise their youth, too young to be veterans of the former Novoyan military, their training however was on par or even beyond those received by the everyday soldier of the Confederation. These were no mere rebels who had stumbled upon a weapons depot, they had been trained to decapitate our leadership.

More rotors are heard from the west, this time flying past the Assembly grounds and heading towards the northern tower. Despite gunships encircling the perimeter to ensure no one can escape, nothing is heard from within, the marksmen realising that resistance would only guarantee their certain death.

With the situation under control, I open a channel, requesting the arrival of reinforcements to secure the prisoners for interrogation. But as the command channel responds to my query, I hear the sound of a disturbance in their background as someone shouts in clear displeasure, but the words are too distorted for even my ears to hear.

"Reaper Wing and Talon from Command, new orders, engage your targets, engage, engage."

Confusion is heard from the channel as a single voice speaks out.

"Reaper One to Command, repeat that command?"

But the opportunity for me to intervene and query is cut short by the appearance of a new voice on the channel, one filled with pain, weariness, and malice. It is a voice recognised by millions, the only voice that could silence my own.

"By my will, you will purge them from our lands, ensure nothing remains."

Within the space of a heartbeat, multiple missiles are launched from the six aircraft hovering over the northern tower, the white smoking trails impacting, sending shockwaves that shatter the glass on every floor. A continuous rain of metal rips through the floors as the under-chin rotary cannons are unleashed to their full potential, the flames billowing out ensuring that no one survives. Despite this, the guns from the gunships overhead remain silent.

"Reaper One to Command. Enemy foot has surrendered and mixed in with civilians. I repeat, surrendered and…"

"You do not question, you obey. Neutralise or I will ensure you join them. No assassins shall be allowed to remain, rip them apart until nothing remains."

I admire the conviction of the gunship commander as his wavering voice fought the moral battle, but no one can stand on those convictions when faced with their own death by someone filled with only malice.

The sudden spinning of rotary cannons causes panic and fear to appear on the faces of the civilians and Insurrectionists below them. There is no time to run before a steady stream of lead rips into the ground, as weapons designed to tear apart armoured vehicles shred everything in their path until nothing but unidentifiable chunks of meat remain.

Though the enemy is clearly dead, the cannons continue to fire, churning up the ground as a wall of red mist is thrown into the air. Behind me, the sound of vomiting and weeping announces the arrival of the requested reinforcements, their arrival in time to see the slaughter of innocents and guilty alike.

"Reaper One to Command, hostiles eliminated."

"Make sure, ensure their termination."

A double volley of missiles is launched from the six gunships, enough firepower to devastate an armoured column. Exploding, they burn the ground, causing the scent of burning flesh to waft in the air.

As the flames begin to settle, there is no trace of either the enemy or civilian dead.

Andros Three removes his helmet and turns to me, indicating with his fingers a single request, using a signal rarely used and known to few. Removing my own helmet, I look at his lips, watching as he speaks without sound. Having passed his message, he places his helmet on his head and moves towards the squad behind me. With a series of commands, he makes arrangements for the transportation of his brethren and the recovery of the scant survivors.

"What have we done Colonel? Is this what we had fought for?"

Silently spoken, those were words that no Praetor should ever utter. If even the indomitable could question, then what happened here today could only ever be seen as a travesty.

As my eyes continue to watch the dancing flames, I notice for the first time the still working cameras in the garden, the green lights showing their delivery of a still live feed. Everything which had just occurred had been broadcasted across the width and breadth of the Confederation.

I knew that the chaos of today was only the beginning, this final strike had given the Insurrectionists and rebels what they had always sought, martyrs. Public sympathy would be directed to their cause and just as the Lord Marshall had begun his war, but the war would not be fought from without but within. I look skywards as I prepare for the coming storm.

Arc 5: Rex Est Promissum

Chapter Thirty Nine

Command Centre, District Headquarters, Starlight City, District 4

52.03, 11.56

1630 hours, 14-11-2177 C.E.

"Welcome to BCBQ News, I am your host Chris Mayer and today we are joined by Executive Joseph Vertes from the Office of Executives."

"Thank you for having me."

"Executive Vertes, with all the ongoing rioting and disorder in the major cities, our viewers are growing increasingly worried. Is there anything we need to know?"

"Now Chris, let me tell your viewers and our citizens clearly, the military is coordinating an effort to restore order. I cannot tell

you more, but let it be clear, this movement is linked to the attempted

assassination of the Lord Marshall."

"Now that is a headline."

"As you can gather, they are highly organised and not just the

usual troublemakers. We will ensure that every single one is brought

to justice, not just those directly involved, but those assisting them."

"The events from two months ago were truly horrific, even now

it shocks me. Can you tell our viewers how the Lord Marshall is

recovering, he has not been seen in public since that day?"

"Of course, it is no secret, he is on the road to recovery and his

personal physician has predicted he will be fully recovered in a

matter of days."

"That is good to hear…"

I allow the channel to continue in the background as my hand

continues to swipe right on the tablet, my eyes flickering as I

continue to scan page after page of incident reports. The news had

remained the same in the days and weeks after the massacre, every

channel reporting the same story, but despite attempts by the

Executives to steer public sympathy, they had been too late.

Across every device, every citizen and every soldier had heard the Lord Marshall's speech, but they have also seen his fall and the devastation and destruction which came after. Though the footage had eventually been stopped, those closest to the scene knew the truth.

Despite the rapid deployment of intelligence agents to round up and detain eyewitnesses, some had escaped, joining the Insurrectionists in the underground as they sought their protection.

Acting no better than the tyrants of past regimes, we had sought to alter the truth, but the Insurrectionists finally had their spark and true victims for their cause, the Lord Marshall had gifted them the ultimate weapon.

Using short ranged radio broadcasts, they spread the testimonies of eyewitnesses, for every dozen signals traced back to their source, another two dozen had been created. Few of the public listened at first to the words, but soon they began to question the truth they had been told. Many were now thinking, what reason did these former soldiers who had fought for their nation to lie?

The truth that it was the Lord Marshall who had ordered the airstrikes, uncaring of the consequences which caused the needless loss of innocents was a bitter pill to swallow for many. His attempts to earn the public's trust and acknowledgement of his humanity by revealing his face had become a double-edged sword, he could no longer hide in the shadows.

The *ding* of an icon appearing on my tablet announces the arrival of another series of reports. I add the majority to the growing pile of unread, but a highlighted page catches my eye, containing words that had responded to an algorithm.

Minor in detail, it reported the attack of a factory that specialised in small arms manufacturing in the Second District. The damage had been minimal, delaying production by twenty minutes, but it was the method, not the result I was interested in.

Similar incidents were happening across the Confederation, the majority in the western districts which had suffered the loss of their Governors. Though small, they had been coordinated and efficient, the Insurrectionists slipping away with little trace. In isolation they could be ignored, but combined, they would slowly grind the behemoth of the imperial war machine to a halt before the new war had even begun.

Those in the east had seen little of the attacks, the rural areas still in the process of being reclaimed and reconstructed. Compared to the inexperienced security forces in the relatively peaceful west, those here were battle-hardened veterans who patrolled a still active warzone.

Here, in the fourth district, the geographical centre of the Confederation, the cities and their streets had remained relatively peaceful. Beyond the newly imposed curfews and increased military patrols as a result of the Omega Protocols, the lives of the citizens had changed little. But this was the result of hard work and a war being fought in the shadows, away from the scrutinising eyes of civilians.

Teams of infiltrators and intelligence agents monitored the work and movements of Insurrectionists within the borders, sifting through and grading any information being received. Whilst Specialist Operation Squads from the Territorial Army, overseen by

Amelia and Squad Gorgo, discretely removed dangerous elements before they became an inconvenience.

But in the last two days, the once constant flow of information, whispers, and rumours had stopped, as if the enemy had suddenly disappeared. Not even the laxest or complacent would greet this news with joy, experience warned me that this was when the enemy was most dangerous, that they were planning something with devastating consequences.

Setting down the tablet, I stretch and swivel my chair towards the window, my eyes gravitating towards the dark needle-like structure which dominated the skyline of the city, Facility 04.

The physical symbol of our power and ambitions, its destruction would cause the splintering and destruction of the empire, or at minimum decades of stagnation and decline. This is where I expected the enemy would strike, the hammer blow being harder than anything seen at the Assembly. That strike had been nothing more than a test of our defences and reactions, whilst exposing our weaknesses.

436

A chime from my desk breaks my darkened thoughts, the nearby monitor revealing a live feed of the corridor beyond the locked office door. The changes in protocol, requiring an invitation to my office had become increasingly inconvenient. I watch as Amelia stands on the other side, immobile as she waits for entry.

Flicking my hand, I de-activate the lock, watching as she enters and locks the door behind her.

"Welcome Colonel, what can I do for you today?"

Nonchalantly I ask the question as her heels create their distinctive rhythmic *clack*.

"Here are the updated reports you asked for."

Having already spent hours reading report after report, I had no wish to continue, instead, I trust in Amelia's work ethic and judgement.

"Is the situation better or worse than yesterday?"

"You can probably guess."

Knowing the answer only causes me to sigh in dissatisfaction, but her unusual response causes the edges of my lips to crease, forming the smallest of smiles.

437

"Is that sarcasm I am hearing?"

"Was it effective?"

"Mildly. Leave the reports on my desk, I will read them later. I am sure you have already disposed of anything irrelevant."

"And how would you like the other matter reported?"

Two weeks had passed since her return, her actions and mission having gone unnoticed, but the results of her efforts were concerning. Though I had known of the myriad of attempts by the Lord Marshall to infiltrate the projects overseen by myself, I had not known of the two "minor" successes.

Though the records of the infiltration had been meticulously expunged, enough remained to allow Amelia to track down those responsible. Though the majority had chosen to self-terminate, three of their number were now guests of our lower levels, watched over by Squad Gorgo and trusted veterans who had served me directly for more than a decade.

Amelia's courtesy had so far revealed the extent of their success, the smallest of errors which had led to the discovery of Orion. But how and why this information had ended up in an abandoned Novoyan facility was yet to be known.

As Amelia removes a series of bottles from a nearby cabinet and takes a seat with glasses in hand, my own hand moves to a circular, gold-tinted disc sat upon my desk. More reminiscent of an archaic coin than of a bullet, I twirl the disc between my fingers as I recognise the threat it represents.

Railgun technology was still relatively new seven decades ago, the smallest practical examples had been fielded on main battle tanks, but the Europa-Novoyan War had led to the development of prototypes small enough to be fielded by infantry.

Directly responsible for the death of a dozen Praetors, though our numbers had been greater then, each loss had been felt keenly. To ensure our battlefield dominance, we hunted down and destroyed every working example, eliminating the researchers and designers to prevent replication.

Only a dozen examples remained, sealed away in time-locked vaults, their locations known only to myself. Even with working examples and original blueprints, no efforts were being made to produce or improve on them, for existing gunpowder weapons were still sufficient and plentiful. Yet, here they were, once again being used to hunt our kind.

I did not yet know the link, if any, between the enemy within and without, from our past and present, but I suspected they were nothing more than aspects of a single entity. With the re-appearance of anti-Praetor weapons, the discovery of the mastermind's identity was now a priority.

Though I suspected the involvement of the Lord Marshall in his own assassination attempt, I did not have enough to challenge him openly and directly. Without evidence, the accusation alone would be viewed as sedition, the punishment being death for myself and everyone connected to me.

Previously, I would have sent Amelia, her skillsets perfect for gathering the information I needed, but with the looming spectre of war, I needed her to remain by my side. I would have to trust another to the role.

Locking the screen, I set aside the tablet and look up at Amelia who sits across from me. Her upright posture is perfect, a legacy of decades of military service and indoctrination. I suspected, no, I knew that even if a peaceful civilian life was offered to her, she would never truly embrace it. My gaze settles on her lips as she takes another sip, though the movement is barely noticeable, I knew immediately that something was wrong.

"Commander?"

As she questions my lingering gaze, I realise that it is a subject that places her ill at ease, one that she is not yet ready to broach.

"What is the mood in the city?"

"Unrest is low according to reports."

"No, I am asking if the people are happy?"

"I do not have that answer, would you wish for me to send out enquiry teams?"

Swivelling in my chair, I turn away from her and look down onto my city, the streets glistening as the winter sun hangs above it.

"Are you hungry?"

"It is still thirty minutes until our scheduled meal, but if you desire, I can request the chefs to prepare something?"

Hearing her response, I wryly smile and shake my head.

"I have been told there is a restaurant in the commercial sector which makes the finest rabbit stew. Would you care to join me?"

"I will make the appropriate arrangements…"

"There is no need, I plan to walk."

"With the current threat, I believe it unwise. A governor is a prize too great for even the wariest insurrectionist to ignore."

"We cannot hide whilst our citizens face such daily dangers, we were not made that way."

Exasperated, she forms a wry smile as she hears my reasoning, she already knows that no amount of "scolding" would alter my course, but that did not mean I did not heed her warning.

My left hand reaches down to the lowest drawer of my desk and removes a package wrapped in blue paper and tied by a ribbon. I throw it towards her and she catches it effortlessly, her eyes open wide in confusion as she notices the weight.

"Open it, it was made for you alone."

Untying the ribbon to reveal a three-piece figure-hugging garment, she runs her fingers across the woven fabric.

"This is…"

"Yes, the Mark VI. After what happened, I designed something new, something light and durable. It is not yet ready for mass production, but this should fit you perfectly."

Though society's attitudes towards genders were not as profound in this age, it would still be regarded as bold for a male to state their knowledge of the physical measurements of a female who was not their life partner. But such common conventions did not apply to Praetors, let alone Amelia. She and I had been together longer than married couples, experiencing moments that no one else had. She was as much a part of me as I was to her, a part that I would always protect.

"Then if I may?"

"You may."

Having gained my permission, she moves towards the entranceway of my private living quarters and unlocks it with her biometrics. Stepping through, she locks the door behind her.

Time barely passes before Amelia emerges from the door, her new armour fitting so perfectly that it is unnoticeable beneath her clothes. Collecting the pair of pistols sitting on my desk, I slide them into the covert holsters built into my jacket before offering Amelia my hand.

"Shall we?"

Wordlessly, she accepts, the smallest hints of a smile on her lips as she walks beside me. Side by side, we step out into the corridor and into the city beyond.

Chapter Forty

Dressed in business and workwear, men and women line both sides of the road, their movements hectic as they head home after a hard day's work. So absorbed in their thoughts, they do not notice the towering forms of Amelia and me as we walk side by side. Those that do, stop, gawping as they stare in our direction, their shoulders getting knocked repeatedly by those walking past them.

Their stares mean little to me, instead my gaze lingers on the trees that line the road, and their almost bare branches swaying side to side as the cold wind blows. The few lingering leaves are stripped away, dancing in the air before falling to the ground.

"You should relax more."

The ever-vigilant Amelia has been tense since we departed from the tower, only relaxing, barely, when we pass through the various security checkpoints.

"I would be more comfortable if we had travelled by convoy."

A wry smile forms on my lips as I continue east, passing through the commercial sector, the buildings bright with freshly painted signs and electronic billboards. Though other areas of the city possessed their own retail outlets, none of them compared to the quality and quantity available here.

Following the scent of freshly roasted game and rapture of laughter, we arrive at our destination, as expected, the interior is busy, the tables and booths filled with a mixture of families and working men and women.

Befitting the ambience, an archaic and rustic jingle comes from the door as I push it open. Barely a heartbeat passes before the laughter and conversation stop and I feel the stare of four dozen pairs of eyes.

"Welcome to Der Jaeger, how can we be of assistance?"

A man dressed in a tailored suit approaches, his bearing and mannerism making it clear he was the proprietor.

"Reservation for two under the name Smith."

Forcibly drawing his eyes away from the pistol at Amelia's side, he flicks through the booking sheets.

"Ah yes, did you indicate a preference for a table or a booth?"

I had never stated a preference, but as my eyes scan the interior, it is obvious from their uneasy stares that members of the military did not come here often.

"A booth, away from the windows if possible."

"Of course, yes, yes. Follow me."

Bobbing his head up and down in relief, he scurries across the room as he guides us to a darkened corner, far from the gazes of anyone entering through the door. Despite his obviously rude intent, the location is to my desire.

"Please be seated, my staff will be with you shortly. Of course, esteemed members of the military such as yourselves will be offered the best bottles as compliments of the house."

Soon a young waitress arrives, her blonde hair tied into a neat ponytail. With a nervous smile, she lights the candle and hands us our menus. Scanning through the diverse selection, I choose a series of simple dishes whilst offering suggestions of my own to Amelia.

Though a decade has passed since the removal of our psychological shackles, I had chosen to maintain a minimalistic

Spartan-esque lifestyle, only indulging when in the company of a select few and on specific, rare occasions. It was an ideology that I forced upon no other, though I believed that some, in their attempts to re-join humanity had begun to over-indulge.

Having noted our order, the waitress returns with a pair of unopened bottles of red wine, both chosen to complement our choices. I recognise the brand and dates stamped on the bottles, rare vintages from a now-extinct Bordeaux vineyard. The cost of a single bottle alone, let alone a crate would have been phenomenal.

With well-practised movements, she uncorks the first bottle and pours before leaving both on the table and moving away, allowing us to converse in private. Neither of us touches our glasses immediately, instead allowing the aroma of a fifty-year-old wine to fill the air.

Raising my glass in a toast, Amelia responds in kind, our glasses *clinking* together as her smiling features are illuminated by candlelight.

Cleansing my palette with a glass of water, I amusingly watch the disappointment on Amelia's face as she stares sorrowfully at her now empty plate. Each of the four dishes had been simple, but each had been seasoned and cooked perfectly with emphasis on the subtle flavours of the main ingredients. Having noticed my smile, Amelia questions me with her eyes as the waitress returns and clears the table.

Offering a pot of tea to complement our dessert, I find it to be rich and citrusy, reminiscent of what was once known as Earl Grey. It's impossible to truly replicate with the extinction of the bergamot orange, but no one under the age of fifty would remember what the original tasted of.

"You should give this a try."

Slicing a piece of her berry pie, she reaches across with her fork and invites me to take a bite. My eyes catch the glances of the waiting staff nearby, I smile wryly as I imagine their thoughts. Accepting the invitation, I bite down, finding the berries to be sweet and refreshing. Allowing Amelia to have a bite of my own dessert, I wave the waitress back to the table, her face etched with worry.

"Is there something wrong?"

Picking up the now empty bottles sitting on the table, I hand them to her.

"This wine was most enjoyable, I would like two to take with me. Can you make the arrangements?"

I watch as her features grow increasingly aghast as she reads the label, likely knowing well the cost of each bottle requested.

"Do not be mistaken, I intend to purchase the other two. Oh and bring me my bill as well."

"Are you sure? The price is quite…"

"That will not be an issue."

Immediately dismissing her concerns, I gesture for her to leave.

"I will speak to the owner."

Scurrying away with the now empty bottles, I soon hear the conversation in the distance as she explains the situation.

"Do they even realise the cost of this!"

Soon the proprietor arrives at the table, his movements doing little to hide his anxiety as he speaks.

"Excuse me, sir, my waitress has informed me that you would like to purchase two of these bottles. This vintage is quite hard to come by and the cost…"

"As I said, price is not an issue."

Sweating profusely, he bows his head in apology and directs the waitress behind him to hand over a pair of identical bottles and the bill. Barely glancing at the cost, I dismiss Amelia's movements as she attempts to pay for her portion.

Though the cost of the meal alone was a significant segment of a junior officer's monthly wage, it had skyrocketed due to the inclusion of the two bottles to something beyond the means of anyone but a senior officer.

Reaching into my inner pocket, I remove a series of glass objects, placing them on the table as the waitress and proprietor look on in confusion, having expected me to pay by card. Soon their eyes widen as they realise the value of what I had placed.

"Your service today was most excellent, feel free to keep the excess."

Extending my hand to Amelia, I lead her out of the booth and towards the door. As the bell rings, I hear the voice of the proprietor behind me.

"Please do come again."

◦◦—◦◦◦—◦◦

Walking shoulder to shoulder as we return to the tower, Amelia leans in close and speaks in a whisper.

"Commander, you do realise we attended a tier five restaurant?"

"Oh, did we now? I only heard the rabbit was delicious, was that pricing excessive?"

"It is a price beyond the means of the majority of the civilian population."

"Well, did you enjoy your meal?"

Feigning ignorance, I attempt to draw Amelia into a conversation about her only known vice. Instead, she continues to face me, her eyes questioning as she probes my intent.

"Civilians also choose to use pre-paid cards rather than currency."

"Oh, I never realised, guess I should use those next time."

Her lips crumple into a frown as she instantly recognises that my last response was a lie. I knew full well that physical currency was a rarity that few could afford. Pre-paid cards issued by banks were secured by biometrics, making it impossible for them to be gained by illicit means. Their use had made crimes of violence and dishonesties effectively redundant.

Physical currency however was made of a glass and plastic polymer with a microchip located at its centre. Highly secure, any attempts to remove the microchip or alter its information would cause it to overheat and render it useless. Ranging in value depending on their shape, squares, triangles, circles and hexagons, their main advantage being their near untraceable nature, compared to card payments which left an audit trail for others to follow.

Despite the value being carried on my person, I held no fear of being a victim of a crime. No thief would approach me or have thoughts of doing so, not whilst armed and dressed as I am. Even the bravest thief know that crimes against military personnel carried harsh penalties, usually death.

THIS IS A PUBLIC SERVICE ANNOUNCEMENT –
CURFEW WILL BEGIN IN THIRTY MINUTES. PLEASE
RETURN TO YOUR HOME ADDRESSES.

The announcement is blared across the street as the few remaining pedestrians hurry onto public transportation services. I watch their movements with sadness as the first of the security patrols drive past, the turrets of the armoured vehicles menacingly sweeping left and right.

This was not the Confederation I had once envisioned, as I glance at Amelia's face, I know that she shares this sentiment.

"Let us go home."

"Yes, Commander."

Chapter Forty One

Locking the door to my office, I turn my back to Amelia as she stands rigid behind me. Despite the silence, I knew she wanted to discuss something, something that others should not hear. With a flick of my wrist, armoured panels descend, isolating the room from the rest of the tower.

Hesitantly, she prepares to speak, but as her lips begin to move, I raise my hand to stop her.

"No, not here."

I point not at the chairs in the corner of my office, but the door leading to my residence. Nodding profusely, she smiles timidly as she understands my intent. Beyond that door was a place where rank no longer applied, a place where words could be spoken candidly.

⚜

Without any need for further direction, she effortlessly moves through my residence. Finding the kitchen, she removes a pair of crystal glasses and begins to pour from the first of tonight's purchased bottles.

Unbuttoning her shirt and hanging her tunic jacket on the back of a chair, she sits cross-legged with her back to the window. Illuminated by moonlight, her relaxed form was awe-inspiringly graceful.

Following her lead, I remove my jacket and tie, place them on a nearby table, and sit across from her. Taking the reserved glass, I take the first sip, the act being enough to break the tension.

"Permission to speak Commander?"

With a sigh, I close my eyes and force a smile, putting the glass down, I reach across and take hold of Amelia's hand. I can feel the tension running through her fingers.

"You know the rules of this place. No ranks and titles, whilst here I am no one but James, just as you are Amelia."

A moment of uneasy uncertainty forms on her face before her features soften. I see behind her visage the small hint of her recovering humanity, a part that has taken decades to form. As I felt the softness of her fingers, I finally realised how vulnerable she was.

456

Unable to look directly into my eyes, her glances are enough to hint at her internal struggle. Finally, having found her resolve, her face hardens.

"Why did you surrender your post as Lord Marshall?"

"Why did you surrender your post as Lord Marshall?"

Sensing my hesitation, she repeats the question whilst taking a firm grip of my hand. I knew now why she hesitated to ask me, she had already waited a decade. Though never expressed, the subject between us had become effectively taboo. Raising my eyebrows, I could only wonder what had caused her to finally ask.

"Amelia, why now?"

"Because too much has happened and I need to know."

"You should know the reason without me saying it."

No other could have asked the question and expect an answer, the ties that bonded us were deep, deeper than any other Praetor. It was beyond mere superior and subordinate, beyond comrade, family or spouse. It was all of those and more.

"I want to hear it from you this time."

"You and I were made for war, and that was our sole purpose. How could I, who has brought so much death and destruction, be the leader of others in this age of peace? I represent everything that had come before, all the pain, all the suffering.

Someone like me is ill-suited for the politics, I do not possess the subtleties, intrigue, and ruthlessness necessary…"

"And you believe Alexander was better?"

Shaking my head, I turn and face her directly as I give my answer.

"My successor was chosen by the Council, the same one that you sat on. You know what was discussed and the choices made."

Knocking back the contents of her glass, she places it heavily on the table as she shakes her head from side to side. As she speaks, her voice grows increasingly higher in pitch as her emotions begin to overwhelm her.

"Only by your insistence! None of us wished for a successor, you were and always will be our leader. His crown, his mantle, everything about him is false and unearned. No matter what the records now say, you were the first and greatest of us…"

458

As her emotions intensify, so does the latent energy emanating from her body. Reaching out, I take hold of her hand, hoping the physical contact would be enough to help her retain control.

"What right does he have to lead us? Where was his voice when the world condemned and abandoned us? It was not he who gave us hope when we were ordained to die. It was not he, who saved what remained of the world and created a dream for us to continue.

How can you watch everything you built become corrupted by that man's ideals and thirst for power?"

Emotions and energy long-sealed within her body begin to seep out as the mental barriers restraining them begin to crack. Moving quickly, I pull her towards me, locking her in an embrace as her voice grows increasingly desperate.

"Have we not fought, bled, and died enough? Are we not meant to be anything more? Do we not deserve peace? You would never have led us down this path…"

"Amelia, stop."

Gripping her tightly, I force my will onto her own as I suppress the energy flowing through her. Only power could suppress power, and only mine was equal or greater.

⋯⋯⋯⋯⋯⋯⋯

Time flows slowly, but I soon feel the arms gripped around my waist loosen as Amelia regains her control. Peering down, I watch as Amelia maintains a downward gaze, refusing to make eye contact as she recovers her steely exterior.

"You have grown."

Smiling, I speak the words I have long wanted to say to her. Designed to kill, designed to be expendable, designed to achieve the impossible, we were made to win wars. But the price of that power was the loss of everything that once made us human.

Our emotions, our thoughts were chained away and buried beneath layer after layer of conditioning. We knew of anger, trained to channel it, but we never knew hate and we certainly never knew love. Now that the chains had been discarded, could we truly control what we have never known or experienced before?

Philosophers once stated that the greatest sin for a soldier was abandoning their nation, but I had willingly made that choice four decades prior, for I believed in a greater sin. The sin of a commander wasting the lives of those under their command.

Ordered to make a pointless last stand, the United European Federation's Special Operations Command or EFSPOC had decided that humanity's greatest scientific achievements were no more expendable than a rifle if it could delay the advancing enemy by a day.

No one expected my treasonous decision, to retreat, to save what little remained and hideaway in time-locked bunkers. Who would have thought it possible that soldiers, indoctrinated, hypnotised, and chemically enslaved into unquestionable loyalty could betray them? They had underestimated us, no, they had underestimated me. I, the first, the progenitor, was something beyond their ability to understand and limit.

⚜ ⚜ ⚜

Upon discovering Amelia's hidden personality, I stroke her cheek whilst smiling in amusement. This sight was only possible after decades of psychological freedom. Whilst we were hidden away and forgotten in a world that was now ash, I had only hoped that my brethren would someday experience and regain their once lost humanity.

But that decision, to end the cycle of drugs, indoctrination and hypnosis had unforeseen consequences. Faults that had remained hidden until the chains had become too loose to be re-applied.

The emotions which allowed humanity to act with honour, courage, and loyalty, also allowed them to act ruthless and jealous. In the weak, such emotions were dangerous, but within the bodies of Praetors, the effects were unimaginable.

"The passage of time has shown that I was wrong. But if given the choice, I would make the same decision again."

Amelia's lips begin to move, to challenge what I have said, but I do not give her the opportunity.

"Despite the decades I have changed little. Even compared to you, I have regained little of my humanity. How can someone who does not understand humanity, lead them?"

Noticing the sincerity behind my words, she hesitates, understanding the differences which still exist between the enhanced and the unenhanced.

"What do you believe makes a human, human?"

Decades ago I had struggled to answer that philosophical conundrum. Even now, the answer I formed was nothing more than a vague concept.

"I have always believed that it was their concept of mortality. Knowing that their time is limited forces them to hurry, to appreciate every moment. Even for our kin, where a month is nothing more than a blink of an eye are not fully immune to the ravages of time."

Turning away from her, I look upwards at the argent moon.

"It could never have been me, nor you, nor even Tria. We near ageless beings who have never felt the spectre of natural death would only become the target of jealousy and displeasure."

With a melancholic sigh, I finish airing my thoughts.

"Those who are short-lived have never been seen as anything more than pieces of a board, to be used where necessary to achieve our goals. Where I am now, hidden away from the public is where I am most suited"

"Do you sincerely believe that Alexander sees them as anything other than that?"

Without any hesitation, I shake my head, removing any misconceptions she may have had.

"No, I never did, but he understands their fears better than any of us. At the start, I did believe he was the most worthy of being my successor, but his ambitions have changed this view."

Hearing that final remark causes her to stare at me, her eyes full of expectation. I already know what she was planning to ask.

"Would you…"

"Only as a last resort and if no other is worthy."

With my true thoughts aired, I turn, avoiding Amelia's gaze and stare at the illuminated tower that dominates the skyline.

"Humanity does not have enough patience. Because of their mortality, they expect results instantly, unable to wait months, let alone years or decades. As Lord Marshall, I would have been a figurehead, aloof and distant, presiding over a stagnating empire."

"But…"

Hesitantly at first, she soon finds the words to express her resolve. Her eyes burning with smouldering anger, one unseen outwith of war.

"Would you have led us down this new path of war?"

Closing my eyes, I consider her question. Alexander's every action has been a miscalculation, from his use of war to distract the citizens from the ongoing internal strife to the revelation of Orion.

Why had he chosen to reveal Orion? It is a question I have been trying to answer daily. Would he place the entire project in a precarious position purely for a political victory, or was there another aim?

But looking into Amelia's eyes, it is clear that the anger within them is unrelated to the deaths of civilians and soldiers in the future, but those much closer.

"Their deaths could not have been foreseen."

Chapter Forty Two

Seigfried Braesail, Phillip Bastogne, names unknown to others until the "Assembly Massacre". Though their names had become immortalised in stone, they were more than Praetors of distinguished service or governors of the second and third districts, they were our closest friends.

"They both died a soldier's death. They had no regrets before the end."

Despite my words, internally, I believed their loss could have been avoidable. If only they had been wearing their armour, if only they had not been placed at the front of the stage, to be used as exhibits for Alexander's political manoeuvers.

"Jam…"

Stuttering, she unexpectedly mumbles my name before placing her glass down on the table. Moving, she stands up, joining me shoulder to shoulder to look upwards at the night sky.

"Do you remember what Alexander's and Anthony's monikers were during the War?"

Nodding, I wordlessly answer her question. How could I forget their morbid monikers? Names which they embraced during their missions within the reconnaissance squads. Anthony "Hound" Oates and Alexander "Reaper" Corsica.

"Do you remember the stories, especially surrounding Oates?"

"High Command investigated them, there was never any proof that he was involved in those massacres."

My words are passionless as I repeat the rhetoric of the time. Despite those statements, I knew the truths behind the rumours. The desperate hierarchy needed victory and would do anything, no matter the cost to achieve it.

Oates was only one of many, each carefully selected to perform "assignments" of which I had no oversight. He and many others working under the supervision of Alexander caused the disappearances of entire towns and villages within the Novoyan Russian heartlands.

All evidence of their crimes were buried and destroyed, ensuring not even a lengthy investigation could unearth the truth. Despite those efforts, the rumours and whispers continued, lingering and tainting the Regiment's battle honours.

Though we were already seen as inhuman, I sought to preserve what little remained of the Regiment's humanity and moved to erase those "mistakes". But the escalation in the war separated us into far-flung bunkers and when we emerged into the "New World", I regretfully needed every Praetor and allowed them to live. That judgement and excuse was my mistake.

"He was already a failure of the indoctrination programme and has only become increasingly unstable. He needs to be removed from his position. Alexander only uses him as his guard dog and assassin, not as an assistant."

"Any formal request would only be blocked, and I no longer have the authority to remove him."

My words have an unexpected effect as Amelia straightens to her full height and takes my hands with her own. Screaming without restraint, tears flow like rivers down her cheeks as her voice becomes laced with countless emotions.

"You cannot wash your hands of this!

With a single word, three-quarters of our remaining numbers would march without hesitation to the Capital. You are Primus, the firstborn, the first and only Colonel of the Praetorian Grenadiers. You are the Daemon of the West, the First Lord Marshall, and Master of the Britannic Confederation, how can you ever say you have no authority!"

Emotionally drained her legs collapse, causing her to fall to the floor as she buries her face into her hands. Crying, she shivers as the adrenaline passes through her body. As her skin begins to glow, I realise the extent of the damage to the barriers restraining her gifts.

Kneeling, I wrap my arms around and pull her in tight. Listening to her cries of anguish, her tears soon soak my chest as I stroke her hair and whisper into her ear, helping her rebuild the barriers from scratch.

"But what of the other quarter? Would you wish for our siblings to fight each other in a civil war?"

Being this close, I feel the whirlpool of emotions raging within her, and I already know the lack of effect my words are having. Closing my eyes, I clear my mind of doubt and settle my conviction. Without hesitation, I speak the words that need to be said, despite the regret I may have in the future.

"Listen well, wherever a tyrant should rise and commit unspeakable crimes, I will slay them. Either alone, or with the armies I command, no tyrant shall escape my sight, and I will not be blind to the plight of the innocent. This I vow with my true name, Primus."

Releasing my grip, I shuffle back and take hold of her right hand with both of my own. Kissing her fingers, I look, expectantly into her eyes.

"Do you, Altera, the other half of my soul, bear witness to this vow?"

On shaking legs, she stands to her full height. Looking downwards, she meets my gaze and nods. In a scene reminiscent of fairy tales, she affirms the vow.

"I, Altera, bear witness to this vow. May you honour it."

The tension that once permeated the room dissipates as Amelia smiles, a pure smile that had been unseen for a century. Now that her eyes have regained their usual composure, I pick up the final bottle and pour a pair of glasses.

"Do you remember the beach we used to walk?"

With a wry smile, Amelia accepts the glass and takes a seat.

◦◦◦ ◦◦◦ ◦◦◦

Amelia lies limp in my arms as I carry her to the bedroom and place her gently on the bed, choosing the side opposite to the one I normally slept on. Her now restored mind would never know the petty trick I had played.

Placed within the subconscious of every Praetor was a series of controls, triggers that would remove all thought and reason. I alone knew of their existence, having stolen the list from our creators. The only remaining record of their existence remained within my memory, to ensure they could never be used against us.

Untying her bun, I allow her long, soft, and luxurious hair to flow down the side of her face, being careful to move the loose strands away from her eyes and mouth. Stroking her sleeping, peaceful face, I look at her with eyes filled with sadness, regretting the myriad of secrets that had to exist between us.

Though my own body and mind were on the verge of exhaustion, I still had business to resolve. Placing the duvet over her body, I kiss her right hand before walking away.

Loosening the muscles of my shoulder, I lean back in my chair and begin to remove the contents of a container that had only just been returned. Carefully placing the navy blue uniform on the table, my eyes are drawn to the metallic threads of the embossed sword and crown as I remember the vivid dream I had experienced.

Beneath, wrapped in cloth is the pendant which Amelia borrowed. Twirling it in my hands, I run my fingers over the engraved *lambda* symbol and the central gem which was more beautiful than any cut sapphire.

Presented as a "gift" to reward my dedication, the gem had been excavated from the ruins of an ancient Spartan temple dedicated to Poseidon, the Greek God of the Sea. Harder than any diamond, its composition was unlike anything Mankind had seen before, and beyond their abilities to replicate.

To the majority, it was nothing more than a benign gem, but when held in the hands of those with certain genetic markers, it would radiate an otherworldly light. The greatest minds could not explain the phenomenon, the only clue to its purpose and origins being an engraving on the altar which housed it.

Ατλαντίδα

Atlantída or Atlantis, a fictional continent from the dialogue and writings of a delusional ancient philosopher. Unconcerned about a land of myths and legends, historians disregarded the etchings and the world would forget of the gem's existence.

That is until a second gem was discovered. Similar in appearance, but different in composition, this second gem was found within an ancient crypt beneath the ruins of the Library of Alexandria.

Volatile and unstable, this second gem was different, containing immeasurable energy which was on the verge of escape. Unable to be examined let alone harnessed safely, it was both a potential weapon and the cure for Mankind's increasing energy demands.

The knowledge of the gems was restricted to a dozen individuals, only three of whom remain alive. Only the "Alexandrian Star" was sealed away in the deepest vaults, never to see the light of day until Mankind's technological achievements reached the stage that it could be examined safely.

Having found that the benign "Lacedaemon Lazuli" glowed when in the proximity of another, acting as a compass, it was given to me. A "gift" to allow the tracking of any others which may exist, to prevent the energy contained within to be misappropriated, for only we were trusted enough to never use them as a weapon or reveal their existence to the world.

⊷⊷——◌⚓◌——⊶⊷

Clamping down on both sides of the pendant, I twist my hands in opposite directions, hearing an audible *click* as a hidden compartment opens. No larger than a fingernail, I remove the card hidden within.

474

An archaic form of memory storage, it takes a while for the files to be downloaded and converted into a modern format. One by one, I scroll through the list of files, each containing forgotten knowledge from an age of science until I find what I am looking for.

Entering the password to break the encryption, the word "CHECKMATE" appears on the screen as the first of a series of videos play. The man at the centre of each is gaunt. His skin is grey, His health is poor as he coughs up blood during every speech. It was a man that I knew well, the adopted father of Amelia and me.

It was recorded as he neared the end of his life with cancer having ravaged him from within. His voice is firm, however, as he speaks of the origins of the Praetors, our true origins, and one which I had kept secret even from her.

As the final video comes to an end, he stares into the camera, as if expecting this moment. He asks a simple question; "Are you ready?"

Without hesitation, I open the final file which contains not only the secrets of creating Praetors, but how to kill them.

Interlude II: Choices

Chapter Forty Three

The scent of uncut wheat and roses causes my nose to twitch, the smell waking me slowly from my slumber. My hands move, feeling the material beneath me, finding it soft and luxurious. The unexpected sensation causes me to gasp, my eyes opening as my heart races in recognition, silk!

The sight which greets me is not the darkness of the open night sky or that of the forest, but the darkness of a marble roof. Turning my head in confusion, the only light that enters the room is from the open window, allowing me to see the faint outlines of wooden furniture.

Pushing myself upright, I allow the covers to fall and I feel an instant chill. Looking down, I wrap my arms around my shivering body and look for something to wear. Gone are the thick furs and winter layers I had become accustomed to, replaced with a thin white chiton that barely covers my body.

As my eyes grow accustomed to the darkness, I see the room clearly. I am alone, no one but me sleeps here. On the other side of the large room is a set of double doors, golden light shining from underneath.

I shout out, seeking assistance, I call for the Captain, the names of my guards, Helena, and finally my sister, but no one answers. I have no memories of coming here, the last being setting camp in the forests of the north after the fall of the fortress and the battle in the clearing.

Pulling down the last of the covers, I expose the entirety of my body. My skin was perfect, unblemished by injury or the bruising caused by wearing armour. If I had been injured, enough time had passed to erase all traces.

A warm wind enters from the open window, causing a stream of rose petals to land on my bedsheets. Picking them up, I find them to be red, delicate and soft to the touch. Flowers such as these do not grow in the harsh northern realms.

As further petals enter the room, swept in by a warm, soothing and familiar breeze. It is far different from the cold, bitter winds of the north, more akin to those of the central realm. The summery scent causes me to feel a familiarity with the room, a feeling which I immediately dismiss as impossible. It was easier to imagine this was the home of a northern noble, only they could furnish a room this finely.

Swinging out my legs, I allow them to drop to the floor before recoiling in shock as my bare skin touches the cold stone. Hesitantly, I place one foot after another on the ground once more, ignoring the cold as I stand on shivering legs.

The bed I had been lying on was long and wide, crafted from aged oak, and carved with half-hidden designs. All the furniture was made of the same material, everything within was fitting for nobility and royalty.

On a nearby table was placed a folded blue robe. Picking it up, I find it to be soft, warm, and made from the finest wool. It was clearly meant for me and as I wrap around myself, the chill which lingers in the air is instantly taken away.

Following the breeze's trail, I stand on the open balcony and look out onto the view beyond the room, the sight causing my heart to flutter. I close and open my eyes repeatedly as I grasp hold of the balcony, unwilling to believe what I was seeing. Before me was the city of my birth, the Crown Capital, a place that could not be mistaken; Artlars.

Tears form in my eyes, growing in volume before bursting and running down my cheeks. My legs grow weak, only the hold on the balcony prevents me from falling. Crawling to the corner of the balcony, I move aside the potted plant. Beneath is an etching, crude in design, the work of a young child. A dry laugh escapes my lips, laughter which lasts until my throat grows dry and I begin to cough. No wonder the room was familiar, I was finally home.

Wiping away the tears, I gaze beyond the balcony to the city below, everyone but a few are sleeping. Those not, are illuminated by torchlight as they cross the numerous bridges which divide the city.

I listen to the flowing waters of the various rivers which run through the city, natural moats which defended it from invasion. The island and the lands surrounding it were natural fortresses, designed by our patron God before his departure to the realms beyond the horizon. They could never be replicated by mortal hands.

A bell tolls in the distance, a chime that carries itself across the expanse beyond the city walls. Beyond, in the darkness, lie golden fields and green meadows, the torches which show the locations of the outlying towns and villages twinkle like flickering stars.

A knock on the closed doors causes me to turn around. The golden light streaming beneath is broken by the shadow of a person. Running quickly, I open the doors, hoping to gain the answers I so desperately needed. But as I fling them open, no one is on the other side.

Looking out, I search for the person who had stood there, but no one is in the corridors and there are no sounds of footsteps. There is no warmth here, only a chill that causes me to wrap the robe tighter to my body as I step out.

The only light comes from above, the warm glow I had seen from the other side of the door is gone. The torches hanging on the walls are long dead, with not even dying embers remaining. Trying the doors on both sides, I find them all locked and no one answers my cries.

At the end of the corridor is another set of double doors, golden light shining from below as the sound of laughter and singing comes from the other side. Desperately, I try the handle, finding it locked. Punching, kicking, I lash out at the door as I scream for the Captain, calling for anyone, but no one answers, despite the moving shadows.

Exhausted, I slide down the length of the door before collapsing on the tiled floor, my limbs bruised and numb. Crying, I stand and turn back, following the corridor back to my room. Whoever brought me here had done so for a reason, they would come for me.

⋆⊰────◯⸙◯────⊱⋆

Locking the door behind me, I collapse onto the bed. Wrapping the covers around me, I hide from the world and begin to cry, crying until my tears soak through the silk sheets.

"*Selesia*"

The voice that calls for me is barely above a whisper, but in this empty room, it was loud enough to hear, even above my whimpers. They sound close as if the person was in the same room.

Peeking out from the covers, I wipe away the tears as I gaze in the direction of the sound, but no one is there. Instead, there is the glint of something metallic, something which was not there before.

Breaking free from my cocoon, I grasp the silver necklace hanging from the wardrobe door. Shaped like a soaring eagle, its talons clutched a single, large amber gem. I recognise it immediately, one of nine counterparts to my ring, the one that was worn by the queen.

As I affix the chain to my neck, wondering why it was here, the wardrobe door creaks open, revealing a set of silver armour, my own. Repaired and burnished, it was as resplendent as the day I had received it. With each revelation, I begin to question the intentions of the person who had brought me here.

Wary, I fit the various sections of armour to my body, the weight and restrictions giving me comfort due to its familiarity. Armed with a sword and dagger on my hip, I was prepared for whoever came through those doors.

"Selesia"

The hairs on the back of my neck rise as I sense a presence behind me. Turning, I draw my dagger and aim it in the direction of the gaze, but no one is there. On edge, I move to the door and confirm it is locked, only the balcony was open, but the cliff beneath was impossible to climb.

Fluttering cloth catches the corner of my eye, drawing them to the table near the balcony. Previously uncovered, now the table was topped with white cloth and a basket of freshly baked loaves and an amphora of wine. The enticing smell causes my stomach to gently growl. Though the intentions of the mysterious patron remained unknown, I did not believe they would go to all this trouble to poison me.

Sheathing the dagger, I tear apart the loaves of bread and place them in my mouth. Warm and with the perfect blend of soft and crunchy textures, it does not take long before the basket is empty. As I wash the final mouthful down with wine, I feel a shiver journey down my spine. This time I do not turn, but stand straight and clear my throat.

"Thank you for your hospitality."

I sense no malice from the lingering gaze, but despite my response, they remain silent. Growing nervous, sweat begins to form on my brow.

"I am aware this is the summer palace, but how did I get here?"

Again there is no response. Growing desperate, I ask the question that mattered.

"Are my sister and lady in waiting safe?"

"For now."

The voice that answers is gentle and disembodied as if the speaker was not really there.

"If I am at the capital, is the war with the Usurper over?"

"Not yet, but it will be soon if you take the wrong path."

The cryptic answer confuses me, unable to resist any further, I turn to face them. Despite the speed of my movements, I find they have already left.

"Come out and see the truth."

A new shiver travels down my spine as I hear the whispered words coming from behind. Understanding how powerless I was, I obey the instruction and follow the voice to the balcony.

Greeted by smoke and ash, my eyes water as I cough, choking on the disgusting smell. Unable to turn back, I wait for the wind to blow and when it does I am greeted by the sight of a burning city.

"Impossible."

Spluttering my response, I look on in despair. Artlars should never have fallen this quickly, but the once-solid walls were cracked and fallen, smoke rising from every corner. No matter where I looked, all I could see and hear was death and destruction.

"Nothing is impossible, anything is possible if a person with power chooses to make it possible."

Turning towards the voice, I draw my sword and dagger. Revealing themselves for the first time is a woman, wearing an almost transparent green dress, her pale white skin is in contrast to her long black hair.

"What is this? What have you done to my city?"

Having barely contained my rage, I scream the question as I step forward, the blades in my hands held threateningly.

Glancing at the sword with a look of displeasure, she raises her hands dismissively, causing a strong wind to blow. Silk drapes fly across the room and wrap themselves around my wrists and limbs, binding and tightening until they force me to release the blades.

"Who are you?"

I knew she was a magician, one who was capable of overwhelming me, but few still lived who could do so. The descriptions of those I knew of, did not match the woman before me.

"You should know who I am, are you not also a wielder of the golden arts? Like your uncle and beloved father?"

"Do not speak of that traitor, tell me, what have you done to my city?"

As if bemused by my question, she glances over my shoulder.

"Done? I have done nothing."

"Do not mock me. If you have done nothing, then why is Artlars burning?"

Drawing a fan, she covers her lips as she laughs in response to my anger. The humiliation causes my anger to grow and I lash out, trying to break free of the binds.

"Your eyes must be mistaken princess, I see nothing burning."

"Are you blind? Can you not see?"

Growling in disbelief, I turn my head, preparing to rebuke her as I remember the sight of the city blanketed in flames and smoke. Instead, I find nothing but serenity, as if the destruction had never happened.

"An illusion?"

No, what you saw was a possibility, of a path that has not yet come to pass. I will now unbind you, but if you wish to know more, you shall not raise your hand to me again."

Rubbing my wrists as the bindings on them loosen, I look at the women, this time unclouded by anger. She is young and beautiful, though she appears to be barely older than me, I can tell from her aura that she is older, much older.

"Why have you brought me here from the north?"

"You are mistaken, you have never left the north."

Despite the fluttering fan hiding her lips, I can tell by her cheeks and eyes that she is smiling. As if she was amused at my inability to understand my situation.

"Everything you have experienced is nothing more than a strand of fate."

"Are you telling me, it is my destiny to see the destruction of my home?"

"Yes and no. Though there are many paths where this fate is averted, they are few and grow fewer with every passing hour."

Pausing, as if in thought, she closes her fan and looks at me. Despite the emptiness I see within them, I cannot look away. Shaking her head, she sighs, giving me an answer to a question I had yet to ask.

"Once a path has gone so far, the fate shown in visions cannot be stopped, no matter how much you struggle. Only your choices early in the path will decide which strands continue and which shall falter, but know that this fate will be the result of your failure."

I shiver in response to her words, the darkness in her eyes are harrowing. A bottomless well of knowledge should not exist behind such a youthful face. Despite knowing that her power is beyond the perception of mortal men and women, I still peek at her essence. The foolish act causes me to cough up blood as I am overwhelmed.

Her soul was enriched with a golden light, a light that should not exist in still living beings. Even royalty whose blood is comparable to those of demi-gods does not shine with such brilliance. I am afraid of the unknown being before me and remain frozen as she steps towards me.

"Foolish child, you have seen something no mortal should see. Are you now afraid, Crown Princess Selesia of the House of Thaeolus? I expected more from someone whose bloodline, though diluted, is descended from the very Gods."

Those words filled with mocking laughter causes my blood to boil. No longer afraid, I stand and begin to chant. Despite knowing the difference in power, I must challenge them nonetheless. The words on my lips flow like music as a growing heat forms on my hands.

"O ágia pnévmata, akoúste tin klísi mou.

489

Sas diatázo na mou dósete dýnami.

Afíste tous echthroús mou sto skotádi…"[6]

Though the chant is long, once complete it is unstoppable, a flame which not even the heroes of ages past could endure without succumbing. Just as the final syllable leaves my lips, she flicks her wrist, trapping me in a whirlpool of wind and slams me into the balcony ledge.

The impact is enough to cause the stone to crack and dent my armour. Coughing up blood, the spell that I had weaved becomes unstable.

"So there is still fight in you. Good, you will need it in the wars to come."

Dismantling the spell with nothing more than a twirl of her finger, she scatters the collected magic. I stare in amazement, for not even my instructors had performed such a feat with so little effort.

---

[6] Ω άγια πνεύματα, ακούστε την κλήση μου. Σας διατάζω να μου δώσετε δύναμη. Αφήστε τους εχθρούς μου στο σκοτάδι ... - Oh holy spirits, hear my call. I command you to grant me strength. Banish my enemies into the darkness...

Walking towards me, she kneels and strokes my face and hair, a glowing smile plastered on her lips.

"I will help you find your path. When you wake, go north. Follow the eagles who bear my message. There you will find me once more."

"You are…"

As she touches my forehead, I feel my body and mind grow weaker. Closing my eyes, her face and voice disappear as I am greeted by darkness.

Chapter Forty Four

A long agonising scream escapes my lips as I awaken. Blinking, I look up at a darkened sky, one created by the canopy of a forest. Staring up in confusion, I feel strong hands grasp my shoulder and hold me in place. Lashing out, I try to fight them off, screaming in anger and fear.

"Princess, wait, it's me. Calm yourself."

Recognising the voice, I stop fighting. Blinking, I clear away the tear and look up at the woman holding my shoulders. With tanned skin and long black hair that accentuated her exotic beauty, it could be no other.

"Artemesia?"

Loosening her grip, she lets out a sigh of relief though the concern is clear in her eyes.

"Did you have a nightmare, your Highness?"

Turning my head, I look at my surroundings, finding only the cold summer sky and roaring fires of the campsite instead of the city of Artlars.

"Yes, nothing more than a nightmare. Please return to what you were doing."

Her examining gaze causes my cheeks to blush in embarrassment. Satisfied, she nods her head before moving away and sits down on a log near the fire. Pouring water over a black block of whetstone, she lathers it completely before sliding her sword up and down it repeatedly.

Standing up, I move towards the fire and sit across from her. Stretching out my arms, I warm my hands close to the flames as I watch her rhythmic movements, the sight relaxing. Though I could not admit it, the dream had unsettled me. Whether real or not, I had seen a glimpse of a nightmarish future.

Shivering, I glance at the sleeping forms of my sister and lady in waiting, who had thankfully remained asleep despite the screams. Walking towards them, I kneel and stroke their hair affectionately.

Instinctively, they smile in response to my gentle touch, the innocent act enough to fill my heart with guilt.

Now unable to sleep, I move away from the group and begin to stretch, following the sequence used by the Captain to loosen stiff muscles. As I lean over and begin to stretch the muscles in my back and legs, I hear the sound of something metallic fall to the ground.

⊶⊰———◉◡◉———⊱⊷

My heart stops as I recognise the light radiating from the amber gemmed silver necklace, how could I not after that vivid dream. Fearfully, I pick it up, cradling it in my hands as my fingers run along the chiselled design.

With grim resolve, I bring the necklace close to my ring, hoping for no reaction. Instead, my heart sinks as they both emit a pale blue light. I fight back the tears as I understand the message hidden within the dream, how could I not, with a royal gem was so far from the presence of the Queen.

"Your Highness, you have grown pale."

Hiding the necklace in the sleeves of my cloak, I turn to face Artemesia, a well-practised fake smile plastered on my lips.

"I am fine, just famished."

She carefully watches me before nodding in satisfaction.

"Please take a seat, I will prepare some food."

Picking up the pot that is hanging over the open flame, she carefully ladles a portion of its contents into a bowl. Though it is nothing more than a simple gruel, I accept it gratefully. Though it had little taste, it is warm and nutritious.

"Go north."

A faint woman's voice is carried by a gentle breeze, a wind that is enriched with the scent of wheat and roses. Though Artemesia feels the breeze, she does not react to the voice or the scent.

"Did you hear that?"

Reacting immediately to my words, she kicks a nearby sleeping guardsman and draws her sword.

"Markos!"

Though he is rudely and abruptly awakened, he reacts instinctively, hefting his sword and shield as he stands. Keeping me in the middle, they wait and listen before relaxing.

"Anything?"

"No, I see and hear nothing."

Satisfied, Artemesia sighs as she sheathes her sword. Turning towards me, she questions what I heard. It is obvious that no one else heard the voice or smelt the unusual scent. I lower my eyes as my cheeks glow crimson in embarrassment.

"I thought I heard something in the wind. It was my mistake, I am not myself tonight."

Noticing my embarrassment, neither choose to push the subject further. Instead, Markos laughs and places the shield back on the ground, forming a makeshift pillow as he prepares to go back to sleep. A wry smile forms on Artemesia's lips as she takes a seat and begins to hammer out the dents in her shield.

"Your Highness, do not leave my side. My people tell tales of wanderers being drawn to the dark hearts of forests by words and songs of spectres and shades, to be consumed and tortured. They would find a bearer of the *sight* an irresistible temptation."

"*Pffft.* Is that the kind of nonsense they teach on an all-woman island?"

Barely muffled laughter comes from Markos as he turns and looks in our direction. The tension which had once existed is ended by a towel being thrown in his face and the first of a series of arguments between him and Artemesia.

Though the mood is lightened, I notice their eyes continue to glance in the direction of the trees. Beyond the boundaries of the campsite, there was only darkness, and it was easy to get lost.

Artemesia's warning is unneeded, I knew better than most the dangers of the northern forests where magic still lingered. But I did not sense any malice from the woman in my dreams or from the voice I had just heard.

I smile as Artemesia's and Markos's bickering comes to an end, the pair leaning back and supporting each other like a married couple. The pride dwelling within both would never allow them to admit the truth which was evident to the eyes of others.

With her tanned complexion, all knew that Artemesia was a child of the island of the Amazons, but how and why she had arrived on our shores was never revealed to me. Stories circulated that she was a slave or prisoner of war who had earned her freedom due to the whims of a noble, but I believed she had sailed to our shores to seek a challenge. Despite my interest, I had not yet dared to ask the question.

The sound of snapping twigs draws our attention to the darkness. Immediately standing, both hold their shields and swords high as they move towards the sound, an ominous tension filling the air as I draw my dagger.

The appearance of five figures, including a giant in silver however eases the tension, allowing us to relax. The Captain noticing that I was awake bows as he approaches.

"We have returned Princess."

I glance over his broad shoulders, checking for any signs of injuries on him or his party. Barely a week had passed since our pyrrhic victory and in the hope of avoiding our many pursuers, we had chosen to use paths known to only a select few.

I smile at the bronze armoured man who kneels to the left of him, a bow and spear strapped to his back. No more than three years older than I, his youthful body was ravaged with scars, each the price of

498

ensuring the safety of those who lived in this realm. Now, out of the thousands who had once guarded the fortress city, he and Eleni were all that remained.

"Belen, you have done splendidly, leading us safely thus far. When this journey is over, I will reward you something befitting your loyalty and sacrifice."

"Your Highness, you exaggerate my meagre skills. Being in your company alone is an honour and privilege. I need no other reward."

A large gauntleted hand lands squarely in the centre of the man's back, causing him to gasp in surprise. Each slap is joined by the sound of laughter from the man beside him.

"Too stiff. Accept the praise, whether you like it or not, you are one of us now."

His laughter is joined by the remaining members of the Royal Guard who have already begun to cluster themselves around the fire.

"Now let us eat."

With a single command, Markos begins to slice and grill the freshly caught rabbits. Not wishing for my sister and Helena to miss the chance to feast on the freshly cooked game, I gently shake them awake.

⋯⋯◦◦◦⋯⋯

As the others enjoy their meal, I remain silent and gaze at the moon, allowing my mind to drift and wander as I remember the dream and vision of the future.

"Go north, but what is north of here?"

Unconsciously, I speak the words too loudly, catching the ears of Helena and the Captain who are sitting nearby. Instantly realising my mistake, I turn away, trying to hide my eyes as the Captain shuffles closer.

"Has something happened?"

My attempts at hiding the truth quickly end under the intensity of his boring gaze. Knowing that I did not have the wit to lie, I repeat what I had said.

"I was asking what is north of here."

Unable to answer the question due to having only a rough knowledge of the area, the Captain instead turns to the ablest person of the group, Belen.

"North of this camp there is nothing."

"Are you sure?"

Sensing a degree of falsehood in his words, the Captain turns to Eleni who shakes her head, the terrain this far from the fortress was unknown to her. Dissatisfied, he questions him further.

"There are no villages, nor towns and cities. The land is barren and desolate and no one willingly goes north of here."

"And what of the unwilling?"

Sensing a play in his words, I lean forward, pushing past the Captain as he tries to hold me back. Noticing my desperation, Belen stares at me, his gaze like that of a hunter sizing up their prey.

"Why do you ask?"

"What insolence…"

Artemesia moves to draw her sword but is quickly restrained by Markos as the Captain waves his hand.

"We will ignore insolent tongue if you answer the princess's question. She would not ask it without reason."

Sensing the murderous mood of those around him, Belen quickly changes tack.

"My apologies, there are secrets that we of the north must keep. Even on the pain of death."

"I had a…vision…."

Nodding his head, he accepts my ambiguous words and smiles, as if he understood the reason behind my desperation.

"As the princess has heard her voice, I will reveal the truth. North of here is a cave, within it, beyond a myriad of mazes and traps is the hidden home of the Oracle."

A single word, a single name was enough to convince the others of the reason behind his willingness to risk his life. The Oracle, a near-divine being, had abandoned her duties and retainers before the start of the Civil War, disappearing without a trace. When the chaos started, many believed she had been murdered by the Usurper, to remove the first of many hurdles to his scheme.

Despite the rumours, I had believed different. Not even my uncle, who was mad in his thirst for power would murder a direct conduit to the Gods. The Oracle was neutral, there was value to him for her continued existence.

"How far away is this cave?"

"Your Highness, if you choose to go there, you will be unable to reach the Kivos Estate before the arrival of the invading armies."

His words pierce my desperate heart, causing me to dig my nails into my arm as I am reminded of the sacrifices made by others. Despite this, I knew I had to go north.

"I will go alone, draw me a map."

"Noooo…"

I feel the arms of my sister wrap around me, burying her face into my chest as she sobs upon hearing my unexpected words. It is an unbefitting display for a princess, but it is clear that everyone else shares the sentiment.

"My sister shall continue as planned and deliver this message with Eleni. It will be her duty also to continue the bloodline."

Though it causes my heart to shatter further, I pry away my wailing sister and hand her over to Helena who cradles her within her arms. Staring at the Captain, I match his stoic glare with one of determination.

"I will not stop you if you explain yourself properly."

Revealing the necklace hidden within my clothes, I hear gasps of recognition from the Royal Guardsmen.

"I have glimpsed upon the strands of fate and been given a warning. From that dream, I have been given this as a reminder."

They look aghast as they understood the meaning of its appearance. Only my sister and Belen do not understand the significance.

"The remaining path to the Estate is three days east. It is so straight that not even a child can get lost. Lady Eleni will be enough to guide you there."

The first to speak is Belen, his words though direct are not immediately understood.

"If you are willing to accept my assistance, I will guide you north."

"And I will be joining you both, for I will not let you go into the darkness alone."

"Captain! We should…"

"Dichas, I am going north and may not return. You are the Captain until we meet again. You and the others will guard Princess

Clariossa and Lady Helena. Deliver that message and survive, do all you must to achieve this."

Noticing his Captain's determined eyes, Dichas falters in his attempts to convince him to change my mind.

"I understand m'lord. I will perform the role until your expected return."

Turning his gaze back towards me, his face softens as he looks upon my welling heartfelt tears. My throat is dry, my words hoarse and barely above a whisper as I attempt to thank him.

"Do not thank me. It has always been my duty, since the day of your birth. We part ways in the morning. Rest and sleep well"

Those final words are not for me alone and the others begin to spread out their bedding. Walking over to Helena and my sister, I tickle her neck, causing her to turn her bright red and wet face towards me. Wrapping my hands around her own, I pass her the necklace that once belonged to her mother.

"This was given to me, so I could give it to you."

"Please do not leave me."

A tender smile forms on my lips as I look upon my sniffling sister. Choking back my tears, I stroke her hair with my fingers.

"My dear little sister, the duties of a princess are many. Know that I am not leaving you because I want to, but rather because I must. I will be with you again, always believe that."

Having let go of Helena completely, I wrap her in my arms and carry her to her bed. As she holds me tightly, I place her gently down on the makeshift bed. Stroking her face and hair, I listen to the sound of her breathing as she falls into a slumber.

"How much you have grown, your mother and our father would be proud. I promise you, I will return."

Lying down next to her, I close my own eyes. My final waking thoughts were of the many who had made such promises and failed to return.

Arc 6: Hidden Consequences

Chapter Forty Five

Residential District, Seine City, District 3

48.85, 2.35

2300 hours, 24-11-2177 C.E.

Pitter-patter

Pitter-patter

The sound akin to falling rain clatters against the hull, their softness belying the truth of the deadly intensity outside. With almost reckless abandon, the convoy of vehicles hurtles through the barricaded streets of a city on the verge of collapse.

"Roadblock! Left, left, left!"

A brief eavesdrop of the broken radio chatter of the convoy commanders is enough to reveal their fears as the vehicles are met by another sequence of explosions, their path followed by tracer fire as they are caught in the middle of another potentially dangerous cross-fire as they move deeper and deeper into enemy territory.

Having taken a route that no strategist would have considered, we had escaped the larger, heavier weapons which could have breached the hulls of the Infantry Fighting Vehicles we were riding in. Soon, we would reach our destination.

I glance at the three figures sitting near me in the cramped confines of the dark interior. Shoulder to shoulder, there was little leeway on either side of them, despite the vehicle's capacity to carry eight.

Working under the illumination of a pair of red lights, each of the three performs their final checks, ensuring they would be ready to fight the second the vehicle came to a stop. Four Praetors, despite the importance of the mission, we could only afford this scant number, the others needed elsewhere to ensure the chaos did not spread beyond this city's limits.

Pop, pop, pop.

A pair of explosions cause our vehicle to jolt sideways, the onboard countermeasures were barely enough to stop the steady stream of missiles hurtling towards us.

"Pegasus one to Ares Commander."

"Go ahead."

"Permission to engage?"

"Denied. Concentrate on speed."

"Acknowledged."

Despite understanding the crew's anxiety, there was too much at stake to allow us to become embroiled in needless conflict.

"IBAS, update."

In response, a stream of data appears on my display. With each upward flick of my eyes, more and more is revealed of the unnatural happenings which had occurred in the twelve hours since the city had become gridlocked by unplanned protests and the six since the eruption of violence.

Small interventions would have been enough to make this situation avoidable, but there was a cancer festering in this city, caused by the lack of clear leadership and endless stalemates caused by those seeking political gains. All foreseeable consequences of the Lord Marshall's unreasonable delay in appointing a new Governor to replace the one murdered months ago.

The Insurrectionists who had gone silent since the "Assembly Massacre", took advantage of the power vacuum, moved in. Biding their time, they lingered in the shadows, waiting for the perfect moment to strike whilst growing their numbers. Today was that moment.

The peaceful protests were used as a smokescreen, the unaware protestors, human shields, whilst they overwhelmed the scattered and complacent garrisons. In a matter of hours, the northern and eastern sectors of Seine City had been overrun until only the Praetor guarded District Headquarters remained as a bastion of order.

I grind my teeth whilst reading of the incompetence of the so-called "leaders" of the District. The Insurrectionists, like parasites, had already begun to gorge on the wealth contained within the captured warehouses and factories. They could not be allowed to grow any further, they had to be dug out even if it meant at great cost.

510

But the armies of the Confederation, though vast, were needed elsewhere, to secure the southern and eastern borders. It would take too long to organise a suitable, sizeable response. Instead, I had chosen this small strike force, barely a platoon. It was a final gamble, a spear to pierce the heart of the beast whilst it was in its juvenile state.

Even this meagre response had been met with political resistance, too many minds arguing for more peaceful alternatives, including the surrendering of the city. Disgusted, I had used my authority as "first amongst equals" to ignore them. I would end this war how I intended.

Twitching my cheek, the broadcasted screams are filtered away as I concentrate on the live image of five buildings projected on my display. Originally a housing complex arranged in the likeness of an open flower, it had become an unintentional fortress.

Forty-three minutes had passed since the secreted agents had reported the appearance of five known leaders of the

Insurrectionists, since then, nothing. The only confirmation of their attendance is the ongoing activity outwith.

With barely a platoon, I could not fight a protracted war, not in the heart of the enemy's stronghold, but the prize was worth the risk, even if it meant sacrificing the final remnants of the city to buy the smallest window of opportunity. Success would ensure the sacrifices had been worthwhile.

The intelligence we had on these buildings was scant, in the decades since the laying of its foundations, modifications had been made. We were effectively fighting blind. Theoretically, the mission was achievable by a fire team of Praetors, whilst supported by the thirty-six members of the Army's SpecOps branch. But there was an expectation that less than half of them, the closest in training and equipment to Praetors, would be returning.

"Meeting heavy resistance. ETA in five, I say again, five."

Acknowledging the message, I disassemble the tablet in my hand, snapping every component to ensure nothing remained which could be extracted by the enemy if we were unsuccessful.

The endless *pitter-patter* of rain grows heavier, becoming more a tropical storm than a shower. Understanding the situation, those beside me heft their weapons, preparing for the unwelcome reception as the interior lights finally change to green.

"Popping smoke."

Having come to a sudden, grinding stop, the rear ramp falls to the ground with a heavy metallic *thump*.

I watch as Sergeants Jesaill and Mynydd immediately disembark and shoulder their rifles, aiming for the figures in the distant tower. Though they, like their targets, were obscured by plumes of thick white smoke, the enemy's heat signatures in the cold winter's air made them as clear as day.

Shocked by our tenacity, the enemy's response is chaotic, offering only sporadic bouts of fire aimed indiscriminately in our direction. Seizing the initiative, our various teams spread and choose their targets, with every exchange of fire being punctuated by the sound of flesh slamming heavily to the ground.

But the enemy's confusion is short-lived, soon the enemy brings their heavy weapons to bear, each capable of penetrating Praetor plate if given sufficient time.

"Pegasus, you are weapons-free. Engage targets two till five."

The IFVs drive forward, sheltering us with their hulls as they turn and elevate their barrels.

"Engaging."

Weapons that were once idle were finally unleashed. Rapid firing autocannons shatter and pulverise the makeshift barricades, the masonry crumbling with each impact of high explosive rounds. Green streaks of tracer fire illuminate the darkness as pintle-mounted machine guns fire at separate targets, neutralising and suppressing those foolish enough to remain standing.

There is no hesitation in the crews' choice of targets, I could imagine their whitened fingers as they unleashed all their pent up anger and frustration after witnessing the destruction the Insurrectionists had caused.

"Squad Charlie, preparing to breach."

Like a well-oiled machine, each of the squads moves from cover to cover, providing suppressive fire as the breaching squad move to the door of the target building. With shields raised, they begin cutting away the barricades with saws and torches whilst positioning the pneumatic ram.

Slam, Slam, Slam, the vibrations are felt even at a distance as the reinforced door buckles. Angry shouts come from within as the door bends out of shape, which soon turns to panic as a grenade is thrown through the gap.

"Breach"

As the door falls with a *clang*, the first of the support squads enter, followed by another and another. With shields held by those at the front, those directly behind carry shotguns and rifles. Working methodically and efficient, they mercilessly neutralise the enemy in a matter of seconds.

"Floor clear."

Following them into the building, I find the walls of the rooms and corridors leading away from the entranceway pitted with scorch marks and bullet holes, all around us the dead lay where they had fallen.

Pausing to only confirm that the dead were truly dead, we advance deeper, leaving the vehicles to guard the entrance. I compare the layout of the floor to those in the blueprints, at first glance nothing appears to be different. Ahead are a pair of stairways, one leading up, the other leading down, both would have to be secured. Deprived of numbers and time, I begrudgingly divide the squads, sending two upwards with another to guard the current floor. The rest would follow us down and into the depths.

With little to no radio chatter, we stalk the narrow, winding stairs, the only sound coming from the muffled clangs of our armoured boots. Room by room, we check every floor, ensuring no one would unexpectedly follow us downwards along the linear path.

Deeper and deeper, we follow the stairs, our radio reception growing fainter as the corridors deviate from the blueprints, becoming older than those built by the Confederation. Static greets those attempting to communicate with those above, the only proof of their continued existence being the series of vibrations. It was clear that the enemy was guarding something and they would not be surrendering willingly.

The air grows increasingly stale as we follow the water-logged path deeper, necessitating the use of respirators to breathe without fear of disease. Though furnished rooms are cut and built into the rock, there is no hint they have ever been used. Cautious of the eerie atmosphere, a series of murmurs come from those in front, questioning the intelligence which had been received. The sparks of dissent are quickly silenced by the growl emanating from Amelia's lips.

A trio of clicks come from the scouts ahead, reporting a door barring our path. Reinforced and made of metal, it led beyond the blueprints and into the unknown. Motioning for the squads to take a position, squad Charlie once again hefts their shields and move forward to cut away at the door.

Click

A warning barely escapes the lips of those standing in front before a stream of heavy calibre rounds shred the door. The red and green tracer fire that illuminates the dark ricochet off the shields and walls. Though the majority are harmless, missing their targets or being absorbed by armoured panels, a few make it through, causing those hit to fall to the floor, clutching their wounds as they scream in pain.

"Air burst."

Sergeant Mynydd broadcasts his warning as he switches to his grenade launcher. With a sound no louder than a popping cork, he fires into the darkness. The pair of explosions that follow tear apart the barricades and eviscerate those behind them in a storm of shrapnel.

Seizing the initiative, the nearest squads to the door burst through. Firing their weapons fully automatic, they dispatch the few remaining defenders. Satisfied, they wave everyone forward before beginning a sweep of the area.

Following them through, I scan the collapsed fortifications, noting the stockpile of food, water, and medication as well as the pair of entrenched autocannons. The presence of these preparations only confirmed my earlier suspicions.

"Governor."

Turning, I acknowledge the presence of the lieutenant who acts as the liaison for the SpecOp teams.

"Two dead, three injured. Charlie is no longer combat effective."

The grim nears is worse than expected. Ahead were a series of tunnels, unmarked on any map, the terrain and the number of enemies unknown. Each factor was enough to make us vulnerable from ambushes and being overwhelmed by sheer numbers.

"Lieutenant, hold this position with the remnants of Charlie and the wounded. Send a runner, have squads Echo to Golf rendezvous here."

It would take too long to wait for the other squads to join us, time was not a luxury we possessed, especially if the enemy were aware of our presence. Only by pressing onwards could we achieve victory.

"Bravo, you take the left tunnel, Delta, the right. Alpha, we will take the centre."

Silently, every squad musters, picking up their weapons and equipment before marching towards their respective tunnels. I watch the backs of the other two squads, though they have not spoken, I sense the anxiety emanating from their body language. Though each was a veteran, they still felt it, the fear of the unknown and the looming spectre of death.

But those emotions were unknown to me or my squad, fear has never entered our minds as we stared into the darkness. For us, there was only the mission, this was no more difficult or dangerous than the hundreds we had fought before. Without hesitation, I step forward.

Chapter Forty Six

I watch the seconds tick by as the timer nears twenty minutes. Though we had followed a nearly straight path without any branching tunnels, we had yet to make contact with the enemy.

Two minutes had passed since we last had contact with another squad, Delta managing only in a broken speech to inform us they were moving uphill. The time since we last had contact with Bravo was longer, only the apparent lack of vibrations and sound of firefights gave the faintest hope of their survival.

Following the narrowing passageway downhill, we crouch as the low ceilings prevent us from walking at our full height. The walls had changed drastically, the red brickwork replaced by white chiselled stone covered in moss.

No longer encumbered by the limitations of the unenhanced, we make swift progress despite the hindrance. Our silent movements are barely above a whisper as we jump across the narrow ravines, the distances insignificant to our enhanced muscles and powered limbs.

Ahead are footprints, the residual heat revealing the recent passage of a large group, with none of the footprints heading in the opposite direction. A series of clicks are heard as our scout raises their left arm and holds up three fingers. Shuffling forward with my pistol drawn, I see what they are seeing, an open door leading into a wide and dark room.

Separating into pairs, we sweep the room for potential threats, but the static and steam plays havoc with our equipment, requiring us to flick open our lenses as they become clouded. Quickly our eyes adjust to the gloom, picking out the shape of archaic oil generators and coal furnaces. Machines were used in humanity's past to boil and funnel water and steam into pipes leading further underground.

This place, with its dark, cramped and confined spaces was too perfect a site for an ambush. Communicating with our hands, our eyes and ears twitch, searching for anything out of place. Suddenly we hear it, something so insignificant that it would normally be drowned out by the noise of machinery.

Pointing in four different locations, we indicate our targets. Pulling the pin from a grenade, I roll it on the floor silently towards the boxes ahead of me. Pistol raised, I wait for the explosion that marks the commencement of the chaos.

Men and women emerge from false walls and from behind boxes as they howl in a mixture of pain and anger. Running, they leap over their wounded colleagues as they hip fire their rifles.

But the darkness is more our ally than theirs, our armour's angular shape making us almost indistinguishable from the other inanimate objects in the room. Like ghosts, we dance around the room, avoiding the stream of bullets as we fire our pistols.

Though more than fifty in number, it means little as their lack of cohesion causes them to fall one by one. Being cut down without causing even a scratch on our armour causes the survivors to scream in frustration. Desperately they begin to throw grenades, each aimed in different directions. The majority land in empty places or too close to their colleagues, showering them in shrapnel.

I dispatch those screaming near me and note their shrinking number, barely half were left. Holstering my pistol, I save ammunition and slash at the nearest two with my darkened blades. The rest of the squad follow my example until only one of the enemies remains. Standing in the centre of the room, his armour and equipment was different from the rest, marking him as someone of minor importance. Seeing me, he yells whilst affixing a bayonet to the end of his rifle and charges.

I avoid his clumsy lunge, stepping through his guard and grab his neck. His muscular, six-foot frame means little as he is lifted, screaming and kicking. The torches at the side of my helmet light up, blinding him as he tries desperately to fire his rifle. Reaching out, I crush his fingers, and the pain causes his grip to slacken and forces his rifle to clatter harmlessly to the floor.

"Check the door, they may have noticed,"

Acknowledging my order, the rest of the squad cover the two known entrances to the room, peering out only to check if anyone was approaching. Turning my gaze back to the struggling man, I watch as he aimlessly strikes out at my shin and groin.

Rummaging through his pockets, I search for anything of value, discarding the hidden weapons and foodstuffs. As I pull out a small green ticket-shaped device and a journal, his movements become frantic. Grabbing hold of my hand with both of his, he tries to break the grip on his neck.

"I see this is important. I have questions and you will answer."

"Never!"

Glowering in anger, he pulls a knife hidden in his sleeve and aims downwards at the apparent gap between my shoulder plate and neck. I make no effort to evade the strike and the thin, cheaply made blade shatters, the pieces being flung in different directions. Staring at the broken knife in disbelief, he stammers a single word repeatedly.

"Monster."

Irritated by his actions, I pull him close, allowing his eyes to stare into the cold lenses of my helmet.

"Tell me, what are you doing here?"

"I'm telling you nothing."

In a voice laced with fury and pain, he howls and strikes out with his hands and feet, striking until his skin breaks and begins to bleed.

"You know it is futile. Answer my question. Why are you here?"

Laughing, he spits at my helmet, the vile saliva tainted in fresh blood.

"Why don't you find out, you false angel. We will eradicate you and all your kind."

Laughing manically, he moves his jaw into an awkward angle and bites down. I pick up the sound of something cracking and soon he begins to spasm and shake. When he goes limp, I shake my head in disgust before dropping his body and kicking it unceremoniously to the side.

"What a waste."

I could not imagine the ideology which could create such zealotry shared by him and other members of the Insurrectionist movement. I had not seen this level of brainwashing since the Wars of Unification, where religious cults worshipped the despair and corruption caused by the nuclear fallout.

"False angel."

I repeat the unusual terminology, unable to understand its more recent origins. Noticing Amelia's gaze, I indicate the body of the man.

"Check the belongings of any others with unusual equipment. We will gather more information before we move forward."

⊷❊——◐\⚓/◑——❊⊷

None of the dead match the criteria I had provided and we did not have the time to search all the bodies. The noise of the firefight would have announced our presence to anyone nearby.

I examine the two items recovered from the man, the first, a green plastic ticket with a single embedded microchip. Too old to be Confederation in origin, it was likely used to unlock a door, I place it in my pocket for the possibility it would be of use. The other is a tattered, leather-bound journal, the pages water-stained and aged.

I flick through the pages, some tearing and crumbling under the touch of my armoured gauntlets. His handwriting is barely legible, those that are, detail his most recent events. The first speaks of his oldest child, the death of his wife, and his struggles for food. It is clear from his writing that he is from beyond the Confederation's borders, but how he entered is never mentioned

As I reach the end, I notice the change in the style and tone. Though the handwriting is the same, the language is more zealous.

17th November 2177

Our glorious Empress has found it!

All those fools, whose faith was not as profound as mine, had been whispering doubts about her after weeks of searching and digging without success. But she said it was there and we found it. I do not know what it is, but I can feel its power, it is something.

20th November 2177

The temple is ancient, I can feel the power within the stone. This must be the temple of the real Gods, not like those false angels. The object was half-buried, but it looked older than anything there, even older than the temple.

As soon as we finished digging, we were told to leave. Only the Empress and those of her inner circle were allowed to stay.

22nd November 2177

I dreamt about the stone I saw last night. It was beautiful, glowing with a light I had never seen before. It must be a divine weapon, made to banish these false angels from these lands.

The captain told me the Empress would be making an announcement soon. I only wish my daughter could see this.

24ᵗʰ November 2177

The Empress told us we were going to play an important role. The artefact was going to be moved to a safer place and they wanted us to protect it from the unbelievers. I can only imagine the glory we will have when the new world begins.

I have been told the false angels die to silver, so I had a blade made especially for them. I can only hope to meet one.

⋇⋯⋯⋯⋇

I close and pocket the journal, though the majority of the words were nonsensical, it had given me enough clues. Those we sought were nearby and having discovered what they were searching for, they would not be leaving without it.

"The enemy is ahead, they have found what they have been looking for. I do not know what it is, but it is most likely a weapon. Our objective remains the same."

"Understood, Commander."

"Praetors, lead the way."

Chapter Forty Seven

The walls continue to change as we follow the rows of exposed pipes. Though crude, they are clearly man-made, with tall archways that allow us to stand at our full heights. Sensing something out of place, I scrape away the layers of thick, wet moss, exposing the painted walls underneath.

Throughout the mission, IBAS had continued to run in my armour's background, despite the drain on its resources. Though it had access to the entirety of our nation's knowledge and records, there was nothing that matched what we were seeing.

This place's non-existence should have been impossible. Seine City, like all the other "New Cities", had been built over the ruins of the "Old World". Every part of the land, including those below the eventual foundations, had been mapped and stored. A tunnel network, as intricate as this, could never have been overlooked. Only by deleting its records from the Central Catalogue could its existence be hidden. Who and why was only another mystery added to the growing list.

Voices ahead cause us to slow our movements, like assassins, we blend into the shadows and take up positions. Shouldering our silenced weapons, we wait, but the voices remain static, neither moving closer nor growing fainter.

Gesturing to those beside me, we slowly creep forward until we catch the glimpse of golden light and three men and two women sat around a table in front of a makeshift shack.

Their idle hands hold not weapons, but handmade cigarettes. The noxious fumes linger in the air as they casually throw down cards. Possessing not a hint of wariness, they could be dispatched or avoided.

But the area surrounding the downward stairway is lit by lamps powered by nearby generators. The effort to slip past them was not worthwhile, instead, I open and close my left hand whilst drawing a pair of throwing knives.

The team follows my example and launch their blades in time with mine. Cutting through the air, they silently embed themselves in vital areas. Collapsing into a heap, each of the guards falls dead, without alerting anyone nearby.

"They were careless"

Amelia speaks in disbelief as she helps move the bodies into the shack, covering them in blankets before moving on.

"We must be deep enough that they believe they would not be found. We can use it to our advantage."

Accepting Amelia's observations, I touch the dark stone pillars that stand on either side of the archways. Scraping away the surface growths, I find words of an unknown ancient script. But despite my curiosity, the sound of distant engines and the hammering of heavy machinery causes me to hold back.

"The enemy is ahead, maintain radio silence. Gamma pattern battle signals only. Understood?"

"Understood."

Our path is blocked by a door, stronger than anything we had encountered before and would need more than the equipment we had brought. Though we could hear the roar of machinery on the other

533

side, I did not believe it would have been enough to mask the sound of explosives.

With a single, well-lit path behind us, there would be no easy withdrawal if we were overwhelmed. Searching for a solution, I soon glimpse a stone more worn than the others.

Unnaturally smooth, a careful examination is enough to reveal the scanner hidden beneath. A technological legacy of the Old World, I was amazed it was still operational. A casual glimpse was enough to confirm the level of encryption, but the time needed to bypass it was time we did not have.

Remembering the green ticket I had taken earlier, I slip it out of the pouch on my belt and examine it closely. Similar in age, there would have been no other reason than this for a mere zealot to possess such an item.

Swiping it across the scanner, an audible *click* is followed by the slow swinging open of the door.

◦◦◦

Having planted a series of booby traps, the door is closed after being marked with a layer of near translucent paint. If the SpecOps teams survived to reach this place, they would see the warning and the directions to find the now hidden key.

The traps were to serve a dual purpose, the first was to ensure any returning enemy patrols would not attack our rear without notice, whilst the second was to prevent the escape of any Insurrectionists during our assault. Whether by being captured or killed, all of them would be dealt with today, none would be allowed to leave.

Two paths lie ahead, both with trails of pipes and electrical cables. Without an indication on which was more important, we take both. Having to split our already meagre numbers, I decide to send Amelia along the lower path, whilst I lead the upper.

Step by step, the roar of engines and the sound of drilling grows louder, loud enough to mask our movements with little effort. Having reached an opening, I peer out and find a ledge without a single rail to prevent the careless from falling.

Below, hundreds of men and women work, moving rocks and wheelbarrows of soil by hand. Using hand tools and industrial lifting and drilling equipment, they expose the remains of bronze statues shaped in the form of rearing horses.

I grimace as I catch sight of the various machines, each too large to have been brought from the surface whole, not along the paths we had travelled. To do so would have required their disassembling, carrying and reassembling here.

Their appearance however explained the tenacity of the city attack. The chaos was nothing more than a camouflage for the noise and vibrations created by the excavation. The planning for this entire operation went beyond a mere insurrection, the true mastermind behind this had a different, unknown purpose.

Feeling a tap on my shoulder, I turn to find Sergeant Jesaill pointing at a ledge higher up. Trusting in their judgement, I follow their lead. Despite the path being well lit, the enemy below was too distracted by their work or too confident in their immunity from infiltration that they fail to notice our presence.

Larger than a stadium, the walls of the room below are built with stone, but due to their age and the work being performed, they are reinforced with steel girders. An intricate dome, rather than a cave roof, looms above us, the religious carvings of immortal beings confirming my thoughts of the buildings original purpose.

Unable to be distracted further, I sling my rifle behind me as I begin to climb upwards. Using the natural holds in the walls, we soon reach our destination, a ledge that overlooked the entire facility.

Crawling along our stomachs, the sergeant and I find the best vantage spot before unslinging our weapons. Unlike the standard-issue rifle that I was carrying, theirs was something more specialised. Unfolding the bipod, they shoulder the marksman rifle which they had adapted over the decades. A weapon which would never be associated with a mission of this nature, in their hands, it was as effective as any other in the chaos of the close confines.

Peering through my scope, I scan the crowd, searching for the targets we had come for. The majority of the four thousand men and women were irrelevant. Meaningless, their torn clothes covered skin that was slick in sweat and mud, for us and those they followed, they were nothing more than expendable fodder.

Above them, standing on the balconies were those worthy of note. Cradling weapons in their hands, each matched the clothing of those who had assaulted the Assembly. As a higher level of threat, they would be the first to be eliminated. Placing my hand on the shoulder of the Sergeant beside me, I run my fingers up and down, allowing them to follow my observations.

As I continue to scan the crowd, I catch movement from the shadows. Subtle but purposeful, they were made to draw my gaze. Hidden behind discards boxes and dormant machines were the unmistakable silhouettes of a pair of Praetors. A faint smile forms on my lips as I admire how close they had approached without being seen.

Having found the presence of our allies, I search for more, hoping for the appearance of other squads, but find none. Only at the end would we truly know their statuses.

A high-pitched screech draws my and the workers' attention onto the balcony. As nine figures make their presence known, the crowd begin to whisper. Of the nine, only one looked important. Dressed in a suit whilst wearing a black and purple robe on top, their appearance was more of a religious orator than a true leader of those assembled here. Tapping the prepared microphone, he smiles as the crowd below gaze upwards with looks of longing.

I watch his smile with one of my own as I confirm the first target, codename; "Demagogue".

Having compared his features to those on file, IBAS confirms the man's identity. With one found, I peer into the shadows, searching for the rest. Behind Demagogue are dozens of figures standing in the shadows. Though many are wearing armour, the rest are distinct enough to identify. We had spent months gathering intelligence on these three men and women that not even the shadows could hide them from us.

Sergeant Jesaill relaxes her muscles and prepares to pull the trigger as I send a series of simple instructions, breaking the enforced radio silence. Counting down, I wait for the end of the Demagogue's religious-like sermon, preparing to use the crowd's wails and clanging of sheets of metal to hide the distinctive sound of bullets when the man steps back and bows to an approaching woman.

Though her features are covered by a silk veil, I can tell they are young. Their clothing, though simple in style is finely wrought and expensive. Carried in their hands is a plain wooden box and despite the distance, I can sense the power contained within. It was a power I had felt before.

All below stand in rapt attention, eagerly awaiting the words of this unknown woman. Lifting the veil, the woman reveals a teasing smile, one normally held by a playful child. Though she appeared innocent, there was something malignant hidden underneath.

This woman was unknown to our intelligence networks, but I knew her identity. She was the one written of by the deceased zealot, the "Empress".

Realising her worth, I change the order of priorities and send the long-awaited broadcast.

"Now."

Chapter Forty Eight

With a sound that is barely a whisper, the first of the sentries touch their chests and notice the red stains on their hands. I watch, emotionless, as their faces fill with despair upon finding the penny-sized holes before they collapse to their knees.

Those standing near them are too enraptured by the speech of their "Empress" to notice, their eyes are drawn to the box as they wait eagerly for the content's revelation. But as more and more of their numbers fall, their weapons clattering to the ground from lifeless fingers, they instinctively begin to feel unsettled.

Turning their heads in confusion, the first of their number notice the discrepancy but before they can shout a warning, hands reach out from the shadows and drag them backwards whilst crushing their throats. Their futile struggles go unheard due to the mindless, frenzied screams of the crowd.

As Amelia and Sergeant Mynydd move closer to the enemy leaders, they pull out a series of grenades and roll them gently in the direction of the masses. I watch as the dark green spheres bob and weave their way down a series of ramps before coming to a natural stop between the feet of the crowd.

Gripping my rifle, I wait for the countdown.

⚬━━◉◟♨◞◉━━⚬

The explosion that follows is deafening, sending shockwaves that travel up the length of the walls, reaching the roof and causing loose chunks of masonry to fall. Those not killed by the blast and shrapnel or crushed by the fallen rocks are knocked to the ground.

Taking advantage of the enemy's disorientation and confusion, a pair of black blurs hurtle forwards, heading in the direction of the balcony. Moving faster than unenhanced eyes can follow, they cover half the distance in a blink of an eye. But their progress slows as those around them instinctively sense the enemy within their midst.

Unable to track their movements, they instead use their sweat-slick, ragged clothed bodies to bar their path whilst swinging fists, pickaxes, and metal poles in their direction. I watch their attempts harmlessly bounce off Amelia's and her partner's armour, the attacks nothing more than an irritation.

Swarmed by a press of bodies, they are forced to use their rifles, firing at point-blank range as they carve a path. Though nothing can stand before the fury of the two rampaging Praetors, who continue to silently and efficiently dispatch those around them, the enemy does enough to slow their progress.

"Praetors."

Those on the balcony stagger to their feet as they speak the words with abject horror, having identified their foe for the first time. I watch as their facial features become etched in fear and their movements grow increasingly frantic.

Following their movements through the lens of my scope, I continue to direct the marksman beside me, ensuring their precise shots are used to remove the more dangerous elements of the enemy.

An officer wearing a peaked cap instead of his helmet begins to shout and bark orders to those beside him, organising a defence whilst pushing his leaders further into the shadows. I end his short-lived efforts with a single pull of my trigger.

"Targets preparing to scatter."

I transmit the message as I continue to fire, aiming into the shadows as I purposely miss. The bodyguards, possessing some level of training, do as expected, dragging those they are guarding behind cover as they turn their ire in my direction.

Corralled and pinned behind walls and machinery, the six targets grow increasingly animated, and whatever unity existed, fractures as they begin to prioritise themselves. The first to move is a middle-aged man wearing thick-rimmed glasses, "Scholar", who drags with him a group of eight soldiers.

Running, he skirts along the path that leads behind the Praetors and towards the security doors. A smile forms on my lips as I turn away from them and continue to target the larger group. It does not take long before the expected explosions occur, causing the already loose masonry to fall once more.

"Scholar eliminated."

Seeing the explosion, the five remaining behind cover understand our plan and become bolder. Shoving the soldiers near them, they direct them towards the temple floor where Amelia was fighting.

Without hesitation, the soldiers callously raise their rifles and open fire, adding machine guns and other heavy weapons to the mix. Uncaring of the casualties, they seek only their survival as they cut down their allies with little remorse.

But Amelia and her partner perform the unexpected, evading the incoming stream of bullets with movements so graceful that they belied their larger frames. Like prima ballerinas, they dance and skirt their way through the press of bodies, pushing and moving those in front of them into the incoming bullets. Step by step, they slowly begin to make ground.

Having watched the ineffectiveness of their efforts, the leaders scream and run in two opposite directions, their bodyguards splitting into three as some remain behind, whilst others follow the two different sized groups.

Emptying the contents of my rifle into a heavy weapons crew, I inform Amelia of the enemy's movements.

"Targets splitting east and west. Category alpha going east. "

"Understood, intercepting east."

Amelia responds without a hint of exhaustion as she leaps over those barring her path. Ignoring their efforts to stop her, she grabs the nearest ledge and hauls herself up, before repeating the process once again.

But before she can continue her pursuit, a squad of soldiers carrying missile launchers emerge and open fire. Whether due to panic or lack of training, they aim too close to the walls behind them. As the backdraft bowls them over, killing and maiming those directly behind, the volley of missiles strike the ground near to Amelia and explode, knocking her off her feet.

"Incoming".

The warning is shouted from the lips of the Praetor beside me as another volley of missiles is launched in our direction. With no choice but to leap down, I land heavily on the ground and roll. Though we had prioritised those carrying weapons capable of penetrating Praetor plate, we had not eliminated them quickly enough.

Shouldering my rifle, I follow the trails and quickly dispatch the launchers before they have a chance to reload. Ducking behind a low wall, I glance in the direction of Sergeant Jesaill and find them already moving to a new position.

Hearing the cheers of the mob below, I look down and scan the room for Amelia and Sergeant Mynydd. Having been emboldened by their apparent success, the Demagogue emerges from a higher floor balcony and begins to squeal in glee. With a sadistic smile on his lips, he begins to orate.

"My brothers and sisters, look at the mortal flesh of these false angels. Kill them for their blasphemy of being a wrongful existence."

Rallying to the honeyed words of their spiritual leader, a thousand men and women begin to converge on the prone Praetors whilst picking up whatever they can find. Still dazed by the explosions, Amelia and the Sergeant stagger sluggishly to their feet.

Noticing the approaching crowd, they shoulder their rifles and open fire.

Surrounded, they slowly walk towards each other until they are standing back to back. Firing until their rifles are empty, they discard them and change to the weapons slung on their backs. Blast after blast, they continue to rack their shotguns, meeting the raging mob who screams towards them with curses on their lips.

Unwilling to do nothing despite the inevitable, I begin to run, leaping from ledge to ledge as I move closer to the two. Firing into the rear of the mob, I add to the pile of dead, but their mindless zeal and deep-rooted hatred cause them to focus only on those in front. As a man clambers over the wall of corpses, Amelia drops the butt of her shotgun onto his head before drawing her combat knives.

Glancing upwards, she sees my approach and shakes her head and points. I follow her gaze and see the escaping leaders.

"The mission comes first, go."

Having understood the situation and their inability to continue, she prioritises the mission over their survival. Answering her message with a series of blinking lights, I change direction and follow the trail of the escapees.

"Do it now!"

Up above, I hear the excited scream of the Demagogue as he stares eagerly at the actions of the crowd. Licking his lips as the Praetors are dragged down by the weight of the mob.

A man who was too full of zeal and too indoctrinated to the cause, he would serve no purpose as a captive for interrogation.

"Alpha four, eliminate Demagogue"

A succession of muffled shots is soon heard, followed by the disappearance of the man and those guarding him. But his legacy remains as those on the higher floors unveil a series of entrenched autocannons, each aimed in the same direction.

Hurrying, I watch as the barrels spit out a hail of heavy calibre rounds. Glancing down, I watch as they cut gouges into the temple floor, missing their targets entirely. Dressed in torn rags, the inexperienced crew haphazardly make adjustments and continue to fire, with each burst the gouges creep closer and closer to where they needed to be.

Just like us, they were willing to sacrifice anything for the mission and cause. Grabbing hold of the ledge, I move from handhold to handhold, climbing until I reach the same floor as the cannons. Leaping onto the balcony, I come face to face with the crew. Meeting their surprised faces with a burst of my rifle, I continue until it is empty.

Dropping the now empty weapon onto the grilled floor, I take hold of the autocannon and turn it upwards, aimed in the direction of the crews standing opposite. So eager were they to claim the glory of a Praetor kill, they had failed to notice the disappearance of those across from them. Pulling the trigger, I listen to the near-endless *chatter* until the belt runs dry and those on the other side are turned into piles of scrap metal and clouds of red mist.

Two sets of arms emerge from the mountain of corpses, slick in blood and offal. Amelia and Sergeant Mynydd confirm their condition before picking up the enemy's discarded weapons. Though cracked and on the verge of collapse, their armour and their bodies were still functional.

"Alpha two and three, okay. Continuing mission."

Having received their message, I drop down to the lower floor. The bodies of the Demagogue and his bodyguards are cold, their hearts and foreheads pierced. Hearing the still braying mob, I kick the corpse of the Demagogue off the ledge, watching as it crashes downwards onto the temple floor.

Wails of grief and denial replace the early zealotry as the still two thousand strong mob recognise the owner of the clothes. Between that and the emerging Praetors, their armour drenched in blood, they begin to waiver, becoming indecisive as they agonise between running and pressing the attack.

Leaving Amelia and Sergeant Mynydd to dispose of the remnants, I set my eyes on the nearest group escaping through the tunnel ahead.

Chapter Forty Nine

Slamming the last of the ambushers into the floor, I turn and listen to the echoes of hurried footsteps and panicked shouts. Though the tunnel had branched into various directions, I was still able to follow and pinpoint their locations. They were still close, but I was not getting any closer.

I admire their tenacity, they had used their superior knowledge of the terrain to launch ambush after ambush, sacrificing their remaining numbers to ensure the survival and escape of their three leaders.

Pausing only to confirm the deceased status of those around me, I discard the now empty rifle in my hand. Wedging it into the wall, I use it as a marker for those who would be following my movements.

Taking the shotgun holstered on my back, I cradle it in my arms as I break into a run, increasing my speed with every step as I follow the still warm trail. Too much time had passed and caution meant little if the prey was allowed to escape.

Ahead, a faint light is seen at the end of the tunnel, barely brighter than moonlight, its presence suggested an exit or a wide-open space. As I approach the end, I instinctively lean back, forcing my body into a slide that continues to the threshold which marks the exit.

Flicking off the safety, I peer out. A glance is enough to confirm my suspicions, ahead were five figures with two operating a heavy machine gun. Out of grenades, I had few options to deal with them directly. Instead, I would have to rely on their highly strung agitation and inexperience. Picking up a nearby rock, I throw it onto the ground in front of me.

As the stone clatters repeatedly on the ground, the gloom is replaced by a light show of red and green. The group fire until their weapons *click* empty before shining torches in the direction they had fired. Gasps and moans of confusion escape their lips as they find nothing but holes in the rock-face.

Seizing the opportunity, I lean out and fire, sending shell after shell of heavy slugs into their bodies before they have a chance to reload. Ejecting the spent shells as the sounds of the firefight is carried further into the network of tunnels, I soon hear the high-pitched shrill of a woman's scream.

"That monster is getting closer, do something about it."

Though their voice has been distorted by the walls, I recognise enough to identify it as belonging to the woman who had the moniker of the "Beauty". For the first time in the pursuit, I had managed to make ground and reduce the distance between us.

Knowing that the resistance would only increase, I load the remaining shells into my shotgun and examine the rifles on the floor. All were examples from the former Novoyan Federation and their effectiveness would be limited. Caked in rust and poorly maintained, the weapons were more a danger to the user than the enemy. But with my supplies depleted, I had few other options.

Choosing two of the best maintained, I sling them over my shoulders whilst collecting all the ammunition I could find. Pulling back the slide of the first rifle, I follow the voices into the tunnel.

"Protect the Oracle. Get on that gun!"

A woman howls in fear as she screams hysterically at those sheltered beside her, demanding they re-crew the now silenced machine gun. Before they have the opportunity, I burst forward, sprinting from cover as my rifle sprays indiscriminately.

"Slow it down. You, go tell the Major to prepare the next position."

As the same woman continues to bark a series of orders, I leap down into a network of trenches. Receiving the impact of a dozen rounds on my shoulder pads, I swing the now-empty rifle like a club, crushing the limbs and skulls of anyone in my path as I engage in a savage display of combat. Step by step, my armour is chipped away until the light on my display changes to amber when I reach the end.

In the gloom ahead, I catch a glimpse of white fluttering fabric and recognise it as belonging to the "Empress". Despite the shadows, her face is clear, etched with fear as she is hauled away.

As another group of armoured figures break away and join the rag-tag army, I heft the machinegun crumpled at my feet. Tearing away the trigger guard, I force my gauntleted fingers into position and pull. Legs braced, I absorb the recoil as it chatters, sending a constant stream of lead that forces those ahead to duck behind cover. Step by step, I stomp forward, ignoring the spontaneous bouts of fire aimed in my direction.

A predatory smile forms beneath my helmet as I spot a man in his late fifties, dressed in a dark red beret and navy coloured uniform. The leader of the Insurrectionist's military arm, the "Major", if he was here, this was truly the last of their resistance.

"It is alone you useless worms, kill it."

Those who stand beside the Major move better than the rest, hopping from cover to cover, as they avoid the incoming fire. "Elites" dressed in armour scavenged from the corpses of Confederation soldiers absorb the few rounds which manage to make it through their movements.

As the machine gun runs dry, I discard it, launching it in the direction of soldiers dressed in rags, the weight and force more than enough to crush their chests as I leap forward with combat knives drawn.

"Kill it now! Kill it now!"

Using movements similar to those displayed by Amelia earlier, I dance the dance of death with those in front of me. Stab, thrust, slice, crush, I repeat the movements as I use their bodies as living shields.

Breaking the arm of a rifleman, I hold it in position as I force his fingers to continue squeezing down on the trigger. Ignoring his screams of agony, I force him to aim at his colleagues as I haul him up and charge towards the so-called elites. His agonising screams end quickly as his body is pocketed with holes.

Dropping his dead weight at the last minute, I sweep into the elites. Aiming for the weak spots of the armour I had designed, I bypass the protective plates and cut them down until only three of the enemy are left standing.

As I stand exhausted and drenched in blood, a series of claps come from the "Major" who stands in the centre of the three, his face calm despite witnessing the slaughter.

"I guess the stories about you monsters are true after all."

The smile on his face could send shivers down the spines of mortal men, it was as if he was a predator who had finally found worthy prey. I watch him warily as he draws the sword from his belt and those beside him heft heavy metal shields and maces. All were weapons that had no place on a modern battlefield.

Charging towards me, I hear the sound of electrified fields being activated from their weighted heads as they swing. Unsure of their capabilities, I choose to evade, dodging their fluid motions as I maintain my gaze on the Major who adopts the stance of a master swordsman. Remaining still, he makes no effort to support his bodyguards, instead, he watches.

Unable to waste further time, I choose to absorb the next strike aimed at my shoulder pauldron, watching as the hit glances off the surface after causing a dent. Now off balance, I hammer my blade into the man's eye before picking up his mace.

Heavier than expected, I use it to parry the strike of the last bodyguard before swinging it down. As the shield crumples under the impact, shattering the forearm of the person behind, I use the momentum of the strike to swing it again, crushing their skull and ending their screams of agony.

"I expected more from my students."

Tutting in disappointment, he looks dispassionately at the bodies of his guards before rushing forwards. With almost superhuman movements, he swings his sword, forcing me to parry with the combat knife in my left hand.

His movements are praiseworthy, emphasising the time he spent honing his craft, but they are still too slow. Disarming him with a flick of my wrists, I grab his mouth, dislocating his jaw as I force it open. Reaching in, I find what I was expecting.

"I have questions, and you will answer".

Prying out the ceramic tooth filled with poison, I crush it in front of his eyes. As his eyes widen in fear, I force him to the ground after snapping the bones in his forearms. Binding his arm and legs with plastic cuffs, I attach an explosive to his body to deter rescue before dragging him into the shadows.

"Stay here, my colleagues will be joining you soon enough."

Ignoring his hate-filled eyes, I wrench my knife from the eye of his bodyguard. Cleaning the blade, I place it back into its sheathe before continuing my pursuit.

Chapter Fifty

The sound of a spluttering engine is heard in the distance as I land at the bottom of a stairway. Having pursued them all this way, I refuse to let them escape and push my exhausted body further, narrowing the distance until I see them barely two hundred metres ahead.

Hearing my heavy stomps, the last of the bodyguards turn and open fire. My unexpected appearance causes them to hurry and as the Empress turns and attempts to escape onto the waiting boat, she trips and falls. Dropping the wooden box, she scuttles after it as it slides along the makeshift dock.

As she is dragged unceremoniously to her feet by her bodyguard, I launch the throwing knives in my hand, the last of my ranged weapons embed themselves in the necks of the closest bodyguards and graze her calf, slicing through her Achilles. Screaming in pain as her white clothes become soaked in blood, she drops the box once more.

"Oracle!"

Seeing their beloved leader's collapse, the remaining dozen bodyguards move to guard her as a woman wearing thin-framed glasses and long brown hair reaches down and picks up the box.

"Leave her, let's go!"

With those words of betrayal, eight of the group turn with her, running in the direction of the waiting boat. As the remaining four stand in a daze, unsure of who to follow, I launch the last of my knives, ending their hesitation.

Ignoring the crumpled bodies and wounded woman, I run to the end of the dock, only to watch as the woman designated "Beauty" cruises off. With every second, she heads further into the underground lake and out of my reach.

With no choice but to end the pursuit, I turn and walk back in the direction of the wounded woman. Bleeding, she drags herself to the rifle held within the grasp of her dead bodyguard and attempts to fire.

Click, click, click, no matter the repeated attempts, it remains empty. Grabbing the barrel, I wretch the weapon away from her and throw it into the water. As she shuffles fearfully back, I could not see the de facto leader of the insurrectionist movements as anything other than a scared child.

Taking hold of her wrist whilst tearing off her veil, I find that she was younger than I originally thought. Grabbing her cheeks, I pry open her clamped jaws and force my fingers into her mouth, checking for signs of poison. Having found none, I remove my hand and lean close, forcing her to gaze into the lenses of my helmet. With her unable to turn away, I give her an ultimatum.

"You have one chance to spare your life, so choose wisely. It is a better offer than those received by others."

Dropping her to the floor, I bind her wrists and ankles as she glares at me with hate-filled eyes. Despite the death stare, she meekly allows me to apply a dressing to her wound before I lift her with both of my arms and carry her like a newlywed bride.

"Don't you dare touch me, let go!"

She flinches as I turn my cold, lifeless eyes towards her.

"W..why are you giving me mercy?"

"Because I have a use for you."

She continues to stare, but her eyes were no longer filled with defiance or zeal, but fear. I had already examined the skin on her arms and legs, there were no apparent scars or deformities, no proof of having lived through hardship. Though she may resist, in time she would answer the questions I needed. But for now, there was only one question that mattered.

"What was in that box?"

The fear she had once shown disappears as a smile forms on her lips, the smile of a child who had played a prank.

"You will find out soon enough.

Epilogue: A Lone Watcher

A lone figure approaches the pool of crystal clear water, their movements silent and deft as they slowly begin to disrobe, their clothes falling and scattering like autumn leaves around the edge of the natural spring.

Kneeling, they run their hands through the water. As they watch the ripples swirl along the surface, their eyes glint with child-like mischief. Satisfied, they untie their long plaited hair and begin to step into the water, before wading into its depths.

As the tips of their hair touch the surface and spread out, a girl-like giggle escapes their lips as they splash the water playfully. Alone, they did not need to watch and listen to their surroundings or conduct themselves as expected, here, only the birds kept them company.

Lying back, they float on the water and look upwards into the cloudless, summer night sky, the twin moons shining radiantly.

"O Theá tou Kynigioú, tha apantíseis poté sta óneirá mou?"[7]

As if responding to their whisper, a blanket of fog hovers over the surface, wrapping itself around the figure, causing their skin to glisten and become almost ethereal.

In times past, a king had once proclaimed their beauty beyond mortal compare, akin to the nymphs of old. To claim the untouchable, they had waged a series of wars, bleeding their nation dry in the pursuit of making them their bride. Few now remember that fool's claim, his nation and descendants long dead. Time had shown again and again that he would not be the last.

The figure sighs as they touch their skin and remember the duty bound to them since the morning of their birth. A duty and vow that was unwanted and unchosen, it was forever etched into their soul. Until their duty was fulfilled, they would forever appear as a young pure maiden approaching adulthood.

To those bound to the whims of mortality and the strands of fate, their eternal youth was seen as the boon of immortality. But to them,

---

[7] Ω Θεά του Κυνηγιού, θα απαντήσεις ποτέ στα όνειρά μου - Oh Goddess of the Hunt, will you ever answer my dreams?

it was a curse that would taint even the purest of hearts. Never would they dream or know the happiness of friendship, the pleasures of companionship, or the joys and pain of childbirth. Their fate was anchored to the abyss of eternal loneliness.

Their sad, lonely eyes gaze into the darkness of the tunnel, searching for the visitors that would never come. Months had passed since they last felt the company of others, and decades since this home had heard the tread of feet that was not their own.

Hidden deep within the territories which the great beasts had claimed as theirs, it was isolated and far from the settlements of Man. Only those possessing bravery, courage, and unparalleled skill with blade, bow, or shield could even begin the journey. With luck and knowledge, they may come upon its entrance, but only those chosen by destiny could enter the door. Without destiny's grace, they would forever remain outside.

Having let out another melancholic sigh, they swim to a throne of naturally eroded stone. Sitting back in the moonlit chair, they allow the water to support their ample, floating bosom whilst shutting their bright green eyes.

As they listen to their beating heart and the songs of chirping night birds, their face becomes the very visage of serenity. But as they edge towards the realm of dreams, their fingers begin to twitch and names that were meant to be forgotten are spoken once more. As the names of the long-lost are heard by no one, a single tear rolls down their cheek.

But before the river flows, the sound of beating wings in the distance causes them to sit up and open their eyes. Feeling the dry thirst that lingers at the back of their throat, they finally notice the red hue that tinges their normally unblemished skin.

Dizzy and their vision blurry, they make their way to the pool's edge on quivering, unsteady limbs. Driven by an almost insatiable thirst, they desperately grab a pouch from a hanging branch and pry open the stopper. Parting their lips, they force the cold, sweet liquid into their mouth, swallowing until the dizziness which had possessed them, vanishes.

⊷⧉——◎⚲◎——⧉⊶

With their vision now clear, they step out of the water and pick up the scattered clothes. Lazily, they dry their dripping body whilst stretching their well-rested limbs. Choosing a fresh blue robe, they drape the thin, translucent material over themselves whilst stepping deeper into the cave which they called home.

Following the scent of untainted trees, they step out onto the moonlit balcony and open their arms in glee as they look out onto the endless forests and mountains. Straining their eyes, they see the faint silhouette of a flying bird. Though the sound of their beating wings was growing stronger, they were still too far away.

Choosing to wait in comfort, they fall into a chair which is sat next to a table, on top, a board of marble. Crafted by their own hand, it was a board of sixty-four tiles, arranged into rows of eight, alternating between black and white. A game from the realms of the Gods, it had changed, evolved, and adapted to the needs of the world's differing cultures. But this board would be different, it would be the closest to the original.

Sorrowfully, they pick up a playing piece, an archer of white, one of the thirty-two that were due to be crafted. Despite the decades of searching, trading, and scavenging, the board was yet incomplete. No ordinary material could be used, for each piece had to be perfect, to contain the strand of fate they represented. Even a lowly foot soldier could change the world if given the opportunity.

Beside each success and the tools to complete them, were the shattered remains of gemstones, each a failure. Many had been chosen over the years to represent the pieces of the board, but due to their imperfections, corruption, or their paths being extinguished prematurely, they had become unsuitable.

Thirty had been completed, sixteen of black and fourteen of white, but the final two could not be rushed, for they were the ones that truly mattered. Raising the two still unfinished pieces, they appraise each for cracks and imperfection before setting them down.

One had been eighteen years in the making, taking the form of a young maiden dressed in light delicate armour. It was carved from the heart of a sapphire that was once guarded by a great beast in the shape of a lion with a silver mane. Of the two, it was the closest to completion, the sole remaining choice is whether it should be carved with a crown or without.

The last however was the source of their anxiety. Carved only months before due to the chance encounter of a ruby buried in the heart of an ancient fallen star. Roughly hewn into a giant wearing exquisitely forged armour of unusual design, in its hands was an unrecognisable stave. The piece was still full of imperfections as if the chosen's role in destiny was yet unknown. Only the most worthy could bear the weight of this piece's responsibility, so it could not be rushed.

The white king and their queen, only when they were finally ready would the game be allowed to start.

[To be continued]

About the Author

Born into a family that was rich in military service, Jeffrey or Jeff MacSporran spent the majority of his childhood travelling the world before settling in the picturesque, but wet, countryside of Scotland, where he subsequently studied and graduated with an Honours degree in Scot's Law.

When not climbing the nearby hills, you will find him nose deep in books; imagining himself a Roman Legionnaire, Greek Hoplite or the hero in some knightly adventure, or rolling a handful of dice as he moves miniature armies across a table.

Initially submitted as a long listed finalist entry for the PageTurner competition. *Praetor's Blood – Shattered Peace* is Jeffrey's first novel.

Thanks for reading! If you loved the book and have a moment to spare, I would really appreciate a short review as this helps new readers find my books.

65856481R00323